GOD

THE RUIN OF
HOUSE HORNBOLT

RYAN HAUGE & IVY SMOAK

This book is a work of fiction. Names, characters, places, and incidents are fictitious. Any resemblance to actual persons, living or dead, events, or locales is purely coincidental.

ISBN: 9781075453014

Cover Design by Ryan Hauge
Illustrations by Ryan Hauge & Eric Gross

2019 Third Edition

For each other.

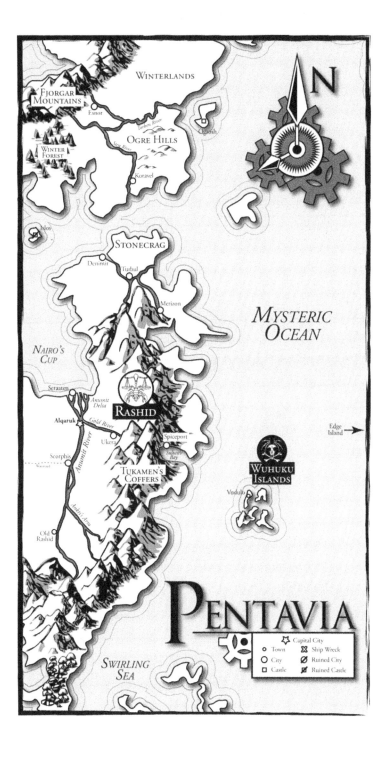

FOR LARGER MAPS, VISIT

WWW.RYANHAUGE.COM

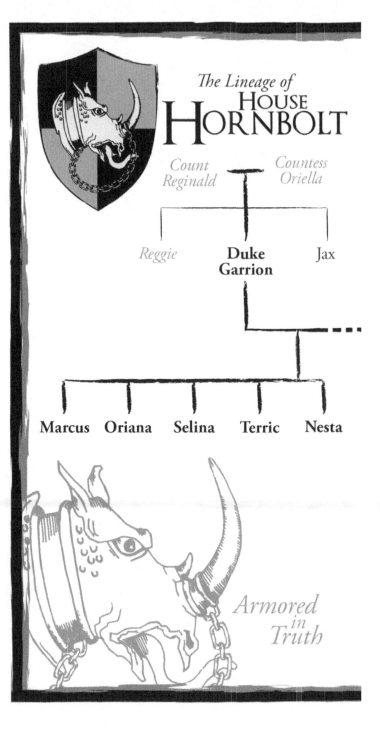

The Lineage of
HOUSE HORNBOLT

Count Reginald — *Countess Oriella*

Reggie — **Duke Garrion** — Jax

Marcus **Oriana** **Selina** **Terric** **Nesta**

Armored in Truth

HOUSE TALENOV

King Bogdan —— *Queen Helga*

Anton *Costel* King Ivan Reavus **Duchess Isolda** Katrina

Crown Prince Rixin

GARRION'S COUNCIL

Sir Aldric Alsight   Father Percival   Brother Savaric   Quentin Harlow   Axion Tobias Crane

HEROVINCI

"Almost there!" yelled Herovinci from the quarterdeck. If his calculations were correct, and they always were, his fleet was minutes away from passing the island that his contemporaries believed marked the edge of the world.

Their claims weren't entirely without merit. It was true that no sailor on record had ever reported sailing this far east into the Mysteric Ocean. It was also true that many ships had left port with the express intention of sailing farther east than Edge Island, and none of them had ever returned.

To the other great minds at the University of Techence, those facts meant that it was impossible. To Herovinci, those facts were an invitation. An invitation to do the impossible and prove everyone else wrong.

Herovinci achieving success would not be unprecedented. At the age of ten, he had created a series of gears that could track time as accurately as the sun's movements, and that was just the first of many inventions that his peers previously thought were impossible. His crowning achievement was the invention of the airship, of which he now commanded a fleet of three on a journey to prove that there was land beyond Edge Island.

Herovinci rushed off the quarterdeck, slid down a ladder to the galley, snaked through a maze of barrels and wood piles, and then finally climbed down another ladder to the crow's nest, beneath the keel of the airship. He should have taken more care to grab each rung, but he was too excited to bother.

"Any sign yet?" asked Herovinci, but no one was there to respond. *Where is she?* he wondered. Lucia should have been keeping watch from the crow's nest, especially when they were so close to Edge Island. Had she fallen overboard? Herovinci hoped not. He never had much luck with women, but he thought he might have a chance with Lucia. If the journey was successful, maybe she would see past his patchy beard and soft belly. Maybe she would see the brilliance that lay beneath.

Herovinci scanned the crow's nest to gather more information about Lucia's disappearance. The spyglass was secured in its leather case, indicating that Lucia had intentionally left her post rather than falling to her death.

Herovinci snatched the spyglass out of the case and put it to his eye. He searched the ocean below for the tiny island. Nothing. He looked off the other side of the crow's nest. Still nothing. And then he saw it. A small strip of land, little more than an uninhabited mound of sand and rock, was rapidly approaching. Edge Island.

"Land ho!" shouted Herovinci.

If he had blinked he might have missed it, but for a moment, the air in front of him rippled and stretched as if the bow of the airship was a needle and the air was a sheet of fabric. A split second later, everything was back to normal. The needle had pierced the fabric.

How odd, thought Herovinci. A trick of the light? A rush of excitement causing him to hallucinate? When he got back to

Techence he'd search the library for mentions of similar phenomena, but for now, there was but one thing on his mind: he had done it. He had done what his peers claimed to be impossible. He had proven that the world doesn't end with Edge Island. There was still more to do - he was going to fly around the entire world - but first he wanted to celebrate with his brother, Enzo.

He climbed back up into the hold and again navigated through the cargo to the engine room at the stern of the ship. He loved the engine room. He breathed in the sweet smell of oil and let the clanking of the gears wash over him. The movement here was a beautifully choreographed dance of finely tuned machinery. It was what transformed the airship from a few balloons and a wooden frame into the greatest invention mankind had ever seen.

"Where's Enzo?" Herovinci asked the engineer.

The enormous man snapped a log in half and tossed it into the fire before turning his attention to his captain. "In your quarters," he grunted with a half-hearted salute.

What's he doing in my quarters? wondered Herovinci. There were a number of possibilities, but Herovinci hoped that it was because Enzo was preparing a celebration. He could picture him uncorking a fresh bottle of the very finest Barcovan wine and raising it in Herovinci's honor.

Herovinci rushed up to the deck and burst into his quarters with a triumphant smile on his face. But that smile faded when he saw what Enzo was doing. He was celebrating all right, but not with wine. He was celebrating with Lucia. She had been given the role of lookout, but really she had been included amongst the crew so that she might sell new fashions to ladies at the stops they had made during their flight east across Pentavia. One example of those fashions, a ruffled white dress with a leather corset, had been hastily thrown on Herovinci's desk.

Herovinci's heart sunk. *Of course that's how Enzo would celebrate.*

The Turbine brothers were both brilliant, but the similarities ended there. Where Enzo was tall and muscular and charismatic, Herovinci was short and weak and awkward. Enzo had earned top marks in every class at the University of Techence. Herovinci had been threatened with expulsion multiple times. No one seemed to recognize his intellect. He was always looked at as the Prime Minister's son, or Enzo's little brother. Or that annoying pest who interrupted lectures to ask questions about flight and elements and how the world worked. But this was his chance to prove them all wrong. This was his chance to explore the world. To change the way men travel. To etch his name in the history books and have a statue of himself erected in Philosopher's Square. This was his chance to show everyone that he, not his brother, deserved to be the next Prime Minister of Techence.

Or was it? When they set sail, he thought this might also be his chance to woo Lucia, and that hadn't exactly worked out.

Herovinci cleared his throat.

Enzo turned to look at him while Lucia let out a mortified squeal.

"I'll be waiting on the quarterdeck," said Herovinci. He turned to leave. "By the way, we passed Edge Island."

"Hero!" called Enzo as Herovinci slammed the door shut.

Herovinci returned to the quarterdeck and pulled the lapels of his long leather coat up around his neck. The wind stung almost as much as seeing Enzo with Lucia.

Enzo appeared on the deck a minute later. Every sailor on deck gave a crisp salute. Herovinci wasn't surprised. The sailors saluted Herovinci because they had to. They saluted Enzo because they wanted to. A decade ago, it would have bothered Herovinci. But by now he was used to it. Or at least, he told himself he was.

"You did it," said Enzo, clapping him on the back. "I knew you would."

Herovinci turned away. "Some way to celebrate. Did you even see the island?"

"Of course I did!" said Enzo. "And about Lucia. You know how women are. She was just excited about passing the island. I happened to be the nearest man for her to celebrate with. I'm sure she would have done the same with you." Enzo flashed Herovinci a dimpled grin.

He wasn't sure if Enzo was serious or not. Was it really that easy for him with women? "Well, you do deserve some credit for this expedition. It wouldn't have been possible without you."

Enzo shook his head. "No. This airship is your design. You're the captain. This was all you, brother."

Herovinci smiled and took the compliment, but both men knew what Enzo meant. Yes, the airship was Herovinci's design, and he had planned the journey, but it was only possible because Enzo convinced their father, Prime Minister Christo Turbine, to fund the expedition. The lure of discovery wasn't enough for the ministry of Techence. They only agreed to fund it when the journey was presented as an opportunity to showcase the technological superiority of Techence and get the bloodthirsty lords of Pentavia excited about the newest toy they might be able to purchase to use to slaughter each other.

"I didn't want to bother you with this until we passed Edge Island," said Enzo, "but earlier today we discovered that some of the wood wasn't loaded."

"How much?" asked Herovinci.

"Almost all."

"I need an exact number so I can calculate..."

Enzo held up a sheet of parchment. "I already did. We have enough wood to stay in the air another four days."

Herovinci scratched his patchy beard. Despite only being in his mid-twenties, it was already speckled with bits of gray. "But we're already nearly four days off shore."

"We are. Which means we need to turn around."

Herovinci grabbed the parchment from Enzo and scanned the calculations. "You didn't consider that we can break down empty food barrels to feed the fire. That'll give us at least another four hours in the air. And if we absolutely need to, we can always tighten the rear valves and downshift the gear ratio."

"Good idea," said Enzo. "I'll have Sergio start breaking those down to use in case of suboptimal wind conditions on the return voyage."

"We're not turning back yet. With that wood, we'll be able to travel another two hours before we have to turn around. There's still a chance we can find land."

"But this trip has already been a success. We made it past Edge Island. We proved it's not the end of the world! We can always come back out to discover more. This isn't the end. But it could be if we don't turn back soon."

"You don't understand, do you?" Herovinci shook his head. "No, of course you don't. You couldn't. You have everything. Everyone at the university loves you. Every girl in Techence loves you. Father loves you. I have none of that. All I have is my brain. All I have is this." He gestured to the ship. "You'll go down in history as the next great Prime Minister of Techence. You'll carry on the family name. I won't. I'll just be a footnote - the crazy son who tried to fly around the world and failed."

"Hero, that's not going to happen." Enzo put his hand on Herovinci's shoulder and gave him a reassuring smile.

Herovinci pushed Enzo's hand away, not at all calmed by Enzo's use of his nickname. "You're right, it's not. Because we're going to keep going, and we're going to find land. And then we're going to sail around the world and show everyone I was right. Now, is there anything else you needed?"

Enzo frowned. "No."

"Good, then I believe you have a job to do. Break those barrels down to use as fuel."

Enzo reluctantly left the quarterdeck while Herovinci stewed in anger. He had meant every word he said, but perhaps reason had escaped him. His legacy was important, but maybe this wasn't meant to be it. He had a dozen more inventions in various states of completion. He still had more to contribute to the world. Was risking his own life and the lives of his sailors really worth proving a few people wrong?

Herovinci looked back to where they had passed Edge Island. It was hardly visible beneath the setting sun. Was the sun also setting on his dream of sailing around the world? He spent the better part of an hour attacking the equation from every possible angle. But as much as he hated to admit it, every calculation led to the same solution: turn back and live to fight another day.

He put his hand on the wheel and prepared to give the order to turn around. Then he saw Enzo approaching.

"If you're here to tell me to turn around..." started Herovinci.

"I'm here to tell you that Lucia just spotted a storm ahead."

"All the more reason..."

"And she saw a pelican."

"Are you sure?" asked Herovinci. If they had indeed seen a pelican, it meant land was near.

Enzo nodded. His pale grey eyes danced with excitement.

"How bad is the storm?"

"It's looks to be mostly nimbus clouds, but it's hard to tell in the dark. No lightning yet."

"So what do you think?"

"I think it's an awfully good thing my brother invented this airship so we don't have to deal with the waves that storm is going to churn up. Let's find land and get these ships stocked with enough wood to fly around the world."

Herovinci smiled. "You're sure? I had already resigned to turning back. I have other inventions..."

Enzo clapped his hand on Herovinci's back. The force of it nearly knocked Herovinci off his feet. "Just promise me I get to be there when we show those smug pipe greasers at the university the proof that we found land."

"Deal."

Herovinci stepped around the wheel to the edge of the quarterdeck. "Gentlemen!" he called.

Some of the sailors looked up. Some didn't.

"Gentlemen, we've spotted a storm ahead. But if we can make it through..."

"We should turn back," mumbled one of the deck hands under his breath.

"You're going to get us all killed," added another. "This is a fool's errand."

Enzo stepped to Herovinci's side. "Your captain wasn't finished speaking yet." His voice boomed across the deck. The entire crew immediately stood at attention.

"If we can make it through," continued Herovinci, "land will be waiting for us. We've seen a pelican."

There were again murmurs among the crew, but this time they were murmurs of excitement.

"Now, let's show this storm what we're made of and re-write the history books." Herovinci was no great orator, but he was satisfied with his speech. For the first time in his life, he finally felt like he had his men's respect.

"What's the plan?" asked Enzo. "Over or under?"

"Over. We'd take on too much rain going under."

Enzo nodded. "Increase altitude!" he yelled as he hurried down the stairs, barking orders to every sailor he passed. Within seconds, the deck was alive with sailors tying ropes, dodging beams, and greasing gears.

The storm was upon them before they could gain enough altitude to fly over it. Herovinci could feel the moisture on his cheeks as the thick grey clouds blotted out the moon. The wind started to pick up. Herovinci had grown accustomed to the wind blowing in his face as the airship sailed eastward during their journey, but this wind was coming from all directions with an intensity he had never experienced. He pulled the thick leather collar of his jacket tight around his neck and tied one of his hands to the wheel to ensure he wouldn't be blown overboard.

Enzo fought to make it up the stairs to the quarterdeck. The wind blew his usually perfect hair into a wild mess and puffed up his coat like it was the main sail of a ship. He gripped the handrail and leaned forward. Every step was a struggle. It was as if an invisible hand was trying to yank him into the sky.

"These winds are too strong," yelled Enzo. "We can't keep this up for much longer!"

"How much..." Herovinci's sentence was cut short by the crash of thunder. A powerful wind gust from the port side of the ship brought with it the first raindrops of the storm. Enzo just barely grabbed the railing in time to avoid being blown away. One of the sailors on the deck was not so fortunate. The sailor caught a rope as he was lifted off his feet, but the rope snapped. The noise from his scream never reached Herovinci's ears. It was swept overboard as easily as the sailor's body, like a mere feather in the wind.

Within seconds, every surface of the deck was slick with water.

"Rusted pipes!" yelled Enzo. "That was one of the ropes holding the balloon."

Herovinci squinted through the relentless rain to survey the damage. It wasn't ideal, but as long as no other ropes snapped, the ship would hold. He looked port and starboard to see how the other two ships in his fleet were faring, but there was no chance of locating them through the oily darkness. He could barely see to the bow of his own ship, much less all the way to the others.

Then a dark shadow in the corner of his eye caught his attention. A particularly dense cloud? No. The hull of one of his other ships? No, not that either.

"Did you see that?" he asked.

"What?" Enzo yelled.

Another lightning strike illuminated the clouds just enough for Herovinci to see it clearly: the peak of a mountain.

"We need to increase altitude," said Herovinci.

"What?" yelled Enzo again.

"Mountain!" shouted Herovinci. "We need to climb!"

"You steer. I'll give the order." Enzo jumped down the stairs and sprinted across the deck, shouting the order as he went.

Herovinci gripped the wheel with both hands and prepared to make a sudden turn, but he knew such a maneuver would be useless. With their current speed in these winds, any course change drastic enough to avoid the mountain would put too much of a strain on the already damaged rigging.

Herovinci shielded his eyes from the torrential rain with one hand as he squinted up ahead to get a better look at the jagged mountain. They were headed directly for the highest peak. Even when Herovinci felt the ship pitch upwards, he knew that they were still doomed.

Most men might have prayed to a god, but Herovinci knew that gods weren't real. Men lived in a physical world. Everything was controlled by equations. Some he understood, others he didn't. But whether or not they had yet been discovered, the equations existed. And they left no room for Arwin or Wazir or any other god to interfere. But maybe, just maybe...

Herovinci shook his head. He couldn't believe he was spending his last seconds thinking about made-up gods. *Think! There must be a solution.*

And then it came to him. It was too late to get over the highest peak. And it was too late for a drastic turn. But their altitude increase coupled with a slight turn might just be enough. He nudged the wheel to the right and held his breath. His stomach twisted into a knot tighter than the knots holding the balloon to the hull of his airship. Not even the final exam to receive the official title of axion from the university had made him this nervous, although at the time it had felt like a life or death situation.

A second passed. Two seconds. They were still alive. Three seconds. The mountain was now visible directly to his left, so close to the ship that Herovinci might be able to reach out and touch it.

And then they were past it.

Herovinci let out the breath he had been holding in. Not only had they avoided the mountain, but as the climbed, the wind and rain began to subside.

His ship was the first of his fleet to poke above the dark grey clouds. He wondered if the others would follow. Either the Eliza or the Christo, the two other ships in his fleet, could have easily been destroyed in the storm or crashed into the mountain. Or just chosen not to climb.

Herovinci looked back and forth hoping they would appear, but lightning bolts streaking between the clouds beneath him were the only thing he could identify in the storm.

The brown balloon of the Eliza finally crested above the storm clouds. Herovinci still thought the silver gear and wrench - the sigil of House Turbine - painted on the balloon was hideous, but for once he was relieved to see it.

The Christo appeared next. At first glance, both airships appeared to have made it through relatively unscathed, but as the Christo gained altitude, Herovinci could see that half the hull had been demolished, sliced off by the peak of the mountain. The balloon and engine room, however, must have remained intact, because the Christo still flew.

That's a mighty fine design of mine, thought Herovinci.

"Hero," said Enzo, gasping for breath.

Herovinci hadn't noticed how thin the air had become. And cold.

"We made it," Herovinci said with a smile.

"No...look ahead."

For the first time since they surfaced above the clouds, Herovinci focused his attention ahead rather than port or starboard.

He didn't think he'd be able to see much of anything at all in the moonlight, but the moonlight was not the predominant light source. An almost constant stream of lightning bolts zapped between the enormous clouds up ahead. Herovinci thought he saw the tops of more mountains between the clouds, but they were in the inverse of how they should have looked. Rather than coming to a peak, they were flat on the top and sloped inward as they stretched toward the ground.

"Now what?" asked Enzo. "Should we climb again?"

Herovinci needed no calculations to tell him that increasing their altitude was not feasible. They would freeze or suffocate to death long before they could fly high enough to get over this storm. They were already higher than they should have been.

"Or maybe we should turn back?"

This time Herovinci did need calculations. Was there enough time to turn back before they reached the second storm? Under standard wind conditions, at normal altitude, with an undamaged ship, there might have been enough time. But when all three of those variables were tweaked, such a sharp turn was much more likely to cause a catastrophic failure of the vessel than be successful. The Christo especially, given its current state, had no chance of a successful turn. It was almost as risky to fly through the thunderstorm, but at least there would be land on the other side, and hopefully answers about those upside-down mountain tops. Herovinci had a hypothesis about their origin. Now he needed to confirm it.

Enzo shook him. "Climb or turn back?" he asked again.

"Neither," said Herovinci. "No time to turn. Straight through is the only option."

"But that's suicide."

"Maybe so, but it's all we've got."

"You're sure?" asked Enzo.

"Always."

Enzo paused to think of other options. "What about landing on one of those...peaks?"

Herovinci shook his head. "Even if we could navigate the landing, the air up here is too thin. We'd all be dead by morning."

"Then we'd better plot a course." Enzo pulled out a sextant and called out coordinates.

Herovinci made the required adjustments until it looked like their course would take them in one of the few paths not occupied by mountains or the thickest clouds. They would still have to contend with some clouds and the possibility of being annihilated by a stray lightning strike, but it was the best they could do.

"How is there so much lightning?" asked Enzo. "Imagine if we could harness that..."

"It's incredible, isn't it? We travel two hours past the supposed end of the world and already we've encountered something that could change the course of history. The Christo will need extensive repairs. We'll need to dock nearby to investigate the cause of the lightning while we get her back to full strength."

"There's no way we can repair the Christo with the tools we have on board."

"I know that," said Herovinci. "But the crew doesn't have to. At the very least it'll buy us a few days before we have to declare it a loss and move on."

The thunder accompanying the constant lightning strikes made it impossible to continue their conversation as they approached the storm.

Herovinci searched for something he should say to his brother in case they didn't make it through the storm. He could have easily conjured an equation or theory - he already had a handful of ideas about the source of the lightning - but when it came to saying something sentimental, his brain failed him.

"Good luck," he muttered as he tightened the rope securing his hand to the wheel.

The wind swirled around the ship. Lightning lit up the sky. Judging by the immediate, deafening thunderclap, the storm was no more than a few hundred yards ahead.

The next lightning strike was even louder. And the explosion of the flammable gas inside the balloon of the Christo was louder still. Herovinci watched in horror as one third of his fleet was obliterated into a million wooden shards. A plank flew by, inches from his face. A smaller piece of shrapnel caught him in the arm. He fell to his knees in pain, and as he did, his hand still tied to the wheel caused the ship to bank hard to the right. The ship rolled. Sailors skidded across the slick deck. Two of them were unable to stop their slide and went tumbling over the railings.

Enzo helped Herovinci to his feet and steadied the wheel, but the damage was already done. Their course had been altered.

"What now?" asked Enzo.

Herovinci didn't immediately have an answer. His mind was stuck in a storm all of its own. The entire crew of the Christo, 22 men, all dead. Three more from his own ship. And who knew how many from the Eliza had perished. Was it real? He wanted to believe it wasn't. He wanted to believe that any minute he'd wake up in the west wing of the University of Techence. He'd go downstairs and eat a big breakfast and then start working on something completely unrelated to airships. His vision blurred and an invisible quill dipped in liquid lightning hastily wrote an array of equations on top of the raging storm. He started to connect the lights below into sketches, like an astronomer drawing constellations in the stars.

Wait...*lights below*?

Herovinci snapped back to reality and his vision sharpened.

"Are there lights down there?" he asked Enzo.

Enzo looked over the edge of the ship. "It's probably just burning shrapnel."

As Herovinci tried to focus on the lights, he thought he saw a lightning bolt originate on the mountain and shoot toward the Eliza. It narrowly missed. Then it happened again, and this time, it didn't miss. It tore through the rigging holding the hull to the balloon. The hull swung down and hung vertically for a moment before the last rope snapped. The balloon floated away into the storm as the hull plummeted to the mountaintop.

"Watch out!" yelled Enzo. He grabbed the wheel and pulled it hard. Yet again, the ship rolled to the right. A bolt of lightning streaking through the sky missed their balloon by a few feet. The thunder left a horrible ringing in Herovinci's ears.

Maybe he wasn't thinking straight from the pain. Or the constant thunder. Or the lack of air. But it seemed like something was targeting them. Even if there was a perfectly logical explanation for it, it was still clear to Herovinci that his airship was a giant floating target for the lightning. Turning around might be too much for the ship to handle, but the chances of being struck by lightning seemed to be quickly approaching 100%.

"Hold on!" he shouted and spun the wheel. More lightning streaked by them.

Enzo must not have heard him, because he was caught unaware by the sudden change in course. He lost his balance and went sliding towards the railing.

Herovinci reached for him, but his hand was still tied to the wheel. Reaching only made the ship roll more. Enzo toppled over the edge.

"No!" yelled Herovinci. Another bolt crashed by the ship. He started to feel lightheaded again. The blood loss from his arm and the thin air were too much. His eyesight started to blur. The ringing in his ears intensified. It almost sounded like birds screeching.

He clumsily pulled out a knife and cut the rope holding his hand to the wheel. As he tried to stumble towards the edge to see if Enzo had grabbed onto something, he tripped on a loose plank and fell. Just as he lost consciousness, he thought he saw the silhouette of a winged man carrying Enzo in his talons.

- CHAPTER 1 -
ISOLDA

Isolda's father once told her that any respectable tournament would feature at least three deaths. Such events were dangerous affairs. A lance could catch a knight in just the wrong spot and find its way through his armor, or a man might take a moment too long to yield in the hand to hand combat. The competitors weren't the only ones in danger, though. Brawls in the stands could often turn deadly. And sometimes people gambled more than they could afford, forcing the debt collectors to take their payment in flesh rather than coin.

Isolda knew that the upcoming tournament would be no exception to the rule of three deaths. It was to be the biggest tournament Treland had ever seen. Bigger arena, more knights, more spectators, and definitely higher stakes. There were even whispers that this tournament was the one foretold in the Prophecy of Arwin. Surely there would be at least three deaths. But who?

The first death, Isolda knew, would belong to her youngest son, Terric. He wasn't going to take a lance through the heart or partake in illegal gambling...at least, she hoped he hadn't gotten into such things. No, his death was of a different variety. He was to take the Oath of Arwin on the final day of the tournament, and with that oath, his dreams of becoming a knight would be snuffed out.

The second death would belong to Isolda's eldest daughter, Oriana. She was of marrying age, and with so many young lords and knights coming to town, it was inevitable that a betrothal would be arranged. Whether it would be to Prince Rixin or some other noble, Isolda was not sure, but either way, the second death would be that of her daughter's childhood.

The third death...Isolda didn't know what the third death would be. She hoped it wouldn't happen at all, but if it had to, she prayed it wouldn't belong to her eldest son, Marcus. His wouldn't be the death of a childhood dream or the death of his youth. He was competing in the tournament, so if the third death belonged to him, surely it would be death in the simplest sense of the word: the end of his life.

A knock on her chamber door took Isolda out of her thoughts. A page handed her a letter sealed with the symbol of a Gargamulan man trap pressed into pale green wax - the mark of Axion Tobias Crane. She broke the seal and scanned the letter. If someone had intercepted it, they would have thought that it was an update on Tobias' tutelage of Terric. He was progressing well in mathematics and showed a great enthusiasm for history and cartography. That was good news, but Isolda suspected that the letter served another purpose. She walked over to the fire and held the paper as close as possible to it without it catching fire. Within seconds, a note written in fire ink became visible in the left margin. *New Market, third alley on the left, second right, one hour.* Isolda committed the directions to memory and tossed the letter into the fire.

What does he want? wondered Isolda. Tobias knew to only summon Isolda for matters of the utmost importance, which meant one of two things. Either her husband's inspectors were dangerously close to exposing the truth about one of her establishments, or Tobias had finally uncovered a clue... No, Isolda refused to let herself dream of such things.

The guard at the front gate of Vulture Keep snapped to attention at the sight of Isolda approaching.

"Good morning, my lady," he said. "I would have had a carriage and escort waiting if I had known you planned on venturing out today."

"That's not necessary," said Isolda. "It's a lovely morning for a stroll around the city."

"That it is," agreed the guard. "Just give me a moment to call for Michael..."

Before the guard could finish, Isolda smiled at him and walked through the gate. She didn't need guards to follow her around the city. She was quite capable of handling herself.

She made it across the bridge and through Sir Garus' square before she noticed the two men watching her. They were both dressed in hooded roughspun cloaks that covered them from head to toe, and by the look of it, they were both armed.

Isolda turned left and headed toward the switchbacks that divided the upper and lower halves of the city. The men followed.

The quickest path to the new market would have been to go straight at the bottom of the cliff, but instead Isolda took a left. The men followed.

Two more right turns brought her back to the main street, the one she would have been on if she had not gone left. Again, the men followed. She quickened her pace. They quickened theirs. She had no doubt that they were following her.

She weighed her options. She could turn down an alley, but they would easily see her and follow. If she ducked into a crowd...no, there were no crowds. With the tournament only a few weeks away, the streets of Arwin's Gate were more crowded than usual, but that still meant that there were only half a dozen people rather than the one or two people that would have been present a month ago. She had no chance of escaping until she reached a busier part of town.

As she approached the new market, the crowds seem to double in size with every step she took. Before construction had begun on the new arena, this part of town had been almost entirely empty, save for unsavory characters that met in crumbling buildings in the wee hours of the morning to sell crossbows, scorpium, and any other contraband they could find. But now it was teeming with merchants hoping to sell their wares to nobles coming to town for the joust and...

"Watch out!" shrieked a woman behind her.

Isolda jumped back. The wagon swerved. It went up on two wheels. Isolda thought for sure that its cargo of colorful carpets would spill out and crush a fruit stand, but the driver was able to stabilize it just before it tipped past the point of no return. He shouted a few choice words not at all appropriate for the ears of a duchess as he turned onto a side alleyway that seemed much too narrow for his wagon.

Isolda let out a sigh and looked down to make sure her foot hadn't been run over. It hadn't, but she was standing on the tail of a very angry looking squirrel. It chirped at her and scurried away as soon as she lifted her foot.

She turned to locate her pursuers and found that they were pushing through the crowd headed straight towards her. As they approached, they pulled off their cloaks to reveal black and grey quartered tunics with a golden rhino head emblazoned on the front.

"Are you harmed, my lady?" asked one of the men.

"N...no," stuttered Isolda. "No, I don't think I am. Just a bit shaken up." She let out a dramatic sigh.

The guard nodded and gripped the hilt of his sword. "How shall we handle that reckless driver? Lord Garrion will surely banish him if you'd have it so."

Isolda considered it for a moment. "I can't help but feel partially responsible. He *was* going too fast, but if I had been watching where I was going, it all could have been avoided."

The guard frowned. "Then just a fine?"

"If you think that's best," said Isolda.

One of the guards started off down the alleyway in pursuit of the wagon. The other stayed with her.

"Are you sure he knows where he's going?" Isolda asked. "I could have sworn the wagon went over there." She pointed at an alley further down the street.

"Are you certain?" asked the guard.

"No, but what harm would it do to check?" Isolda suppressed a smile as she watched the second guard run off into a dead-end.

That was easy, she thought. After years of practice, Isolda had become quite adept at spotting the guards that Garrion sent to protect her whenever she left the castle. They always wore cheap hooded cloaks to try to blend in, but to her trained eye, that only made them stand out. She had confronted Garrion about it once, but he just feigned ignorance. After that, she had made a point to lose the guards whenever possible, whether she was having a clandestine meeting with Tobias or merely enjoying a morning stroll.

Before the guards could return, Isolda ducked into the third alley on the left and went through the second door on her right. It was immediately clear to her that the room hadn't been occupied for years, not since the gold mine went dry and practically turned Arwin's Gate into a ghost town overnight.

The only part of the room not covered with a thick layer of dust was a vanity in the corner of the room stocked with make-up, a wig, and a neatly folded pile of clothes.

Isolda's transformation began by exchanging her shimmering golden dress for a pair of black pants, a dark grey corset, high-heeled leather boots that reached to mid-thigh, and long leather gloves to match. She wiped off her usual bright red lipstick in favor of a more subtle pink. A bit of powder on her cheeks quickly removed her tan glow. The last order of business - and probably most important - was her hair. Isolda removed her black ironwood hairpin, being careful not to poke herself with the razor sharp point. It had been a gift from her father before he sent her up north to find a husband. "As long as you have this, you'll always be safe," he had told her. His promise hadn't been entirely true, as the hairpin had done little to protect her from being imprisoned at the end of the Wizard's War, but at least it had kept her alive. She tucked the pin into the front of her corset before securing her long golden braids underneath a curly black wig. A pair of odd little spectacles and a long brown cloak finished her transformation from Lady Isolda Hornbolt, Duchess of the Shield, to Lady Marsilia, the most notorious crime lord in Arwin's Gate.

Isolda had no trouble spotting Tobias on the crowded market street. His short stature would generally make him difficult to locate, but his tan top hat was more than tall enough to make him appear at least a normal height, if not taller. Tobias adjusted his glasses as he inspected the offerings of an ink merchant. As soon as Isolda caught his gaze, he finished his purchase of a new quill and walked in the opposite direction.

Isolda followed behind him. It probably wasn't necessary to keep such a distance, but she could never be too cautious. Her husband already had an innate distrust of anyone from the godless city of Techence. Rumors of Tobias being mixed up with Lady Marsilia would only deepen that distrust.

At first Isolda wasn't sure which of her establishments Tobias was heading towards, but as they continued, it became clear that he was taking her to their newest venture, the Razortooth Tavern.

The mud brick walls, thatched roof, and arched windows of the tavern matched the rest of the buildings in the city, but that was only because they weren't finished with the details yet. Men were hard at work fitting iron grates to the windows and chiseling away at a larger-than-life statue of a razortooth tiger standing guard at the entrance. Isolda waited a few minutes and then followed Tobias through the doors.

"Welcome to the Razortooth Tavern, Lady Marsilia," said Tobias with a grin. "What do you think?" He gestured around the tavern. The tables were all new, the seats looked as comfortable as you could expect at a tavern, and the bar was well stocked with everything from Fjorking ale to Barcovan wine.

"Everything looks just as it should," said Isolda. "But I assume you haven't brought me here to impress me with..." Isolda picked up one of the bottles she didn't recognize and read the label, "...Kraken Tooth rum."

Tobias adjusted his glasses and looked down. "I'm sorry, I didn't mean..."

"I'm not upset, Tobias. I just want to know what was so urgent."

"Of course you do. I would have just sent a letter about it, but I wasn't sure...well, you should just come look." Tobias led Isolda upstairs and ushered her into room 17, which turned out to be a secret passage to an entirely separate part of the tavern where patrons could purchase services that weren't entirely legal. After navigating a maze of hallways and staircases, Isolda arrived in a cavernous room bigger than the grand hall of Vulture Keep. Most of the foliage that would soon decorate the room was still in enormous crates and barrels, but it was doing its best to break free. Vines and leaves poked through every available hole or crack in the containers, and when their containers had no more cracks, the wild plants made their own. Soon they would be free to grow wild, blossoming into flowers the size of a man and climbing up the pillars to drink up as much sunlight as they could from the windows in the domed ceiling. Isolda wanted to open the crates and inspect the exotic plants, to get a taste of the poison jungles far to the south that only the bravest men in the kingdom would dare visit, but for now, she was content to follow Tobias to a small room off to the side that apparently held the mystery of why he had called on her for this meeting.

The room had been furnished with a tan carpet, an overstuffed sofa, and a lush bed, but they were all askew. It looked like the table setting a few years ago after Terric had attempted the old jester's trick of pulling the tablecloth off the table without disturbing any plates or cups. They had all gone crashing to the floor in a heap, just the way the furniture had been sucked into a sinkhole in the corner of this room.

"What am I looking at?" asked Isolda.

Tobias pointed into the pit. "There was a collapse this morning."

"I can see that. Was anyone hurt?"

"Only one. But the reason that we're really here is what they found in the pit."

"Which is?"

Tobias grabbed a lantern off the wall and handed it to her. "Take a look."

She bent over the edge and peered into the pit. Through the darkness, all she could discern was the faint glimmer of gold behind a pile of rocks.

"Leftover gold from the old mine?" asked Isolda.

"Can you not see it?" Tobias shook his head. "More rocks must have come loose. I'll call for Owen to clear the path."

"No need," said Isolda. She handed the lantern back to Tobias, slipped out of her boots, and began climbing into the pit.

Tobias let out a little gasp. "My lady, are you sure that's safe?" Beads of sweat began forming under the brim of his hat.

"No, but I hope it is." When she reached the bottom, she turned back to Tobias. "Are you coming?"

"I, uh," started Tobias. "Climbing isn't really..."

"Then at least hand me the lantern so I can see."

Tobias refused. She insisted. He refused again. Eventually he found a rope and used it to lower the lantern to her. With the cavern now lit, Isolda picked her way through the rocks until she was face to face with a yellowed corpse dressed in golden armor.

She gasped. Not because it was a corpse. She had seen plenty of corpses during her time in the dungeons of Icehaven in the final months of the Wizard's War. No, she gasped because of *which* corpse it was. The body of Arwin.

Isolda had only seen it once when she was a young girl. As far back as she could remember, she had always begged her father to let her into his reliquary to see the corpse. But as much as she had begged, he had always refused. It wasn't until her tenth birthday, the day before she was to be sent to Icehaven in hopes of a betrothal to one of the Fjorking princes, that he allowed her to finally see it.

"This is the body of the one true God," he had told her. "Don't let those northerners poison your mind with thoughts of Throg or that two-headed ogre god. This is the one true God."

But to Isolda, it didn't look like a god. It looked like a decaying corpse dressed in a suit of bloodied golden armor. For years the image of the corpse had worked its way into her dreams, morphing them into horrific nightmares.

Isolda shivered at the thought and lost her grip on the lantern. The glass shattered against the rocky floor. The pit was bathed in darkness once more, but the sight of the corpse was seared into her memory and the icy feeling remained in her veins. She quickly turned and climbed out of the pit.

"Are you okay?" asked Tobias. He grabbed Isolda's arm to steady her. "Forgive me, I didn't realize it would frighten you so."

Isolda took a deep breath and tried to clear her head. How had her dead father's most prized relic ended up here in Arwin's Gate?

"How many people saw what's down there?" asked Isolda.

"Just you, me, Foreman Owen, and Henry. A couple others might have seen it, but I think they were more focused on helping Henry. His leg was crushed in the collapse. Compound fracture of the tibia and fibula. I fear there's more damage than that, but I won't know for sure until the swelling..."

Isolda waited for Tobias to finish his longwinded medical analysis of Henry's injuries. When she was sure his full attention had returned to her, she said, "Word of this must not get out. Do you understand? Tell Foreman Owen that I'm holding him personally responsible for the silence of his men."

Tobias nodded. "Yes, my lady."

"How many keys are there to this room?"

"Just this one."

"Good. No one is to enter this room." Isolda took the key, locked the door, and began the walk back to the dusty old changing room. Along the way, she tried to wrap her mind around what she had just discovered. For the first time in twenty years, she had a sliver of hope that she might solve the mystery of her father's murder.

Isolda's father once told her that any tournament worth talking about would feature at least three deaths. The first would be her son's dreams. The second would be her daughter's childhood. And with any luck, she'd find her father's assassin and drive her hairpin through his blackened heart. His death would be the third.

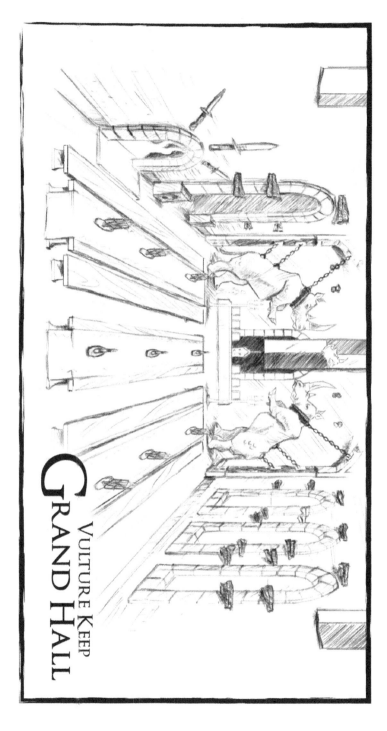

VULTURE KEEP
GRAND HALL

- CHAPTER 2 -
TERRIC

"I win!" shouted Warin as he dumped his final bucket of manure over the cliff.

Terric put his hands on his knees and looked back at his own side of the stable. Half the stalls were still filthy. Warin's side was spotless. "How is that..." He gasped for breath. "How is that possible?"

Warin laughed. "That's what years of practice does for ya, mate." He clapped Terric on the back. "Either way, I appreciate the help."

"I'll beat you next time," said Terric. "I was just distracted."

"By what? Did you climb over the bathhouse again and get another look at Bella dressing?"

Terric turned away so that Warin wouldn't see him blushing. "That was one time! And I didn't even mean to." It really had been an accident. He had been trying to climb back into his room in the castle, but a few vultures were blocking his usual path. He couldn't find any loose rocks to toss at them, so he altered his route. Along the way he happened to peer into the steam vent above the bathhouse and caught his older sister's handmaiden getting dressed. So yes, it had been an accident. The three times after that, however, had not been accidents.

"Suuure," said Warin. "Are you also going to claim that it was disgusting? Maybe you should show me how to climb up there so we can have a more educated discussion."

"Are you trying to end up in the stocks?" asked Terric. "I'd get a stiff warning from Mum if I got caught, but if someone saw you up there..."

"Yeah, yeah. I know they'd banish me. Maybe if your parents caught you, they'd finally realize that you weren't meant to be a priest. Watching ladies bathe is quite unpriestly."

"True, but it's not very chivalrous either. Really, if I got caught, Father would probably think a demon had made me do it. He'd lock me in the temple until I was declared demon-free." Terric shuddered at the thought. "Is there a demon in me?"

"If there is, it certainly hasn't made you any better at sword fighting."

"You sure about that?" Terric grabbed the two pieces of wood that they often used as swords and tossed one to Warin. "Defend yourself, Sir Wilmarc."

"You shall perish at my blade, Sir Oleg," declared Warin.

When the boys practiced sword fighting, they always pretended to be their favorite knights from the stories. Warin had no noble blood, but his ancestors were from the Huntlands, so Warin pretended to be Sir Wilmarc of Whitehall. A man besting an ogre in hand to hand combat was almost unheard of, but Sir Wilmarc had managed to kill three all at once.

Terric, on the other hand, had nobility on both sides of his family. His father's house, House Hornbolt, had been the dukes of Arwin's Gate for generations, bravely protecting the

Shield from the Rashidi raiders to the east. There were countless stories of Hornbolts heroically defeating Rashidi, all with varying degrees of believability. And the Hornbolts had been in charge of erecting Arwin's Wall. But the tradition of second born sons in House Hornbolt becoming priests dampened his enthusiasm for that side of the family.

Terric found his mother's house, the royal House Talenov, much more appealing. He loved the stories of his grandfather, King Bogdan, leading expeditions into the poison jungles of Tujira, but most of all, he loved the story of Sir Oleg of Bloodstone, the man who brought House Talenov to prominence. At that time, the Talenovs were a minor house in the Shadowlands, so poor that Oleg was sent out to collect wages as a blacksmith's apprentice. When Oleg's father died and Oleg inherited the estate, he decided to sell it, and with the proceeds of the sale, he convinced the king to sell him a thousand acres between Ghostwood and the east face of the Deadstones. The land was thought to be haunted - the river there ran red, supposedly caused by giants on the Deadstones eating humans and spitting their remains into the river. The other nobles mocked Oleg, taking bets on how long he would survive. But Oleg knew better. From his experience as a blacksmith, he suspected that iron deposits were the cause of the red rivers. And how right he was. He founded the village of Bloodstone and began mining the rich iron ore deposits. Blacksmiths from all over flocked to Bloodstone, and before long it had grown into a thriving city. Even to this day, Bloodstone swords were unrivaled in quality and value.

Terric loved the story of Oleg. The storybooks never told of his ability with a blade, but Terric imagined that Oleg was quite a clever swordsman, able to take advantage of even the smallest weakness that his enemy presented. As such, Terric practiced dueling with that philosophy in mind. Pure skill was only a part of swordsmanship. The rest was about being clever and making use of your surroundings. His favorite trick was to push Warin into a spot where he would be momentarily blinded by the sun shining in between the cracks in the thatched roof of the stable.

As soon as Warin had a grip on the sword, Terric lunged at him. Warin easily parried it, riposting with a strike of his own.

The match went on for quite a while as Terric slowly worked Warin into the beams of sunlight. The sun was enough of a distraction for Terric to register the first strike of the day, even if it was merely a glancing blow on Warin's left arm.

"Well played, Sir Oleg," said Warin with a bow.

"Thank you, Sir Wilmarc. You fought valiantly. Another?"

Warin raised his sword and the two boys resumed fighting.

"How do you think I'd fare against Prince Rixin?" asked Terric in between lunges.

"The Shadow Prince has won every tournament he's entered."

"He has. But I haven't been a part of those tournaments!"

"Oh, right. He's only been jousting against the best knights of the realm. Yeah, you'd probably beat him." Warin laughed, and Terric used his friend's momentary lapse in concentration to slash at his arm.

Terric smiled triumphantly. "If he's as distractible as you, I think I'd have a pretty good chance."

The sound of the noon temple bells cut his victory short. Terric knew that he had to begin climbing back into Vulture Keep at the sound of the bell if he wanted to make it to the grand hall in time for supper.

He hated the bells ringing. Sometimes when he heard them, he thought about taking one of his father's horses and riding off. And as it began to seem more and more unlikely that he'd be able to avoid becoming a priest, his thoughts of running away intensified. He had even stolen a map from the library to begin charting his escape route. His most recent plan consisted of heading north through the Shield into the Hunt-lands. His reason for that was twofold. First, he knew that Warin would be more likely to come if he was going to the birthplace of the great Sir Wilmarc. But more importantly, the Huntlands were controlled by King Felix Gormont rather than King Ivan Talenov, and thus the lords there would be less likely to honor a request from the Talenovs to send Terric back to Arwin's Gate. Terric's father frequently referring to the Huntlands as a "lawless wasteland filled with thieves and back-stabbers" concerned Terric slightly, but no plan was perfect.

"Better luck tomorrow," said Terric as he darted out of the stables toward the castle.

"Say hi to Bella!" called Warin.

Terric didn't bother responding. He was tempted to climb past the bathhouse windows, but he decided to take the other route. Terric had made a point to *not* memorize the verses that he would be required to recite before taking the oath of Arwin, but he couldn't help pick up bits and pieces of it during his weekly lessons with Father Percival. One thing he noticed in the stories was that sinners always got punished. Even if he didn't put much stock in Arwin's teachings, he couldn't help but think that he was tempting fate by spying on Bella while perched precariously on a slippery wall thirty feet above the ground.

Avoiding the bathhouse, Terric climbed up the west tower of Vulture Keep. When the castle was originally constructed, the sheer limestone walls would have been nearly impossible to climb. But centuries of harsh sun and even harsher summer thunderstorms had eroded the rock, necessitating patches of mud and plaster. Eventually they had added wooden beams to serve as a sort of permanent scaffolding to facilitate easy repairs. Those beams just so happened to also facilitate easy climbing. Despite that, Terric's muscles were on fire by the time he reached his room.

"Terric? Are you in there?" asked his mother through the door.

Just in time.

Terric wiped the dirt off his shoes, smoothed out his trousers, and sat down on the sofa with the Book of Arwin.

"Terric?" asked his mother again, jiggling the doorknob. "I'm coming in."

Terric jumped in surprise as she entered. "Oh, Mum! You startled me."

His mother raised an eyebrow. "Is that so?"

"I was so enthralled with..." Terric stole a look at the page to see what part he had opened to. "...With Arwin's journey to Mount Peleus."

"You were enthralled by the story of Arwin spending fifty days in solitude? Don't tell your father, but I fell asleep when I tried to read that. I wish we had a copy of Throgtome so I could read you some real stories. Throg made a journey to a mountain too, but his ended with him fighting a dragon rather than reflecting in silence."

Terric perked up at the mention of Throg, the god of the Fjorkings. His mother mentioned him often, but only when his father was nowhere near.

"Can you tell me one of those stories?" asked Terric. "Please?"

"Haven't you had enough stories for one day? You've been reading since sunrise."

"Yes, but these stories are boring."

"If I tell you a story, will you be on your best behavior while we're preparing for the tournament?"

Terric nodded.

"And during the tournament?"

Terric nodded again, but less enthusiastically. Would running away to the Huntlands be considered bad behavior?

"Okay. Let me think." His mother scrunched her face to the side and adjusted her braids over her shoulder. "Have I told you the one about where your name comes from?"

Terric's eyes lit up. "No. Tell me!"

His mother moved the Book of Arwin off the sofa and took a seat next to Terric. "There was once a fearsome warrior who lived up north in the frozen city of Icehaven. He had hair of gold, and he was as tall as a sheep."

"A sheep? That means he was like four feet tall. He was a dwarf!"

"He may have been short in stature, but he was a clever man. His name was Terric the Terrible."

Terric crossed his arms. "I was named after a terrible dwarf?"

"He was invincible to most things, but he did have one weakness... Tickling!" His mother reached over and tickled Terric. He tried to push her off but soon gave in to a fit of laughter. She didn't stop until Terric looked like he might pass out. "Now, don't lie to me again. Just because I'm lenient doesn't mean I'm stupid. I know that you sneak out to sword fight with Warin every chance you get. You come back covered in sweat and dirt every day. What am I supposed to think, that you work up a sweat reading?"

"You know and you still let me?"

"Of course. It pains me to see you stuck in here reading while your brother is out there getting to live out *your* dreams. But you're the second born, and in your father's family, that means you're destined to be a priest."

"Can't you talk to Father?"

"I can. But talking to him and changing his mind are two very different things. And I have to admit, as much as I want you to be happy, I also want you to be alive. I don't love the idea of you running off into battle as the squire of some lord I've hardly met. I'll sleep much better at night knowing that you're right here in Arwin's Gate."

"But I don't want to be safe. I want to be a knight! I want to see the world. I want to fight dragons like Throg did! Even Oriana and Selina and Nesta are going to get to see more of the world than I will. I just have to sit in this stupid city my whole life. It's not fair."

Terric's mother ruffled his shaggy blonde hair. "Okay, I'll talk to him. But let's leave out the part about Throg and dragons. If your father does let you become a knight, he'll make sure you're fully dedicated to spreading the word of Arwin. Now, clean up and get ready for supper. Whether you're a priest or a knight, your father won't stand for you coming to the grand hall looking like this." She stood up and left the room.

Terric glanced at the other tunics that had been laid out for him, but he didn't feel like changing. Instead he just brushed the dirt off himself as best he could. It wasn't like his father was going to pay him any attention at supper anyway. He probably wouldn't even look his way.

Supper wouldn't be a total waste though. He was hungry, but more importantly, Bella would be there. His heart started to race at the thought of seeing her. Would she talk to him?

He looked back at his other tunics. Maybe he should change after all. Which one would Bella like the most? There wasn't really much variation - they were all black and gold with rhinos incorporated somehow. He finally settled on the one he had been wearing two weeks ago when Bella had smiled at him. It was hot and itchy, but if Bella liked it, that was good enough for him.

When Terric entered the grand hall, his mother looked up and smiled at him. She was seated next to his father at the head table on the dais. Just as Terric had predicted, his father didn't even look his way. He was too busy discussing something - probably Marcus - with Sir Aldric Alsight, the master-at-arms. As always, one of Aldric's prized hawks was perched on one of the two rhino statues that stood on their hind legs and formed an arch over the dais. The hawk's eyes immediately began tracking Terric's every movement, and so did Sir Aldric's. Terric felt like he was always being watched by Sir Aldric, or the Hawk, as he was often called.

A few years ago, Terric had been fascinated with Aldric. The knight was everything Terric wanted to be, with all his battle scars and his awesome helmet shaped like a hawk's head. He even told stories about his exploits in the Wizard's War. Aldric had put an arrow in the heart of all three Zaberwald triplets, and rumors had spread amongst the Huntlands that Aldric could see through the eyes of his hawks. That was how he'd been able to find and kill the Zaberwalds in battle. When Terric had asked him if it was true, Aldric had just smiled.

Terric had asked for more stories, but Aldric just wanted to tell that same story over and over again. Eventually Terric got bored with him.

Now Aldric was Terric's nemesis. The hawk was always watching him, always trying to prevent him from doing anything fun.

Terric looked down to avoid Aldric's gaze as he walked to his table. He usually sat at the table with the knights and squires, including his older brother, Marcus. But their table was empty. Terric frowned. Now Marcus was allowed to skip supper too? Terric didn't want to admit it, but he wasn't just upset that Marcus got special privileges. As jealous as he was, Terric still liked eating supper with him and the other men. They always had such entertaining stories of patrolling the savanna or hurting each other during training. One of them even had a story about visiting a brothel.

With his usual table empty, Terric either had to sit by himself or sit with the girls. Yes, he would have loved to eat with Bella, but he didn't want her to think he was girly. And he certainly didn't want to look like a loner. There was only one option. He grabbed a loaf of bread and a turkey leg and headed back to his room. His plan to escape to the Huntlands still needed work.

- CHAPTER 3 -
GARRION

Garrion nodded in approval as his youngest son exited the grand hall. Terric was proving to be quite dedicated to his studies. This wasn't the first time the duke had seen him sneak out during supper to go back to his readings. He knew Terric was enthralled by the words of Arwin, much as Garrion had been in his youth. The two had so much in common. Why then, Garrion wondered, did he find it so difficult to talk to the boy? No matter what he did, Terric always seemed upset with him.

Why can't he see how proud I am of him? Maybe all of that would change once Garrion told him the good news. Tradition held that the earliest a boy could take the oath of Arwin was on their thirteenth birthday. Under those rules, Terric would have had to wait nearly six months for his big day. But there was no need for that. Terric was devoted. Terric was ready. Garrion was sure of it. And so he had written a letter directly to Arwin's Voice to petition for an exception. Just that morning he had received word back: his request had been granted. Terric would be permitted to take the oath in front of all the lords of Treland immediately before the final joust of the tournament.

Garrion took a sip of wine from his goblet. His life hadn't gone the way his young self had expected. He had grown up thinking he would be a priest, but when his older brother fell ill and died, he was forced to trade his books and verses for a sword and shield. As cruel as it was, that was the path Arwin had set for him. He prayed every day that Terric wouldn't suffer the same fate. He would do everything in his power to ensure the boy got everything he was promised. Terric was the lucky one. He would get everything Garrion never had. Everything Garrion had ever wanted.

Garrion was gripping the stem of his goblet so tightly that his knuckles had turned white. He exhaled slowly. It did no good to think of the past. No good at all.

He glanced at his wife. Her mere presence calmed him, even if he couldn't tell her everything that troubled him. He put his hand on her knee. Maybe he hadn't gotten everything he wanted as a child, but that didn't mean he wasn't lucky. He still thanked Arwin every day for sending him Isolda. "You look beautiful this evening, Issy."

"You're too sweet," said Isolda. "But flattering me won't make Conrad any less insulted when your plate comes back full. I would have thought you'd love that cheese."

"What?" asked Garrion.

"You've barely touched your food."

"Oh, right." He picked up a cube of cheese and bit into it. "I was just distracted thinking about delivering the good news to Terric."

"About that..." Isolda folded her hands on her lap. "I was thinking. We never really asked Terric if it was what he wanted. I think that maybe his heart craves a lance."

"Craves a lance?" Garrion burst out laughing. The thought of Terric with a lance was preposterous.

"I'm serious," said Isolda.

Garrion continued laughing. "Are you sure you don't have him confused with Marcus? You know, our other son? The one who's spent the last year training day and night to win the tournament. Now *that* boy...he's meant to wield a lance. Isn't that right, Aldric?" Garrion turned to his oldest friend, Sir Aldric. The two men had become brothers while fighting in the Wizard's War, and Garrion had rewarded his loyalty with a seat on his council and the title of master-at-arms.

"His dedication is unrivaled," said Sir Aldric, tossing a chunk of turkey to one of his hawks. "But he still has work to do. Arwin willing, I shall have him ready for the tournament."

Garrion nodded his approval. "I knew you'd make a knight out of him. He was born for it, just as Terric was born to be a priest. Everything is turning out exactly as Arwin intends." He touched Isolda's knee again and gave it a reassuring squeeze.

"I just want him to be happy," Isolda said.

"I want him to be happy too. Which is why I want him in the temple, far away from the death and destruction of a battlefield. Marcus must already bear that burden."

Isolda didn't respond. At first Garrion just thought she was busy eating, but then he saw the worry in her eyes. He had been so caught up in his own thoughts that he hadn't noticed her distress.

"Issy," he said and grabbed her hand underneath the table.

"Hmm?" she asked, turning to him but not really looking at him.

"Is something the matter?"

"What? No. Why do you think..."

Garrion raised an eyebrow. "I've been your husband for nearly twenty years. I know when something is bothering you."

"It's nothing." Isolda placed her hand on top of his and smiled up at him. "I'm just distracted."

"By what?" asked Garrion. He never wanted his wife to want for anything. His subjects and his faith were important to him. But nothing was more important than his family.

"Really, it's nothing. I was just…thinking about the fabric for Oriana's dress. It came in the wrong shade of blue."

"Then we'll purchase another color. Brother Savaric is tight with the purse strings, but I'm sure I can wrestle a few drachmas from him."

"I hope so. Oriana will be devastated if she looks anything less than perfect for Prince Rixin."

Garrion frowned at the thought of the prince looking at his daughter. "On second thought, maybe I won't. She can wear the ugly blue."

Isolda shoved his arm and laughed. "Do you want none of your children to go off into the world?"

"I should rather like to keep them all right here in Vulture's Keep. But I know that's not possible. It's just…I still see our girls as babies."

Isolda shook her head. "She's sixteen."

"Much too young to be betrothed."

"You're impossible. Look at her." She gestured to the table where their three daughters were seated.

Oriana was easy to spot in the grand hall. Her blonde hair was striking, and her blue eyes had so much warmth. She was laughing with her handmaiden, Bella. "She looks just like you did at that age," said Garrion.

"She does, doesn't she?" Isolda didn't wait for Garrion to respond before turning back to him. "And you're sure about Terric? What if we're wrong? What if…"

"Straying from Arwin's path leads only to ruin!" He hadn't meant to raise his voice. He wouldn't have even realized that he had if Aldric hadn't awkwardly cleared his throat.

Isolda frowned and Garrion grabbed her hand again. He hated when she looked like that. He hated when she looked at him like his soul was damaged.

"I just meant that he should learn from his older brother," he said. "Marcus has embraced his destiny as the next Arwin's Lance. I can't wait to see the look on Prince Rixin's face when Marcus unhorses him. If Rixin even makes it that far in the tournament. With Reavus training him, I doubt he will."

"You better not let Reavus hear you talk like that. Do try to be civil when he arrives, won't you?" Her smile was back. But her words made Garrion's disappear.

The thought of having to see Isolda's younger brother, Duke Reavus, made Garrion's blood boil. Garrion would never forgive Reavus for the atrocities he committed at the end of the Wizard's War.

Garrion still remembered every detail of those final days of the war. He remembered the shock when he heard that King Bogdan Talenov had been assassinated. And he definitely remembered when one of his spies informed him that King Philip Hyposa of the Shield, a man who Garrion thought of as a second father, had been conspiring with the Rashidi to sack bloodstone and wipe out the Talenov bloodline. But most of all, he remembered marching his army south and slaughtering the entire Rashidi army. What happened after that, what Reavus had made him do, he prayed every night he could forget.

He balled his hand into a fist, letting his nails dig into his flesh. *Don't think about that night.* "Civil?" Garrion said. "How could I possibly be civil around that man? After Marcus wins, Reavus will probably claim that I conspired with the Rashidi to fix the tournament." *The same way he accused me of being in league with the Rashidi after I saved his life.*

"Garrion, please. I admit that Reavus does sometimes let his temper cloud his judgment, but you need not sink to his level."

She was right. His beautiful wife was always right. "Perhaps someday Reavus will find Arwin's path. I still can't believe King Ivan allowed Rixin to squire for Reavus. One can only hope Reavus hasn't already poisoned his mind."

Isolda laughed. "Yes, one can only hope."

Garrion looked over at Oriana once more. He had always assumed she would marry Prince Rixin and someday become the queen of Treland. Even if Rixin strayed from the path of Arwin, Oriana would make sure that their sons were raised properly. Garrion glanced back at his wife. Yes, the years had aged her. But she really was every bit as beautiful as the day they'd wed. Prince Rixin would be a lucky man to marry Oriana. Marrying a Hornbolt would be the best thing that ever happened to the young man. Garrion prayed King Ivan could see that, although rumors had been swirling that Ivan was considering a marriage between Rixin and a Rashidi princess. The thought of a Rashidi being the queen of Treland made Garrion's stomach churn.

"My lord," said a young page. "Axion Tobias said to inform you that your merchandise has arrived." The page bowed and ran off.

"It's about time," said Garrion. "I was beginning to think that he wasn't going to deliver."

"You really think the armor will be as good as he claimed?" asked Aldric. "I don't trust that little weasel for a second."

"After how much it cost, it better be the finest armor ever made." Garrion turned to Isolda and brought his lips to her ear. "Aldric's just jealous that I didn't buy him a new suit of armor." He kissed her cheek. "And don't worry about Terric. He's on Arwin's path. I'm sure of it."

Servants began clearing all the plates as Garrion and Sir Aldric stood up.

Isolda grabbed a skewer of beef and handed it to Garrion. "Have Marcus eat this, would you? He must be hungry."

They found Marcus and the other squires practicing archery in the courtyard. Marcus loosed an arrow into the bulls-eye of his target.

They watched him shoot two more bulls-eyes, including one that split an arrow, before Garrion whistled to get his attention.

"Your mother is worried about you not eating." He handed him the skewer.

Marcus took a step closer to the two men and lowered his voice. "Really? Now they're gonna tease me for days."

Garrion laughed. "A little teasing will give you thicker skin."

Marcus puffed out his chest. "I have the skin of a rhino. Just like you."

"Thatta boy. But that's enough for today," said Garrion and slapped him on the back. "Put away your bow, I want to show you something."

"Now? But the sun won't set for another two hours," said Marcus. "Actually, I've been thinking. Maybe I should stay out past dark to make sure I'm ready for any conditions. If the summer rains start early, it could be black as night during the tournament."

"That's an excellent idea," said Garrion, "but I didn't mean for you to stop entirely today." He lowered his voice so just Marcus could hear. "I just meant that you should accompany us to the armory." He raised both his eyebrows. It was hard to contain his excitement.

"My armor came?!" asked Marcus. He turned to the other squires. "Come on, boys. Let's go see it."

Garrion let out a sigh. Marcus wasn't supposed to tell anyone about his new armor. One of them could easily be a spy for Reavus, Or maybe the whole lot of them were spies. Really, he'd expect nothing less.

"Armor? What armor?" asked Garrion.

"His armor was dented the other day," said Sir Aldric, instantly noticing that Garrion was trying to cover up for Marcus' carelessness. "We've been waiting for the smithy to mend it."

"Oh, right. Yeah, that's what I meant," said Marcus. The other squires all looked confused. It was obvious to Garrion that Marcus had gone against his word and told them about the armor.

"Just come with me," said Garrion.

Marcus followed his father and the Hawk out of the courtyard and down the long hall to the armory. It wasn't the quickest path, but Garrion had chosen it for a different reason. They walked past the ten foot tall stone statues immortalizing great Hornbolt men.

"This could be you one day," Garrion said and gestured to the statues as they walked through. "You'll be the first Hornbolt man to ever hold the title of Arwin's Lance. Eight of us have gotten close - all the way to the final joust - but none of us have succeeded. You'll succeed where I failed."

"I will, Father," said Marcus.

Garrion believed him. But he still wondered sometimes if Marcus was really ready for the responsibility. The boy had grown into a talented warrior, but he was only eighteen. He had been born in a time of peace. He had never seen a real battle. He couldn't possibly understand what it was like to ride into combat with thousands of good men, knowing that half of them might not return.

Garrion hadn't even realized that he had clenched his hand into a fist until his nails bit into the skin of his palm. He quickened his pace, ignoring the rest of the statues. Could a man who had never experienced combat really be ready to bear the burden of Arwin's Lance? To have the sole authority to declare a holy war in the name of Arwin? Garrion had a fortnight remaining to prepare him for that responsibility.

His thoughts dissipated when he entered the armory. "What in Arwin's name is this? Is this some sort of joke?"

"It's so...thin," said Marcus as he ran his fingers across the metal. "How am I supposed to compete in this?"

"I knew Tobias couldn't be trusted," said Sir Aldric. "A lance will split this armor in two."

Garrion could picture it happening. He had seen so many deaths. So much blood on his hands. He wouldn't let anyone else die. Especially not his son. Not at a tournament held in his city. Not with him watching in the stands. His hands had started to shake. "That fool will pay for this!" growled Garrion. "Aldric, come with me. Marcus, go back to your training. And next time, when I tell you to keep a secret, you better keep it. Do you understand?"

Marcus nodded. "Yes, Father." He bowed and left the armory.

Garrion walked over to the fragile suit of armor and picked it up with one hand. His anger increased with each step he took on the way up to Tobias' chambers, and unfortunately for Tobias, that was a lot of steps. His chambers were at the very top of the Axion's Tower, the tallest tower in Vulture Keep. The last time Garrion had been up there, he had accused the previous axion of trying to convert his children into godless monsters. After dangling the axion off a balcony, Garrion had heard the confession he knew to be true. The axion had immediately been sent back to Techence. The tower stayed vacant until Techence had sent Axion Tobias Crane.

Garrion barged into the room and threw the suit of armor on the floor. It smashed into a desk and sent glass bottles crashing to the ground.

Tobias let out a shrill scream and jumped up from his chair. Garrion's piercing stare nearly knocked him back into his seat. Tobias started for the door, but Aldric blocked his path.

Garrion's chest heaved with each breath he took. When he finally spoke, his words were quiet and slow.

"Axion Tobias," he said. "I understand that you have odd customs in Techence. I tolerate you prancing around my court in that leather corset and ridiculous hat that you wear to try to appear to be of normal stature, but only because of the valuable services you provide."

Tobias stood and smoothed his waist-length, sleeveless tunic. This was not the first occasion that Garrion had voiced his opinion of his clothes, but Tobias always insisted that his tunics were the latest fashion trend from the Isles of Invention and that they were superior to customary tunics in both functionality and comfort. On this occasion, though, he did not speak up in defense of his fashion.

Garrion pointed to the heap of armor on the ground. "When you try to dress my son in armor this thin, I have to wonder about your continued presence here in Arwin's Gate. Did you get confused and think he was fighting a clowder of kittens rather than entering a joust?"

"Forgive me, my lord," stammered Tobias. He was shaking so badly that he had to keep pushing his glasses up his nose to prevent them from falling off. "I thought..."

"Did you see the armor?" asked Garrion.

"No, my lord. But I was promised by my father that it would absorb..." Tobias paused and produced a sheet of parchment from a hidden compartment in his tunic. He adjusted his glasses and continued. "The force absorbed by the armor should be 2.315 times greater than his old suit of armor, assuming the angle and surface area of the impact stay constant. And if the angle changes..."

Garrion slammed his fists on the desk. The flasks jumped as high as Tobias.

"Enough of this nonsense," bellowed Garrion. "I don't care about calculations. I care about how things work in the real world. I care that my boy doesn't get skewered by Prince Rixin's lance in front of every lord in Treland." He tried to swallow down his rage, and his throat made an odd groaning noise. *No one will harm my son.*

"His armor should easily withstand one and a half times the force generated by a lance before you even see a dent."

"How confident are you of that?"

"Well it does depend on the angle of the lance, but..."

"Are you confident enough to try it yourself?" asked Garrion.

"Garrion," Aldric said and placed a hand on his friend's shoulder. "Maybe we should…"

Garrion shrugged Aldric's hand off. "Answer me!"

"My...my lord," stammered Tobias. "I'm not a knight. And even if I was, the armor wasn't designed for me."

"You're asking me to risk my son's life on your calculations, but you won't risk your own?" Garrion felt like someone was strangling him. He was moments away from completely losing control.

"That's not what I meant. I just..."

"Good. Aldric will help you into the armor. For your sake, I hope it's as strong as you claim."

Garrion paced around the room while Aldric adjusted the straps on the armor to fit it to Tobias' slight frame. Eventually they settled on just dressing him in the chest plate. It hung well below his hips.

"This will have to do," said Aldric.

"Are you sure..." started Tobias.

In one motion, Garrion drew his sword from its sheath and channeled all of his anger into a swing aimed directly at Tobias' midsection. The blow lifted the little man off his feet and propelled him into the stone wall just below a stuffed boar's head. Tobias crumpled to the ground while the stuffed head teetered and then fell on top of him.

"I think you might have killed him," Aldric said. "Are you okay?"

"I'm fine," growled Garrion. The room was eerily quiet. His words seemed to echo around him. All Garrion could hear was his own breath. *Death.* He was always surrounded by death. He looked down at his hand clutching his sword. His knuckles were so white that they looked like they were about to burst through his skin.

Finally there was a small grunt from within the armor. When Tobias had hit the wall and slid down, the loose-fitting chest plate had moved up to cover his face.

"And Tobias is fine too," said Garrion. But for a moment, he hadn't been sure. His hand shook as he sheathed his sword. He needed to get out of this room. He needed fresh air.

"How is that possible?" asked Aldric, inspecting the armor.

"What?" asked Garrion.

Aldric waved him over. Somehow, the armor hadn't been destroyed. Not even a little bit. In fact, there wasn't a dent to be found.

Tobias poked the top of his head out of one of the armholes. When his eyes found Garrion's sword safely in its sheath, he exposed his head the rest of the way. There was a hint of a defiant smile playing on the corners of the axion's mouth.

"Arwin smiles upon you this day," said Garrion. "And so do I. It will require some more testing before I trust it enough to let Marcus wear it in the joust, but for now, it appears to have worked." He took a step back, needing to be rid of this room. To be rid of the blood searing through his mind.

"I'm glad to have been of service," said Tobias. "Perhaps next time you should trust..."

"Don't push your luck," warned Garrion. "And see to it that the armor makes its way back to the armory."

Tobias reached his arm through the neck hole and groped for the straps. "I think I might need some help getting this off," he said. But Garrion and Aldric had already left the room.

Garrion took the stairs two at a time. His head was spinning by the time he pushed through the doors into the gardens. He gasped for air, but the fresh air did little to calm him. Nothing could erase the images of death.

- CHAPTER 4 -
ORIANA

Oriana stared at her reflection as her handmaiden, Bella, braided her long blonde hair. It felt like she had been sitting in this same seat her whole life. Always waiting. But now that the wait was almost over, there was a pit forming in her stomach. What if she wasn't ready?

"Were you thinking about something like this, m'lady?" asked Bella.

Oriana looked at the elaborate braids, twisted in almost the same way her mother wore them. Her whole life she had done exactly what was expected of her. Now, if things went as planned, she'd marry Prince Rixin. The only problem was that she wasn't sure if things would go as planned.

It had been years since she had last seen Prince Rixin. Even so, it wasn't easy to forget the fact that he hadn't seemed interested in her at all. They had just been children then, but she'd still noticed the way his eyes seemed to gravitate to Bella instead. She looked up at her handmaiden.

"Actually, I was thinking about trying something a little different." If she wanted the prince to notice her, she needed to do something bold.

"What did you have in mind?" asked Bella.

Oriana thought about it. She had hoped Bella would just come up with something. Then she remembered how Bella used to wear her long, dark hair in loose curls. Oriana had always thought it was so beautiful. "What if we try more of a crown of braids with some soft curls?"

"That would look lovely. Let me see what I can do." Bella began to undo the braids.

Oriana watched as her appearance started to transform. She knew she was overthinking things, but she couldn't seem to stop. Last time she had seen the prince, she had been going through an awkward stage. It was no wonder that Prince Rixin hadn't given her the time of day. But she wasn't the girl she used to be. And she was certain the prince wasn't the same boy. She had heard the stories about his skills with a sword and his reputation in the joust. Just thinking about Prince Rixin's eyes on her made her pulse race. She remembered his smile and how it lit up his whole face. And his laugh. She bit the inside of her cheek.

Oriana still had almost two weeks to perfect her hair before the prince would arrive for the joust, but she couldn't help but feel like it wasn't enough time. She needed to calm her nerves, and playing with her hair was the only thing that seemed to help. She had to look perfect. It was easy to remember his smile and laugh. But time changed people. What if he wasn't the same? What if he wasn't the one? She bit her lip. That wasn't really what she was worried about. She was terrified that *she* wasn't the one *he* wanted.

"Ori!"

She looked in the mirror to see Nesta, her youngest sister, skipping into the room. Oriana breathed a sigh of relief, happy for the distraction.

"I'm hungry," said Nesta.

"But we just ate supper," said Oriana.

"I know. But Papa finished eating too quickly. I didn't even get to the whole left side of my plate."

"How about we sneak down to the kitchen after Bella finishes my hair?"

A huge smile spread across Nesta's face. "Okay." Then her smile turned quizzical. "Why are you doing your hair after supper?"

"I'm just trying a few new styles."

"For the knights competing in the joust?"

"No...just...to try." Oriana bit her lip. Nesta was too intuitive for a six-year-old.

"Are you really going to marry Prince Rixin?" Nesta asked as she twirled around in a circle, her long skirt lifting around her the way she enjoyed so much.

Oriana's spirits sunk again. She shook her head and turned toward her little sister. *I hope to Arwin that he'll ask for my hand.* "Don't be ridiculous, I haven't even seen him since we were children."

"But I heard Mama and Papa talking about your betro...betroth...betroval?"

"Betrothal, m'lady," said Bella.

"Don't encourage her, Bella." Oriana turned back toward the mirror. Her stomach had been twisted in knots all day and this was making matters worse. It wasn't as though she hadn't heard the rumors. She just thought they were a little premature. Nothing was set in stone yet. Really, it was out of her hands completely. It was up to King Ivan, if he was even still alive. He hadn't made a public appearance in years, not since the death of the queen. Now he just sat in his castle all day doing Arwin knows what. Some people said he reads books all day. Others claimed he ate children. Some people even whispered that he was dead. Whether or not the king was alive, it wouldn't hurt if Prince Rixin wanted to marry her. Surely the prince would have some say in his own future.

"I heard he's very handsome," said Nesta. She continued to twirl around until she got too dizzy to stand. She fell to the floor. "And he *is* the prince."

"And I heard he's the best swordsman in the realm," added Selina.

Oriana looked up to see Selina walking into the room. Selina was her younger sister, but only by two years. Ori and Nesta had gotten their mother's blonde hair and high cheekbones, while Selina had the misfortune of being stuck with their father's dull brown hair and strong chin.

"Now you're encouraging her too?" asked Oriana.

"I was merely stating a fact. He's coming here for the tournament, after all. Just be yourself, you have nothing to fret over," Selina said with a pat on Oriana's shoulder. "If you follow Arwin's path, all will go as it should." She gave her older sister an encouraging smile and then turned to her younger one. "Now, Nesta, it's time to practice your stitching. Sister Morel will have a fit if you show her another crooked seam." She held her hand out and helped Nesta to her feet.

Oriana smiled, but it didn't quite reach her eyes. It didn't matter if Prince Rixin was handsome or the best swordsman. She hadn't seen him in years. She didn't even know if they'd have anything in common. Things were already working out grandly for him. She just wasn't sure if she had any part in his life.

Bella finished the final twist of Oriana's hair and held up a mirror. "How is that, m'lady?"

"It's the perfect hairstyle for sneaking some chocolate out of the kitchen." Oriana winked at Nesta.

Nesta laughed and dropped her needle and thread onto the floor.

"Nesta!" said Selina as she picked up the discarded items.

"Oh, one day I hope I get to marry a prince too," Nesta said as she rested her hands on the arm of Oriana's chair. "Hopefully he'll eat slowly enough so that I can finish my whole supper."

Oriana laughed. "One day I'm sure you'll find your prince. Until then, Selina is right. We must both behave ourselves." She tapped the tip of Nesta's nose.

"Well, maybe we don't have to behave ourselves too much," Selina said. "Some chocolate does sound good right about now."

Nesta giggled.

Oriana glanced once more at her reflection before standing up. The curls looked romantic. They somehow made her look innocent yet more grown up. She suddenly had new confidence. *Maybe everything will work out for the best.*

"Come on," Nesta said and slipped her hand into Oriana's.

Nesta's laughter was contagious. Oriana couldn't help but smile too as her sister pulled her down the hall with more strength than she realized Nesta could muster.

"Shouldn't we clean this up first?" called Selina before giving in and running after the other girls.

Oriana needed to stop obsessing over things beyond her control. What was there to be nervous about, really? Oriana had a great life here in Arwin's Gate. Besides, there would be plenty of handsome knights and lords at the tournament. Just the thought made her stomach twist back into knots. She only had eyes for one lord. She had been smitten with Prince Rixin since the first moment she saw him. *Please let him feel the same way about me now.*

BODY OF ARWIN

- CHAPTER 5 -
ISOLDA

"And how many meat pies should we cook on the second night of the tournament?" asked Conrad the cook.

Isolda sighed. She had planned to go to the library immediately after supper, but Conrad had accosted her before she could make it out of the grand hall. He had a seemingly endless list of dishes and apparently no idea how many mouths any of them would feed.

"Twenty meat pies," said Isolda. "Just assume a packed hall for every meal."

"Okay. Do you know what kind of desserts King Ivan prefers? I've always thought of him as a strawberry sort of man, but on second thought, I think I remember hearing from the new chef at Bloodstone that he was going through a blueberry phase. And King Bogdan always loved spiced cattails..."

"Conrad, you're the best chef I've ever known. I'm sure whatever you make will be perfect. Just don't serve Princess Navya any nuts."

Conrad scribbled something on the back of a sheet of parchment and scratched his beard. "Nuts? I thought it was shellfish. Now I have to rethink the entire menu."

Isolda gave him a reassuring smile. "It'll be okay, Conrad. But I have to go. Other business requires my attention."

Conrad bowed as Isolda left the grand hall.

Finally. She loved Conrad's food, but sometimes his indecisiveness made her want to smack him with his rolling pin.

Isolda walked as fast as she could down the short hallway between the grand hall and the stairs to the library. A few paces from the stairs, her three daughters came racing down the hall. Nesta ran into Isolda's legs and fell backward onto the floor.

Rather than crying, Nesta popped back up and giggled. "Oops. Sorry, Mama."

Isolda patted her on the head. "It's okay, sweet one. What are you girls up to?"

"Choco..." started Nesta, but then her eyes got big and she clapped both hands over her mouth. "I mean...um."

"Are you girls going to pilfer chocolate from the kitchen?" asked Isolda. "How many times has Conrad told you not to do that?"

Nesta put up five fingers and counted them. "Four times." She scrunched up her face. "No, wait. Six."

Oriana and Selina looked at each other and shook their heads.

"We're sorry," said Oriana. "We just needed a little break from sewing and..."

Isolda smiled at her girls and made a mental note to never trust Nesta with any secrets. And she'd have to tell Sister Morel to give Nesta a few extra lessons on counting.

"No need to apologize," said Isolda. "Unless you weren't planning on getting any for me?"

The girls looked relieved. "We can do that," said Selina.

"Good. Just don't get caught. Maybe the mystery of his missing chocolate will keep Conrad from worrying about the tournament menus for a few days." She turned to Oriana. "Your hair looks beautiful like that."

"Thanks," said Oriana. "I don't know if I like it..."

"Yes you do!" said Nesta. "And Prince Rixin will too!"

"Nesta, please!" said Oriana.

Selina laughed.

"I think the prince will like that style very much," said Isolda. "Just try not to get your hopes up too much. Your father is keen on the match, but ultimately it's up to King Ivan and Prince Rixin, and I've heard rumors that the king is considering marrying him to Princess Navya instead." As soon as Isolda said it, the crushed look on Oriana's face made her wish she hadn't.

"But Navya's a *Rashidi*," said Oriana. "Surely Father wouldn't stand for that."

"Your father might not stand for it, but unless you're the one that Rixin decides to marry, your father has little say in the matter. And anyway, it's just a rumor. I shouldn't have mentioned it." Isolda looked down at Nesta. *So much for that secret.*

"But how..." said Oriana.

"You'd make a much better match for Rixin," said Isolda. "I'm sure the king will see that. Now, go get that chocolate."

At the mention of chocolate, Nesta yanked Oriana's hand and took off running down the hall.

After all the distractions, Isolda finally made it to the library stairs. It was time to get some answers about the body of Arwin.

Isolda held her nose as she wound down the stairs deep into the underbelly of Vulture Keep. Despite Arwin's Gate being so dry, the parchment of the books still managed to smell old and musty. Or maybe it was the monks who looked after the books. Either way, the smell was unpleasant.

Isolda cursed under her breath when she saw Father Percival sitting at a table between two rows of bookshelves. She knew she would likely encounter at least one holyman during her mission, but she had hoped it wouldn't be Percival. He was the Master of Truth on her husband's council. Officially, he was on the council to provide Garrion with guidance from the good Lord Arwin. Unofficially, he was in charge of a vast spy network of priests, monks, and missionaries spread to the far corners of the known world. While Isolda was generally unimpressed with his abilities as a spymaster, she assumed he was competent enough to sniff out odd behavior right under his nose.

"Another map missing," grumbled Father Percival as Isolda approached. When she was a few steps away, he looked up, startled. "Forgive me, my lady. I didn't hear you approach."

Some spymaster. How can Garrion trust him to keep tabs on lords on the other side of Pentavia when he couldn't see me coming from five feet away?

Percival grabbed his cane from the side of the table and used it to balance himself as he slowly stood. Isolda couldn't tell if the creaking sound was coming from his bones or from his chains. Like all priests of Arwin, Percival's wrists were shackled and chained to a metal band around his head. The band had four screws in it, and whenever he told a lie or had an impure thought, he was expected to tighten one of the screws. Isolda always found the idea of it repulsive and nonsensical. Eventually she had convinced herself that the screws were actually just there to keep the old priest's drooping skin from sliding off his face.

"What brings you to the library today?" asked Percival.

Isolda had known this question would come, and she had prepared an answer before entering the library. "I worry about Terric."

"For what reason? Is he ill?"

"No, no. Nothing like that."

"Does his faith in Arwin waver?" Percival sounded much more concerned by this than the possibility of Terric being sick.

"Sometimes I fear it does. I'm sure Arwin will show him his path in due time, but I worry for his happiness in the meantime. Adjusting to life after taking the oath might be difficult for him. I was hoping to find a story or two to show him how rewarding the priesthood can be."

Percival stepped closer to Isolda. His cloudy grey eyes looked deep into her soul. She felt like he could see that she wasn't telling the truth. Maybe he was more proficient at spycraft than she had realized.

Isolda turned and looked at one of the shelves. Had she overdone it? While she did usually try to sound like a believer - lest Garrion would have her banished over the wall for heresy - it was known amongst the priests that she was not the most devout follower. Talking about Arwin's path might have been too much.

"If the boy needs inspiration, he need only read the Book of Arwin," said Percival.

"He has..." Isolda stopped short. She needed to tread carefully. If she made it sound like Terric wasn't a believer, he might spend the rest of his childhood locked in the temple reciting verses. "He reads it every day, your holiness. But supplemental texts can give one such a deeper understanding of Arwin's teachings."

"Hmph. I must agree with you on that point. Let me find something..."

Isolda put a hand on Percival's bony shoulder. "Please, I didn't mean to disturb you. I'm sure I can find something on my own."

Percival nodded. "As you wish." As he started to sit down at the table, he muttered, "Maybe you'll learn something about Arwin too."

Isolda walked over to the dusty old shelves. She couldn't even read the titles of some of the books through the thick layer of dust on their spines. The waning daylight creeping through the tiny windows did little to help.

"Now how are these ordered?" asked Isolda softly, trying to remember the system that the old axion in Icehaven had taught her.

Isolda had loved the library in Icehaven. Actually, that's not entirely accurate. She loved the *contents* of the library in Icehaven, and once she had found a wonderful story, she loved taking it back to the great hall, curling up by the hearth, and getting lost in a magical tale. No matter how cold it got in Icehaven, no matter how many layers of ice and snow covered the city, a good book always warmed her soul. But the library in Vulture Keep was not like the one in Icehaven. The one in Vulture Keep was strictly curated by the priests to only contain books that glorified Arwin. The result was a library whose shelves mainly just contained records detailing the locations of various relics rather than anything actually worth reading.

But in this case, that was exactly what she needed.

After over an hour of searching, Isolda came across *The Body of Arwin*, written by Father Osbert of Bloodstone. She remembered the priest well from her youth, especially the disappointed look he would give her whenever she fumbled over her words while reciting boring passages.

Isolda grabbed the book and started flipping through the pages. It began with a graphic description of the Battle of Arwood, in which Arwin heroically sacrificed himself to turn the battle against the Sky Islanders.

She skimmed over the details - she had heard the story a thousand times. Everyone knew that Arwin had been dressed in a great suit of golden armor. Everyone knew that Voltanis had slit Lord Arwin's throat and drank his blood. And everyone knew that Arwin's self-sacrifice had miraculously sapped Voltanis of all his power.

But not everyone knew what happened to Arwin's body afterward. Actually, no one did. The Barcovan Empire fell into ruin after the end of the Sky War, and thus the relic was lost. Some speculated that the body was simply buried in a graveyard near Arwood. Other's thought that some lord kept it hidden away in his private collection. Some historians who had no qualms about weaving a bit of fiction into their works even claimed that the House of Wisdom - a mysterious group of magicians from Rashid - had possession of the body for some time.

Isolda flipped ahead hoping to find...well, she didn't know exactly what she was hoping to find. Ideally, the book would have ended with something that led her right to her father's assassin. Instead, it merely ended with a sketch of the skeleton and armor.

Great.

She slammed the book shut and sent a cloud of dust billowing into the air.

Thanks for your help, Father Osbert, thought Isolda as she put the book back on the shelf. But then she got an idea.

This library was filled with record books from all over. She suspected it was one of the ways monks passed information to Percival. Even the most overzealous soldier trying to root out a spy wouldn't think to check for secret messages embedded in the mundane records of a monk.

It was possible Percival had records from the Bloodstone reliquary.

Isolda searched for the section labeled "Records" and scanned the spines for any mention of Father Osbert. There were at least a hundred books authored by him. She grabbed the one she needed, *Bloodstone Reliquary, 1300 - 1310 AE*, but her heart sank when she saw that the cover was locked shut by a thick strip of metal.

She assumed Father Percival had the key, but what reason could she give for wanting to read it? Meticulous record keeping of the contents and visitors of a reliquary was the exact opposite of something that would get Terric excited about becoming a priest.

"Can I help you with that?" asked a voice behind her.

Isolda turned to see Father Percival studying her. How long had he been watching? Maybe he was a better spy than she thought.

"Odd choice," said Percival, grabbing the book out of her hands.

"This?" asked Isolda, trying to stall while she thought of an excuse. "You know, I was thinking. When I was a child, I always loved my father's relics. They all had such a rich history. So why not teach Terric by showing him objects that Arwin actually interacted with? I just wanted to make sure that all of my favorites are still there. It would be a shame to travel all the way to Bloodstone only to be disappointed by an empty reliquary."

"An excellent idea, my lady. Perhaps I've underestimated your devotion to the good lord." He gestured for her to follow as he hobbled through the maze of shelves back to the table at the center. He unlocked a cabinet to reveal hundreds of keys hanging from hooks. "Sometimes I wish the reliquary here was more impressive. Maybe that would get the boy to show some interest."

Isolda nodded. The reliquary at Arwin's Gate was indeed sparse in comparison to the one at Bloodstone. It was hardly a reliquary at all, really. The Bloodstone reliquary was a grand chamber filled with suits of armor and golden swords and ornate robes. The one at Arwin's Gate was little more than a closet with a rotted bandage and a gnarled wooden dagger. The bandage had supposedly been used to save the decaying arm of a man suffering from the crimson thirst. Isolda found the story of it to be even less interesting than the Book of Arwin.

The story of the dagger, on the other hand, Isolda could not forget. It began over twenty years ago, before the Wizard's War, during a time of relative peace. A great wealth of gold, jewels, and spices had just been discovered deep in the jungles of Tujira, and all of the royal families scrambled to stake their claim. Isolda's father, King Bogdan, made a handful of journeys, but as his health declined, Costel, his second son, offered to go in his stead. On his first expedition, he returned with a ship full of gold and claimed that he could have brought three times as much if he'd had three more ships. So he went back, but on the return voyage, his ship was lost at sea. King Bogdan blamed Barcovan privateers and demanded they be arrested immediately. Barcova refused, Bogdan called for his bannermen, Barcova did the same. Then the Zaberwalds joined on the side of Barcova, and thus began the Wizard's War. There are countless tales of bravery and betrayal that occurred during the war, but alas, the story of the gnarled wooden dagger is not one of them.

The story of the dagger didn't resume until many years after the war, when Garrion's younger brother, Jax, went back to the site of the shipwreck. He hadn't really expected to find much. At best he thought he might find a few gold coins hidden in the trousers of the dead crew. The treasure chests, he was sure, would have been plundered long ago. But oddly enough, he found the entire ship had been untouched. Even more oddly, all of the treasure chests were completely empty. Except one. That was where he found the gnarled wooden dagger. And as it had belonged to Isolda's brother, Jax thought it fitting that she should have it.

At least, that was the story Jax had told. Everyone knew that Jax's stories were often laced with a bit of fantasy, and this story was no different. Garrion told her that Jax had probably been beaten to the wreck by scavengers and didn't want to admit it, or that he had kept all the real treasure for himself and then gambled it all away. But what if the story really was true? What if her brother Costel really had valued that dagger so much that he decided to return home with no other treasure? Isolda couldn't crack the riddle, so she had locked the dagger away in the reliquary. She had hoped it would at least draw a few extra visitors to Arwin's Gate. It hadn't.

"Ah, there we are," muttered Percival as the lock on the book clicked open. He set it near a dim lamp so that Isolda could read the contents.

Isolda sat down and scanned the pages, searching for any mention of the body of Arwin. At first it appeared on every page. She even saw her name scrawled on the page from the day her father had finally let her see it. But then, in 1304 AE, at the end of the Wizard's War, all mentions of the body of Arwin ceased. She flipped back to the last time it had been mentioned.

She almost missed it, but at the bottom of one of the pages, in smaller letters than most of the records, was a note about the body:

Body of Arwin: transferred.

She had seen a similar note about a few other relics while she was scanning the records, but all of those said *where* the relic was transferred. This one didn't.

Isolda flipped back to the previous entry about the body:

Visitor: Duke Garrion of House Hornbolt

Reason: View the body of Arwin

What? That didn't make any sense. She stared at Garrion's name on the page. Her husband had been the last one to visit the body before it was mysteriously transferred. Or stolen. Why else would the body be listed as transferred with no destination listed? Father Osbert certainly wouldn't have told everyone that the body of Arwin, the most prized relic of her father's collection, was stolen under his watch.

"Is everything okay?" asked Percival. "You look pale."

Isolda started to slam the book shut, but she froze when the date at the top of the page caught her eye. The day that Garrion visited the body was the day before her father was murdered.

Did Garrion murder her father and steal the body of Arwin?

No, he couldn't have. That was ridiculous. Isolda knew Garrion. He wouldn't do something like that. He had his faults, but he was a good man. A peaceful man. He was the one who had warned her brothers that Philip Hyposa and the Rashidi were planning to assassinate them.

Isolda shut the book and handed it back to Percival. "Sorry, I think I need to get some air. Thanks for your help."

- CHAPTER 6 -
TERRIC

Terric's head hurt. He had been staring at his stolen map all afternoon, but he didn't feel like he was making any progress.

The basic path was fairly straightforward. He had to start out going north on the Grass Road, which he'd traveled occasionally with his father on their way to visit the surrounding villages and manor houses. But they had never gone more than half a day's ride in any one direction, and therein lay the problem. Terric had rarely left Arwin's Gate. All he knew of the world was from stories he had heard, and he had no way of knowing how accurate those stories were.

He had been told that Seawatch had been built to guard against the Rashidi potentially invading from Nairo's Cup. He assumed Seawatch had a fleet of war galleys for that purpose, but did they have a bustling port? If they did, it would make his trip simple. He could just take the Grass Road north to the ruins of Deseros, cut east to Seawatch, and then take a ship all the way to Horn Harbor. At that point, he'd be in the Huntlands. Easy.

But what if Seawatch was nothing more than a glorified watchtower on the edge of the Shield owned by some grumpy old lord just waiting to die? There would be no ships, and Terric would have wasted...well, he didn't know how long that detour would take. He didn't know how long any of it would take. But on the map it looked like it was pretty far.

Then Terric's mind started to wander. He pictured himself and Warin arriving at Seawatch and meeting the grumpy old lord. The lord, as it just so happened, was in need of some adventurous young lads. His daughter, a beautiful maiden who, in Terric's imagination, looked almost identical to Bella, had been kidnapped by Rashidi pirates, and any man who could save her would be given her hand in marriage and would inherit all of Seawatch...

A knock on the door brought Terric out of his daydream.

"Terric?" called the high-pitched voice of Axion Tobias.

"One moment please!" yelled Terric. He hastily rolled up the stolen map and shoved it under the bed. "Okay, come in."

Tobias walked in with an inkwell in one hand, a quill in the other, and a stack of parchment tucked under his arm. What happened next was the most glorious feat of coordination Terric had ever witnessed. As Tobias put the quill and inkwell on Terric's desk, the ink started to spill. He adjusted his arm to try to balance the inkwell, but as he did, the papers came loose from under his arm. And then he tried to grab the papers with the same hand that was carrying the inkwell. Papers and ink flew everywhere.

It took all of Terric's self-restraint to keep from laughing. But he knew better than to laugh at Tobias' clumsiness. Two weeks ago Tobias had tripped over his own feet, spun around, and somehow wrapped himself five times in Terric's bed curtains. Terric had laughed at him, and that night Tobias had forced him to write twice his usual amount of multiplication tables.

Terric wasn't looking forward to whatever Tobias had planned for him to do with the quill and all those papers, so he tried to be on his best behavior. He rushed over and helped the flustered axion gather all the papers and wipe up the spilled ink.

When they were finished, Tobias adjusted his glasses and straightened his ink-covered tunic. "Well then, I thought this evening you should copy the writings of Cornelius Turbine. Do you know who he is?"

"Cornelius Turbine was the Prime Minister of Techence during the War of Gears."

"And?" asked Tobias.

Terric racked his brain. "And...he was really smart?"

Tobias sighed. "No. He was..."

"What do you mean no?" asked Terric. "How could a prime minister of Techence not be smart?"

"I didn't mean that. Of course he was smart. He was one of the greatest gristologers ever! If not for his invention of the floating caltrop, the Huntlands might have taken over."

Terric snapped his fingers. "Ah, I remember now. Cornelius Turbine was best known for his invention of the floating caltrop."

Tobias looked at his young pupil. Terric couldn't tell if the axion was annoyed or impressed with how easily Terric had tricked him.

"That's correct," said Tobias. "Now, I thought tonight you could copy some of the letters that Cornelius wrote to Axion Dennis Frost while designing the floating caltrop. I think you'll find that they are both eloquently written and gristologically stimulating."

"You mean these papers?" asked Terric, holding up three sheets of parchment badly stained with ink. The pages were closer to the color of Tobias' dark skin than the natural color of parchment. Only a handful of words on the pages were still legible.

Tobias let out a high pitched gasp and snatched the papers from Terric. "No! My caltrop letters! I must try to salvage these!" He hurried to the door. Terric thought he was going to get out of any lessons, but just before Tobias exited, he said, "Just write someone a letter tonight."

Terric stared at the papers. To whom was he going to write a letter? It wasn't like he knew anyone from a faraway land to communicate with. And if he needed to talk to anyone in the castle, he could just have a conversation with them rather than writing them a letter like a weirdo. Then an idea struck him. What if he could write a letter to express his feelings to Bella? He always found himself horribly tongue-tied in her presence, but if he could take the time to compose his thoughts in a letter...

My Dearest Bella,

I've always loved you. Your hair is like the tail feathers of a vulture...

No. Terric tore the parchment in half and started over.

Lady Bella,

I know that you probably only know me as Oriana's little brother who will someday be a priest. But that's not the truth of it. I'm not going to take the oath of Arwin. I'm going to run away, and I want you to join me. I haven't figured out the entire plan yet, but you and I and Warin can all sneak away. We'll go north to the Huntlands. Or whatever you want, really.

I would cross the entire Rashid desert just to make love to you...

Terric shook his head. *Too forward.* And now that he was thinking about making love to Bella, he knew he was in no state to write a proper love letter. His next attempt would probably end up reading like an obscene limerick comparing her breasts to Conrad's chocolate pastries. Both were fantastic in their own right, of course. But which was better? He pondered the question for a moment, but then he realized the answer didn't matter. In his current position, he couldn't have either. He had asked Conrad for chocolate pastries a hundred times, but the cook always just shooed him out of the kitchen. All the while, Conrad was happy to make Marcus anything he asked for. Fresh bread? No problem. Berries and cheese? Gladly. Gazelle steaks? Conrad would probably try to chase one down himself just to give Marcus what he wanted. That was how it was. Marcus was the heir. Marcus got everything. As Terric thought about it, a horribly wonderful idea started to take shape. He suddenly knew exactly what letter he would write next. He steadied his hand and tried to emulate the way he believed Prince Rixin would write:

Lord Marcus,

I know I'm not expected at Arwin's Gate for another week, but I've come early to watch you. You are a fine warrior, but you are not my equal. You have no chance of besting me in this tournament. But luckily for you, I care not for the title of Arwin's Lance. My mantle is already full of trophies and my bed is full of beautiful women. But my belly...my belly has never experienced your cook's fine chocolate pastries. So my proposal is this: leave a plate of chocolate pastries in the stairwell to the guest tower within two hours, and you have my word that I will allow you to win the tournament.

His Royal Highness,

Rixin of House Talenov

Crown Prince of Treland, Duke of Arwood, Blood of Arwin, Distinguished Knight of the Order of Chains, and Defender of the Wood

Terric read over the letter and nodded in approval. *Yes. It's perfect.* Then he made one final addition.

P.S. It will be embarrassing for me to lose, so I shall require your embarrassment in return. As such, you must remove your trousers and wear them on your head until the pastries have been delivered.

Terric rummaged under his bed for the bow and quiver that he'd pilfered from the armory a few months ago. By the time he found it, the ink on the letter was dry. He wrapped the letter around the shaft of an arrow, sealed it with a bit of hot wax, and then extinguished all the lamps and candles in his room. With his room now dark, he walked over to his window and took aim at the courtyard. His arms still burned from climbing earlier as he pulled back the bowstring.

As soon as he let the arrow fly, he realized he probably shouldn't have aimed quite so close to Marcus. He was relieved when the arrow stuck harmlessly in the ground.

Terric ducked. He waited half a minute until he peered back through the window. Marcus was reading the letter. Terric couldn't quite make out his expression, but by the tilt of his head, he could tell that Marcus was confused.

Marcus looked around nervously, and then, much to Terric's amusement, he removed his trousers and put them on his head.

Success!

Terric raced down the stairs toward the kitchen. He wanted to see the look on Conrad's face when Marcus showed up pantsless and demanded chocolate pastries. Right before Terric got to the kitchen hall, he skidded to a stop and peered around the corner. The timing was perfect. Conrad had just opened the door. But he didn't even look surprised. He just smiled and nodded and said "Yes, my lord. Chocolate pastries coming right up."

Then it all went wrong. Conrad's smile changed to a frown, and he pointed down the hall right at Terric. Marcus turned and locked eyes with Terric. He looked furious.

Uh oh.

Terric took off running in the opposite direction. He was quick for his size, but Marcus was so much bigger and faster. Every step of Marcus' was equal to two of Terric's. The distance between the two quickly disappeared. Terric knew he would be caught within seconds, so he ducked into the first doorway he came across. As Marcus ran past, Terric jumped on his back and pulled his pants down over his eyes.

"Terric!" yelled Marcus. "I'm gonna kill you!"

Terric tried to use the distraction to run away, but Marcus was too quick. He grabbed him by his collar and pulled him back. Then he raked his knuckles over his head.

"Stop!" cried Terric. He *hated* when Marcus did that. It was so humiliating. He would have preferred to just get punched in the face.

"What's going on out there?" yelled a deep voice from down the hall.

Marcus froze. "Aldric's coming. Get in there." He opened the door to the storeroom and tossed Terric inside.

Terric was thankful that he landed on a bag of flour. He took a moment to dust himself off and then pressed his ear to the door to see when the coast was clear for him to come out.

"What are you doing prancing around with no pants on?" asked Aldric.

"Sir, I uh..." Marcus paused. "I had a scorpion in my trousers. I shook it out, though."

"And where is it now?"

"It was just over there."

"There's no scorpion there."

"It must have skittered away," said Marcus.

"Hmmph, okay. Get your pants back on. We need to test your new armor."

New armor? Why did Marcus get new armor? He had just gotten new armor less than a year ago.

Terric waited until he heard Aldric and Marcus walk down the hall before he emerged from the storeroom. He should have gone back to his room and been satisfied with making Marcus run around with no pants on, but his curiosity got the better of him. He walked to the armory and peered through the keyhole. Inside, he could see a golden suit of armor fitted over a bag of hay. Marcus took a swing at it with his sword, but other than the ear piercing clang of metal on metal, there didn't seem to be any effect. Next Marcus took a spear and stabbed at the armor. Again, no damage.

"That's incredible!" said Marcus. "This is the strongest armor I've ever seen."

"It does appear to be," agreed Aldric. "And that's not even the best part."

"It's not?"

Aldric shook his head. "No. The best part is the way it looks."

"Thin and unimposing?" asked Marcus.

"Exactly."

"How is that good?"

"Have I ever told you the story of how my father died?" asked Sir Aldric.

"No," said Marcus.

Here we go, thought Terric. He was sure this would be another retelling of how Aldric killed the Zaberwald triplets. The old knight really needed to come up with some new stories.

Sir Aldric's golden eyes stared into the distance. "When I was a young man, no older than you, I was out hunting in the savanna with my father. He looked like a true knight, dressed in expensive leather armor with our family sword on his hip. I had been wearing armor when we started out, but I had gotten too hot in the afternoon sun and complained until my father let me remove it. When we were attacked by raiders, they put an arrow through my father's heart before we even saw them coming. But they didn't touch me. They figured they'd lasso me and take me as a slave." Aldric whistled and one of his hawks flew down from the rafters of the armory and landed on his arm. "They did lasso me, but they only made it about ten steps before my birds tore their throats out."

"That's horrible," said Marcus. "I'm so sorry about your father. But what does that have to do with my armor?"

"Being underestimated can be just as powerful as being feared. You just need to know how to leverage it. So let the other knights laugh at you. Let them think they're going to skewer you with their lances. Let them call you names. Use your enemies' ignorance like an invisibility cloak. Mask yourself in it. And after the joust, when they're lying on their backs and you're hoisting Arwin's Lance, you'll have the last laugh."

"You really think the armor is that silly looking?" asked Marcus.

"Oh yes. I dare say it would be less embarrassing to show up for the joust in a dress. At least that way everyone would think you were trying to be funny. This armor though...you'll be the laughing stock of the tournament."

Marcus glared at the armor. "Well that's not acceptable. I can't have everyone laughing at me if I'm going to be the Duke of Arwin's Gate someday, now can I?"

"Hmm," said Aldric, stroking his pointy beard. "I hadn't thought of it that way. No, I suppose you can't. Roger?" he called.

A minute later the blacksmith appeared from between two racks of halberds. "Yes, sir?"

"We need to make a few additions to Marcus' armor."

"Does it not fit?" asked Roger.

"He hasn't tried it on yet," said Aldric. "But..."

"He'll need to try it on before I make any adjustments." The blacksmith easily lifted the armor and started buckling it on Marcus. Roger's years at the forge were chiseled into his muscles and caked on his skin in a thick layer of soot, but the ease at which he lifted the armor still surprised Terric.

"It's so light," Marcus said as he lifted his arm. He knocked his fist against the metal. "This is incredible."

"Good," said Aldric. "The lighter it is, the more we can add before it becomes unwieldy. Let's start with the shoulders." He pointed to two thick metal plates on the wall. "Can you turn those into rhino horn pauldrons?"

"We could probably make that work," said Roger. "Or maybe I could polish parts of the breastplate to form the Hornbolt sigil. It's a new technique out of Techence, but I'm sure some knights' armor will feature it for the tournament." He walked over and grabbed a sheet of metal. Part of it was rough, while other parts were polished into a smooth, reflective surface. It created a striking black and white pattern.

"I like that," said Marcus. "And with the gold of my armor, it would look even better."

Sir Aldric shook his head. "I thought you didn't want to look ridiculous?"

"I don't. Roger said that other knights will be wearing it."

"Maybe the ones who can't afford something better," said Aldric. "If you showed up to the tournament in that, people would begin to gossip that the Hornbolts were on the edge of bankruptcy. You don't want to end up like Lord Barkridge, do you?"

"Lord Barkridge?"

"A few years ago someone started a rumor that he was going bankrupt. He wasn't, but it didn't matter. The other lords and merchants stopped trading with him out of fear that he wouldn't be able to pay his debts. It turned out to be a self-fulfilling prophecy. He was bankrupt within the year. Bandits overran his estate and seized control of his lands. King Gormont is offering titles and lands for anyone who can bring the bandits to justice, but with the state of things up north, no one has the troops to spare. Last I heard, the bandits were still in control."

Marcus gave some proper response, mourning for the honorable Lord Barkridge. Terric didn't listen though. He was already halfway down the hall, and in his head, he was already making plans to find Lord Barkridge's estate so he could defeat the bandits and earn the reward.

- CHAPTER 7 -
ISOLDA

Isolda rolled over and tried to get comfortable for the tenth time that night. But when her eyes fell on Garrion, she had to roll back in the other direction. He was the reason for her troubled sleep.

Was he really a murderer?

He couldn't be. He had his faults, as everyone did, but deep down Isolda knew he was a good man. He cared about her. He cared about their children. And he was a devout follower of Arwin. Isolda didn't agree with all of Arwin's teachings, but at least Arwin taught his followers not to assassinate kings.

Despite her sound reasoning, ever since she had seen Garrion's name in that record book a few days ago, she had found sleep utterly impossible. During the day she was able to distract her mind with preparations for the tournament, but at night, when she was left alone with her thoughts, all she could picture was her father's blood on Garrion's hands. She squeezed her eyes shut. It was as if she were forced to watch the same play over and over again with no escape.

Enough. Isolda knew that she couldn't continue like this. But how could she get past it?

If Garrion really had murdered her father, then everything she ever knew about him, every good memory she had with him, had all been lies. That was not something she could simply choose to forget. She needed to talk to someone, but who could she trust? Garrion was always the person she went to when she needed to talk. Just the thought made a lump form in her throat.

Maybe she should just ask him about it.

Isolda played out the scenario in her head. First, she imagined Garrion was innocent. He would laugh at the question. Maybe he'd get angry. But either way, she wouldn't know for sure if he was telling the truth.

Then she imagined that he had, in fact, killed her father. He would deny it, but he would start to worry that she suspected him. He wouldn't want her to tell anyone about it, and, being a killer, he would have no aversion to adding another body to his tally. So maybe she wouldn't wake up in the morning, having died from a horrible heart attack in the middle of the night. Or maybe she'd mysteriously fall down the stairs and break her neck. One way or another, her murderous husband would see to it that she was silenced.

Isolda pushed the sheets off. It was stifling to be in the same bed as Garrion. She couldn't bear to lie beside him for one more second, to stare at the face she thought she knew. What if her whole life was a lie? No matter how hard she tried to swallow it down, the lump in her throat wouldn't go away.

As she got out of bed, Garrion rolled over and grabbed her arm.

"Where are you going?" he mumbled, his eyes only half open.

"I just need some water," said Isolda. "Go back to sleep."

"Want me to come with you?" His eyes opened a little more and a mischievous smile started to form in the corners of his mouth. "Maybe we can sneak down to the kitchen like we used to." He reached for Isolda's breast, but she pulled back.

Usually the thought of sneaking down to the kitchen and making love on the table would have made her smile, but tonight she had to force the smile to come. "Not tonight," she said and pulled the covers up to Garrion's chin.

He grunted and closed his eyes. A second later his snoring resumed.

Isolda wrapped a shawl around her shoulders and exited their room. She didn't know where she would end up. She just couldn't be in her room with Garrion. Maybe a drink of water would help calm her nerves.

But her feet didn't carry her to the kitchen. Instead, she found herself walking up the winding staircase to Tobias' chambers. She had only been to his room a handful of times, and never alone. Their secret meetings about her establishments were generally conducted far from the castle. On the few occasions when urgent business had forced them to meet in Vulture Keep, they had always met in the bathhouse. It was the one place in the castle where anyone respected her privacy.

Isolda knocked gently on the door, but it creaked open. The lock had been smashed when Garrion had barged in and nearly killed the poor man. She shook her head at the thought. Just more evidence that maybe Garrion was a murderer after all.

"Hello?" said Tobias. His voice cracked halfway through the word.

"It's just me, no need to be afraid," said Isolda as she pushed the door open the rest of the way.

Tobias was sitting on the balcony next to his telescope. He immediately jumped up and bowed. His long nightcap flopped in front of his face and nearly knocked off his glasses.

"My lady," said Tobias. His eyes got wide and his face turned dark red when he looked up and saw she was wearing only a chemise and a shawl. He immediately covered his eyes. "You're not...this is...improper," he stuttered.

"Oh please," said Isolda. "You don't have to cover your eyes. It's not like I'm here to seduce you. I just need someone to talk to, and you're the only person in this city I can trust." Yes, she considered some of the other ladies at court her friends. But she couldn't trust them with something like this. It would be too dangerous if they told their husbands, which she was almost sure they would do.

Tobias uncovered his eyes, but Isolda could tell that he was staring past her at the wall.

"Do you mind if I join you?" asked Isolda. Before Tobias could answer, she grabbed a chair from his desk and dragged it out onto the balcony.

They sat in silence for a moment.

"The stars are a funny thing," said Tobias.

"How so?" asked Isolda.

"When I was at the university, I used to study them. The astrologers would tell me that the movements of the stars could be used to predict major events."

"And can they?"

"Maybe. They have equations that show how past events have correlated with certain celestial movements. One star in particular, the eye of Krakos, seems to be related to wars. The last time it came to prominence, the Wizard's War began within a month."

"The eye of Krakos?" asked Isolda. "Can we see it now?"

"Yes. If you look..." Tobias looked through his telescope and made a few adjustments. "If you look here, you'll see it starting to appear. Between Cynigma and Chalkos."

Isolda bent forward and peered through the lens. It hadn't been visible to the naked eye, but through the telescope, she could see the red star. "I remember this star," said Isolda. "When I was imprisoned in Icehaven, I would always watch the stars at night. This was my favorite one. I thought the red was so pretty. They called it Flameheart up there."

"It was my father's favorite star too," said Tobias. "But that's not surprising. He loved anything that brought war, because war in Pentavia meant plenty of lords willing to throw drachmas at Techence in exchange for better weapons."

"You said it was starting to appear," said Isolda. "When will it be visible to the naked eye?"

"I haven't done the calculations, but an initial estimate would put it at..." Tobias paused to think for a moment. "...Seven hundred and twenty-three days."

"Do you think it will really bring war?"

Tobias shrugged. "How could a star have the ability to bring war? The Marinthians believed that its presence in the sky meant that Krakos was angry. And when he was angry, he would fill their heads with thoughts of war."

"How often does it appear?"

"It varies, but on average, about two decades."

"The amount of time it takes for a new generation of warriors to be of fighting age," said Isolda. She thought of her oldest son, Marcus, born just after the Wizard's War. There were thousands more like him, born all over Pentavia to warriors coming home after a long war. And soon those children would be looking to make a name for themselves. The thought gave her chills.

"An astute observation, my lady."

"What else can you divine from the stars?" asked Isolda.

"What do you want to know?"

"Is my husband a murderer?"

Tobias coughed. "I'm sorry. My hearing must be following the path of my eyesight. I thought you said..."

"Is Duke Garrion Hornbolt a murderer?" said Isolda. "Did he murder my father?" Saying it out loud made the possibility seem more real.

Tobias adjusted his glasses and looked at her for the first time that night, finally moving past the fact that Isolda was dressed in her nightclothes. "What would make you think...?"

"In the Razortooth Tavern," said Isolda. "That hole. The body of Arwin was down there."

"But that relic belonged to the Talenovs."

"It did. It belonged to my father. Yet there it was, under a half-built tavern here in Arwin's Gate."

"How is that possible?" It was obvious that gears were turning inside of Tobias' head to connect the pieces.

"I didn't know either," said Isolda, "so I went to the library and looked at some old records. The body was listed as being 'transferred' a few days after my father was killed."

"To where?"

"It   didn't   say."

"Odd," said Tobias. "Arwinian monks are known for their precision of record keeping. An omission such as that, about such an important relic...that seems an unlikely mistake."

"The kind of mistake that would only be made if the body had been stolen and they didn't want anyone to know."

"Yes, perhaps. But what does that have to do with Garrion?"

"He was the last one listed as having visited the body of Arwin. The day before my father was murdered."

Tobias shifted uneasily in his chair.

"I want to believe that Garrion isn't a killer," said Isolda. "But all of the evidence points to him. We know he was at Bloodstone the day before the murder occurred. We know that the body of Arwin went missing at the same time, or at least very soon after, my father was killed. And we know that the body is now here in Arwin's Gate, the city controlled by Garrion."

"And his motive?" asked Tobias.

"To steal the body of Arwin."

"It's possible," agreed Tobias. "But why kill the king too?"

"Who knows? Maybe my father caught him in the act." Isolda shook her head. "But then there's also the story that my little sister, Katrina, told me. She saw a man in a red hooded cloak by her bedside right before she got up and found my father lying dead in his bed."

"Him lying in bed contradicts the theory that he was collateral damage from the theft. That sounds more like a cold-blooded assassination."

"Does Garrion seem like a killer to you?" asked Isolda.

"A killer? Yes," said Tobias. "I'm sure he has taken many lives on the battlefield. He even almost killed me the other day in a fit of rage. But is he a calculating assassin who would murder a sleeping man? I think not."

Isolda breathed a sigh of relief. "I agree. It just doesn't add up. I must be missing something."

"What if the body isn't real?" asked Tobias. "What if what we found is a replica?"

"But it looked just like it."

"That's the whole point of a replica. You'd be amazed what a skilled gristologer can do with proper motivation. You could buy a small castle with the gold you'd earn for selling such a piece to the right buyer."

"So you think it's a fake?" asked Isolda.

"I do not know. But I think we would be wise to find out before accusing Lord Garrion of regicide."

Isolda considered the idea. The thought that it might be a fake already made her feel better, although a part of her was disappointed. After all, if it *was* the genuine body of Arwin, it was the first real clue to the unsolved murder of her father. "How can we determine for sure if it's a fake?" she asked. "I've seen both, and they look identical. Can you run some tests on it?" She motioned to the beakers scattered around the room filled with various colored liquids.

"I could test to see if it was made of gold rather than some cheaper alloy. I could even tell you if the blood on it was real. But if you want me to divine if Arwin ever wore it...I'm afraid they don't teach such flimflammery at the university."

"Are you sure?"

"I'm sure. The only one of my professors who would have dared even entertain such a question would have been my oratology professor. He would have used logic rather than alchemy to argue that Arwin never existed, so by the transitive property, Arwin never could have worn the suit of armor in question."

"Ignoring a question is not answering it."

Tobias laughed. "You sound just like Wymund. He was always arguing those points. That's probably why he got expelled. A lad like him belonged at the House of Wisdom rather than at the university."

"Do you have any way of contacting him?"

"Wymund? No. He was always one of the popular lads. He didn't have time for the likes of me. Why do you ask?"

"The House of Wisdom. They're who we need. Aren't they supposed to know all about relics?"

"Some people think that, yes," said Tobias. "But then again, some people think that they fly on magic carpets and summon genies. Depending on what sources you read, they've been credited with the assassinations of at least three sultans throughout the years. The truth is, no one really knows what they do."

"So you're saying you don't think they exist? And by the transitive property, a group that doesn't exist can't help us?

"No. Not at all. In fact, I believe they do exist. I can't be sure if it was real or not, but I was approached by one of their recruiters during my third year at the university. He showed me a few parlor tricks and promised me answers to things that the books and equations at the university couldn't even begin to explain. I told him I wasn't interested. At the time I believed it was just a test by my father to see if I was dumb enough to go off chasing magic."

"What did he want you to do to join?"

"He never said. But he did leave me a message the next morning. It was written in fire ink. Gave instructions on how to contact him if I ever had a change of heart."

Isolda's eyes lit up. "Do you still have that letter?"

"No. Rusted pipes, no. I threw it in the fire the second after I read it."

So much for that.

"But I remember exactly what it said. I can't promise any results, but I could contact him if you'd like."

"Can you do it without Garrion knowing?" asked Isolda.

"I believe so, yes."

"And how long will it take?"

"Under standard wind conditions, a carrier pigeon should be able to make the journey to Alqaruk in approximately 16 hours. So there and back would be a day and a half. I know nothing of magic, but common sense tells me that they will need to see the corpse to determine the authenticity. If we're lucky enough for them to have an agent stationed in Arwin's

Gate, we could theoretically have an answer within two days. But given Garrion's ban on Rashidi, I'd guess we'll have to wait a bit longer. If they have to come all the way from Alqaruk, it could take a month or more."

"Then let's hope there's one here in Arwin's Gate." Isolda couldn't imagine having to wait an entire month without knowing if Garrion was a murderer or not. She couldn't go on like this. "Let me know as soon as you hear back."

- CHAPTER 8 -
ORIANA

Princess Navya. How could King Ivan even consider such a match for Rixin? It was positively preposterous. Oriana slammed her book shut. There was no point in trying to focus on the words when her mind was consumed by other thoughts. She tossed the book on her bed and started pacing back and forth in her bedchamber.

No matter what she did, she couldn't stop thinking about Princess Navya. She had never met the princess, but she had seen a few Rashidi women before. The one thing they all had in common was long, beautiful dark hair, just like Bella's. And she remembered perfectly well how much Prince Rixin couldn't keep his eyes off Bella when they were children.

This was ridiculous. Oriana was going to look beautiful at the joust. She had been working on her dress for months, making sure every part of it was perfect. The meticulous stitching had taken her countless hours and she only had the sleeves left before it would be finished. If anything could take her mind off her troubles, it was focusing all her attention on looking perfect for the big day. A new hairstyle and a new dress were all she could do to tip the scales in her favor. She bit her lip. She didn't need any more reminders that her whole future seemed terribly out of her hands.

Oriana opened the chest at the foot of her bed, but she froze when she saw the dress wasn't laying on top where she'd left it. She threw dress after dress out of the chest. Where was it? *This can't be happening.* She grabbed the bottom of her skirt to pull it out of the way and ran out of her room.

"Bella! Bella, have you seen my dress? Bella, where are you?" Oriana ran over to Selina's door and banged on it with her fist.

Selina opened the door with a smile. The corners of her mouth immediately changed direction when she saw the look on Oriana's face. "What's..."

"Have you seen my dress?" asked Oriana.

"Which one?"

"What do you mean which one? The one for the joust! Have you seen Bella? I need Bella!"

Selina put her hand on Oriana's shoulder. "I haven't seen her. But I'm sure your dress hasn't gone far. Maybe Bella went to wash..."

"It didn't need to be washed. Bella wouldn't have done that. It's never been worn! It's not even finished!" Panic was starting to rise in Oriana's chest. Where could it have gone? She walked away from Selina and knocked on Nesta's door.

"Oriana, calm down. I'm sure it was just misplaced," said Selina from behind her.

"Secret password!" said Nesta from the other side of the door.

"For Arwin's sake," Oriana mumbled and opened the door without attempting to play along.

Nesta was standing in the middle of the room wearing Oriana's dress. She had a needle in one hand and a spool of thread in the other.

"Nesta." All the air seemed to be knocked out of Oriana. The dress was a complete disaster. Nesta had added sleeves that were horribly asymmetrical. The beautiful material was wrinkled around Nesta's feet because it was way too big for the young girl. And the new stitches were just as crooked as Nesta's stitches always were.

Nesta looked up with a huge smile on her face, proud of what she had accomplished in such a short amount of time.

"What in Arwin's name have you done?" asked Oriana.

"I wanted you to look beautiful so that Prince Rixin will choose you."

Oriana didn't know what to say. Nesta had just been trying to help, but the dress was absolutely hideous. She couldn't show up to the joust wearing *that*. She pressed her lips together to make sure she didn't say something she'd regret.

"It's okay, we can fix it," Selina whispered with another pat on Oriana's shoulder. "It's going to be fine. Just a few alterations. We can do it together in no time, I'm sure of it."

"Isn't it beautiful?" Nesta said. She turned in a circle and tripped over the long material. As she fell to the floor, a terrible ripping noise echoed in Oriana's ears.

No.

Selina gasped.

"Oops," Nesta said. She shoved the dress over her head, leaving it in a ruined heap on the floor.

"Sister Morel is going to be furious," said Selina.

"I can fix it. Where'd my needle go?" Nesta stared at the ground.

"Nesta, stop," said Oriana.

Nesta turned to her older sister, her eyes starting to pool with tears. "I'm sorry, Ori. I thought you'd like it." She ran over to Oriana and threw her arms around one of her legs.

"No, no, it's beautiful. Thank you, Nesta." Oriana patted her sister's head as she tried to hold back her own tears. Nesta had just been trying to help. But Selina was right, Sister Morel would not be pleased. Oriana needed to fix it before the nun found out so Nesta wouldn't get in trouble. "You know, I just remembered that I need to get something at the market. I'll be back in a bit, okay?"

Nesta reluctantly let go of Oriana's leg.

"Let's find Bella to escort you," said Selina.

"I don't have time to wait for Bella. I have no idea where she is. She didn't even answer me when I was calling for her."

"But Mum and Father will be..."

"They'll be fine if no one tells them," said Oriana. "I'll be back as soon as I can." What she wanted to say was, "What's the worst that can happen when the unthinkable has already occurred?" Instead, she bit her tongue and left the room. She only had a week to sew a brand new dress. She couldn't afford any delays.

***

Oriana draped her shawl over her head as she stepped into the new market. She had never strayed this far from Vulture Keep alone, but then again, she had never had a reason to be out here when it had been an old abandoned gold mine. Usually Bella and a few guards accompanied her everywhere and made all of her purchases. Sister Morel insisted that the vendors would haggle Oriana into spending more gold if they recognized her. Hopefully her disguise would work.

She wound her way through the other shoppers on the street, ignoring the vendors calling out their prices and waving their wares in front of her face as she passed.

"Fresh spiced chicken skewers!" called one vendor as he cut the head off a live chicken. Oriana turned away and nearly tripped over the end of a five-foot-long razorwood trumpet. The musician played a few angry notes as she quickly apologized.

The next booth was selling "the finest quality swords east of the petrified passage," but even Oriana's untrained eye could tell that they were cheaply made.

Eventually she stopped at one of the tables to examine a shimmering golden cloth that had caught her eye.

"Two gold drachmas for the beautiful lady," said the vendor with a crooked yellow smile.

Oriana immediately shook her head and took a step back. "I'm just looking."

"Nonsense, the color matches your golden hair." He smiled again.

She looked back down at the fabric. Maybe she could use it to patch the tear. A few designs sewn into the dress might be just what it needed. She ran her fingers across the smooth silk. The way it caught the sun truly was gorgeous. How could Prince Rixin's gaze not fall on her in something so lovely? But would it be enough fabric to cover the tear? She had planned to sew a whole new dress, so she hadn't measured it. And this wasn't nearly enough fabric for an entire dress. Oriana thought about the plain dresses that most of the women wore in the castle. Having a design would help her stand out. Or would it look foolish since no one else was wearing such a thing?

"Two gold is a good deal," said the merchant. "Usually I'd charge twice that, but I have a soft spot for women with blue eyes."

She thought of the three gold drachmas sitting in her coin purse. It was meant for a whole spool of fabric, not just a swatch.

"Get back here!" a deep voice boomed from a nearby merchant stand.

Oriana turned her head just in time to see a dirty little squirrel, with what appeared to be a vine of grapes in his mouth, scurrying toward her. It dashed across the fabric merchant's table like a miniature sandstorm. One second it was crawling up a spool, then the next it was jumping onto a pile of fabric. The fabric teetered and fell onto the dusty ground. The merchant grabbed for the rodent, but he ended up with only a fistful of air. Oriana screamed and stepped back, tossing the swatch back onto the table. And then, just as quickly as it had come, the squirrel leapt onto a carpet on the side of the booth and disappeared onto the makeshift roof over the next vendor's table.

"Your pet just ruined everything!" yelled the fabric merchant, waving a dagger in the air.

"My pet? I've never seen that creature before in my life." Oriana looked around at the mess. Pieces of fabric were strewn in the dirt. Tiny brown footprints dotted the cloth left off the table. And the carpet now featured little tears where the squirrel's claws had dug into it on its way up to the roof. Oriana started to walk away, but the vendor grabbed her wrist.

"You have to pay for that," he snarled.

"Let go of me." She tried to pull her arm away, but the merchant tightened his grip.

"Two hundred gold for the lot of it."

"But it wasn't my fault."

"That animal of yours ruined everything. This is my livelihood!" He yanked her back toward the table.

Fear gripped her heart. Three gold was all she had. Why had she ventured out alone? "I only have three."

"That one swatch alone was worth twice that."

"I don't have the money, but I can get it. If you just let me go to the castle..."

"The castle?" he practically screamed. "You're not going anywhere until I get what I'm due." He pushed her against the table. "If I can't have it in gold, I'll take it in flesh."

She knew the punishment for stealing. But she hadn't stolen anything. Why was everyone just watching this? Why was no one standing up for her? She knew in her heart that Arwin wouldn't let anything happen to her. He was fair and just. But her belief waned as the vendor gripped the dagger tighter in his hand.

A whistling sound pierced the air. She turned to see who had produced the shrill noise. Was it a guard coming to stop this madness?

Before she could locate the source of the whistle, the fabric merchant started screaming behind her. But this time it wasn't directed at her. She turned back to see the squirrel had returned, dangling by its mouth from the merchant's ear.

A strong hand slipped into Oriana's. "Hurry, this way," said the stranger's deep voice. Before she could even turn to look at the man, he had already pulled her into the crowd away from the fabric merchant.

"I'm not going anywhere with a complete stranger," she hissed. *And certainly not a strange man!* It wouldn't be proper. She pulled her hand away.

He turned to face her. He had a smile and dimples worthy of any royalty. "Are you trying to get yourself killed?" He backed away from her, slowly disappearing into the masses of patrons.

Of course I'm not trying to get myself killed! Especially for a crime she didn't commit. Arwin must have sent this man to save her. She took a step toward him. He winked and took off in the opposite direction, as if he'd known she'd follow him all along.

The nerve of him. But she didn't have time to overthink her decision. She needed to get away from the fabric merchant. She quickened her pace as she caught up to the only man offering her any help.

"This way." The stranger grabbed her hand again as the two of them ducked beneath a weathered canopy. He may have had the face of a prince, but she knew he was not one. His hands were rough and calloused from years of labor. And his clothes were torn and dirty. She shook away the thought, not knowing why she was analyzing him when she should be focused solely on escaping.

"Stop them!" yelled the fabric merchant from somewhere far behind them.

The stranger pulled Oriana down a side street, away from the market. He kicked open a door and she followed him in just as the merchant tore around the corner.

"That way!" yelled the merchant. He had amassed an angry mob.

Oriana struggled to keep pace as the stranger dashed up a flight of stairs two at a time. They burst through another door onto the roof of the building. He dropped her hand and jumped across a gap to another roof.

Her feet skidded to a stop.

"You have to jump!" he called to her.

She heard the merchant's voice again. He seemed even closer. *Oh bother.* She grabbed the hem of her skirt and lifted it to her knees. With a deep breath, she took a step back and then ran as fast as she could. She leapt across the small divide. Her momentum made her stumble to her knees as she landed.

The stranger pulled her to her feet before she had a chance to recover. They burst through another door and ran down the stairs. The thick sheets over the windows rendered the room almost completely dark.

"This'll do." He caught her arm and pulled her into the corner of the room.

Oriana started to protest, but the stranger pressed his finger against her lips. "Shh," he whispered into her ear.

She swallowed hard as she looked up at him. Her heart seemed to skip a beat. Yes, a face worthy of a prince indeed. Although, no prince she had ever imagined would dare find himself in such a situation.

His finger fell from her lips but his body stayed pressed against hers.

"I should probably..." she tried to duck away from his arms.

"Just one moment," he whispered. The warmth of his breath against her ear sent a shiver down her spine.

Suddenly it sounded like a herd of rhinos was stampeding across the roof. She threw her arms around his neck and didn't protest at all when he held her firmly against his chest. She didn't want to imagine what the fabric merchant would do if he caught her. What had she gotten herself into?

"Shh," he whispered again. The words and warmth comforted her slightly.

As the silence settled around them once again, the stranger took a step back from her. "Are you alright, m'lady?"

"Yes. I'm fine." A little bruised and scraped, but nothing lasting. "And you?"

He laughed. "I've been through worse."

Her eyes slowly began to focus in the dark. She couldn't seem to stop staring at his disarming features.

A smile spread across his face as he watched her.

"What's your name?" she asked.

"Bastian." He took her hand and brought it to his lips. "It's a pleasure to make your acquaintance." He placed a gentle kiss on her hand.

The gesture sent a chill down her spine.

A squeaking noise made them both turn their heads. The same squirrel from the market scampered down the stairs toward them. Oriana squealed and took a step back, slipping on an uneven patch of floor.

Bastian easily caught her with one arm.

She momentarily lost her breath as her hands wrapped around his biceps.

Bastian laughed as he held her body against his. "It's quite alright. It's just Nut."

It only took Oriana a moment to realize that she was clinging to a man she didn't even know. She immediately took a step back. "Nut? It has a name?"

"Of course he has a name." Bastian squatted down and held his hand out toward the squirrel. "Don't you, boy?" The squirrel jumped up onto his shoulder.

"That...that animal almost got me killed!"

Bastian patted the squirrel's head as he stood up. "He also saved you." Bastian pulled a grape out of his pocket and handed it to the squirrel. Nut grabbed it with his greedy little paws and nibbled away at the outside of the grape.

"I wouldn't have needed saving if...wait a second. You made that rodent attack."

Nut stopped nibbling mid-bite.

"Rodent?" Bastian said. "That's a little harsh. Although he is in desperate need of a good bath."

Nut threw the remaining piece of grape at Bastian's cheek.

Bastian laughed. "You know I'm just kidding with you," he said and patted the squirrel's head again. "Besides, Nut's distraction also allowed me to get you this." He pulled out the golden fabric that the merchant had been trying to sell her.

"But I...I didn't pay for that."

Bastian winked. "It can be our little secret." He pushed the fabric into her hands. "It really does match your hair perfectly."

The dark room suddenly felt stifling. Their eyes locked. No one had ever looked at Oriana the way Bastian was staring at her. It made her heart race. And her palms felt sweaty. This was how she desired for Rixin to look at her.

"I should probably get back," Oriana said. She pressed her lips together, wondering why she had broken the spell. Bastian was making her incredibly nervous.

He took a step back from her, pushed a tattered curtain to the side, and looked out the window.

Oriana smoothed out her skirt while his eyes weren't trained on her.

"It appears everything has settled down. You should be safe to go." He turned back toward her and gave her another charming smile.

"I don't know how to thank you." She looked down at the cloth in her hands, unsure whether a thank you truly was in order. He was a thief. A thief who had saved her life. With a smile that could light up this dark room.

"No need to thank me. It was my pleasure, my lady." He winked again and jumped onto the window sill.

"But..." began Oriana. But before she could say another word, he was gone.

- CHAPTER 9 -
GARRION

Garrion grunted and rolled over at the sound of the temple bells. He pushed his pillow over his face to block out the morning sun streaming through the window. He felt like he hadn't gotten a good night's sleep in over a week. Isolda tossing and turning had made it impossible to fall asleep. He had asked her countless times what was bothering her, but she wouldn't give a straight answer.

It was always, "I'm worried about the joust," or if he pressed for details, "I'm worried about you and Reavus." He would try to ease her concerns, but she never wanted to discuss it.

Worse yet, her worries had started to creep into his own thoughts. As the days passed, Garrion found himself tossing and turning at night too, worrying about what would happen if Marcus lost the joust. Would Prince Rixin, or whoever might win, use their position as Arwin's Lance to start a war against the Rashidi? Maybe even Marcus would start a war if he won the title. Garrion had done his best to guide Marcus along the path of Arwin, but Marcus was only 18. Would he be able to avoid the temptations that life would throw at him?

It also didn't help that Father Percival's spies in Rashid had gone silent a few days after Isolda began acting strangely.

Garrion needed to find a way to relieve his stress. He reached over for Isolda, but his hand came up empty. Of course she wasn't there. She was never there in the mornings anymore. Where did she go during the night?

Garrion's squire helped him dress and then accompanied him down to the temple to say their morning prayers.

Father Percival was already deep in prayer, kneeling directly in front of the marble altar at the front of the temple. Marcus and a few of the other squires knelt in prayer as well. The young men were always the first ones to the temple. He hoped that they were there out of eager devotion rather than the desire to be finished with prayers as quickly as possible so that they could begin training.

Garrion took a moment to enjoy the relative emptiness of the temple. In a few days, with all the visitors arriving for the tournament, the temple would be packed every morning. They might even have to move the morning prayers out to Garus' Temple to accommodate the extra guests. That was assuming that Reavus and his court even bothered with morning prayers. They probably didn't.

Garrion knelt and shackled his wrists to chains attached to the altar. It took him longer than it should have to focus completely, but eventually, he was able to push through the fog in his mind to connect with Arwin. *Why is Isolda so distant?* he silently asked Arwin, but no answers came forth. The good Lord Arwin would reveal the answers in his own time.

Yet again, the temple bells came far too soon, signaling the end of prayers and the start of a council meeting.

The five men sitting around the strategy table all stood as Garrion strode into the room. He swept his golden cloak to the side and took a seat at the table. The other men followed his lead and waited for him to begin the proceedings.

"Father Percival, status report?" asked Garrion as his eyes scanned the position of the colored pawns on the strategy table.

Garrion could practically hear the sound of creaking bones as the old priest stood. Percival transferred his weight from his cane to the side of the table and then used it to point to the black figurine shaped like an anvil. It was positioned just north of Arwin's Gate on the map.

"Duke Reavus is on the grass road, a week past Deseros," said Father Percival. "Barring any unforeseen delays, he should be here in three days."

Garrion turned to Quentin Harlow, the steward of Vulture Keep. "Are accommodations ready for their arrival?"

Quentin rose and pushed a loose strand of his long brown hair out of his eyes. "Yes, my lord. Some of his knights will have to stay in the east pavilions, but we do have room for Reavus and his court in the guest tower. At first I wasn't sure what to do with Princess Navya, but Sister Morel suggested she stay with the girls."

"The Rashidi wench is coming?" asked Garrion. He turned to Percival. "I thought I told you to find a way to keep her from attending."

"I'm afraid that as a hostage of the crown, she is to be treated with the same respect as other members of the royal family," said Percival. "You will be pleased to hear, however, that Reavus has seen to it that she is receiving a proper Arwin-ian education."

"Reavus doesn't care about the word of Arwin. He's probably just trying to bait Sultan Zand into breaking the treaty of Islos and attacking us."

"Arwin works in mysterious ways," said Percival. "Regardless of his motives, Reavus raising the princess as Arwinian could prove to be a huge blow to the false god Wazir."

Garrion and Sir Aldric both spat on the floor at the mention of Wazir.

"And what of our spies in Rashid?" asked Garrion. But he already knew the answer. The purple scorpion figurines that represented the sultan and his generals were nowhere to be seen on the map. Instead, Rashid was covered in question marks. "Have you been able to reestablish communications?"

Percival shook his head. "I'm afraid not."

"How is that possible?" asked Garrion.

"I only report on that which the good Lord Arwin reveals to me. I do not speculate on his reasons."

Garrion pushed his fingers against his temples. He hated uncertainty, especially when it came to the Rashidi. "Very well, I want you to find and eliminate all Rashidi spies within our walls."

"That would be nearly impossible, my lord. We don't even know how many..."

"Then it would be equally impossible for Sultan Zand to do the same to our spies. So our assets are still alive, but their messages aren't reaching us. Are we receiving communications from other realms?"

Percival nodded. "Yes, of course. Just yesterday I received word that the lords of the Huntlands have voted to keep Felix Gormont as their king." Percival went on to detail many other lords' movements to make his point that messages were still being received. Just that morning a pigeon from Icehaven had delivered a letter from Isolda's younger sister, Katrina.

"Very good," said Garrion. "We're still getting messages, so our lack of communication from Rashid is not due to someone here targeting incoming pigeons. That means someone in Rashid must be hunting pigeons, and they're doing a rather good job of it. Do we have any other ways to make contact with our assets in Rashid?"

"Yes, but it will take some time."

"How long?"

"A week, Arwin willing. Maybe a month or more."

"That's not good enough. Sultan Zand surely knows of this tournament. He'll know that every lord in Treland will be present. And thanks to Reavus attempting to convert Princess Navya to Arwinism, the Sultan will stop at nothing to get his daughter back before she can see the light of Arwin. Meanwhile, we're just supposed to sit here and hope Zand doesn't launch an attack?"

Axion Tobias cleared his throat, which sounded more like the squeal of a mouse, and stood. "If I may, this lack of communication indicates that Zand *is* planning something. Why else would he go to such great lengths to make us blind to his movements? That would be wasteful if he's not planning an attack."

"A fair point," said Garrion. But he knew not to take Tobias' advice too seriously. Tobias had once convinced him of impending war and sold him three wagons full of the finest halberds that Techence had to offer. The war had never happened.

"With your permission, I can contact my father to see if he has any new technology that we might find useful against the Rashidi. I know he's been working on..."

Garrion shook his head. *That greedy little weasel.*

"My lord," said Brother Savaric, the master of coin. "We could only afford a purchase from Techence if Minister Crane would be so kind as to allow delayed payment. Between the new tournament grounds, the mummers for the Skyfall parade, and Marcus' new armor, we're a bit low on coin. The revenue from the tournament will be significant, but those drachmas won't fill our coffers until the tax collectors are finished making their rounds well after the tournament has finished. Not to mention that it would be impossible to transport weapons that quickly. My fleet is the fastest in Pentavia, but even they cannot make the journey from Techence to Port Garza in less than a month, and then the journey up Katra's Crossing would add another week at least."

"I have no intention of making any purchases from Minister Crane," said Garrion.

"A wise decision," agreed Brother Savaric. He pulled a gnarled twig from his robes and began chewing on it.

Sir Aldric stood. "We could double the guard. Wages aren't paid until the end of the month, so by then we should have plenty of gold."

Garrion nodded. "Good idea. Let's triple them. If Zand so much as steps foot in the savanna, I want to know about it."

The temple bells ringing signaled that it was almost supper time. Garrion put his hand on his stomach. Being nervous made him hungry, and recently, he felt like he was always starving.

"Anything else we need to discuss?" asked Garrion.

The council was silent.

"Good. Father Percival, come directly to me if you hear word from Rashid."

Tobias and Quentin were the first to leave the war room, followed shortly by Brother Savaric.

Sir Aldric turned to Garrion. "I didn't want to mention this in the meeting or we would have had to listen to three hours of Tobias running through calculations, but the additions to Marcus' armor are complete. Prince Rixin is going to fill his drawers when he sees Marcus charging towards him."

"Excellent. I'll have to..."

Before their conversation could continue, Father Percival hobbled between them. "My lord," said Percival. "Can I speak to you for a moment?"

"Of course," said Garrion. "What is it, Father?"

"I'm concerned about Terric. Isolda came down to the library the other day looking for books to make him more interested in Arwin. She fears for the boy's happiness after he takes the oath."

"Ah yes. Did she tell you that nonsense about him wanting to be a knight rather than a priest?" Garrion laughed at the thought. "She mentioned that to me the other day too."

"What books did she end up taking?" asked Aldric.

"Some record of relics from Bloodstone," said Percival. "She thinks seeing relics will pique Terric's interest. Whether or not she's correct in her worries, I'm sure Arwin will show Terric the path. But some encouragement from his father couldn't hurt."

"I'll talk to him," said Garrion, realizing that he had been so distracted by Isolda's odd behavior that he hadn't yet told Terric the good news that he'd be taking the oath right before the final joust.

"May Arwin be with you." Father Percival bowed and walked away.

"What do you make of Isolda's strange behavior?" asked Aldric as he gathered a few sheets of parchment off the strategy table.

"She says she's anxious about the tournament. Maybe she's projecting her own anxiety onto Terric."

"Are you sure that's all it is?"

Garrion thought about it for a second as the two men stood and walked toward the door. "You know how she gets whenever her brother Reavus is coming. She thinks the two of us are going to rip each other's heads off."

"Is that not a possibility?"

"He certainly deserves it. Can you believe he's trying to start a war by converting Navya?"

"Why wouldn't he?" asked Aldric. "After all, Vulture Keep is the first line of defense. He'll just sweep in at the end and save the day. The bards will all sing of Reavus the Savior."

"Good point. Either way, I can't wait for this joust to be over and for everything to be back to normal with Isolda."

"What if Reavus is responsible in a different way for Isolda acting strange?" asked Aldric.

"How so?"

"I don't know. I have no idea what that little rat is up to. But maybe he's blackmailing her to get leverage against you."

"Hmm..." Garrion considered the thought. Reavus certainly wouldn't hesitate to use Isolda against him. And what if Reavus was somehow behind the lack of information coming from Rashid? "I think you might be onto something. Isolda has been leaving our room at night, and I don't know where she's been going. Have a pair of guards watch her at all times."

Wanted
Lady Marsilia

Verily for
Gambling, Hedonism, & Crimes Against Arwin

- CHAPTER 10 -
ISOLDA

Isolda looked around the market. With the tournament less than a week away, the streets were packed almost to maximum capacity. It had made it easy - almost too easy - to slip away from the guards following her. Usually she would have been disappointed by the lack of the challenge, but today she didn't mind. All she cared about today was if Tobias had received a response from Wymund.

"Pssst," said a voice behind her.

She spun around and saw Tobias. He still had his glasses and his trimmed beard, but that was about all of his appearance that she could recognize. He was dressed in brown monk robes. And he was about a foot taller than usual.

"How are you so tall?" asked Isolda.

"Oh, just some stilts I've been working on," said Tobias. "They're a bit hard to walk in, so you'll have to bear with me, but they do make an excellent disguise if I dare say so myself."

"Impressive," said Isolda. She was glad Tobias hadn't made her wear stilts too, although the heels on the shoes he usually gave to Lady Marsilia were so tall that they might as well have been stilts. There was no time to dwell on disguises though. In his message, Tobias hadn't told her what this meeting would be about, but she hoped it was about the body of Arwin. She leaned in closer to Tobias and dropped her voice. "Is Wymund here to meet with us?"

"Not exactly," said Tobias. "But I have received word from him. He's agreed to send one of his colleagues to meet us, just not in Arwin's Gate. Garrion's ban on Rashidi in the city makes them too nervous to come here."

"Please don't say he wants us to meet him in Alqaruk."

"No. They want us to meet them in the savanna. We must bring a piece of Arwin's armor for them to inspect. And fifty gold drachmas."

"Fifty?" asked Isolda. "Just to tell us if it's real or not?"

"That's the price he demands. He didn't leave much room for negotiation, and even if he had, letters from Rashid have stopped arriving. I don't think it's a completely unreasonable price, though. I believe the high fee is not for their time, but rather for their discretion and reputation. I'm sure there are plenty of people out there willing to appraise it, but we couldn't be sure that they wouldn't tell anyone. Or just kill us and take it for themselves."

"And how can we be sure Wymund's colleague won't do that?" asked Isolda.

"We can't be. But do we have any other options?"

"I suppose we have no choice but to pay his price. Is the Razortooth Tavern operational?"

"Yes, my lady," said Tobias. "It opened two days ago."

"Then while we're there to get a piece of the armor, we can also collect our profits so far."

Isolda and Tobias began walking to the tavern. Tobias' stilts might have made for a good disguise, but they required a degree of coordination far above that which Tobias possessed.

He had to hold on to Isolda's arm the entire way there. What should have been a ten-minute walk took almost half an hour.

"So when is this meeting set to occur?" asked Isolda. She had been so focused on the price that she couldn't remember if Tobias had told her the time or not.

"Ah, yes. I suppose I should have mentioned that. The meeting will take place at the Last Oasis on the morning of the next full moon."

"That's Skyfall. The day of the joust," said Isolda.

"It is."

Isolda started going over every possibility of how she could slip out unnoticed that morning. She had seen the schedule that Garrion's men had devised. The morning was packed with a grand breakfast before the competitors paraded through the city to the tournament grounds. She would be expected to be part of the parade, waving to the crowd as they went. "How am I supposed to sneak away that morning?"

"Feign illness?"

"No," said Isolda. "Garrion wouldn't leave me unattended in the castle if I was ill."

"True."

"And if Sir Aldric is to be believed, Marcus has a good shot at winning the tournament. I would never forgive myself if I missed Marcus' joust only to discover that I just wasted fifty gold drachmas to be told the body is a replica. The only option is to send someone else to the meeting." Isolda looked at Tobias, but he turned to avoid her gaze.

"Please don't say you're considering sending me," said Tobias.

"I was."

"But...there are bandits and razortooth tigers out there. I'd be more likely to get eaten alive than find Wymund's colleague."

Isolda didn't doubt that was true. And Tobias did bring up a good point. It wasn't just walking to a meeting. The Last Oasis was at least an hour's ride to the east. And there *were* tigers and bandits. She would need to send at least a few capable warriors to ensure that they even made it to the meeting. But who could she trust? Right now she felt like she could only trust Tobias, and he didn't quite fall into the category of a capable warrior.

"Here we are," said Tobias. "You really think I'd fair well against one of those?" He gestured to the razortooth tiger statue guarding the entrance to the Razortooth Tavern. It really was impressive. And terrifying. The tigers lived on the other side of the hundred foot wall that separated the Shield from the savanna, the civilized from the uncivilized. Executions were against the word of Arwin, at least, that's how Garrion interpreted it, so serious crimes in Arwin's Gate were punished by exile over the wall. Everyone in the city would gather on the wall to watch as the criminals were lowered into the savanna on a platform. Sometimes they'd survive, but usually, they'd be eaten by tigers before the platform even hit the ground. Banishments were the only times Isolda had seen one of the beasts in person.

It was no wonder that Tobias didn't want to go into the savanna to meet with Wymund.

They entered the tavern and pushed through the crowd of men standing around the bar. The clientele was mostly merchants and squires, but that didn't bother her. The men with real money to spend, the ones that would make the tavern successful, would be in the back room.

Tobias was unable to get the bartender's attention. Isolda, on the other hand, knew exactly what to do. She dropped three golden drachmas on the counter, making sure to have them create the irresistible clang of gold on gold. The bartender immediately turned to look at her.

"What'll ye be having?" he asked. "Our ale is the finest in all of Treland."

"I'd like a room for the night. Room 17, if you please," said Isolda.

The bartender grunted, took the drachmas, and replaced them with a bronze key. "Enjoy."

"Hey!" protested one of the squires. "I thought you said all your rooms were sold out."

"If you looked as good as her, maybe I'd make an exception," said the bartender. "Until then, sit down, shut up, and drink your ale."

Isolda and Tobias took the key and went to Room 17, which was really the passage to the back half of the tavern. It was the same as it had been when they were there a few days earlier, but now it had been decorated to make it seem like they were slowly being transported into a deep, dark forest. At first the transition was subtle - a few vines hanging from the ceiling - but then branches started jutting out from the walls, and the tan stone floor changed to plush green carpet that felt almost like real grass. Just when Isolda was beginning to feel like she was truly lost in Arwood Forest, the hallway opened into a grand room.

A stunning woman with flowery vines twisted into her long blonde hair stood in the center of the room. Her corseted dress looked like it had been made completely out of foliage. Two women with similar hair and attire sat cross-legged on a plush sofa to the side of the room. One of them plucked a grape off a vine and seductively fed it to the other.

"Welcome to the Viriphyte Palace," said the blonde.

One of the girls on the couch stood up and walked toward Tobias and Isolda. She ran the back of her hand down Tobias' face and bit her lip. "I want this one," she said.

"Now now, Lily," said the blonde. "Give him a minute to get comfortable before you jump all over him. He might prefer one of the others."

"That doesn't mean he can't have me too."

Isolda had to stop herself from laughing at Tobias. The poor little man looked like he was about to soil his pants with excitement. She was also amused by how little attention the girls paid to the fact that he was dressed like a priest. It almost seemed like the presence of a priest at such an establishment was a rather common occurrence. Just the thought of that would have made Garrion have a heart attack.

The blonde smiled at Tobias. "Don't worry, she won't bite."

"Unless you want me to," added Lily. She leaned in to nibble on his neck.

"My friend here is actually looking for something more exotic," said Isolda. "He's always wanted to be with a red-head."

Lily pulled back, went over to the couch, and popped another grape in her mouth. She let the juice from the grape run down her chin and drip onto her ample cleavage. "I'll be here when you change your mind."

"You can find Rohesia upstairs," said the blonde. "If none of the other girls grab you first." She winked and motioned for them to go up the grand staircase wrapped along the back wall. Scantily clad women danced in vine-covered iron cages along the length of the staircase.

"So what do you think?" asked Isolda as they ascended. "Do you still stand by your theory that men won't like the viriphyte theme?"

Tobias didn't immediately respond. Isolda looked over at him and found him staring at the girls in the cages. He tripped and had to grab the rail to steady himself.

"I guess that answers my question," said Isolda.

"It's the stilts," muttered Tobias.

Isolda smiled. When she had first told Tobias her idea to theme the tavern around the old wives tale of the viriphyte seductresses, he had insisted she was mad.

As the tales went, a thousand years ago, Treland was covered in dense forests and haunted by viriphytes - nefarious demons whose life forces were tied to their trees. They were immensely powerful near their trees, but if they ventured too far, they would die.

Any man who dared go too close to a viriphyte tree risked being seduced into following them back to their tree. Some accounts claimed that merely looking into the eyes of a viriphyte was enough to put you under their spell, while other works were adamant that a kiss from a viriphyte was required. Either way, the result was the same. Any man who went with a viriphyte would never be seen again.

Isolda had read of plenty of contemporary viriphyte sightings in Arwood Forest, and as much as she enjoyed them, they were generally regarded to be the ravings of madmen. Most people believed the viriphytes never existed in the first place. They claimed they're just an old wives tale told by women to caution their husbands against running off with some young trollop.

That was why Tobias thought it was a terrible idea for a tavern. The viriphytes were created to caution men against infidelity, not encourage it. But Isolda suspected the opposite was true. Making it taboo and forbidden made it even more appealing. Having the women dress in exotic plant outfits and act aggressively was all part of the fantasy. And based on Tobias' reaction to Lily and the girls in cages, Isolda had been right.

As long as they didn't stay true to the part of the story where the viriphytes murdered the men after having their way with them, Isolda was sure the Viriphyte Palace would be a huge success. And she was even more sure of it when she saw the grand hall.

The room was a maze of plant-covered platforms connected by branches and bridges. Gorgeous women dressed as viriphytes were scattered throughout the room. Some sat near the main entrance ready to grab new patrons. Others sunbathed nude on the platforms, a homage to the stories of viriphytes bathing in sunlight rather than eating.

"Can I trust you to go collect the money from the back room while I get a part of the body?" asked Isolda.

"Of course," said Tobias. "You think I'm going to run off with the money?"

Isolda glanced at an approaching woman. "I'm more worried about you running off with one of these girls."

Tobias adjusted his glasses. "I wouldn't...I..." he stuttered.

Isolda laughed. "Meet me back here in five minutes." She pulled the key out of her corset and walked toward the room that housed the body of Arwin.

She passed a crowded bar on the way. Unlike the bar downstairs, this one featured a board at the back with the sigils of the great houses of Treland paired with their odds to win the title of Arwin's Lance. Patrons jockeyed for position, holding up drachmas and calling out bets. As the bets came in, a viriphyte standing on a table behind the bar continually swapped the positions of heraldry on the board. First she swapped the spider of House Black with the rabbit of House Quigley, and then she moved the grotesque mask of House Mobek up to fourth place at the expense of House Charo.

Among all of the movement, two positions never changed. The bat of House Talenov stayed in second, and the rhino of House Hornbolt stayed in first.

Wait...*first?* That meant Marcus was favored to win the tournament. Over Prince Rixin. Was her son actually favorite, or had her bookie here suddenly gotten addicted to scorpium?

Isolda nudged one of the men at the bar. "Excuse me, I'm a bit new to all this. Why is Lord Marcus favored to beat the prince? Isn't Prince Rixin undefeated?"

"Crazy, right? I'm starting to believe it could happen, though. They're saying that he's the second coming of Arwin."

"And why would they say a thing like that?"

"The prophecy, of course," said the man.

Even though Isolda wasn't a devout Arwinian, she still knew the prophecy. Everyone in Treland did.

When the servants of evil spread their wings,
And the ground splits open,
A hero shall descend into the depths.
The ground will tremble at his feet,
A king will fall,
Fire will engulf the land.
And in the darkness,
When he is surrounded by death,
He shall bathe himself in gold,
And drain himself of blood.
Then he shall steal the wings of death,
And he shall rise.
And when he returns,
Warring kingdoms shall unite,
And a new dawn will rise.

According to the Book of Arwin, the prophecy foretold the return of Arwin. And so for the last thousand years, people had periodically claimed that the prophecy was being fulfilled.

"What makes you think it's about Marcus?" asked Isolda.

"What *doesn't* make you think it's about Marcus. Everything fits."

"Have Voltanis' thunderkin returned from the sky islands? Last I checked, the sky was clear."

"That's not what it's talking about. Don't you remember the stories about that axion inventing an airship?"

"That was twenty years ago."

"And now the arena was built in the old gold mine. To build it, the ground was split open."

Isolda pursed her lips. "That's quite a stretch. And that has nothing to do with Marcus."

"That part doesn't. But the next part does. The prophecy says that a king will fall. That must be talking about Prince Rixin. And fire engulfing the land...there's a wildfire up north. Some farmers were burning and it got out of hand. I saw it with my own two eyes on my way here."

"That could still be about any knight in the joust," said Isolda.

"True, but what of the part about bathing in gold? There are whispers out of the castle that Marcus just got a brand new suit of armor from Techence, and it's made of solid gold."

So much for that armor being a secret.

And the wings of death," continued the man. "That's talking about the winged wreath that the victor wins."

Isolda shook her head. It was a novel theory, but Isolda wasn't convinced. Prophecies were nothing more than an exercise in wordplay. It was too easy to twist the words to fit whatever theory you wanted. If she really wanted to, Isolda could probably make a convincing argument that the prophecy clearly pointed to Nesta being the second coming of Arwin.

Either way, she had heard enough. She turned away from the gambling board and got back to the mission at hand: gather a piece of the body to be evaluated by Wymund.

She grabbed a lamp off the wall and opened the door to the room. It looked exactly like it did a few days before, with the carpet and furniture sucked into the pit. Well...maybe not *exactly* the same. The furniture seemed like it had been moved.

Isolda held the lamp over the pit. She expected to see the sheen of gold in the flickering light, but there was nothing.

The body wasn't there.

PRINCE
RIXIN

- CHAPTER 11 -
TERRIC

"What about here?" asked Terric, pointing to the far east on Axion Tobias' map. Beyond the Rashid Desert. Beyond the Mysteric Ocean. Beyond Edge Island. The map just ended. Surely there was something out there.

"First calculate how far Edge Island is from Arwin's Gate, and then I'll tell you what I know of it," said Tobias. As always, getting any useful information out of him was nearly impossible. Terric had been trying to learn about prospective destinations for his escape for months, but Tobias always found a way to shift the lesson away from the interesting bits and back to math or science. Tobias had taught him how to find the bearing at which a pigeon must fly to get from Arwin's Gate to Whitehall, and the North and South latitudes of the Huntlands, but nothing actually useful. Nothing Terric could use to decide if the Huntlands should be the final destination for his escape.

Terric impatiently held his index finger up to the scale in the bottom right-hand corner of the map and then figured how many finger lengths could fit between Arwin's Gate and Edge Island.

"About 3000 miles," said Terric.

"Correct. But next time, use your ruler like I showed you." Tobias pushed the flat wooden ruler towards Terric.

"Okay. But now it's time for you to tell me what's beyond Edge Island." Terric's eyes were big with anticipation.

Tobias adjusted his glasses and looked down at the edge of the map as if that would help. "Many sailors have tried and failed to get past the island. In most cases, the ships were never seen again."

"But some returned?"

"Oh yes. One time a giant wave forced a ship to turn back. And on multiple occasions, crews have mutinied, stranded their captains on the tiny desert island, and then sailed their ship back to Pentavia. And then there was that one time where the ship washed up on the shore near Spiceport with no sign of a crew. They just vanished. Poof." Tobias made an exploding motion with his hands.

Terric pursed his lips. "So you don't actually know anything about what's out there?"

"Well, there was Herovinci's expedition. But he was mad. Murdered his own brother. Telling his story is a waste of time..."

"No it isn't! I want to hear it."

Tobias took his glasses off and rubbed his eyes. "Very well. But you have to promise to focus more tomorrow."

"Fine."

"Okay. Almost thirty years ago, Herovinci Turbine, the second son of Prime Minister Christo, invented an airship."

"An airship?" asked Terric.

"Yes. They're quite similar to normal ships, but rather than sailing through the ocean, they sail through the sky."

"They can fly?! How have I never heard of this before? Why doesn't Father have one?"

"The expedition didn't go quite as planned. He was supposed to fly around the world, but he never made it. He arrived back at Techence a few weeks after leaving port. His ship was half destroyed and only a few of his crewmates remained alive. The other two ships in his fleet and the rest of his crew, including his older brother, Enzo, were never seen again. He claimed they found land beyond Edge Island before being attacked by winged men in the middle of a thunderstorm. Of course, the Ministry of Techence realized his story was a bunch of nonsense. He could have been put to death for the murder of Enzo, but there was insufficient evidence for such a harsh punishment, so instead he was banished."

"Over the wall?" asked Terric.

"No, no. Just banished from Techence."

"That doesn't seem fair. What if he really had been attacked?"

"What could possibly attack an airship? Certainly you don't believe in the stories of thunderkin."

"You just told me that Herovinci invented a ship that can fly. Why couldn't there be men out there that can fly too?"

"Bone density, for starters. The size wings you would need to lift a 150-pound man would be enormous."

"So what happened to the airship?" asked Terric. Wherever it was, he wanted to go find it.

"It was destroyed, and the schematics were sealed by the ministry. None have been built since."

"That's stupid. Can't you design one? You're supposed to be the smartest man in Arwin's Gate."

Tobias laughed nervously. "That would be most unwise. Techence takes the unsanctioned use of sealed technology very seriously. I don't want to get a visit from the collectors."

"The collectors?"

"A group of assassins tasked with controlling the spread of unsanctioned technology. The same way the king would execute a deserter, or the temple would execute a priest who breaks his oath, the collectors ensure the swift termination of any axion who breaks his oath and gives illegal technology to the lords of Pentavia. I'd rather not receive a visit from them."

Terric swallowed hard. His eyes were wide with intrigue. He was all too familiar with the idea of oath-breaking priests being executed. The image of himself standing in front of the temple and being forced to turn the screws on his headband until they pierced his skull often haunted his dreams.

"Is Herovinci still alive?" asked Terric. If he was, finding him and commissioning an airship was an awfully tempting idea.

Tobias thought for a moment. "That's a good question. For a while axions were reporting seeing him in various places across Pentavia, but he's settled down somewhere now..." Tobias snapped his fingers. "That's right. He's the head of security at the First Bank of Arwood."

"What's Arwood like?" asked Terric. He knew exactly where it was on the map, just at the northern tip of Treland on the edge of Arwood Forest. From his studies with Percival, he also knew that it was the birthplace of Arwin and the current seat of Arwin's Voice, the figurehead of the temple. If Terric couldn't escape and was forced to be a priest, and if he could rise high enough in the ranks, he might someday live there. But he'd much rather go there as a free man so that he could commission an airship from Herovinci.

The noon bell rang.

"That will have to wait for another day." Tobias began gathering all his things, including rolling up the wonderful map. Terric had stolen one from the library, but this one was twice the size and way more detailed. Tobias' map, drawn by the famed cartographer Henricus, even had little drawings of the major landmarks of each city.

"Wait," said Terric. "Can't you leave your map?"

"Why would I do that?" asked Tobias.

"Um, uh..." The ruler on the table caught Terric's eye. "I want to practice measuring distances. I'm tired of always using my fingers to measure."

Tobias smiled. "Well that's wonderful. I'm glad to see you taking some initiative with your studies. Yes, I suppose I can leave the map with you for a few days."

Yes! Terric turned away so that Tobias wouldn't see his smile. "Great, thanks," he said casually. If he was too excited about studying, Tobias would know he was up to no good.

Tobias finished packing up and then they headed down to the grand hall for supper.

Garrion intercepted them just after they entered the hall.

"Terric, we need to talk," said Garrion.

Tobias looked relieved when the conversation was directed at Terric rather than him. He excused himself and went to find his seat as Garrion pulled Terric aside.

Terric didn't know what to say. His father hardly ever talked to him, and when he did, it was usually to reprimand him or bore him with talk of Arwin.

"I was talking to Father Percival..." started Garrion.

Oh no. He knows about the stolen map! Terric looked around the hallway for any possible distractions.

"And he told me that he's concerned about you. He thinks you might be feeling anxious about becoming a priest."

Terric tried to get a read on if his father was upset about what he just said. Garrion's face was stoic and unexpressive, which Terric guessed was better than flushed and angry.

"I know I don't always show you as much attention as I show Marcus," said Garrion. "That's not because I'm not proud of you. In fact, I'm quite proud of you. Jealous, even."

"Jealous?" asked Terric.

"Yes, jealous. Did you know I was the second born too?"

"You were?" *How did I not know this before?* Terric's head was spinning. First Tobias told him that airships existed, and now this. What else didn't he know?

"My older brother, Reggie, died when I was ten. He was perfectly healthy one day. The next day he had a cough. The third day he was dead. It was devastating. And it meant that I would no longer get to be a priest. I had looked forward to it my entire life, and it was taken from me in an instant. I was suddenly the heir to Arwin's Gate. My dreams of serving Arwin were torn from me and replaced with the responsibility of being a lord. I've done my best to serve Arwin as the lord of this city and the Duke of the Shield, but it doesn't compare to what I could have done as a priest."

"But I don't want..." started Terric.

"When Father Percival told me that you were anxious, I knew what it must be. It's hard for you to commit fully to the idea of being a priest when it's not set in stone. I know we had been planning for you to take the Oath of Arwin on your thirteenth birthday, but I have some good news. I spoke with Arwin's Voice, and he's agreed that you can take your oath early. You'll get to do it right before the final joust of the tournament, in front of all the lords of Treland. That way there's no more waiting, no chance that it will be taken away from you like it was with me."

What?! Terric tried to digest what his father just told him. There were still six months until his thirteen birthday. But now the time he had to plan his escape had been cut to less than a week. Despite the grand hall not being particularly hot, Terric was suddenly sweating uncontrollably. He had never heard his father tell a joke, but he hoped this was his debut act as a jester.

"Don't look so surprised," said Garrion. "I know I can be harsh, but I just want what's best for you."

Terric searched for the words to tell his father that he didn't want to be a priest. But before he could find them, Quentin entered the grand hall and cleared his throat.

"Lords and ladies," said Quentin in his best steward voice. "Crown Prince Rixin of House Talenov."

Terric looked over to the entrance of the grand hall where his cousin had just been introduced. He hadn't realized Rixin would be arriving so soon, but he was glad that he had. As Duke Reavus' squire, Rixin had traveled all over Treland and beyond. He would have a wealth of knowledge about all sorts of different places. And with Terric's escape now having to occur within the next week, that information would be invaluable.

Everything about Rixin was awesome in Terric's eyes. His black leather armor studded with blood gold rivets was unlike anything Terric had ever seen, but the best part was the shadowy tooth that served as a clasp for his red and white checked cloak. It was like the tooth was made of liquid shadows, changing shape slightly as the candles in the grand hall flickered. Was it a shadow beast tooth? Had Rixin slain a shadow beast? Or maybe he crawled through the twisted bone swamp and bravely yanked it from the beast's mouth while it slept. And his helmet... Unlike the helmets worn by the Hornbolt soldiers - nothing more than cheap brown leather caps - Rixin wore a segmented helmet that resembled the thick scales that protected the heads of swamp lizards, complete with tiny slits for the eyes.

Terric had always looked up to Marcus, but he suddenly had a new hero. Rixin was everything Terric wanted to be.

Isolda rushed down from her seat on the dais to greet her nephew. Garrion walked over to him too, albeit less enthusiastically than Isolda.

Out of the corner of Terric's eye, he saw Oriana duck behind a table and crawl out of the grand hall. Where was she going? It seemed like all she ever did was talk about Rixin. And now that he was here, she was running away from him. How odd. Normally Terric would be curious enough to follow her to see where she was sneaking off too, but Rixin had his full attention.

"Your Highness," said Isolda with a curtsey. "It's wonderful to see you again."

Rixin removed his helmet and held it in one arm. "Aunt Isolda, the pleasure is all mine." Rixin leaned forward and kissed her hand.

"I'm afraid we weren't expecting you so soon," said Isolda. "If we had known you would be here today..."

Rixin smiled. "My apologies. I should have sent word that I was riding ahead. I just couldn't stand to spend another three days riding next to those dreadfully slow wagons."

Garrion knelt down on one knee before the prince. "Your Highness, welcome to Arwin's Gate."

"Thank you, Uncle," said Rixin.

"You're here just in time for supper," said Isolda. "I'm sure Conrad made plenty of extra soup." Isolda's eye caught Terric's. She waved him and his sisters over.

Terric wanted to run to meet his cousin, but he restrained himself and instead approached with what he hoped was a relaxed swagger.

"Hey there, little man," said Rixin. "I've heard you've grown into quite the swordsman."

Terric tried to hide his confusion. Had Isolda told Rixin that he'd been sneaking out to practice sword fighting? Terric glanced up at Garrion to see what he thought of the comment. It appeared that Garrion just thought Rixin was being friendly.

Nesta knocked on Rixin's leg armor. When he didn't notice her, she headbutted his leg and fell backward. "Oof," she muttered.

Rixin looked down and smiled at the young girl. He knelt, grabbed her hand, and kissed it. "My lady," he said.

Nesta giggled and ran away.

"Well she's every bit as cute as your letters describe," said Rixin to Isolda. His eyes then fell on Selina. "And you're every bit as beautiful, Lady Selina." He flashed her a charming smile and kissed her hand.

Selina executed a perfect curtsey. "Your Highness."

"Where are Marcus and Oriana?" asked Rixin.

"Marcus is out practicing his archery," said Garrion. "He's not going to roll over and let you have the title of Arwin's Lance, Your Highness."

Rixin smiled. "I would expect nothing less. And Oriana?"

"I saw her duck behind..." began Terric, but Selina cut in before he could finish.

"I'm afraid she wasn't feeling well," said Selina.

"Oh no," said Isolda. "I should go check on her."

"It didn't seem serious," said Selina. "I'll bring her some food after supper."

"Speaking of supper," said Garrion. "We should eat before the food gets cold."

"I appreciate your generous hospitality," said Rixin, "but with your permission, I'd like to go join Marcus. It's been far too long since I've seen him."

"Of course," said Garrion. "Quentin will show you to your chambers and then out to the courtyard."

Terric watched as Rixin left the grand hall. He had so many questions for the prince. And time was running out before he had to make his escape or be condemned to a lifetime of priesthood.

- CHAPTER 12 -
MARCUS

"Who's next?" asked Marcus. Three of his friends knelt nearby, breathing heavily after being outdueled by Marcus.

"I'll go," offered Peter Harlow, the steward's son. He picked up a wooden sword and got into a defensive stance.

Marcus smiled. All of his friends were decent with a sword, but Peter was the only one to give him real competition. Marcus pressed on the attack.

"So did you hear you're the favorite?" asked Peter.

"Says who?" asked Marcus. He dropped his voice a bit and shot a glance to the side to make sure Sir Aldric wasn't nearby. "Ajana?"

Peter laughed and just barely parried one of Marcus' strikes. "Sir Aldric is going to kill you if he hears you talking about his daughter like that. You should really go after someone else, anyway. You realize she's just gonna get fat like her mum, right?"

Marcus scowled and put a little extra power behind his next swing. "No she won't. Seriously though, who said I'm the favorite?"

"It's the talk of the taverns," said Peter. "They think the prophecy is about you winning the tournament."

"What prophecy?"

"*The* prophecy. The second coming of Arwin."

Marcus' eyes got big. "Don't joke about stuff like that."

"I'm not joking," said Peter. "They really think it's about you. They think you're going to kill Prince Rixin." Then he went pale and dropped his guard.

Marcus slashed his wooden sword against Peter's arm before turning to see what his friend was gaping at.

"You're going to kill me, eh?" asked a young man dressed in a checked red and black tunic. He narrowed his bright blue eyes and scowled at Peter. The man was quite a bit older than the last time Marcus had seen him, but he knew exactly who it was.

"Your Highness," gasped Marcus, immediately kneeling. Peter did the same.

"Forgive me, Your Highness," said Peter. "I didn't mean that Marcus is going to actually kill you. It was just a figure of speech. Like, he's going to beat you really badly. But I don't mean that either. That's just what they're saying in the taverns. I'm sure you'll beat Marcus easily."

Marcus nudged Peter in the ribs.

"I mean, not easily. It's going to be a brilliant match. Between the two best swordfighters to ever live."

Rixin held his scowl for a moment longer and then burst out laughing. "That was priceless," he said when he recovered from laughing. "You should have seen the look on your face."

"So you're not going to have me beheaded?" asked Peter.

"Sweet Arwin, no," said the prince. He turned to Marcus. "Cousin, what have you been telling your friends about me? Have you made me out to be some sort of monster?"

"No, Your Highness," said Marcus.

"Call me Rixin. And stand up, would you? You're making me feel weird."

Marcus and Peter stood.

"So back to that bit about killing me," said Rixin. "I can't say I'm fond of the idea, but you're welcome to try. Just so I can better prepare myself, when do you plan to do it? During the swordfight, or during the joust? Or were you planning on 'missing' one of your shots and putting an arrow through my heart? I suppose that would be effective, but rather unsporting."

"He's better with a sword than the lance," said Peter, "so I suspect it would happen during the hand-to-hand combat."

"Ah, a man after my own heart. I've always liked sword fighting the most too. What was that stance you were just using, by the way? I've come across it in some old books, but I've never seen it used in practice."

"This?" asked Marcus. He crouched down into his aggressive stance, just the way Sir Aldric had taught him.

"How interesting," said Rixin, circling Marcus to inspect him from different angles. "Where'd you learn that?"

"I've made some adjustments of my own, but Sir Aldric taught it to me originally," said Marcus.

"Who?" asked Rixin. "Oh, you mean the Hawk? Uncle Reavus told me stories about him. I always pictured him as more of an archer than a swordsman, though."

"Do you have a better technique?" asked Peter.

"More modern, perhaps. But that doesn't necessarily mean better. I could show it to you if you'd like."

"If it's not too much trouble..." said Peter. He waved the rest of their friends over. They had been respectfully watching from afar, not wanting to offend the prince. "Hey lads, the prince is going to show us a new stance!" They all rushed over.

"Alright, so to begin, you want to stand with your feet apart..." began Rixin.

And just like that, all of Marcus' friends started learning Prince Rixin's technique rather than Marcus'. *What is happening?* thought Marcus. His entire life his friends had looked up to him, and now, within five minutes of the prince arriving, they'd all abandoned him.

Marcus didn't bother to learn the new technique. Instead, he walked over to the table where Conrad had set out some perfectly medium rare gazelle steaks, just like he had asked. He cut off a thick slice and took a bite.

"Mind if I join you?" asked Rixin. "I showed them the basics, but they'll be practicing for a while. Figured it would give us some time to catch up."

"Sure," said Marcus. "All the steaks are medium rare, though. I assume you like your steak well done."

Rixin laughed. "What? Has someone been spreading nasty rumors about me? Please tell me that your sister doesn't think I like my steak well done."

"Which sister?"

"The lovely Oriana, of course."

"What do you care about Ori?" asked Marcus, feeling rather protective.

"I don't know. I've heard that she's grown into quite the beautiful young lady."

Marcus shrugged. "Don't ask me. She's my sister. I don't see her like that. And anyway, aren't you going to marry Princess Navya?"

Rixin frowned. "I wouldn't know. Ask my father."

"Have you not asked your father?"

"No. That would require him to be in the same room with me, which is apparently too much to ask for."

"It seems to me like you should just be able to choose. I mean, you're going to be the king some day. Ori might kill me if she heard me say this, but wouldn't Princess Navya be the obvious choice? Your marriage could create peace between us and the Rashidi. I'm talking *real* peace. Not this fragile peace created by the Treaty of Islos."

"True, but Navya is just so... Well, I guess I feel the same way about her as you do about Oriana. We've grown up together. She's like a sister to me."

"But don't you always declare that you're jousting for her?" asked Marcus.

"Yes, but something about this tournament...it just feels different knowing that Oriana will be in the stands."

Marcus decided to change the topic. "So what are you going to do if you win the tournament?"

"I haven't given it too much thought. I'm sure Uncle Reavus will have me throw some sort of grand ball back in Bloodstone to commemorate the victory. Or maybe they'll have it in Arwood. Maybe both." Rixin shrugged.

What? "I meant with the title. The ability to declare a holy war."

Rixin sighed. "Not you too."

"What?"

"Sorry, Uncle Reavus has been talking about that nonstop. He can't wait to march an army across the desert."

"And you don't want to?"

"No. Why in Arwin's name would I give up jousting to ride 700 miles across a giant desert?"

Marcus breathed a sigh of relief. It felt like a weight had been lifted from his shoulders. His father had convinced him winning the tournament was the only hope the kingdom had to avoid war with Rashid. Now that he knew Rixin was on his side too, he could breathe easier.

"As soon as this tournament is over," continued Rixin, "Sultan Zand will triple his patrols in the desert and the Jagged Sea. He'd know we were coming the minute we stepped foot into the desert. But between you and me, I have a better plan."

"Oh?" asked Marcus.

"In my grandfather's writings, he mentioned that there might be a path through Tujira. If we could find that path, they'd never even see us coming. It would be a Franking worthy of General Frank Sappington himself."

Rixin was right. Such an attack wouldn't just be any old flanking maneuver. It would be so dirty and unexpected that it would be on par with the tactics of the great General Sappington, perhaps even enough that the history books would refer to it as a Franking rather than just a flanking.

But wouldn't it be better to just keep the peace?

"I was actually thinking that if I won, I wouldn't declare war," said Marcus.

"Clever," said Rixin. "Lure him into a false sense of security while we find the passage...let him think the new Arwin's Lance is going to be peaceful. And then *boom,* surprise attack on Spiceport! Brilliant."

"No. I meant like...no attack at all."

"Right," said Rixin with a wink and a mischievous smile. "No attack." He lowered his voice. "Good call...there might be spies around. I had heard you were clever, but now I'm seeing it with my own two eyes. I'll be proud to have you as one of my generals. Or if you're as good as your friends say you are, maybe *I'll* be *your* general. We'll go down in history, right next to General Sappington."

Marcus found himself smiling. The thought of conquering Rashid, of finally putting an end to the threat of invasion, was awfully enticing. And with the proper strategy, they wouldn't even lose that many men.

"How would we keep control?" asked Marcus. He wasn't saying yes just yet, but it couldn't hurt to plan. "Conquering it is one thing, but ruling it is another. The Barcovan Empire conquered Rashid once, but they couldn't hold onto it."

Rixin clapped Marcus on the back. "How would you like to be the king of Rashid? I may think of Navya as a little sister, but I've seen some other Rashidi women. And if I'm not mistaken, Rashidi women aren't opposed to their men having multiple wives."

"Prince Rixin!" Terric called as he ran across the courtyard.

Both Rixin and Marcus turned to see Terric duck underneath the fence and scramble on his knees for a moment before joining them. His face was red like he had run all the way from the grand hall.

"I was hoping to talk to you," Terric said.

"Hey, Terric," said Marcus. He was happy to see his little brother. Even if Marcus' other friends were so easily enamored with Rixin's fancy new stance, Marcus knew that Terric would be more loyal. "Want to see me hit a bulls-eye?"

"Not right now," said Terric.

"I'll even do it without looking." That was Terric's favorite trick.

But Terric wasn't interested. Instead, he was completely transfixed on Rixin.

"You've traveled a lot, haven't you?" asked Terric to Rixin. "Have you ever been to the Huntlands?"

Rixin smiled. "I've traveled all over. And yes, I've been to the Huntlands."

"What was it like? What was the best place you've been? If you could choose one place to live for the rest of your life, where would it be?"

Rixin laughed.

"What's gotten into you, Terric?" Marcus asked. "Did you sneak some of that fermented giraffe milk again?"

Terric exhaled like he had been holding his breath. "I just have a bunch of questions and I don't have much time."

Marcus frowned. "Not much time? What does that mean?"

"Nothing, I just meant...it'll be bedtime before we know it."

Rixin smiled. "Thalencia is my favorite place. I'd choose there if I could live anywhere."

"Really? What's so great about Thalencia?" Terric asked. "Isn't it similar to here?"

"No, it's quite different. There are a lot more..." he looked around, "...trees. And although I've tremendously enjoyed being a part of Reavus' court, I do miss my home. If I could choose one place, Thalencia would certainly be it."

"And what about the Huntlands? Is it really a lawless wasteland filled with thieves and backstabbers?"

"Of course it is," said Marcus.

"I wouldn't say that," said Rixin. "I mean, every place has a few bad seeds. It's rather unfair to write the whole kingdom off just because of a few scallywags."

"Is it safe for someone say...my age traveling alone or with another person my age?"

"Are you planning on going somewhere?" Rixin asked.

"No, that would be insane. Right? Or would it be very reasonable? I'm just curious."

Rixin laughed. "I don't think two kids should be traveling anywhere alone. Unless you have a proper knight with you." He winked at Terric.

"If you need to go somewhere, I'm happy to escort you," said Marcus.

Terric frowned, either disappointed by Rixin's response or by Marcus claiming he was a proper knight. "But you're not a knight," said Terric. "You're still Sir Aldric's squire."

Ouch. So much for having a loyal little brother. Marcus glared at Rixin. For a second, he had actually been starting to like him. But now he realized it was all just a trick to make Marcus lose focus on the tournament. How could he have been so blind? He had to win the tournament. He had to win the title of Arwin's Lance. He had to stop Prince Rixin from starting a war.

- CHAPTER 13 -
ORIANA

Oriana's hands were shaking as she tucked a flyaway hair behind her ear. Why was Rixin here so soon? She was supposed to have two more days to prepare. Oriana needed those two days back. She wasn't ready. Her stomach grumbled. She had left supper so quickly that she hadn't even touched her food. *Left.* That was an understatement. She had crawled out of the grand hall on her hands and knees to avoid Rixin seeing her. What had she been thinking?

"What if he saw me?" Oriana said and turned to Bella. The hunger and nerves were making her feel slightly dizzy. She put her hand on her stomach.

"I'm almost certain he didn't see you, m'lady. When I came after you, no one had even turned your way."

"Are you sure?"

Bella nodded. "He was distracted by introductions. Let me go fetch you something to eat. You must be starving."

Oriana didn't protest as Bella left the room. As soon as she was alone, she started pacing back and forth. If Rixin had seen her on her hands and knees, there would be no way to repair the damage. Just seeing him had set her heart in a fit. And her palms had gotten all sweaty. She fanned her face, trying to calm herself.

It was similar to the way Bastian had made her feel. She immediately dismissed the thought. Just thinking about how she had acted with Bastian made her face flush. She had been terrified. But that was no reason to break all rules of decency. She had even wrapped her hands around his neck, for Arwin's sake. She shook her head. There was nothing to even compare between Bastian and Rixin. Any tiny amount of desire she had felt toward Bastian had probably just been heightened by her fear.

She sighed and sat down on the edge of her bed. Why couldn't she stop thinking about him? She had even dreamed of him last night. And the feeling of his muscles. She groaned and lay back onto her bed. *What is wrong with me?*

There was no point in asking the question. Oriana knew exactly what was wrong. She was just nervous. That was it. She was worried about her future with Rixin. And terrified to meet the other contender for his hand. *Princess Navya.* What kind of name was Navya anyway? *The kind of name that belonged to a girl with long dark hair, just like Prince Rixin prefers.*

Oriana sat up and got off the bed. This was pointless. She was driving herself mad for no reason at all.

The door to her room burst open and Nesta came running in. "Ori, Ori! You missed everything!" Her little sister's feet slid across the floor until she stopped right in front of Oriana. "He kissed my hand!" She squealed with delight. "The prince kissed my hand!"

Oriana knelt down and put her hands on Nesta's shoulders. "What else? Tell me everything."

"He called me 'my lady.' " She giggled and her cheeks turned rosy.

Oriana smiled at her sister. "What a gentleman. Did he say anything about me, by chance?"

Nesta shook her head. "Selina said you weren't feeling well though. Are you okay?"

"She was just covering for me. I got so nervous when I saw him."

"Because you're in love?"

"No." *I don't know.* "I just...I wasn't ready."

"Because of your hair?"

"What about my hair?" Oriana tucked the flyaway behind her ear again. She was still used to having it set in braids. The loose curls were starting to make her nervous. What if Rixin didn't like them? What if he wanted her to have the same fashion as the rest of the women in Arwin's Gate? She shook her head.

"You've just been changing it a lot lately. I like it." Nesta pulled on one of the loose tendrils.

"Thank you, Nesta." Somehow her sister had said the exact right thing to momentarily calm her down. "Did he say anything else?"

"He didn't say anything about you not feeling well. But it was because he wanted to go practice with Marcus. He was probably really worried about you like I was."

Oriana smiled. "I promise I'm okay."

Nesta nodded. "I stole some food from supper today just in case Papa finished early. But I'm not hungry. Do you want it?" She pulled out half a loaf of bread from a hidden pocket in her skirt.

"This is just what I needed." Oriana tore a piece of the bread off and put it in her mouth. "Delicious."

"Do you want to come help me practice my stitches? Sister Morel says I need to get them straighter." Nesta furrowed her brow, deep in thought.

The sound of an arrow hitting a target outside made Oriana glance out the window. "Actually, I think I might go for a walk. Can I join you later?"

Nesta nodded. "Can I marry the prince if you decide you don't want to? He's really handsome."

Oriana tried to stifle her laugh. She never realized how consumed Nesta was by looks. "Of course. He'd be all yours. Well, you'd probably have to fight Princess Navya for him."

Nesta scrunched up her nose. "I don't fight. I'm a lady."

"One with very straight stitches."

Nesta giggled. "Soon! I'll go practice. I'm glad you're not ill." She ran from the room, leaving the door open behind her.

Oriana shook her head as she walked out into the hall. Now when she finally did get introduced to Rixin, he was going to think she was ill. She should have just introduced herself like a normal person. The thought of actually talking to him made her palms feel sweaty again.

***

Oriana peered around the stone arch and stared at Rixin. She wasn't sure how long she'd been standing there. But it was certainly long enough to count as spying. For the second time that day, she wondered what she was doing.

She bit her lip as Rixin notched an arrow and pulled back on the bowstring. He had rolled up his sleeves just enough for Ori to glimpse the tight muscles in his forearms. His biceps bulged under the fabric of his shirt. But what really got her were his eyes. The light blue irises were striking against his inky black hair, which he had grown long and pulled back into a bun. And his skin... At first glance you might describe it as pale, but that would do it a great disservice. Selina was pale. She was always inside reading and never got any sun, so her complexion was pasty and colorless. And if she ever did venture out into the sun, she'd get all red. Rixin's skin, on the other hand, was more of a silvery white. And if the sun hit it just so, it almost seemed to shimmer.

As Rixin pulled another arrow, her eyes wandered back to his muscles. They were every bit as big as Bastian's.

Stop thinking about Bastian! She put her hand to her forehead. Maybe she *was* ill. Or maybe she was going mad.

Either way, she shouldn't be spying on the prince. Someone might think she was an assassin. She laughed at the thought. After watching Rixin hit another bulls-eye, she reluctantly turned away. She had told Nesta she was going for a walk, but she knew she had come out here exclusively to stare at Rixin from a safe distance. Now that she was outside though, a walk might do her some good. She needed to clear her mind.

She didn't know what was going to happen with Rixin. And she had absolutely no control over the outcome. Oriana wandered through the main gate and down the path that twisted around the base of Vulture Keep. If Rixin liked her, maybe he'd beg his father to let them marry. Who could deny true love? She knew she was getting ahead of herself. She hadn't even been formally introduced to him yet, at least not since they were small children. But she could see it. She could see a future with him, and that was what made her so incredibly nervous.

Oriana turned around the bend. She was finally far enough away from the castle that she couldn't hear the twang of the arrows. She kept walking through another gate, across the bridge, and into Garus' Square. And she didn't stop there. Her feet carried her through the square, down the switchbacks, and through the increasingly crowded streets until she found herself in the heart of the new market. It was even more crowded than last time she had been there. Her senses were over-whelmed by it all. Her eyes couldn't focus on any one thing. At first her eyes gravitated to the blood red crystal, practically the size of her head, set into an obelisk in the center of the market. Then the sparkle of a jewelry stand caught her eye. Her ears found it impossible to discern between the merchants yelling and the chatter of customers. Even her nose was overwhelmed by all the smells wafting through the market, although the most prevalent smell was that of body odor. Didn't these peas-ants ever bathe?

Oriana stood there, wondering again what she was think-ing. Make that three times today that she had thought that. Her eyes scanned the market. While she was there, it didn't hurt to look for Bastian. It's not like she was going to talk to him again.

She closed her eyes. *I'm definitely losing my mind.* She had wandered farther away from Vulture's Keep than she had in-tended. Bella was probably wondering where she had run off to. She turned around to head back to the castle and ran straight into someone.

Strong hands gripped her arms.

"I'm sorry," she started to say, but immediately stopped when she looked up into the handsome face that had brought her here in the first place. *Bastian.*

"Back to see me so soon?" A smile spread across his face.

She responded with a small peeping noise. Because the truth was, he was every bit as handsome as she had remem-bered. She wasn't imagining things at all. And she did like the feeling of his hands on her. Nerves about Rixin had nothing to do with it. *Oh no, Rixin.*

"M'lady." Bastian took a step back, grabbed her hand, and kissed it.

She felt the same tingle as the first time his lips had touched her skin.

She abruptly pulled her hand away.

"Although you did look beautiful in rags, this dress quite suits you."

Oriana bit the inside of her lip. "Thank you." It came out as more of a whisper than anything. "I should probably be getting back." She shouldn't have come here. It was wrong, seeking him out like this. She had no place here.

"I knew you wouldn't be able to stop thinking about me," Bastian said before she took even a few steps away.

Oriana turned back toward him. She couldn't seem to stop staring at the way his hair fell onto his forehead. Or his charming smile. Or his piercing brown eyes. *How does he know?*

"Come see me again when you have more time to spare," he said.

Her heart was practically beating out of her chest. "I can't...I..."

He stepped toward her and lightly placed his fingers under her chin, tilting her gaze back toward his.

She should have slapped him. She should have. But his touch made it hard for her to breathe. Her lips parted, but she immediately closed them again. She didn't want his fingers to fall from her skin.

"Tomorrow," said Bastian. "Same place. Same time. Wear your shawl so that we won't be noticed."

"I'm practically betrothed." She had finally found her voice again.

"That's very different than being betrothed, m'lady." His fingers shifted slightly under her jaw. "You were here looking for me, were you not?"

"I was just on a walk. To...clear my head."

"I don't think you need to clear your head. Your eyes defy you. I can tell exactly what you want."

There was so much heat in his gaze. He was right. She was looking for him. She just didn't know why. "I'm sorry. I really have to go." Oriana grabbed her skirt and took a step back from him.

"Tomorrow then," he said with a wink.

She turned and walked away as quickly as she could. She hadn't said yes to him, but it seemed like he already knew she'd show up. The audacity of it all. Her heart seemed to be drumming even faster. But he was right, wasn't he? How could she not show up when she hadn't been able to stop thinking about him either.

It was like Bastian had ignited a spark in her. And she wasn't sure if she wanted it to be extinguished.

- CHAPTER 14 -
BASTIAN

Nut scurried across a row of tables, creating havoc as he went. Some merchants shouted obscenities, others tried to swat at him. But he was too quick. And he was also the perfect distraction. Because as the merchants focused all of their anger at Nut, Bastian walked along and pilfered whatever he wanted.

He grabbed an apple from one shop, tossed it to his other hand, and took a huge bite. The next vendor had a delicious selection of bread, and another had some dolls. He absentmindedly grabbed something from each shop. Usually he would have been more choosey, but his mind was elsewhere. He couldn't stop thinking about Oriana. The fact that she had been too shocked to even respond made him smile. He took another bite of the apple. There was no doubt in his mind. Oriana's reaction to his words said it all. She couldn't stop thinking about him either.

Eventually he had to stop taking things simply because he couldn't carry anymore. Bastian looked at the doll. Why did he even steal that? He certainly wasn't going to play with it. Nut might enjoy gnawing the buttons off, but he didn't want the poor little guy to choke on one.

Bastian tossed the doll to the first young girl he passed. The child smiled up at him and he patted her gently on the head. He continued on towards a small bridge. To most people, the bridge was just a bridge - a way to cross one of the many chasms that had been cut into the market district back when it had been a gold mine. Most people probably didn't even realize they were crossing a bridge. But to Bastian, the bridge was home. Or at least, under the bridge was home.

Bastian glanced around to make sure no guards were watching him. When the coast was clear, he jumped off the side of the bridge and swung down onto a narrow platform directly under it. He pushed one of the stones on the side of the ravine and a hidden door swung open.

In case anyone found the secret entrance, the first stretch of old mine shafts were unlit. But as Bastian and Nut went deeper underground, they soon encountered a few dim lanterns.

I wonder what Oriana would think if she ever saw my home, thought Bastian as he wove his way through the tunnels. On more than one occasion he was so lost in thought that he almost stepped in the wrong place and triggered one of the traps. Was it one of the nets, or was it one of the darts? Getting stuck in a net and having to be rescued by one of his comrades would have been embarrassing, but getting shot in the neck by a poison dart would have been deadly.

After half a mile of evading traps, Bastian and Nut finally arrived at a sturdy wooden door. He knocked four times in rhythm.

A little slot on the top half of the door slid open. "Password," demanded a gruff voice.

"Bangers and mash," said Bastian, reciting that month's ridiculous password. Whoever chose them had an odd fascination with the culinary arts, because it was always some sort of dish. Last month it had been rhino stew on a bed of garlic parsnips.

The door swung open and Bastian entered. He gave the imposing doorman a nod of respect as he passed. Besides reciting silly passwords, Bastian had never spoken to him. Some of the other thieves would greet Bastian with friendly banter, but the doorman always just stood there eyeing Bastian suspiciously and gripping the daggers strapped all over his body.

Really, the doorman's personality was not out of place at the Thieves Guild. The bartender was always friendly, and each thief tended to have one or two close friends, but beyond that, everyone operated independently. That was by design in case anyone got captured. At worst they'd crack from torture and give a few names. Arwin have mercy on any guards tasked with trying to navigate the old mine shafts to find the guild, though.

Bastian climbed a staircase lined with razortooth tiger teeth and scanned the main hall for his friend, Logan. Two of the three tables - upside-down barrels with candles on top - were unoccupied. The third was, as usual, being used as a card table by two men in hooded black tunics and skull masks. Bastian often wondered if the men ever actually did any thieving or if they just played cards with each other all day. Bart the bartender stood behind a counter on the far wall. It was just as easy to purchase a mug of ale as it was to purchase a disguise or a dagger. In fact, three daggers and a flask of poison sat on the counter right next to some empty flagons.

Another thief was throwing knives at a bulls-eye next to the bar, while another attempted to pickpocket a dummy without ringing any of the bells attached to it. The frequent sound of bells jingling indicated that the practice was much needed.

The chief thief's balcony, a small platform that overlooked the entire guild hall, was currently unoccupied.

Good.

Bastian wasn't quite ready to tell the chief about his latest treasures.

Just in case the chief thief did decide to make an appearance, Bastian hurried out of the guild hall and into a mine shaft lined with a series of doors. The fifth door on the left was his.

Logan was sitting cross-legged on the ground snorting a line of scorpium from a heavily worn end table. Bastian had been trying to get Logan clean for months, but now wasn't the time to press it. Not with the nasty stab wound in Logan's arm. Bastian might have even given in and tried some scorpium to dull the pain of a wound like that.

"Who's there?!" asked Logan frantically. His hand went for his dagger and knocked over a vial of scorpium.

"Whoa, calm down," said Bastian. "It's just me."

Logan sheathed his dagger and wiped some white powder off his nose. His eyes were big. "You're gonna get yourself killed sneaking up on people like that. Next time at least knock or something."

"Sorry, I..."

"So how'd it go with the princess?" interrupted Logan. He grinned and the flickering lantern light shining off his silver tooth nearly blinded Bastian.

"She's not a princess," said Bastian. "She's a lady."

Nut jumped off his shoulder and crawled into the canvas bag in the corner of the room. Nut loved anything golden, and the bag happened to be filled with gold.

"And how'd you know I met with her again?" he added.

"What? I'm not allowed to follow you?" asked Logan. "You forget you're surrounded by thieves here, mate."

"Shouldn't you be spending your time thieving rather than spying on me? At least spy on something that could prove valuable, like that new tavern."

"Oh, I've already spent plenty of time at the Viriphyte Palace," said Logan. "In fact, I came out with three times as much gold as I paid."

"I don't want to hear about you giving out favors," said Bastian.

"I didn't give anyone any favors."

"Right, I guess it's not a favor if they're paying. Either way, you should have asked for more money."

"What? No, I stole the money. I wasn't giving out...wait, did you hear that I was? I don't fully remember that entire night..."

Bastian laughed. "Whatever you say. Just one of the many reasons you should stay away from scorpium."

"Back to the princess," said Logan. "I want to hear all about it."

"There isn't much to tell. I was tailing a nobleman who wasn't paying attention to his coin purse. Just when I was about to grab it, I noticed Oriana. She was just standing there, right in the middle of the market."

"So you didn't get the coin purse then?"

"No, of course not. I went to talk to Oriana."

Logan shook his head. "You barely even know her and she's already taken your mind away from what's important."

He stared at Logan. "Are you sure you were following me? Because if you had seen her, you'd understand why I was so distracted. Talking to her again was worth missing out on a bit of gold."

"Whatever you say, mate. So you think she came back just to look for you?" asked Logan.

"I do, yes." Bastian smiled to himself. "Because right after we talked..."

Nut pulled on Bastian's pant leg and chirped at him.

"Not now, Nut," said Bastian. "Anyway, right after we talked she just went back to Vulture Keep. She never bought anything. And the way she looked at me..." Bastian's voice trailed off as he pictured her blue eyes looking up at him. She definitely wanted him. It wasn't even a question.

"So ya think the princess is gonna run off with you, eh? I feel like you're forgetting something, like...oh I don't know. The fact that she's a princess. You think she's just going to give up everything to be with the likes of you? She's probably wasted more gold than you or I could steal in three lifetimes."

Bastian clenched his fist. "You didn't see the way she looked at me." But deep down, he knew Logan was right. Whatever he had with Oriana, it wasn't going to last. At best, she might come back to see him one more time. Maybe she'd even kiss him, but after that, she'd come to her senses and he'd never see her again. At worst, she'd come back with a dozen guards ready to mount his head on a spike.

Maybe before the war, before his useless father lost everything, Bastian would have had a chance with her. But now he was nothing more than a street rat. Stealing apples and trinkets was one thing. Stealing Oriana's heart was another.

"And she said she's going to meet me again tomorrow," said Bastian. Even if he knew he couldn't have her, he still liked talking about her. Giving his fantasies a voice made them seem more real.

"Good. Do you have a present for her? That vase you stole last week might work."

"You think so?" asked Bastian. He hadn't considering giving her a gift.

"Yeah. If you're lucky, she might even use it as a chamber pot." Logan grinned at his own stupid joke.

Nut chirped louder. Bastian finally looked down and saw that his squirrel had something gold in his mouth.

"What's that you've got there, boy?" asked Bastian. He reached down and Nut spit the trinket into his hand. Bastian turned it over. The gold necklace was shaped like a burning sun pierced by a sword. A ruby was set in the middle and surrounded by smaller ones. It took him a second to remember where he recognized the symbol from. His earliest memory of it was during his journey south from the Huntlands. The Legion Road, one of the few paved roads still remaining from the Barcovan Empire, was fortified with guard towers every so often, and the soldiers that built them often carved the symbol of Barcova into the stones.

The necklace looked like it was real gold. He put it in his mouth and bit it softly. Yup, definitely gold. And the rubies...they weren't just any old gemstones. They were masterfully cut, and they were big. Big enough to be fit for a lady of Oriana's standing. "Where'd you get this?" asked Bastian.

Nut turned and shook his tail towards the bag.

Bastian held it out to show Logan. "Was this in there?"

Logan shrugged. "Beats me. Nut must have found it the other night. One of those idiots probably dropped it when he stabbed me. Man, I can't believe we let them get away. Can you imagine how much that whole suit of armor would have been worth?"

Bastian grabbed the bag and pulled out a golden gauntlet. The other night they had been watching the back door to the Viriphyte Palace when they saw a few men come out carrying a golden suit of armor. He and Logan tried to set a trap for them, but the men got away. All they managed to get from them was the gauntlet and a stab wound on Logan's arm. And now the necklace, thanks to Nut.

"We really should turn this stuff in," said Logan. "Can you imagine how much the chief will pay for this? It makes me nervous having it here. You can't trust the thieves in this place."

"Everything makes you nervous when you've been doing scorpium. And yes, he'll pay a lot. But we could get more from a private buyer."

"I don't think it's worth the risk to wait. That necklace alone will..."

"What necklace?" asked Bastian with a grin.

Logan reached for his dagger again. "If you think you're gonna give that necklace to the princess without paying me for half of it, you're out of your mind."

"Fine, fine." Bastian gripped his own dagger. "I'll pay you for it. Just give me a little while to find a buyer for the gauntlet. Then we'll both have more money than we know what to do with."

SHADOW BEAST

Cloak of Invisibility

- 4 pounds Shadowbeast Scales -
- 1 Mandrake Root
- 1 pound Cave Bat Droppings
- 2 cloves Black Lamb's Wool
- 1/2 pint Bonesap
- 1 Tactaflame Bloom
- Cheetaur Sinew

During a new moon after nightfall, ground the scales mandrake root and tactaflame into a fine powder. Let rest for one hour. Add one fifth of droppings Repeat four times. Add bonesap until thickened Immediately spin into thread, then combine with root. Bury in the swamp at a depth of eight feet. Let sit for one cycle, then sew with the cheetaur sinew

- CHAPTER 15 -
ISOLDA

Isolda paced around the bathhouse. Everything in the room was damp from the steam rolling off the surface of the hot water. *What's taking him so long?* she thought as she dipped her toe into the bath.

After she had discovered the body was missing, she'd told Tobias to have the madam ask all the girls at the Viriphyte Palace if they had seen anyone near that room or anything else out of the ordinary.

Now she was waiting in the bathhouse for Tobias to report what he had learned. The anticipation was excruciating, but the steamy room calmed her nerves somewhat. Arwin's Gate had little in common with the frozen city of Icehaven where she had spent her teenage years being courted by Fjorking princes. One thing both cities did have in common, however, was that they had both been constructed on hot springs, even if the springs served a very different purpose for each city. The hot springs here were an important source of water in case the castle was ever under siege. The springs in Fjorkia, on the other hand, were used for their warmth rather than for their water. In a place where the sun would some-times disappear for twenty hours a day and the temperature never went above freezing, heat was a valuable commodity.

Isolda remembered sitting in the pools in Icehaven think-ing about her suitors and devising ways to toy with them. How fun and carefree those times had been. Before the war. Before her father had been assassinated.

Will Tobias have the killer's name for me? wondered Isolda. Surely he'd at least have a description of the person who'd stolen the body. Isolda had made it a point to have all of her best girls working at the Viriphyte Palace. They'd all been trained to extract secrets from their clients, and also to re-member faces. It would have been impossible for someone to slip by her girls with an entire golden suit of armor without being noticed and remembered.

It was really just a matter of how much information the girls would provide.

But what would Isolda do with the information once she had it? It depended on what Tobias had learned. If the thief was clearly working for Garrion...

Isolda sat down on a bench to try to process the thought. She was perhaps moments away from learning that her hus-band of almost twenty years had assassinated her father. She always thought apprehending the assassin would feel so satis-fying. She'd pictured the moment countless times. She would arrive with an army of guards at her back. The shocked look on that smug scoundrel's face when he realized he had finally been caught...it would be priceless. But not if it was her hus-band's face. She absentmindedly started to tap her foot on the tile floor. The thuds matched her racing heart.

She jumped up from the bench when she heard the knock on the door.

"Occupied," she called.

Another three knocks in quick succession signaled that it was Tobias. Isolda opened the door and allowed Tobias to slip in. Then she locked it, and just to be extra safe, she removed her ironwood hairpin and jammed it into the lock. No one was going to walk in on their conversation, even if they had a key to the bathhouse.

She turned back to Tobias. He was staring at the floor rather than at her.

Bad news.

"I'm sorry, my lady," said Tobias. "The girls saw nothing."

"*Nothing?*" asked Isolda.

"Nothing. They mentioned some patrons with pretty disturbing fetishes. And some scorpium addict had to be thrown out for trying to grope the other patrons. But other than that, they had nothing to report."

Isolda shook her head. "That's impossible. Someone dragging the body out of there would have had to pass at least half a dozen girls, if not more."

Tobias used his sleeve to wipe the condensation off the wall and then rolled out a floor plan of the Viriphyte Palace. "Right, I thought the same thing. But just to be sure..." He adjusted his glasses and ran his finger across the map, tracing paths from the room with the body of Arwin to each of the exits. Each path yielded the same result: someone would have seen.

"So they didn't walk out with the body," concluded Isolda. "That leaves...magic?"

Tobias made a high-pitched noise that was a cross between a laugh and a snort. He turned it into a cough when he looked at Isolda and saw she was completely serious.

"What's that all about?" asked Isolda. "You didn't seem to think magic was fake the other day when we were talking about the House of Wisdom."

"It's the House of Wisdom that I believe to be real. Their magic on the other hand..."

"Wait, so you're telling me that we're going to pay fifty golden drachmas to have a fraud look at the body? If we can even find it."

"No, not at all. If Wymund represents one of their average members, then they're a very smart group indeed. And I believe they *do* put a great deal of effort into studying relics and things of that sort. I just don't think they use magic to evaluate it. I suspect he'll use some sort of chemistry. Maybe some scribology as well to check for markings on the armor. Some sort of trademark from the craftsman who made it, perhaps. Or maybe certain dents or scratches that only the most learned historian would know about."

"Well you might not believe in magic, but I do. I've seen it with my own two eyes. When I was little, before the war." Isolda smiled as she thought of her father's old jester and his red and white hat with the bells. "He would never do it in the castle, but sometimes, when we'd be out in the forest away from prying eyes, Father would let Knobbly Knees do one or two tricks for me. One time he opened his palms and created fire out of thin air. Another time he made sparks shoot from his fingertips. I know I was young, but I'm sure it was magic."

"Mere tricks, my lady. Don't you think I could make Nesta believe in magic with a few devices hidden under my sleeves?"

Isolda sighed. She would have expected such a response from most axions, but she thought Tobias might at least entertain the thought. The University of Techence must have done a better job than she realized in convincing their students that magic did not exist in any form. "Shouldn't we at least consider it?"

"If you're talking about a mechanical device that could render the thief invisible..."

"No. I'm talking about pure magic. The kind where some-one says a word and poof, they're gone."

Tobias squinted and stared at nothing in particular. That was the face he made when he was deep in thought. "If you believe in magic, do you also believe in the shield crystals?"

"Yes, of course," said Isolda. The shield crystals, as she had been taught, had been created after the Great Purge and dispersed all across Pentavia. Most major cities had at least one on display near the city center. She still remembered the odd reddish glow emanating from the one in Bloodstone, almost like the shell of the crystal was made of blood. There were countless tales of men casting spells near a shield crystal, and all of them ended in disaster. It was said that any magic used within a certain radius of a shield crystal would summon Green Cloaks, who would subdue the deviant and transport them to a magical prison. "The shield crystals are why Knobbly Knees would only do magic in the woods, far away from the city. He didn't want to accidentally summon the Green Cloaks."

"Okay, then that rules out magic. There's a shield crystal in the new market less than a mile from the Viriphyte Palace. Anyone trying to escape through magical means would have been detained."

"The Green Cloaks could have taken the body," said Isolda.

"Don't you think we would have heard about it if an ancient society of wizards appeared in the streets, or in the Viriphyte Palace, to arrest someone? Everyone would be talking about it."

"Then what about an invisibility cloak?" asked Isolda. "Those are made from the ground-up scales of a shadow beast, so using one isn't magic. It wouldn't trigger the shield crystals."

"My lady, please forgive me. But shadow beasts don't exist."

"How do you know? You of all people should know that it's very difficult to prove an absolute negative."

"You're correct. I cannot say with certainty that they do not exist."

"There have been many sightings," said Isolda. "I think I even saw one as a girl. And Prince Rixin's cloak. There are rumors it's made of spun shadow scales. They say that if the light hits it just so, it renders him invisible."

"Let's assume for a moment that shadow beasts *do* exist. Who's to say that you could make a cloak out of their scales? It seems to me that grinding the scales into a powder would destroy the structure that creates the illusion of invisibility. I can't say for certain that shadow beasts don't exist, but a lot of assumptions are required to arrive at the conclusion that invisibility cloaks are real. "

Isolda adjusted her braids. She hated when Tobias made so much sense. "Fine. Then what do you propose happened?"

Tobias didn't answer. He was staring at the map again.

"Tobias?"

He tapped his finger on the room. "What if they didn't leave through one of the exits. What if they left through the old mine tunnels under the brothel. That's where the body was hidden in the first place."

Isolda tried to picture the sunken floor. Was it a closed chamber, or were there tunnels that led to it? "No, I don't think there were any openings. After I discovered it was gone, I looked around to make sure I wasn't looking in the wrong place. Unless it was a hidden opening, I would have noticed it."

"Okay," said Tobias. "Then I know who took it."

"You do?"

"Yes. It must have been Foreman Owen. Think about it. He was the only one who knew about it. After his workers finished building, he could have easily sneaked in and grabbed it."

"So he lied about giving me the only key?"

"He must have," said Tobias. "And whether or not he knew what it was, the fact that it was made of gold would have been motivation enough for him to take it."

"Or he was working for whoever assassinated my father. Either way, I want to find out what he knows."

"Should I inform him that Lady Marsilia would like to offer him a free night at the Viriphyte Palace to congratulate him for a job well done?"

Isolda smiled. She always appreciated how Tobias was one step ahead of her. "My thought exactly," said Isolda. "By morning our girls will know every secret he's ever had. Including where he took the body."

Isolda removed her hairpin from the lock and peered into the hallway. When she saw it was empty, she slipped out. She should have been satisfied with their conclusion about Owen, but something didn't feel right. At first she couldn't put her finger on it, but then it came to her. Foreman Owen wasn't the *only* person that knew about the body. Tobias did too. And as she had just realized a moment before, he was always one step ahead of her.

- CHAPTER 16 -
GARRION

While Quentin gathered the council to discuss the unexpected arrival of Prince Rixin, Garrion took a walk around the gardens of Vulture Keep to calm his nerves.

The red mist clouding his vision and the blood pumping through his fists told him to storm into the war room and split Father Percival in two, but he tried his best to push that aside to take a calmer approach. Father Percival had been a trusted servant of his, and of Arwin, for many years. But the old priest was slipping. First he had lost all communication with Rashid, and now he had let Prince Rixin, a man that he was supposed to be watching closely, arrive at Arwin's Gate without notice. That was two major blunders in as many days. What was next? Sultan Zand arriving unannounced at the wall with ten thousand men? He could have been marching through the desert at that very moment, and Father Percival probably wouldn't have known.

Garrion stopped in front of a patch of spear lilies and picked one. To everyone else in the castle, they were merely a pretty plant, but to Garrion, they marked the grave of his closest childhood friend and the girl Garrion once loved. Their bodies, of course, were elsewhere. Reavus had made sure of that.

The memory of his friends usually helped remind Garrion that violence was not the answer, but in this case, with Reavus arriving in a few days, it only made Garrion more angry.

Reavus, thought Garrion. *Reavus must have arranged for Rixin to come early. But what's his angle? Is it just to unsettle me? Or is he planning something more sinister? Perhaps sabotaging Marcus in some way...*

Garrion looked down at the spear lilies. In the red mist, his mind wandered back in time, to the final months of the Wizard's War.

***

The memory began, as it always did, with Garrion and his best friend, Julian Hyposa, drinking ale in a war tent on the side of the Legion Road. It had been over a month since they had left the front. They'd been battered and bruised. They were exhausted. But they had succeeded in killing the Zaberwald triplets and destroying Scarfort. They had done their part, and now the war was nearly won. King Zaberwald just had to surrender.

Garrion couldn't wait to return home. Or at least, he couldn't wait to return to his adopted home of Deseros. That was where Dory was waiting for him. He still had to ask Duke Philip Hyposa for Dory's hand in marriage, but he was quite certain Philip would say yes. Philip was like a second father to Garrion.

But before all that, he and Julian were on their way to complete their final mission - to deliver the sword of Crown Prince Anton Talenov to Bloodstone. The bards were already singing songs of how Anton fell bravely in battle, but the truth of it was that he had been hit in the head with a rock when Scarfort inexplicably exploded.

Garrion thanked Arwin that the war was drawing to a close. He couldn't stand to see any more needless death.

"So what's the first thing you're going to do when we get home," asked Julian. He leaned back and took a big swig of ale.

Garrion took a moment to consider the question. It had been so long since he had been home. What was home to him, even? He had been born in Arwin's Gate, but after his older brother died, he'd gone to squire for Duke Philip in Deseros. And met Dory. Who was he kidding? Garrion knew exactly what he'd do when he got home.

"I'm gonna ask your father for Dory's hand in marriage," said Garrion.

Julian snorted. "I wondered if this war would turn you into a man. I guess it has. I'll be proud to have you in the family. That reminds me. Do you remember at Port Claudius when that soldier played dead and then tried to stab me in the back?"

"Yeah." Garrion remembered it well. The man had sneaked up on Julian, and Julian had spun around and split his head in two.

"Good." Julian grinned. "Because you'll suffer the same fate as him if you mistreat Dory."

"I'd expect nothing less," said Garrion. He knew his friend was all talk, though. They were like brothers. Julian would never hurt him. "What about you? What are you going to do when we're back?"

"Take a bath. And get a nice shave." He picked at his thick black beard and pulled out a crusty breadcrumb. "I still have last night's supper stuck in this mess. I am going to miss this, though."

"You're going to miss picking food out of your beard? I dare say you could do that at home if you wanted to."

"No, you swine, I'm talking about this." He gestured around the tent, or maybe he was gesturing to the vast camp of soldiers that surrounded them. The thin fabric of their tent did little to muffle the sound of their soldiers' drunken singing and arguing. "Something about being out here, talking strategy with you. Drinking ale whenever we feel like it. I'll even miss the battles. There's no thrill quite like having a thousand men all trying to kill you."

"We'll still be able to talk strategy back at Deseros. It'll just be a different kind. There are thousands of people in Tujira just waiting to learn the word of Arwin. Imagine if we could help them see the path."

Sir Aldric poked his head through the flaps of the tent. "Got room for one more?"

Julian waved him in. "We were just talking about what we're going to do when we get home."

"I haven't really thought about it," said Aldric.

"Do you mean before or after the king awards Aldric a castle for killing all three Zaberwald heirs?" asked Garrion.

Aldric smiled. "Funny you should mention the king. Just a few minutes ago, a rider delivered this letter." He pulled a letter out of his pouch and tossed it to Julian. It was sealed with a bat sigil pressed into bright red wax.

"Zaberwald must have finally surrendered," said Garrion. It felt like an entire castle had been lifted off his shoulders. No more war. No more bloodshed.

"That's my guess," said Aldric.

Julian broke the seal and started reading. "Duke Julian," he began.

"You're a duke now, eh?" interrupted Aldric. "The end of the war must have the king in awfully high spirits if he's going around handing out titles. Although I don't know how your father would feel about you being given *his* title."

"What's wrong?" asked Garrion. Julian's skin had turned paler than a Talenov's.

Julian didn't respond. He just handed the letter to Garrion.

Duke Julian,

I regret to inform you that your father died fighting bravely at Horn Harbor. You have my word that his sacrifice will not be in vain. Baron Pudlock has assumed command of the army and is marching on Whitehall. The Zaberwalds will pay for this.

His Majesty,

Bogdan of House Talenov, First of his Name

King of Treland, Lord of the Trelish, the Shielders, and the Coastmen, Blood of Arwin, and Defender of the Realm

"Philip is...dead?" asked Garrion. He couldn't believe what he had read.

"That can't be!" said Aldric. He snatched the letter from Garrion and read it. His face was somber by the time he got to the end.

They all sat in stunned silence for a moment. Then something hit Garrion. "Wait a second," he said. "Who did it say was in charge?"

Aldric glanced down. "Pudlock."

"Why would Pudlock be given command?" asked Garrion. "He's two ranks below my father." He already knew the answer, though. "My father's dead too, isn't he?"

"It must have been a slaughter if Pudlock is the highest ranking lord remaining," said Aldric.

"Or maybe my father just got hurt," said Garrion. "Can you ride after the messenger to see if he has more information?"

"Sure thing," said Aldric. "My hawks will stop him within the hour." Aldric got up and left the tent.

Julian read the letter again and smashed his mug of ale on a rock. "King Bogdan has to pay for this. He didn't have to make them attack Horn Harbor. The blockade was enough. The Huntlands were done."

"We don't know that," said Garrion. "Maybe something changed since we left the front."

"Please," spat Julian. "The only thing that changed was Prince Anton's death. King Bogdan sent our fathers into a slaughter just to spite the Huntlands for killing his precious Anton."

"How many more people must die?" asked Garrion. He was feeling lightheaded.

"Three," said Julian.

"Three?" asked Garrion.

"Yes." Julian held up three fingers. "King Bogdan, Prince Ivan, and Prince Reavus." He put one finger down with each name.

"That's treason," gasped Garrion. "You're talking about killing our king."

"He's no king of mine. Not after he killed my father.."

"You're not thinking straight," said Garrion. "I know it's shocking, but..."

"No, I am thinking straight. I'm the Duke of the Shield now. My subjects look to me to protect them from harm. How can I look them in the eye if I bend the knee to a mad king that marches his own soldiers into a slaughter?"

"I can't believe you're even talking about this." Garrion stood and started to leave.

Julian grabbed his arm and pulled him back. "Who's next? What's to stop King Bogdan from sending us back to the front? In the words of Lord Arwin, 'He who steals a loaf of bread has committed a wrong, but he who wastes the gift of life is the greatest criminal among us.' Does that not condemn the actions of our king?"

"If King Bogdan has lost the way of Arwin, his path shall lead him to ruin," said Garrion.

"If not by our hands, then by whose? Just think...you and I could rule the kingdom together. We could bring Arwinism to the people. I'm not talking about the Arwinism that Bogdan follows. That's nothing more than a façade to keep the support of Arwin's Voice. I'm talking about *true Arwinism*. I'm talking about making the kingdom a better, safer place. A place where the lives of men like our fathers are respected rather than tossed into the privy."

The more Julian talked, the more sense he was making. Was assassinating the king truly the path that Arwin had set for him?

Garrion dropped his voice to a whisper. "I'm not agreeing to it yet. But if I did, how would we do it?"

***

Two weeks. Garrion had two weeks until he was supposed to assassinate King Bogdan. But he still wasn't sure if he could go through with it.

Please, Lord Arwin, give me a sign, prayed Garrion silently.

He glanced up at the dais. King Bogdan was seated between his youngest daughter, Princess Katrina, on one side, and a Rashidi ambassador on the other.

What kind of sign is that? If Arwin's Path had been a road on which Garrion was traveling, that sign was equivalent to one that pointed to his destination being in two opposite directions.

If anything, it was a painful reminder that his plan with Julian was rather half-baked. All they had decided was that Garrion would deliver Anton's sword to King Bogdan to gain entry to Bloodstone, and then reward the king's hospitality by taking his life. Meanwhile, Julian was one of the few people who had been entrusted with information that Crown Prince Ivan and his younger brother, Reavus, were hiding in Bone-garden, so he would go there and assassinate them.

If they timed it right, all living male Talenov's would be wiped out in one night.

But they hadn't discussed the daughters. Katrina was only sixteen. She wasn't as lovely as Dory, but her curly black hair was quite striking against her pale skin. Killing the king was one thing, but killing Katrina? The thought of it made Garrion ill.

And then there was still the other Talenov girl, Isolda. Last Garrion had heard, she'd be imprisoned in Icehaven when Magnus Frostborn overthrew the old regime.

"You'll have to excuse me," said Garrion.

Aldric nodded, not even turning to look at him. A group of Talenov soldiers had gathered around their table to hear Aldric's stories about how he killed all three Zaberwald triplets. A serving girl sat next to Aldric and practically swooned after every word he said.

Garrion grabbed one more spiced cattail and walked out of the grand hall.

He went outside to get some fresh air, but the thick fog wafting off the swamp surrounding the castle could hardly be classified as such. And the giant stone bats guarding the bridge made Garrion feel uneasy. He knew they were just a homage to the Talenov sigil of a crowned bat, but to Garrion, they seemed too similar to the grotesque winged men described in the book of Arwin as fighting for the evil Voltanis.

It wasn't just the bats that bothered Garrion. It was every-thing about this place. The dark stone, the sun being constantly blocked by the impenetrable fog, the blood-red water of the swamp below...it was all so unsettling. The red and white checked onion domes on top of each tower at least provided a pop of color in the otherwise dreary landscape, but those bothered Garrion too. They were nearly the exact same shape as the domes that were so common throughout Rashid. At least, that was how Rashid was depicted in the paintings Garrion had seen.

No more procrastinating, Garrion told himself. He knew what he had to do. He had to go to the temple. To face Lord Arwin. To own up to the countless Huntlanders he had killed in bat-tle. To confess to what he and Julian were planning.

He made his way back inside and wound through the cas-tle towards the temple. A week ago, he would have gotten lost, but he had made a point to find and memorize every passage-way in Bloodstone Castle to maximize his chances of escape after the assassination.

Garrion entered the temple and was greeted by a serious looking priest who was easily in his late seventies, if not older.

"How may I help you, my child?" asked Father Osbert in a slow, gravelly voice. One of his milky eyes seemed to be look-ing at Garrion, while the other wandered.

"I..." Garrion searched for the right words. "It's been some time since I've been in a temple. How can I face Lord Arwin after what I've done at war?"

Father Osbert raised a hand and grabbed Garrion's shoul-der. Garrion couldn't tell if it was supposed to be comforting or if the old priest was using him as a crutch.

"Lord Arwin was a peaceful man," said Father Osbert. "But our enemies are not. Are we to just sit back and watch as they spread their evil?"

"But why must we kill?" asked Garrion.

"If you were surrounded by cheetaurs, what would you do? Try to sooth them with words, or fight for your life?"

"Fight, of course. But they're beasts. Not men."

"Are they so different than our enemies? The Zaberwalds put magic before Arwin. And Rashid worships Wazir. They are beasts. They have not seen Arwin's path. It's our duty to show them the way. Come, let me show you something." The priest hobbled over to a wooden door reinforced with steel. He fumbled with some keys attached to the chains that ran from his iron headband to his bracelets. Eventually he found the right one and awkwardly contorted his body to be able to put it into the lock.

The door swung open to reveal a cavernous chamber filled with swords, robes, urns, and more. Relics of all sorts lined the walls. But one in particular drew Garrion's attention: a suit of armor covered by a white sheet. *The body of Arwin.*

Father Osbert walked over to the body and removed the sheet to reveal a corpse dressed in bloodstained golden armor. "This is what Arwin wore when Emperor Ocidius turned him over to Voltanis. It had been Arwin's father's armor. The soldiers dressed him in it to mock him for renouncing his title."

Garrion nodded. He may not have been in a temple for some time, but it was ridiculous for the priest to think that he had forgotten this story. Everyone knew the story of Arwin's sacrifice.

"Arwin went peacefully as they turned him over to Voltanis. But Voltanis double-crossed him. The minute he had him in his grasp, he bit his neck and drank his blood. You can still see it on the armor." Father Osbert pointed to the deep red stains on the chest plate.

Chills went down Garrion's spine. He had heard the story a million times, but actually seeing the blood on the armor changed it. It made it more real. "So what are you saying?" asked Garrion. "Arwin's peaceful sacrifice destroyed Voltanis, didn't it?"

"It did. But that alone didn't win the war. It took thousands of brave soldiers to push back the forces of Voltanis. If not for them, Arwin's sacrifice would have been in vain. Until the truth of Arwin is in the heart of every man, there will be a need for both priests *and* warriors. Do you understand?"

"I think so," said Garrion. He wished he could ask if assassins were needed too.

"Good, good," muttered the priest as he walked over to a book and quill by the door to the reliquary. He dipped the quill into an inkwell and got ready to write. "What is your name, knight?"

"Garrion Hornbolt."

"Garrion of House Hornbolt," said the priest as he wrote it into his book. "Wait...that name sounds familiar."

"I'm sure you've heard of my family. My ancestor Garus founded the city of Arwin's Gate."

"Ah yes. He's an excellent example of how a warrior can do the work of Lord Arwin. But I meant that *Garrion* sounded familiar." The priest paused and his wonky eye wandered around the room. A second later the eye snapped back to Garrion. "That's it," said Osbert. "I have something for you. From Father Percival." The priest shuffled out of the room.

Being in the famed reliquary of Bloodstone should have been one of the most interesting moments of Garrion's life. He should have delicately inspected each of the relics. He should have taken time to honor the revered men that had helped reveal the path of Arwin to the world. But all he could seem to do was look for hiding places and secret passageways. In a moment of weakness, he even wondered if after the assassination he could dress himself in Arwin's armor and hide under the sheet.

Father Osbert returned a moment later and handed Garrion a letter.

Lord Garrion,

I suspect you've already heard, but I have received confirmation that your father was one of the many great men that was taken from us at Horn Harbor. He was a wonderful man and a devoted follower of Arwin. His loss is a loss to us all.

-Father Percival

Garrion nodded. He had been quite certain that his father was dead, but getting the final confirmation was still painful. It was so...final.

Something about the message struck Garrion as odd, though. Why was the letter from Father Percival, and why had he sent it to Osbert? Priests often exchanged records and religious writings with each other, but they didn't often send each other letters to give to lords. It would have made much more sense for a steward to send the letter through the proper channels. The contents of the letter weren't even *that* important. Yes, it was horrible that his father was dead. But the letter even began with Percival saying that he suspected that Garrion already knew.

Everything about it was odd. There was only one explanation.

The letter must have been delivered by a priest because it was a sign from Arwin. Maybe not knowing if his father was truly dead was what was making Garrion feel uneasy about assassinating King Bogdan. Maybe this was the push he needed to go through with it.

"Thank you for delivering this message, Father," said Garrion. "And thank you for showing me the reliquary. You have given me great clarity. May Arwin smile upon you."

"You are welcome, my son. I am sorry to hear about your father's death, but I think you will find there is more to it than meets the eye. Go, take a moment to yourself. Sit by the fire and reread the letter, and perhaps Percival's words will take on new meaning."

What? "I will do that. Thank you."

"Go forth and follow his path," said the priest.

Garrion left the reliquary more confused than when he had entered. For a moment he thought he knew what he had to do, but then Osbert had said all that nonsense about different meanings in Percival's letter. What other meaning could it have? It was pretty clear: Garrion's father was dead. Or did it mean something else? *His loss is a loss to us all.* Was that code that Garrion needed to go looking for his father? Was his father somehow still alive?

Not knowing what else to do, Garrion decided to follow Osbert's strange advice. He went back to his room, sat by the fire, and reread the letter.

Nothing seemed different. There was no hidden meaning. Until...

What's that? thought Garrion. Black smudges had started to appear at the bottom of the page. And then they turned into words:

Forgive me for using your father's death as a pretense for this letter, but I fear it was the only way to safely pass you this information. Last night, Duke Julian was here. He opened the gate and allowed an army of ten thousand Rashidi to enter. They were gone by morning.

Garrion had to read it three times to process the information.

Julian had betrayed him. And to make it worse, he had sided with the Rashidi.

***

Garrion didn't want to think about his friend's betrayal. About the death of King Bogdan. About all the bloodshed when Garrion led an army to intercept Sultan Zand's army outside of Bonegarden. There was no point in questioning his decisions now.

Nonetheless, his stomach was in knots as he crept through the halls of Castle Deseros. He had done so on countless nights before the war, but that had been to sneak into Dory's room. Now, he was an intruder, and he wasn't alone. Reavus and a small force of elite soldiers were at his back. They were there to arrest Julian for his crimes.

"That's it up ahead," said Garrion, pointing around the corner to the door to Julian's room. "Should we try to distract the guard?"

"No need," said Reavus. He raised a crossbow and shot the guard in the neck. The guard slumped to the ground.

"You didn't have to do that," said Garrion.

Reavus shrugged and motioned for his soldiers to advance. Within seconds, they were in Julian's room. Reavus turned to Garrion. "Awaken him."

Garrion stepped forward and cleared his throat.

"Who's there?" asked Julian, still half asleep.

"I'm sorry, brother," said Garrion.

Julian blinked and looked around the room. The soldiers clad in black were just barely visible from the moonlight streaming in through the open windows. "What's the meaning of this?"

"We know you were working with the Sultan," said Garrion. "We know you were behind the assassination of King Bogdan. And we know you were planning to kill Ivan and Reavus."

"That's preposterous. Guards! Arrest these intruders!"

"Your guards are dead," said Reavus.

Julian reached for the dagger he kept under his pillow, but Garrion put his sword to his throat to stop him.

"Easy, Julian," said Garrion. "We aren't here to hurt you. Reavus said he would be merciful if you confess. Sultan Zand already told us about your involvement. About how you helped his troops slip through Arwin's Gate."

"So after all these years, this is how it ends?" asked Julian. "With you letting Reavus come kill me in my sleep?"

"It's not like that," said Garrion.

"You sealed your fate when you conspired with Zand," said Reavus.

Julian spat at Reavus. "If you want to arrest me for treason, I demand a trial by combat."

Reavus wiped the spit from his face. "No."

"No?" asked Julian.

"No. I'm not going to grant you a trial by combat. But if you tell me who else was working with you, I might grant you a quick death."

"You said you'd show mercy if he confessed," said Garrion.

Julian turned to look at Garrion. "I'm sorry, brother. It wasn't supposed to happen like this. I wish I could explain." His eyes were filled with sadness. "Protect Dory."

"Who were you working with?" asked Reavus.

Julian shook his head. It looked like he was about to open his mouth right as he stood up into Garrion's sword, driving the blade down through his collarbone and into his own heart. Garrion would never forget the sickening squish or the way the blood splattered on his face as he pulled back. Despite the room being dark, the blood was a bright crimson in his memory. It splattered everywhere. On his face, on the bed sheets. Even on the wall. It was the red mist that haunted him.

"What have you done?" asked Reavus. "He was going to name his conspirators. And you killed him."

"I didn't..." started Garrion.

"It makes me wonder," said Reavus. "Who was he going to name? Perhaps he was going to name *you*."

Garrion gripped his sword tighter. He was at a loss for words. And then he heard the screams. Horrible, ear-piercing screams coming from outside. "What's going on?" demanded Garrion.

Reavus smiled. "Did I forget to mention I was going to raze the city?"

Garrion lunged for Reavus but two guards intercepted him and tackled him to the ground. "Those people are innocent," yelled Garrion.

"I want every knight, every soldier, and every peasant out there to know that treason will be handled swiftly and without mercy. Someone in this city knew what Julian was up to, but no one spoke up. If they had, they would have saved my father. And they would have saved the entire city. Maybe that someone was *you*?"

"I'm the one that warned you the sultan was attacking, you fool. I saved your life. How dare you accuse me of treason!"

"I have to wonder...how did you know the sultan was attacking? Did you help plan it and then have a change of heart?"

Garrion tried to throw the two guards off of him so he could get to his sword.

"Don't worry," said Reavus. "Once you execute Dory and end the traitor's bloodline, I'll believe you're innocent."

"Leave her out of this!" yelled Garrion. "If you harm one hair..."

"I'm not going to harm any of her. You are. And if you don't, I'll have you beheaded."

"Then you might as well take my head right here. I won't kill her."

"That would mean you're guilty of treason as well. And I think you've seen how we handle the subjects of traitors." Reavus motioned for his men to take Garrion to the window.

Garrion could hardly look at the destruction below. Reavus' troops swept through the city, throwing torches into houses and cutting down any survivors. They didn't stand a chance against Reavus' men. One minute they had all been sleeping peacefully, the next minute their houses were on fire and their families were being torn to pieces.

"My lord," said Quentin.

Garrion gasped for breath. He could still taste the smoke in his lungs from the burning city.

"My lord," said Quentin again a little louder.

The red mist cleared from his sight and the Vulture Keep garden came back into focus. He unclenched his fist and let the crushed spear lily fall to the ground.

"Are you okay?" asked the steward. "You look pale."

"I'm..." The word was barely audible. Garrion cleared his throat. "I'm fine."

"The council awaits your presence." Quentin bowed and backed away.

Garrion was thankful that Quentin had interrupted him when he had. The rest of the memory...with Dory...it was unbearable to relive those moments.

After the destruction of Deseros, Garrion had nearly killed himself. He had gone home to Arwin's Gate to get the affairs of the city in order before he left this world to finally meet Arwin. But then he had spoken to Father Percival. The priest had convinced him that he still had something to live for.

"You can still save Treland from Reavus," Percival had told him.

At the time, he'd taken that to mean he could still get revenge on Reavus. But over time, as Garrion reread the book of Arwin, he realized what Percival had really meant. He wasn't talking about inflicting physical pain on Reavus. He was talking about bringing light into the world to oppose Reavus' darkness. Despite sometimes succumbing to his anger and getting lost in the red mist, Garrion tried to provide that light.

The war room was tense when Garrion entered. Even if Percival hadn't known Rixin was coming, he surely knew by now that the prince had arrived. And he would have known that Garrion would not be pleased that it was a surprise.

"Father Percival," said Garrion. His words were slow and measured. "Why did you not inform me of Rixin's arrival?"

Percival put his weight on his cane as he stood. "My apologies, my lord. Rixin's departure from Reavus' caravan was done with great secrecy."

Garrion could feel the blood rush to his hands. He gripped the side of the strategy table to avoid reaching for his sword. *He's a man of Arwin. He's a man of Arwin,* repeated Garrion in his head until his breathing slowed. "Have we received any communications from Rashid yet?"

"No, not yet. But I'm working on it."

"My lord," said Savaric from across the strategy table. He removed a chewed root from his mouth and stood to address Garrion. "I have good news. A shipwreck pigeon arrived at the docks this morning."

"How is that good news?" asked Garrion. Brother Savaric had come up with the idea for shipwreck pigeons a few years prior after two of their ships had mysteriously disappeared in the Tujiran Sea. Both ships had been filled with gold, and Savaric very much wanted to send expeditions to recover the contents of their holds, but they had no idea where to look. Savaric raised dozens of carrier pigeons at his offices at the north docks, while Tobias designed bird cages that would open if a certain portion of them became submerged in water. Each pigeon had a scroll permanently tied to their legs, and it was up to the captain to update it daily with coordinates of the ship. "Doesn't that mean one of our ships sank?"

"More or less," said Savaric. "It wasn't officially one of our ships, but we did have a stake in the venture. Anyway, the important part is that the ship was just outside the Sultan's Bay when it sank. And before it went down, the captain recorded more than just his coordinates. He wrote that a terrible storm had crushed an entire Rashidi fleet near the Wuhuku Islands and that he was going to try to outrun it. Based on his coordinates, he was able to sail west towards the Sultan's Bay before the storm overtook him."

"A Rashidi fleet sinking is indeed good news," said Garrion.

"It is. But I think there's more information to be had from this pigeon. The storm was heading west. If the storm was fierce enough to sink an entire Rashidi fleet, it's possible it made it over the Ushurka Mountains without losing too much strength."

Savaric pointed with the half-chewed root to the mountain range running down the east side of the Rashid Desert. "If it did, it could have created a sandstorm for the ages. And if that storm hit Alqaruk and continued west into the desert, it could be blocking pigeons from reaching us."

"Axion Tobias?" asked Garrion. "Have you checked the validity of this theory?"

Tobias nodded and his top hat nearly fell onto the strategy table. He quickly straightened it. "Yes, my lord. Weather is a funny thing to predict, especially when I don't have any actual numbers to go by. But even using conservative estimates, what Brother Savaric is saying is quite possible."

"It's not a bad theory," agreed Sir Aldric. "I've seen sand storms out in the savanna. No pigeon is flying through one of those."

"That's not all," said Brother Savaric. "The dock at Tus-kacia just received a work order from the crown to patch parts of the hull of the King's ship."

"So he's coming then?" asked Garrion.

"Quite the opposite. Those repairs will take weeks. I think that's confirmation that he's *not* coming."

Garrion shook his head. King Ivan was the one man who could keep Reavus in check. Reavus listened to him. At the end of the war, Reavus recommended that Garrion be arrested as a traitor. Instead, King Ivan rewarded Garrion for his loyalty by elevating him to the rank of Duke of the Shield.

Without King Ivan coming, Prince Rixin would be the highest ranking lord at the tournament, followed by Reavus. That could prove to be a serious issue for the safety of Garrion and his family.

"Do we know why he's not attending?" asked Garrion. If they knew, maybe they could send a pigeon to change his mind.

"I'm afraid not, my lord. My sources are limited to gossip at the docks and my shipwreck pigeons. Perhaps Father Percival has more information?"

Garrion looked expectantly at the old priest.

Percival spread his hands wide, as if to say, "I have no idea."

"What am I supposed to do with that response?" demanded Garrion. "You haven't heard *anything*?"

"I think Father Percival might be overworked," suggested Brother Savaric. "Between the dovecote, the library, and his duties as high priest of Arwin's Gate, he's carrying quite a burden. Perhaps I could help lighten that load."

"What would you have me do?" asked Garrion. "Are you asking me to dismiss Father Percival and install you as the master of truth?"

Savaric looked shocked. "No. No, I wouldn't ask that of you. Father Percival has been a trusted servant of Arwin since before I was born. His information is invaluable. And most of my time must be devoted to the exploration of Tujira and the administration of the docks. But just as I helped us find gold in Tujira after our goldmines ran dry, I believe I can help us find new sources of information now that our current source has run dry. "

"Very well," said Garrion with a nod. "Quentin, see to it that Brother Savaric receives a key to the dovecote. And Father Percival, I appreciate everything that you've done for this city. And for me. But one more mistake, and I'll have no choice but to dismiss you from your duties as master of truth. In dangerous times such as these, we can't afford to be blind to our enemies movements."

- Chapter 17 -
Terric

Terric sat on a ledge and pretended to read the book of Arwin, but really he was just watching Sir Aldric put Prince Rixin, Marcus, and the other men through a series of training exercises.

Archery, push-ups, then right back to archery. And then some dueling with the wooden practice swords.

Rixin wasn't as fun to watch as Terric had hoped. He had a suspicion that the prince was holding back. He had hit mostly bulls-eyes, but he wasn't splitting his arrows. And while he was clearly the best swordsman, his opponents *had* registered a few strikes against him.

It was a smart strategy. Showing your opponents all your best moves during training was a waste. It was better to save them for the tournament. That's what Terric would have done.

But no, he'd never get that opportunity. Terric looked back down at the stupid Book of Arwin. The most strategizing he'd get to do as a priest would be finding ways to convince particularly sharp-witted skeptics to follow the path of Arwin.

Boring.

Terric kept hoping Prince Rixin would take a break from training so that he could ask him more questions about prospective destinations, but the opportunity never came. Unlike Marcus and the others, who would strain themselves in the hot sun and then break for water, Rixin kept himself positioned in the shade and paced himself so that he'd never need any breaks. Or maybe he just wasn't exerting himself. Either way, his lack of exhaustion was more evidence that he was holding back.

"Alright men," barked Sir Aldric. "Time for the real training." He whistled for Warin to bring them their horses.

Warin guided the horses out from the stables, and when his work was done, he jumped up onto the ledge with Terric.

"Where ya been?" asked Warin. "For a few days there I thought you got caught spying on Bella and ended up in the stocks."

"Enough with that already," said Terric.

"Sorry I brought it up. It was just a joke," said Warin defensively.

The two boys sat in silence as Rixin spurred his black stallion into a gallop. Halfway across the courtyard, he lowered his red and white lance and took aim on the quintain. He hit the target right in the middle. As the counterweight swung around, he shifted in the saddle to avoid being unhorsed.

"He's awesome," said Warin.

Terric shrugged. "He's okay. Nothing that special."

"What's your problem today?" asked Warin.

"Nothing. He's just not that good. He lifts his chin right before he strikes." Terric grabbed a pebble off the ledge and tossed it into the dirt.

"Okay, well, I guess I better get going. Sir Aldric is gonna get mad if I'm up here for too long." Warin jumped off the wall.

"Good," muttered Terric.

Warin started towards the stables.

What's wrong with me? thought Terric. He shouldn't be pushing Warin away just because his plan wasn't coming together. This was when he needed Warin most.

"Wait," called Terric.

Warin spun around. "What?"

"I'm sorry." Terric patted his hand on the ledge where Warin had been sitting. "I'm just in a bad mood."

"What's got you down?" Warin jumped back up onto the wall.

"Father moved up my vows. I'm set to become a priest on the final day of the joust."

"No you aren't," said Warin.

"I am."

"Not if you escape."

A smile returned to Terric's face. "Does that mean you'll come?"

"Depends on the plan. Maybe you can get some ideas about where to go from Prince Rixin. I bet he's been all over."

"I thought the same thing. But he's useless. All he told me was that Thalencia was his favorite place and that two kids our age shouldn't be traveling anywhere without a proper knight at their side."

"I wouldn't call that useless," said Warin.

"How so? Thalencia isn't an option. There's no way we'd make it more than ten minutes there without getting grabbed by some lord eager to return me to my father to gain a bit of favor. We have to leave Treland. That leaves the Huntlands as the only real option, unless you want to try your luck in the savanna."

"For someone so clever, you're being pretty dense right now. You just have to convince the prince to take you on as a squire. It's the perfect solution. You'd get to go to Thalencia, and you'd be traveling with a proper knight at your side."

"And Rixin outranks my father."

"Welcome to the conversation," said Warin. "Glad you finally caught on."

"So how do I get Rixin to make me his squire before I take the oath of Arwin? He already has one."

"You just have to show him how qualified you are. You can read and write, you can sword fight, you know about jousting. You've even started studying cartography and politics."

"Yeah, but his squire has probably done all of that too. And more. Not to mention that his squire already has experience with him. He probably knows exactly what Rixin wants even before Rixin asks for it. Look, here he comes now."

A lanky fellow in a perfectly crisp tunic strode into the courtyard and approached Rixin. He had a letter in one hand and a red candle in the other.

"Your Highness," said the squire. "I've drafted this letter to send to Duke Reavus. He requested you notify him upon arrival."

Rixin took off his right gauntlet and reached down from his horse. His squire handed him the letter.

"Thank you, Nigel," said Rixin. He scanned the paper. When he was finished, he folded it up and held it down to allow his squire to drip red wax on the fold. Nigel held it steady while Rixin pressed his ring into the hot wax.

"I also brought you some honey bread," said the squire. He handed a perfectly golden brown loaf of bread to Rixin.

Rixin smiled and took a bite out of the bread. "I don't know what I'd do without you."

Nigel bowed and backed away.

"I'm sure he didn't mean that," said Warin. "He'd get on fine without Nigel if he had you instead."

"I'm not so sure about that." Terric grabbed another pebble off the ledge and tossed it into the dirt. "Unless Nigel dies in a horrible squiring accident during the joust, I don't stand a chance." A squire getting hit in the neck with a stray splinter or getting trampled by a horse wasn't unheard of, but it wasn't a common occurrence either. And he definitely wasn't going to perish from helping Rixin seal letters with hot wax. *Hot wax.* "That's it!"

"What?" asked Warin. "You sound like you just came up with an idea that I'm not going to like."

"I did. What if I wrote a letter recommending me as a squire and then sealed it with Rixin's ring. With a letter like that, any knight in Treland would be happy to take me. We could do it for you, too." Terric couldn't believe he hadn't hatched this plan the other night when Tobias had forced him to write letters. He even had leftover parchment and ink that he could use.

"That's a great plan, but how are you going to use his seal?"

"Steal it," said Terric.

"Off his finger?"

"I don't know. I haven't thought out all the details. But if I can pull it off, will you come with me?"

Warin scrunched his mouth to the side. "It's risky. If we got caught..."

"Oh come on! This is perfect. When else are you going to get the chance to be a squire? You could even be a knight someday."

"I'll think about it. But first you have to get your hands on that ring."

"Deal." Terric smiled triumphantly. It felt like he was closer than ever to becoming a knight. And more importantly, he was closer than ever to *not* being a priest.

- CHAPTER 18 -
RIXIN

Prince Rixin glanced over his shoulder at his young cousin, Terric, who had been sitting on the wall all afternoon watching him and the other men practice. Terric seemed to be lost in discussion with the stable boy and they both kept frowning at his squire, Nigel Quigley, not at all attempting to hide their disapproval.

"On second thought," Rixin said as he tossed the remaining bread back to Nigel. "I'll need to add a bit to that letter." He lifted his leg over his horse and jumped down. Nigel helped him remove his other gauntlet.

"Quitting so soon?" Marcus said with a triumphant smile as he galloped over.

"Not quite yet," said Rixin. "But I do need to take a break to let Uncle Reavus know that I've arrived safely."

Marcus nodded and urged his horse forward. He galloped off, his lance held at the perfect position, and made direct contact with the quintain.

Rixin nodded approvingly. Almost all the knights he had faced fell into one of two categories. First, there were those who lacked the skill to properly challenge Rixin. Since he was a boy, he'd received instruction from the best tactologists and swordsmen in the realm. Most other knights hadn't had that luxury. The second group, on the other hand, had the proper training, but they were too timid to use it properly against their crown prince. This group drove Rixin mad. There was nothing less satisfying than beating someone who refused to give it their all.

Marcus, it appeared, fell into a rare third category. He had the skill, and based on their training, he wasn't going to hold anything back.

Finally some real competition. Rixin was glad he had arrived early so that he'd have a few days to figure out Marcus' weaknesses. But first he had to deal with Reavus.

He turned back to Nigel. The squire had a quill in his hand and was ready to make whatever changes Rixin deemed necessary.

"Actually, I'd prefer to make the additions myself," Rixin said and held out his hand.

"Of course, Your Highness." Nigel handed him the quill and paper.

Rixin found a spot on a nearby staircase where he could sit and compose the letter.

Uncle Reavus,

I have arrived safely at Arwin's Gate. As you had hoped, I caught our hosts unaware. While they were flustered to greet me properly, that seemed to be the extent of it. Upon my request, the steward immediately took me to the guest chambers. You'll be disappointed to hear that there were no booby traps or hungry razortooths waiting for us. The only oddity I encountered was Terric. I think he might be addicted to scorpium. And he's definitely planning on running away. But he's hardly a threat to the kingdom.

Duke Garrion is a perfectly harmless host, and unless you stumble upon some *real* evidence, I expect you to treat him with the utmost respect. Whatever past history the two of you have, you must set it aside. The man is your sister's husband, our host for the tournament, and the father of a woman who may be my future queen.

Not only is it safe for us here, but it is safe for my father as well. Please send for him to come. I should like to have him here to see me win Arwin's Lance.

Rixin reread the letter and signed his name and titles. He probably shouldn't have even bothered with the last bit about his father. He had more important things to occupy his mind than whether or not King Ivan was going to grace Arwin's Gate with his presence. Rixin had learned a long time ago that nothing he did was ever good enough for his father, and that a promise from him was rarely upheld. But against his better judgment, Rixin kept getting his hopes up. *Maybe this time he'll come,* he thought. After all, the king's sister was there. And it *was* the tournament for Arwin's Lance. It was going to be the biggest tournament in the past decade.

Even if the letter didn't get his father to come, he at least hoped it would make Reavus behave. Rixin was so tired of hearing his uncle go on and on about how he was going to finally find evidence that Garrion had murdered King Bogdan. Enough was enough. It had been twenty years and no evidence had been found.

He looked up to wave Nigel over, but the squire was already in front of him. *Was I this good a squire to Reavus?*

Nigel dripped hot red wax on the fold of the letter and Rixin pushed his signet ring into it to emboss it with the Talenov bat sigil.

"Will that be all, Your Highness?" asked Nigel.

Rixin was about to respond when something caught his eye. Maybe he was imagining it, but he thought he kept seeing a flash of golden hair. He had seen it earlier behind the wall around the archery targets. And now he kept seeing it in one of the tower windows. If the rumors were true, Oriana had turned into quite the beauty. It was hard for him to imagine. The last he'd seen her, she'd been chubby and was still playing with dolls. But that had been many years ago.

"Your Highness?" asked Nigel.

"What?" Rixin looked at him. "Oh, right. Actually, yes, there is one more thing you could help me with. I was wondering if you had heard if Lady Oriana is feeling better?"

"I haven't, but I shall check." Nigel bowed and left the courtyard.

Rixin mounted his horse, Midnight, and went to grab his lance, but then he realized that he'd been so caught up in dreaming of Oriana that he had forgotten his gauntlets. *Get a grip, Rixin,* he told himself. *You're supposed to be finding Marcus' weaknesses, not presenting him with your own.*

He looked around the courtyard to see who might be able to help. Nigel was long gone, but Terric and the stable boy were sitting on a nearby ledge.

"Terric!" he called. "Could you hand me my gauntlets?"

Both boys leapt off the wall at lightning speed and ran over to Rixin. Terric lifted one gauntlet and the stable boy lifted the other.

"What's your friend's name?" Rixin asked as he put out his hands.

Terric was surprisingly quick at fastening the gauntlet. Was that a symptom of being high on scorpium?

"This is my friend, Warin," Terric said as he secured the other gauntlet.

Rixin nodded. "It's a pleasure to meet you, Warin."

"The pleasure is mine, Your Highness." Warin bowed awkwardly.

"Thank you for taking good care of Midnight." Rixin patted his horse's neck. Her shiny black coat was slick was sweat. "Sometimes she can be a bit fussy around new grooms, but she seems to like you. Will you boys hand me my lance?"

Terric lifted up the lance. Warin helped him give it an extra push up to the prince.

"Thanks, boys," said Rixin. He tugged on the reins to get Midnight moving back towards Marcus and the other men.

"Welcome back," said Marcus. "Everything okay? I saw that you forgot your gauntlets for a second there."

"Everything's fine," said Rixin. "Just wanted to give your little brother and his friend some excitement. Figured I'd pretend to forget my gauntlets so they could lend a helping hand."

Marcus nodded skeptically. "If you say so."

"Quit your jabbering and get back to training," barked Aldric. "Prince Rixin is your competition, not your girlfriend."

The other men laughed and Marcus' face turned slightly red. He shook the reins and took off towards the quintain.

Practice went on for a while longer. Most of the men did decently, but Rixin and Marcus were the only two to hit the quintain every time. They kept going until Peter Harlow misjudged the counterweight and ended up flat on his back. Sir Aldric helped him hobble into the castle so that Axion Tobias could take a look at his bruises.

Rixin hadn't been able to test Marcus' weaknesses while Sir Aldric was there watching. Even if the knight was past his prime, he'd still be able to spot the tactic and warn Marcus not to be rattled by it. But now that Aldric was gone, Rixin could have a little fun.

He waited until it was Marcus' turn, and then, just as Marcus was about to strike the quintain, Rixin said, "When does Oriana usually go to bed?"

Marcus hit far to the left and just barely avoided suffering the same fate as Peter.

Rixin smiled to himself. *There it is. Marcus' weakness.* He had noticed Marcus get protective of Oriana during their earlier conversation. Now he had the confirmation he needed.

"Sorry about that, mate," said Rixin as Marcus brought his horse around. "Poor form for me to talk right before your strike."

"Don't sweat it," said Marcus. "I suspect the crowd will be cheering quite loudly for me, so it's good to practice jousting with a little noise."

Rixin nodded. He didn't want to push the Oriana topic too hard or Marcus might notice what he was up to. Speaking of Oriana... Rixin could have sworn he saw another flash of golden hair up in the tower.

How much longer was Marcus going to keep him out here practicing? Now that he knew Marcus' weakness, all he wanted to do was check on Oriana, to see if the rumors about her beauty had been exaggerated. He hoped they weren't. He hoped his father would come, and that he'd allow Rixin to marry Oriana rather than Navya. But even if Oriana wasn't to be his bride, she'd still make his time in Arwin's Gate more enjoyable. There hadn't been a woman yet who had turned down his advances. Oriana would be no different.

- CHAPTER 19 -
ORIANA

Same place. Same time. Oriana took a deep breath as she rummaged through the chest at the foot of her bed. She wasn't sure why she was even thinking about the nonsense Bastian had said. There was no way she was going to meet him again. Just the thought was preposterous.

Yet she found herself pulling out a shawl. She stared down at the fabric. *It would be easy enough to sneak away...*

She threw the shawl back down into the chest and slammed it shut. What was she thinking? She bit the inside of her lip. That was the problem. She wasn't thinking. At least, not about what she really wanted. Rixin. Oriana sighed and sat down on top of her chest, dropping her chin into her hand. She couldn't have feelings for another man when she was practically betrothed to Rixin.

But that was the whole problem. Practically was a whole different thing than actually. For Arwin's sake, that was exactly what Bastian had said. She sighed and walked over to her door. What she desperately needed was a distraction from everything. A walk was out of the question. She was worried her feet would just force her to walk to the market. Which she definitely didn't want to do. Or did she? *Ugh!* She knocked on her youngest sister's door.

"You may enter, noble warrior!" Nesta called from the other side.

Oriana laughed and opened the door. "Nesta, what are you doing?" She wasn't really sure why she bothered asking. It was clear that Nesta was recreating a joust with her dolls. An oversized needle was sticking out of one of their stomachs and Nesta was making neighing noises.

"Ori!" Nesta immediately got up off the ground and ran over to her sister. "Look what I made! Mama thought that I'd do better if I was making something I actually wanted. So I made a beautiful dress for Nessy." She held the doll up to Oriana's face. The doll had been given to Nesta when she was born and it had the same blonde hair and blue eyes as its owner. As soon as Nesta could talk, she had affectionately named the doll after herself. But the years of use had left one of the doll's eyes lopsided and some of the stitches on the mouth were unraveling. For years the stuffing had been slowly falling out through a gash in one of the arms.

The stitching on the doll's dress, however, showed signs of improvement. "This is really great, Nesta. Sister Morel is going to be very pleased with your progress." It was almost completely straight. Just a few stray stitches.

Nesta smiled so hard that the tendons in her neck stood out.

Oriana tried to stifle a laugh. "Were you pretending to joust?" She glanced over her little sister's shoulder at the carnage.

"Mhm. I was pretending to be Prince Rixin." She held up her doll again. "And that's Marcus." She pointed to the doll lying on the ground with a needle in his stomach.

"Nesta!"

"What? Prince Rixin is going to win."

"He is not. Your brother is going to win."

"No, Prince Rixin is. He's a *prince*."

"That doesn't mean he's a better jouster than Marcus."

"Yes it does, Ori. Princes are better at everything."

"That isn't true. Just because someone isn't born into nobility doesn't mean they aren't as good." *Where had that come from?*

Nesta frowned. "You'll see. He's going to beat everyone."

"Don't let Marcus hear that you're rooting against him. Or anyone else for that matter." She shook her head at her little sister. This conversation wasn't helping Oriana feel any better. Maybe she just needed to get everything off her chest. She sighed. What she needed was to talk to Selina. Selina was always reasonable. She'd know what to do. The problem was, Oriana knew exactly what Selina would tell her. And it involved avoiding the market for the rest of her life.

She looked down at the doll in Nesta's hands. Fixing it up for her would be a great distraction. The stitches were so small. It would be tedious, horrible work. *Perfect.* "Do you mind if I borrow Nessy?" she asked.

"But I wasn't done playing yet. I still have three more opponents to destroy. Please, Ori! Sister Morel said I could play until supper."

"I just wanted to fix her beautiful smile for you. You can keep playing with the rest of your dolls."

"Oh." Nesta looked down at Nessy.

"So that she looks more like you." Oriana tapped the bottom of Nesta's chin.

"Yes, please." She shoved the doll into Oriana's hands, ran back to her other dolls, and collapsed onto her knees with a loud neighing noise.

Oriana smiled to herself as she walked back into the hall. This really would be the perfect distraction. She would need to borrow some of her mum's thread, though. She was almost out of this shade of red. She was staring down at the doll when she turned the corner of the stairs and collided with someone. Hard. The force almost knocked the breath out of her as she stumbled forwards and started to fall down the stairs.

"Are you alright?" a deep voice said as an arm caught her around her waist to keep her from falling.

Oriana put her hand on her chest to steady her breathing. She was so embarrassed she couldn't even look up to see who she had run into. "I'm so sorry." She stepped away from his arm and almost tripped again, but quickly regained her balance.

"It was my fault," said the man. "You have nothing to apologize for."

"No I should have been looking where I was going, I..." her voice faltered when she finally looked up. "Rixin." Oriana completely lost her breath again when she looked into his pale blue eyes. She swallowed hard. It looked like he had just come in from practicing. A bead of sweat dripped down his forehead. He casually wiped it off with the back of his hand and flashed her a charming smile. She cleared her throat. "I mean, Prince Rixin." She quickly curtseyed. "I mean, Your Royal Highness. Sir." *Stop talking!* She did another awkward curtsey.

"Lady Oriana. You look every bit as lovely as I remember."

She laughed. "You never thought I looked lovely." She clasped her hand over her mouth. Had she really just said that out loud? Had she completely lost all reason?

A smile broke over his face. "I don't think that's true. But either way, you are beautiful in every sense of the word now." He grabbed her hand and placed a soft kiss on her knuckles.

She felt like she was going to melt into the floor.

Rixin kept her hand in his and ran his thumb along the spot where he had just kissed. "Truly breathtaking."

Oriana's face was slowly turning the same shade of red as Rixin's tunic. "As are you," she whispered.

"You think I'm beautiful?" The playful smile on his face made it hard for Oriana to breathe.

"Handsome. You're every bit as handsome as I remember, I mean." Except his jawline was sharper. And the muscles in his arms were larger. And he towered above her, emanating the strength she knew he possessed.

"One thing hasn't changed, though," Rixin said. "You're still playing with dolls."

"What? Oh." She pulled her hand out of his and picked up the doll from the ground. "It's my little sister's. Nesta, not Selina. Obviously. I promised her I'd fix some of the stitching."

"Mhm. Sure."

"I don't play with dolls. I'm not a child anymore, Rixin."

He raised his eyebrow. "I can see that."

Is he trying to see how red he can make my face?

"I should probably go get cleaned up before supper." He wiped another bead of sweat from his forehead.

Oriana clenched her hand by her side in order to restrain herself from wiping his sweat for him. She wondered how soft his skin would feel. She immediately shook the thought away. "Right. And I have to stitch up this doll that is in no way mine. I'll see you at supper."

He lifted up her hand once more and placed another gentle kiss on her knuckles. "It's a date, my lady."

A date. *I have a date with the prince!* It took every ounce of her resolve to not squeal.

***

Oriana pushed her half-eaten roast around with a piece of bread.

"Are you going to talk about why you're barely eating? Or are you just going to keep sighing?" Selina asked.

Oriana looked over her shoulder at the spot where Marcus usually sat. If Rixin was going to show up, he probably would have sat right next to him. As it was, neither of them were there, and neither were any of the other knights or squires. She dropped the bread on her plate and turned back to Selina. "I ran into Rixin this morning and I thought we had a nice conversation." *Or did I just completely embarrass myself?*

"That's great. So why do you seem...not great?"

"It's nothing. Foolishness, really." Oriana pushed her plate away.

Nesta grabbed the piece of bread Oriana hadn't eaten and shoved the whole thing in her mouth. "What?" she said with her mouth full when both of her sisters stared at her.

Oriana shook her head and smiled. "Nothing, Nesta."

"You're not getting out of this conversation that easily, Oriana," Selina said. "Tell me what's wrong. Maybe I can help."

"Like I said, it's nothing. He had just implied that he'd be here during supper. And that maybe we'd have another opportunity to talk."

"Oh." Selina gave her a sympathetic smile.

"Yeah. Oh." Oriana glanced once more over her shoulder. "It doesn't matter. I made a complete fool of myself. I literally ran right into him and then he saw me with Nessy and thought it was mine. And I couldn't keep myself from rambling. No wonder he's avoiding me."

"I'm sure he's not avoiding you. He's just training. When he saw that Marcus was skipping supper to keep training, he must have decided that he should too. That's all. You know how Marcus has been. He's so worried about losing."

"He should be," Nesta said. "He's going to lose to Rixin."

"Shh," Oriana said and put her hand on her youngest sister's shoulder. "Don't let father hear you talking like that."

"What happened to family allegiance?" Selina said and scowled at Nesta.

"But he's a prince. And he's so handsome."

Selina laughed. "Really, Nesta, not everything is about looks."

"Then why do my stitches have to be just so? And why do I have to wear this dress instead of running around in my knickers? And Mama always makes me scrub my face until it's red." She crossed her arms over her chest and slumped in her chair.

"Sit up straight," said Selina. She immediately laughed. "Actually, I see what you mean. Maybe you have a point. We do have an awful lot of rules to follow."

"Marcus is going to win the joust." *And show Rixin not to mess with the Hornbolts.* "If you'll both excuse me," said Oriana as her plate was cleared away.

"I'm sorry," said Selina. "If you want to stay a little longer and talk, maybe he'll show up late?"

"I'm not waiting any longer. Clearly he stood me up." She rushed past the empty table where Rixin should have been and retreated toward her bedchamber. She felt so foolish. After they had run into each other, she had gotten her hopes up. But obviously Rixin didn't mean a word he'd said. He still saw her as that awkward young girl who played with dolls in the corner and stared at him. What would he possibly see in her? She felt tears stream down her cheeks.

This was ridiculous. She immediately wiped the tears away and peered out the nearest window. Sure enough, Rixin and Marcus were wielding their swords below, completely entranced in their practice. It should have been a relief to see that Selina was right. But it wasn't. It just further proved that Oriana meant nothing to Rixin. Surely missing training to eat supper with her wouldn't have had that much of an impact on the outcome of the joust.

Rixin was just playing games with her head. He wanted her to think she had a chance when, in reality, his hand was probably already promised to Navya. She watched him perfectly parry Marcus' advance.

She knew the answer to her question. It stung because she'd had a crush on Rixin ever since she was a little girl. She probably used to talk about it as much as Nesta did. And the truth was, she could lean on this window sill and stare at him practicing and be perfectly content. A chill ran down her spine. Watching him from a distance was as close to marrying him as she'd ever get. The thought made her chest hurt. It felt like she was falling to pieces as she stared down at him. She couldn't do this.

Oriana grabbed the bottom of her skirt and ran to her room. She threw open her chest, grabbed the shawl that was still lying on top, and headed back the way she had come. She needed fresh air. It suddenly felt like she couldn't breathe. Her future was slipping away. She took a huge gulp of air as soon as she stepped outside. The clanging of the swords echoed in her head. She needed to get as far away as possible. Grabbing her skirt again, she started walking in the opposite direction of Rixin.

The farther away she walked, the easier it was for her to breathe. Maybe Selina was right. Maybe Rixin just didn't want to look weak in front of Marcus. That would make sense. Was she reading too much into him missing supper? *Probably*. Or was she just finally realizing that she never had a chance with him in the first place? *Ugh*.

The worst part was that getting stood up didn't alter her feelings. Yes, she was mad at him. But she still longed for him. She still couldn't stop thinking about his perfect smile. Or his enticing laugh. Or how strong he was.

Oriana didn't stop walking until she was several paces away from where she had run into Bastian the other day. *Same place. Same time.* It was as if she had been drawn to this spot. Drawn to him. She looked down at the shawl in her hand. Oriana had told herself that she just needed air. But the truth was, there was another smile she liked. Another enticing laugh. Other muscles. She swallowed hard. She had even gone to grab her shawl before leaving Vulture Keep.

She had been thinking about Rixin a lot that day, but Bastian was still in her thoughts too. And honestly, it was nice to be wanted. Especially by someone so handsome. She rolled her eyes at herself. She sounded just like Nesta.

She could still turn around. But after being stood up by Rixin, she didn't want to do that to Bastian. She knew how badly it hurt. That's what she told herself as she wrapped the shawl around her head. That she just didn't want to hurt his feelings. But the way her heart was beating with each step closer, the truth was very clear. She had feelings for Bastian. A part of her had been looking forward to this moment just as much if not more than supper with Rixin.

Oriana stopped in the same spot she had run into Bastian yesterday. The crowd of the market swirled around her. Any minute Bastian would appear in front of her. But he didn't. Oriana waited. And waited. And waited. Until her heart stopped hammering against her ribs. Until she had made her lip bleed as she bit it with worry. Until she realized that she had just gotten stood up for the second time that day.

She was just about to head back to Vulture Keep when she saw a squirrel scurrying around the corner. *Nut?* She walked toward him.

As she approached, Nut stuck his head around the corner, then immediately disappeared. A smile spread across Oriana's face. Nut wanted her to follow him. Surely he would lead her to Bastian. She picked up her pace and turned the corner. It was a side street, but it appeared that the market had spilled over into it. She was jostled to the side by a group of drunkards. She quickly stepped back away from the crowd. Nut was nowhere to be seen. Neither was Bastian. Maybe it hadn't even been Nut. It wasn't like he was the only squirrel in Arwin's Gate.

She had been stood up. Again.

But this time, she didn't feel the same anger coursing through her veins. She just felt defeated. What was the point of getting her hopes up only to have them stomped upon? There was no point. Her fate was out of her hands. It was up to her father and King Ivan. And if Bastian didn't want to see her, that was up to him. She had no idea where he lived. She couldn't just walk into the market and expect to run into him every time. It wasn't like he had a spy network to trace her movements. She might never see him again. The thought made her chest ache. She sighed as she looked up at the castle. It was like all her dreams had suddenly been swept away. She might end up spending her whole life in Vulture Keep.

***

With each step up the stairs, her fate grew more and more dim. She'd spend the rest of her days stitching up dolls. Was something really so wrong with her? Was she somehow appalling? She followed all the rules that Selina had talked about at supper. She always did what was expected of her. Maybe that was the problem.

She reached into her pocket for the key to her room. But instead of the key, she felt something else. Oriana pulled out a note with a necklace tied to it. Her jaw dropped slightly. It wasn't just any necklace. It was the most beautiful thing she had ever seen. And definitely the most expensive piece of jewelry she had ever touched. She didn't even know rubies that big existed.

Oriana quickly opened up the note.

My lady,

A little something beautiful for the most beautiful woman in the realm.

I'll be seeing you soon,

-Bastian

The fact that he had stolen the key to her bedchambers was not lost on her. She looked down at the keyhole to her door, knowing perfectly well that even though it was locked, it wouldn't keep Bastian out. She swallowed hard. What in Arwin's name was Bastian thinking? He had clearly stolen this necklace. He was planning on sneaking into her room. The scandal of it all! So why was she smiling? She should have been reporting the incident to Sir Aldric so he could lock down the castle. Instead, Oriana found herself turning around to search for Bella. She needed the spare key to her room as soon as possible so she could get in and make sure there were no dolls visible when Bastian arrived.

I ‑ CHAPTER 20 ‑ SOLDA

Isolda tossed and turned in her bed. No matter what position she turned to, the sheets were too hot. Or too cold. Or her pillow was too lumpy. Or she was too close to Garrion. There was no way that he'd murdered her father. *Right?* She pressed her lips together. That thought was the thing really keeping her from finding sleep. It felt like she was getting no closer to an answer.

The search for Foreman Owen was thus far unsuccessful. His wife hadn't seen him in days, and neither had his workers.

Of course.

He had taken the body and ran. Or maybe Tobias had taken the body and framed Owen.

By Throg's beard, who can I trust in this infernal city?

Reavus was scheduled to arrive that morning, but even though he was her beloved brother, he couldn't exactly be trusted to act in her best interest. She had no doubt that he would be eager to help her find proof that Garrion was guilty of killing their father. And she was sure he'd find that proof, whether it was real or fabricated. No, going to Reavus wasn't an option. Not until she was sure Garrion was innocent. *Or guilty.* She sighed and rolled over in bed again.

The main problem was that she felt like the trail was going cold. A week ago, Isolda and Tobias had a trail of bread-crumbs laid before them, guiding them through a forest she had been trying to navigate for nearly two decades. But suddenly, the breadcrumbs had disappeared. Tobias was still there to guide her, but when the light hit his face just so, she thought she saw hints of something more sinister beneath his friendly, timid disguise.

Why had Tobias come to Arwin's Gate in the first place? She tried to think back to when he'd first arrived. Three years ago. They had been without an axion in Vulture Keep for a few years before that. The official reason was that there was a shortage of new recruits, but Isolda knew the real reason was that no axion was willing to risk their life working for Garrion. Not after Garrion had dangled the previous axion off a balcony.

Tobias had gone through his first few months at Vulture Keep hardly making a noise. He'd looked like he was on the verge of getting ill every time Garrion walked into the room. Isolda tried to be friendly to him, but he seemed just as terrified to talk to her.

Isolda still remembered the night he'd opened up. It was about nine months after he had first come to Vulture Keep. She encountered him in the hall outside Terric's room. He was sitting on the floor weeping, his glasses in one hand and a snot covered rag in the other.

Isolda sat down next to him. They sat there for a while, maybe an hour, without saying a word. And then he started talking.

As his story went, he had been one poor test result away from expulsion from the University of Techence. He always studied hard, but when it came to taking tests or giving oral presentations, Tobias cracked under the pressure. The only thing that saved him was his family name. His father, Mobius Crane, was one of the three members of the Ministry of Techence, and as such, he held considerable sway at the university. By greasing just the right gears, Mobius arranged for Tobias to be granted the title of axion on a temporary basis, with the remainder of his studies to come in the form of real-world experience.

As with everything in Techence, Tobias' success was measured with empirical data. The main function of an axion, at least as far as Techence was concerned, was to sell technology. Tobias was tasked with generating more gold than 50% of other axions currently in service. Based on the size of Garrion's estate compared to those of minor lords, it should have been easy. But it wasn't. Garrion saw no need for Tobias' contraptions.

In his first nine months at Vulture Keep, Tobias hadn't earned a single drachma. The university had notified him that he would be terminated if the situation didn't change. It was unclear if termination meant being stripped of his title and recalled to Techence, or if the Collectors would make him disappear.

Isolda had been able to convince Garrion that ordering a shipment of new halberds from Techence would help strengthen their defenses on the wall, but it wasn't enough. Tobias remained in the bottom 50%.

That was when Isolda had hatched the idea to pay Tobias to be the liaison for her illegal business ventures. Up to that point, she had been disguising herself as Lady Marsilia to collect her profits and information from the brothels, but it was a risky business. If Garrion had caught her, he might have sentenced her to banishment in the Razortooth Savanna. Would he have really banished her? She didn't know. Their love was strong, but his temper was, at times, stronger. Using Tobias as a middleman greatly decreased her risk.

Over the next few years, Isolda and Tobias had grown into dear friends, bonded together by the secret of the brothels. She could trust him more than anyone. Or so she thought. Maybe her trust had been misplaced. Maybe, when he had seen the body of Arwin, he had seen an opportunity to steal it and make a great fortune. With the kind of money he'd earn from that, he'd be able to buy enough technology to catapult himself up the charts into the ranks of the most successful axions.

Or maybe he really was her friend.

Isolda tugged on the covers and rolled over. Not being able to sleep was driving her mad. An obvious clue could have been right in front of her and she might not have seen it through the fog that had taken up permanent residence in her brain.

"Trouble sleeping?" asked Garrion.

Isolda jumped and let out a squeal. She hadn't realized Garrion was awake too. "Yes."

Garrion gave her a reassuring smile. "Me too. Every time I close my eyes, I see Reavus and..."

Isolda nodded. He didn't have to say it, Isolda knew he was picturing his old friend Julian.

"I feel like Reavus is planning something," said Garrion. "But I can't figure out what it is. Why would he send Rixin early? That has to be a clue."

"Maybe Rixin really did want to come practice. I bet he wanted some extra time to scout out Marcus. There's no reason to be suspicious." *Or is there?* Rixin had arrived after the body was discovered missing. But what if he had been in the city before that? What if he took the body? She shook her head, dismissing the thought. She was losing her mind.

Garrion pushed his pillow up against the headboard and sat up. "No. No, there has to be more to it than that. Reavus has been trying to go to war with the Rashidi ever since Zand stole Tarini from him. He wouldn't leave an opportunity like this up to chance."

"Then it's a good thing you're married to me. He would never let his plan slip in front of you, but if I talked to him one on one, sister to brother, I might be able to get some information out of him. If I get him talking about the joust, I might be able to get a hint out of him. Even if it's just a nervous tic when I mention something related to his plan."

"Are you sure you're up for that? As our master of spies, that might be a job better suited for Father Percival." Garrion shook his head. "Or maybe Brother Savaric would be better. I hate to say it, but I think old age might finally be catching up to Father Percival."

Isolda had to hold back a smile. If only Garrion knew what she did in her free time. She was twice the spy Percival or Savaric would ever be.

And then it hit her. She couldn't believe she hadn't thought of it sooner. If she could pick up on a nervous tic of her brother, whom she'd hardly seen in the past twenty years, she'd surely be able to pick up on a nervous tic of her husband. She just had to think of a way to bring up the body of Arwin without actually mentioning it...

Isolda snapped her fingers. "You know what, I might not even have to talk to Reavus. I think I might already have a clue. The other day, Tobias mentioned that there had been a few cave-ins under the new construction around the tournament grounds." Isolda watched Garrion closely as she spoke, hoping for any little change in his expression.

Nothing.

"The old mine shafts just aren't strong enough to support the weight of the new buildings, according to Tobias," added Isolda, hoping that might elicit more of a response.

Still nothing. Isolda grabbed his hand to see if she could feel his heartbeat accelerating. She knew how the blood rushed to his hands when he got angry. But his pulse felt normal. If he had hidden Arwin's body in the tunnels, the thought of it being uncovered in a collapse would have worried him.

"Hmm..." Garrion stroked his chin. He looked pensive. Not nervous or upset. "What would be Reavus' angle with that?"

"I don't know," said Isolda. "It might just be a coincidence."

"Maybe he's planning on using that as an excuse if Rixin loses. He'll try to invalidate the results of the tournament on the grounds that the city was unfit to host the tournament."

"Let's sleep on it. It looks like the sun isn't going to rise for another hour or two." Isolda gave Garrion a quick kiss on the lips, but he grabbed her hips and pulled her back, kissing her harder.

It was easy for her to get lost in the kiss. But as soon as their lips parted, she felt the suspicions creep back around her. And she felt guilty for suspecting him in the first place. It was as if she carried an unbearable guilt on her shoulders. She closed her eyes and rolled back onto her side, trying to distance herself from Garrion. But it gave her a momentary sense of peace when he shifted closer and wrapped his strong arms around her. She wasn't totally convinced Garrion was innocent, but his lack of reaction to the mention of the tunnels collapsing was worth clinging onto if it allowed her to finally get some sleep. And she needed the support that only his arms could seem to give her.

With Reavus coming to town, she had a feeling sleep would be hard to come by for them both.

VULTURE
KEEP

- CHAPTER 21 -
GARRION

"Are you sure this is necessary?" asked Isolda. "You look like you're going to battle rather than greeting a guest."

"When the guest is Reavus, there's a good chance it could devolve into a battle," said Garrion.

"Please try to be civil. You haven't seen him in eight years. A man can change a lot in that time."

"Give me one example."

Isolda walked over and helped Peter tighten the straps on Garrion's armor. "Just look at you. You've practically out-grown your armor since you last put it on."

Garrion shifted uncomfortably in his armor. Isolda was right, it hadn't been nearly this tight last time he wore it, which had been... He could hardly remember when he had last worn armor. Had he really become one of those lords that just sits in his castle getting fat? "It's muscle," said Garrion defensively.

"Oh yes, I'm sure it is. Shoveling all those meat pies into your mouth looks quite grueling." Isolda smiled playfully.

Garrion might have been offended, but he was just glad that Isolda was acting normal again. He would endure her insults all day long if the alternative was having her be cold and distant like she had been for the better part of the last fortnight.

"If Reavus tries to crawl under your skin, just look at your sword," said Isolda, handing Garrion his sheathed sword. "You are Arwin's Rhino. You are armored in truth, not in anger."

Those were the same words Isolda had spoken to him when she had given him the sword on their first wedding anniversary. Garrion took Horn from her and pulled it a few inches out of the leather sheath. It wasn't as balanced or as sharp as his family's ancestral blade, Razorclaw, but Garrion's best friend hadn't impaled himself on it either. It had a perfectly reflective blade and a dark red rhino head hilt, with its horn protruding perpendicular to the cross guard. Isolda claimed the polish was to force him to look in the mirror before resorting to violence.

"I know, I know," said Garrion. "I haven't hurt a fly since the end of the war."

Isolda eyed him skeptically. "What about your little incident with Tobias?"

Garrion shrugged. "I knew the armor would keep him safe. Do you think I have no faith in our esteemed axion's talents?"

"Either way, I had Roger buff the polish."

"Good. That way I can use it to apply some mascara after I take Reavus' head off."

"Garrion!"

"I only jest. I hardly even know what mascara is, much less how to apply it."

"That's not the part I was upset about." Isolda yanked the strap on Garrion's chest plate to make sure it was extra tight.

"Okay, okay," conceded Garrion. "As long as Reavus doesn't bring up the Hyposas..."

Three trumpet blasts at the entrance to Arwin's Gate ended their conversation. Reavus had arrived.

Garrion and Isolda were the last Hornbolts to arrive in Garus' Square. A combined force of Hornbolt soldiers and Reavus' elite guard, known as the Blacksmiths, kept eager peasants from getting too close to the approaching caravan. Garrion couldn't help but notice that the Blacksmiths were much more effective than his soldiers at keeping the crowd at bay. While the Hornbolt soldiers acted as individuals, the Blacksmiths moved as one, as if they were all controlled by one mind. Or maybe the Blacksmiths just looked more unified in their identical black metal armor studded with bloodgold rivets. Garrion's soldiers, on the other hand, each wore individually crafted leather armor and caps. Each piece looked somewhat similar and met certain guidelines, but it didn't have nearly the same effect.

Garrion turned to Sir Aldric. His blue and silver armor was closer to the standard of the Blacksmiths' armor. *Why aren't all of our soldiers dressed like Aldric?* "Are these really our best soldiers?"

"No, my lord," said Aldric. "Our finest troops are patrolling the savanna. The Sultan won't be embarrassing us with any surprise attacks. That I assure you."

"Good, because our soldiers' uniforms provide enough embarrassment for one day. See to it that our men are all in full armor from now until the joust."

"With pleasure."

Isolda shoved Garrion lightly in the ribs. "Please tell me you aren't already comparing the size of your swords before Reavus even exits his carriage."

Garrion ignored the comment. Instead, he puffed out his chest and straightened his shoulders.

Reavus' bard spurred his black stallion in front of the wagon. He played a few blasts on a trumpet to make sure he had everyone's attention, as if his red and black halved tunic wouldn't have accomplished that on its own, and then cleared his throat.

"My lords, my ladies," began the bard. "It is with great pleasure that I present to you...Treland's master-at-arms, Duke of Bloodstone, distinguished knight of Arwin's Temple, Prince of Treland, eradicator of treason, The King's Hammer: Lord Reavus of House Talenov."

Eradicator of treason? That wasn't an official title. It was a reminder of what Reavus had done to the Hyposas. Garrion started to feel the blood rushing to his hands.

The crowd cheered enthusiastically as a soldier opened the carriage door. Reavus stepped out and waved to the peasants. Garrion hated the sight of him. The greasy black hair, the crooked smile. Most of all, he hated Reavus' shifty black eyes. But there was something different about Reavus. Unlike the blacksmiths, and unlike the last time Reavus and Garrion met, Reavus was dressed in a simple black tunic with red trim. It wasn't classless or garish or insulting. In fact, it was similar to what most lords wore when they traveled. But it was odd to see Reavus dressed in such a manner. Garrion had expected him to be dressed in full armor.

What's he planning?

Garrion reluctantly bowed as Reavus approached. As much as he hated it, Reavus did outrank him as a direct member of the royal family.

"You may rise, Duke Garrion," said Reavus. Then he turned and embraced Isolda. "It's been too long, sister."

"It has," said Isolda. "It's a pleasure to have you here. Isn't it, Garrion?"

"It is," said Garrion through gritted teeth.

Reavus shook his head. "It shouldn't be. Not after..."

Garrion stared at him.

"Well, we won't speak of that. I was foolish back then. Young and brash. I didn't know what I was doing. Hell, I still don't get it right all the time."

"We've prepared the guest tower for you and your court," said Garrion, ignoring Reavus' half apology. He was determined to not let Reavus crawl under his skin.

"That's very kind, but I can't accept the hospitality of a man I've wronged. Not until my apology is complete."

Garrion lowered his eyebrows. "Go on then," he said.

"I shouldn't have handled the Hyposas the way I did," continued Reavus. "Having you put your friend to the sword...it was brutish. Unbefitting of a knight. I was caught up in the moment. I was angry that my father had been killed. And I thought you were responsible."

Garrion's hand shifted to the hilt of his sword. "I wasn't."

"I know that now. You've been a loyal servant of the realm for years, and King Ivan and I thank you for your loyalty. If you give me a chance, I think you'll find that I've changed."

"That doesn't..." Garrion took a deep breath to try to clear his head. The red mist was starting to cloud his vision. "That doesn't bring Julian and Dory back."

Reavus raised an eyebrow. "Nor should it. Don't mistake my words - as long as I'm alive, I'll make sure no traitor escapes punishment. The Hyposas were traitors and their deaths were deserved. But the way I went about it was wrong. Brute force is required in some situations, but it's so much more satisfying to lie and wait. Even the most careful traitors slip up eventually. And when they do, I'll be there to catch them." The corner of Reavus' mouth turned up ever so slightly as he spoke. His apology was nothing more than a thinly veiled challenge. He wasn't talking about catching traitors. He was talking about catching Garrion. But what snare would he set?

Garrion gripped Horn tighter. With one swing he could put an end to this miserable snake of a man...

Reavus put his hand on Garrion's shoulder. "I'll understand if you can't forgive me right away, but I hope we can move past it eventually. This tournament isn't about the mistakes of old men. Such a distraction would do a great disservice to the brave young men vying for Arwin's Lance."

Garrion's hand bumped against the rhino carving on the hilt of Horn. *You are Arwin's Rhino. You are armored in truth, not in anger.* Isolda's words cut through the red mist. He forced a smile and looked into Reavus' mocking black eyes.

"You are most generous, Your Highness," said Garrion. "I agree that nothing should take away from Marcus' impending victory."

"You must not have watched Prince Rixin practice yet," replied Reavus. "Perhaps we should make a wager..."

"There will be time for such things later," said Isolda, stepping between Garrion and Reavus, "but first we should get you settled." Isolda looped her arm in her brother's and led him through the gate and over the bridge. The Blacksmiths and three carriages full of Reavus' court followed.

Garrion hung back to talk to Aldric. "What do you think he's planning?" he asked.

"I actually don't think he's planning anything."

"What? Why not?"

"I've seen the prince train. He's hardly been trying and he's still miles better than the rest of the boys."

"Not Marcus though, right?"

Aldric shook his head. "He's closer than the rest, but he's still no match for the prince."

"Even with a few more days of training?"

"Impossible. Do you remember when you jousted against Obasi Mobek?"

"Of course." Garrion instinctively flexed his leg at the mention of it. The bone still ached sometimes. Apparently the axion who set his leg after Obasi had unhorsed him hadn't done it quite right.

"You described it as trying to joust against the wind. That's how Marcus is going to feel."

"There must be something we can do."

Aldric stroked his pointy beard. "In the words of General Sappington: 'Every enemy can be beaten if you know where to strike.' "

"That's all well and good. But do we know what Rixin's weakness is?"

"I have a guess," said Aldric.

"Then tell me."

Sir Aldric smiled and pointed to where the carriages were unloading at the main gate to Vulture Keep. Arwin's Voice had just emerged. Garrion was surprised by how fat he'd gotten, but more-so by all the jewels that adorned his traditional priest chains. It would have been an audacious display of wealth for any man, much less Arwin's Voice. He was supposed to live a life of poverty and service. Not a life of gluttony. *This must be the work of Reavus,* thought Garrion.

"You think Rixin's weakness is Arwin's Voice?" Garrion was shocked at the thought of it. "Are you accusing them of buggery?" *I guess that would explain all his gaudy jewelry...*

Sir Aldric stifled a rare laugh. "Forgive me. I was trying to point to Lady Oriana."

The thought of Rixin and Oriana still bothered Garrion, but it was slightly less appalling than his previous assumption that Arwin's Voice was a boy plonker.

"How sure are you?" asked Garrion.

"Not entirely. It's just a hunch."

"I'll need more than a hunch if I'm going to go dangling my daughter in front of the prince like a piece of meat. Can you find out with certainty?"

"Of course. He can't hide his weaknesses from me. No one can." Aldric pointed to his golden eyes.

"Speaking of hiding from you...are those birds still nesting in the ceiling above your room?"

"That was last year," said Aldric.

"Oh."

"But they're back, and they're just as annoying as they were before. I still think that cleaning up that nest would be the perfect punishment next time I catch Terric climbing the walls. It'll kill two birds with one stone, so to speak."

Garrion frowned. "I've told you before, we're not risking Terric's life just to silence a few birds. And anyway, those birds might prove useful yet."

"How so?"

"The birds keep you from sleeping at night, right?"

"Yes."

"Perfect. We'll move Rixin's room there, and then he'll be the one not getting any sleep."

"And where am I to stay?"

"I don't know. Aren't there some empty rooms somewhere?" He noticed Quentin Harlow off to the side. "Quentin!" called Garrion.

The steward rushed over. "How can I be of service, my lord?"

"Are there any empty rooms in the castle?" asked Garrion.

Quentin flipped through a few sheets of parchment. "Just a few in the servant's quarters. The entire guest tower is going to be filled to the brim with Reavus' court."

"Very well," said Garrion. "I'd like to move Rixin to Aldric's room. And I guess Aldric will move to the servant's quarters."

"But my family is coming tonight," said Aldric. "You'd have my girls sleep in the same room as Evelyn and me? In the *servant's quarters?*"

"Can you think of another way?" asked Garrion. "Maybe you could stay with Tobias..."

"Sweet Arwin, no," spat Aldric. "The servant's quarters will do just fine."

- CHAPTER 22 -
ORIANA

Oriana tried her best not to stare at Rixin. She kept her eyes trained on the carriages. Any moment now Navya was probably going to appear. She'd finally see the reason why Rixin had stood her up.

Just thinking about yesterday made color rise to her cheeks. She was so foolish. She had let herself get her hopes up with Rixin. And then did the same with Bastian. *Twice.* She'd even had improper thoughts of Bastian sneaking into her room last night. Which of course he didn't do. Because she was the only one who had lost all reason.

The waiting was the hard part. Waiting for Rixin. Waiting for Bastian. Waiting for stupid Navya to be introduced. Oriana already knew Navya would be beautiful. She'd probably have perfectly smooth dark hair and big eyes and the latest fashions. She'd be everything Rixin actually wanted. Because clearly it wasn't Oriana who he liked. She let her gaze wander to Rixin.

Clearly, indeed. Rixin was standing with Marcus and a few other squires. They were all laughing and talking. They were having a wonderful time. *Unlike me.* Not once had Rixin's gaze wandered in her direction. Despite how much she tried to look away, she just couldn't. His pale skin almost sparkled in the sun. All she could think about was touching it. How was she supposed to ignore such perfection? She willed her feet to stay still so she wouldn't do something she would regret.

"Ori, can we go back to play now?" Nesta asked and tugged on Oriana's arm.

"Not yet," Oriana whispered. "We have to wait to greet Uncle Reavus." *And see Navya.*

"But I don't wanna."

Oriana turned to face her sister, happy for the distraction. "Nesta, we haven't seen our uncle in…" her voice trailed off as she looked at her youngest sister. "Well, actually you've never met him. We also need to meet Navya."

"I know. And I don't wanna. Let's go." She tugged on Oriana's arm again.

Oriana laughed. "Nesta, what has gotten into you?"

"Papa said the Rashidi wench…"

"Nesta!" Oriana clapped a hand over Nesta's mouth and looked over her shoulder to make sure no one had heard. Everyone seemed to be enthralled by the bard introducing lords and ladies from Reavus' court. "Where'd you learn to say a thing like that?"

"Papa," Nesta mumbled against Oriana's hand. When Ori didn't move her hand, Nesta licked her palm.

Oriana groaned and wiped her hand off on her skirt. "Well, don't say it again."

"But Papa…"

"I know. But we're ladies. And we don't use words like that."

Nesta shrugged. "Oh! The prince is coming over to talk to me!" She started to jump up and down.

Oriana looked up to see Rixin approaching them. Her heart thumped against her ribcage. She felt dizzy and nauseous at the same time. He probably was just coming to talk to Nesta. She grabbed the bottom of her skirts and was about to run when she froze. What in Arwin's name was she doing? She shouldn't be the one that was embarrassed to see him. He was the one that needed to apologize. She let her skirt fall back in place and then turned away from him, focusing instead on the bard's introductions.

"My lady," she heard Rixin say.

"Prince Rixin! What is Uncle Reavus like?" Nesta asked. "And what is Navya like? My papa called her…."

Oh, no. Oriana quickly turned around. "Nesta, what did we just talk about?"

"I wasn't gonna say it." She turned back to Rixin. "My papa called her something I'm not supposed to repeat because I'm a lady."

Oriana covered her face with her hands. *Why, Nesta?*

Rixin laughed. "Well, it's good you didn't repeat it then. Do you mind if speak with your sister for a moment?"

"Mhm. I'm gonna go meet Uncle Reavus." Nesta hummed as she skipped away.

Oriana lowered her hands but kept her face turned away from Rixin. She wasn't going to pretend any longer. She wasn't some little girl with a crush on him. She was Lady Oriana of House Hornbolt and she did not get flustered by the prince.

"My lady?" Rixin said.

She didn't respond.

He lightly touched her shoulder. Just the smallest touch and it felt like her skin was on fire. She turned around, embarrassed by the flush that she knew was on her cheeks. He was staring at her so intently that she took a step back.

"Your Highness," she said and curtsied. "Selina's around here somewhere. I'll go try to find her for you." She turned to leave when he caught her hand.

"You know that I meant you," he said.

Oriana pulled her hand away. "Actually, Your Highness…"

"Rixin," he corrected.

"Fine. *Rixin.* I did not know if you meant me. And I would never be so presumptuous to think so."

"I owe you an apology."

"Yes, you do."

He smiled. "The other men were practicing late and I didn't want to be the first one that retired. But if you think for a second that I'd rather be with them than a beautiful woman like yourself, then you are sorely mistaken."

Oh my. She took a deep breath. "Well, maybe I'm sorely mistaken, then." *What did I just say? Did I just contradict the prince? Kill me now.*

Rixin smiled. "Lady Oriana, you are very different than I remember."

In a good way or a bad way? She couldn't seem to speak, terrified that she'd say something else insulting. She turned away and found herself staring into the golden eyes of Sir Aldric. A chill went down her spine. Why had he been watching her so intently?

"May I help you?" asked Oriana.

"Forgive me, my lady," said Aldric. He bowed his head slightly. "I had hoped to speak with the Prince to extend him an invitation for this afternoon's training."

"I'll be right there," said Rixin. "If you'll excuse me, Lady Oriana." He grabbed her hand, placing a kiss against her knuckles. "I meant you've changed in a good way," he whispered against her skin before dropping her hand and joining Sir Aldric.

Did I just imagine that? She rubbed the back of her hand with her fingertips, relishing the feeling of his warm breath against her skin.

"Ori, Ori, look!" Nesta came running back over to her and pointed toward the gate.

Two beautiful white stallions pulled the final carriage into position. All of the carriages had been impressive, but this one was different. It had been crafted from thick planks of dark ironwood embellished with bloodgold trim. Even the wheels had bloodgold detailing on the spokes.

A footman hurried to put a little staircase covered in red velvet in front of the door to the carriage while another rolled out a plush carpet between the stairs and the front gate.

The footmen stepped to the side and the bard blew thrice on his trumpet. "Presenting the daughter of Sultan Zand Sakar and hostage of the crown: Princess Navya of House Sakar."

Duke Reavus opened the door and offered Navya his hand.

Wait...that's Navya?

Ori couldn't believe her eyes. Navya's fancy dress did little to hide the fact that she had the physique of a scrawny ten-year-old boy. And her hair...it was long and black, but it was nothing like Bella's. It was wild and frizzy. Her dark olive skin might have been beautiful, but Oriana had trouble seeing it beneath the dark hair on her arms.

"The wench is ugly," Nesta said.

"Nesta!" But Oriana couldn't stop the laughter that bubbled out of her. She had never felt such relief. Navya was not at all beautiful. She was an odd little monster girl.

"Sorry, Ori. I forgot. I won't use that word again. But Rixin will definitely choose me over her! I'm beautiful."

Oriana laughed. "You're very pretty. But let's not talk about our guest that way."

Isolda and Selina were some of the first to greet Navya, and then they brought her over to Ori and Nesta.

"Ladies, I want you to meet Princess Navya," said Isolda.

Oriana curtseyed. "It's a pleasure to meet you."

The pleasure is all mine," said Navya. "Really, I mean that. I read that the people of the Shield have hated the Rashidi for centuries." She lifted up the book in her hand. "So you're either being polite or dishonest." She pushed a frizzy strand of hair out of her face.

"Is that an original volume of The Second Sand War by Omar Ryphib?" asked Selina. "I've been asking Tobias to get me a copy of that for years."

"It is," said Navya proudly. "Is it still common practice here to tie Rashidi to poles and bet on which will be eaten by a razortooth tiger first?"

"Did we really used to do that?" asked Selina.

Isolda cleared her throat. "Navya, we're very pleased to have you. We've made arrangements for you to stay in Nesta's room."

Nesta looked at Navya and then back at Isolda. "No, thank you."

Isolda crouched down next to her daughter. "Nesta, the two of you will get along grandly. How about you show her to your room?"

"But Mama, no one's allowed to know my secret password. So she can't stay with me."

"I'm sure we can make an exception for our guest."

"No."

"Nesta…"

"She can stay with Selina," Nesta said and pointed up at the two of them talking about the history of Trelish cruelty towards the Rashidi. "Ori and I are too busy. She's fixing Nessy and I'm learning my stitches."

Isolda sighed.

"It's okay, Mum," Selina said. "I don't mind. I'll show Navya the way now. She said she'd let me borrow her book." Selina was smiling.

"If you're sure that's alright?"

"Of course. Come with me, Navya," Selina said. "I'll show you around the castle."

"Thank you," Isolda said as she watched them walk away. Then she turned toward Nesta. "Why didn't you want to share a room with Navya? And I know it's not because of the password. You always tell me your passwords." She ruffled Nesta's hair.

"Ori said I shouldn't use the word wench because I'm a lady. But if I can't use the word, I shouldn't be able to share a room with one."

Isolda looked up at Oriana.

"Don't look at me," Oriana said. "She learned it from Father."

Isolda sighed. "Just this once, don't listen to your father. It's not nice to call people names."

"Yes, Mama," said Nesta.

"Now go get back to sewing. Sister Morel will expect to see some straight stitches." She kissed Nesta on the cheek.

Nesta nodded. As soon as Isolda had walked away, Nesta grabbed Oriana's hand. "Let's go play now." She pulled Oriana away from the crowd.

"You just told Mum you were going to practice your stitching. And we haven't greeted Uncle Reavus yet."

"Mama won't be mad. Ori, the prince is going to choose you or me."

"That's not necessarily true." But Oriana couldn't ignore the tingle on her skin where he had kissed her. Or the way that he smiled at her. Or how he thought she had changed in a good way. She had to swallow the squeal that wanted to escape her throat. He had even asked her to call him Rixin.

"It is true," said Nesta. "Navya's yucky. And he kissed my hand! And he kissed yours too. He loves us."

If only it were that simple.

- CHAPTER 23 -
BASTIAN

Bastian twisted his key and pushed the door open. He was greeted by darkness, just like he was every evening. He lit a candle and let his room flicker to life. Yesterday had been great. Picturing Oriana pacing back and forth in the spot he had promised to meet her put a smile on his face. She had waited for quite a while before giving up. And she looked just as cute when she scowled as when she smiled. If only his evening could have been as good.

Finding a buyer for the golden gauntlet had proved more difficult than Bastian had anticipated. He'd spent all night going from fence to fence, but they all gave him the same answer. Selling stolen trinkets and jewelry was relatively safe. But selling stolen armor? That was a great way to have an angry knight take your head off. At least, that was what the fences had all told him.

He sat down and stared at the vials of scorpium on the wooden table. He'd managed to scrape together enough drachmas for the scorpium. But guilt started to creep into his mind as he waited for Logan. He knew Logan would be desperate for a fix. When he had seen him yesterday, he was scratching his arms and mumbling nonsense. He was in withdrawal. If he hadn't found any by now, he'd probably give up a limb for a single dose. Bastian had hoped it wouldn't come to this, but it was the only way he could think to pay Logan for his half of the necklace. It would have to be enough.

Besides, one day, he'd be out of these tunnels. He'd get Logan clean and take him with him. Maybe he'd even have Oriana. Just the thought of her smiling up at him put his mind at ease. She liked him too, despite what Logan thought. He had a real shot with her.

Nut scampered through the small hole in the door and hopped onto Bastian's lap. The squirrel immediately spit an acorn onto the front of Bastian's trousers and looked up at him expectantly.

Bastian patted Nut's head and grabbed the acorn. Bringing him food was Nut's way of showing his loyalty. Or maybe Nut was trying to take care of him. Bastian patted the squirrel's head again. What Nut didn't realize was that Bastian eating raw acorns would make him sicker than Logan's horrible withdrawal symptoms.

When there was a knock on the door, Bastian took advantage of Nut's distraction and slid the acorn into his pocket. "Come in," he said. He loved his squirrel, but he didn't want to spend the night hunched over the privy. His fingers wound around the key in his pocket. He was going to visit Oriana. He just hoped it was the key to her bedchamber and not the kitchen pantry. Although, a warm meal wouldn't be the worst thing. Bastian had used all his money to purchase the scorpium for Logan. The apple he'd swiped for lunch was all he'd eaten all day. Bastian grabbed both vials of scorpium, slid one into his pocket, and stood up just as Logan entered the small room.

Logan looked even worse than he had yesterday. There were now red lines down the fronts of his forearms, some deep enough to show blood. The scratching was a sure sign that Logan hadn't found another source of scorpium yet. And Logan needed the drug just like Bastian needed a proper supper.

Bastian held out the vial. "Payment for your half of the necklace."

"I thought we agreed to..." Logan stopped talking. "I can't remember."

"Good thing I got you two then," Bastian said and pulled the second vial out of his pocket.

Logan nodded eagerly and grabbed the vials. "You have yourself a deal. When are you going to give the princess the necklace?" He poured one of the vials onto the table.

Bastian ignored the temptation to argue over whether or not Oriana was a princess or not again. "Tonight." He had already slipped Oriana the necklace, but he didn't want Logan to know that he had done it before paying him for his half. Besides, he was planning on seeing Oriana tonight anyway. It was barely a lie.

"The rubies will look nice with her pretty blonde hair," Logan said. "And it'll look even better dangling between her perky breasts."

Bastian tried to hide his scowl. He didn't like hearing other people talk about Oriana that way. But he had no claim to her. *Yet.* "I should get going," Bastian said.

Normally Logan would offer to come with him. He was a great lookout. But Bastian knew that tonight, no offer would come. Logan had a date with those vials.

"Wait," Logan said and grabbed Bastian's arm. "Where did you get these? I thought you didn't know any dealers."

Bastian shook his head. There was no way he would tell Logan about his source. If he did, Logan would waste away into nothing. Bastian had seen what the drug did to people. Or, more accurately, how it slowly killed them. It was better that Logan had to search the city to get one vial of the toxin. "I just got lucky. Saw a trade going down in an alley nearby and knew you needed some."

"Which alley?" Logan scratched his arm, making another line of blood appear on his flesh.

"I don't remember."

"Well, what was the dealer wearing?"

"A tan cloak." *Just like every other criminal in this city.*

"Tan cloak. Alley nearby." Logan nodded eagerly. "Got it. Does that mean you were able to find a buyer for the gauntlet? If the chief thief catches us with that..." He started nervously scratching his arm again.

Bastian looked away. "Yeah, I found a buyer," he lied. He just wanted Logan to stop scratching his skin before there was none left. And he was worried that Logan might get paranoid and tell someone about the gauntlet if he thought they still had it. Bastian would never be allowed back in the guild if he was caught hiding his loot from the chief. And even though his room was cold and barren, it was still his home. He didn't want to be out on the streets again.

"Where's my half for that, then?" asked Logan.

"I don't have it yet. But the drop is set for tomorrow."

Logan nodded. His attention had turned to the scorpium that he'd poured out. He was looking at it like he was in love. "Isn't it beautiful?" he mumbled.

"You said you'd cut back," said Bastian.

"I know, I know. I'm trying. But I just get this itching for it..." His eye twitched.

Bastian walked past his friend and patted him on the shoulder. *One day we'll both be rid of this place,* he vowed silently. It kept his guilt at bay as he walked through the tunnels with Nut scurrying at his side. Before he knew it, there was a slight pep in his step. He wound his way through the hidden traps that lined the tunnels on his way to see Oriana. Images of her flooded his mind. The curve of her hips. The softness of her skin. Her big blue eyes blinking up at him, so innocent, yet longing for more.

***

When Bastian reached the gate outside Vulture Keep, he paused. He was planning on sneaking into Oriana's bedchamber. Surely that wouldn't end well if he got caught. He imagined what it would be like to be banished over the wall. If the razortooth tigers didn't get him, unquenched thirst surely would. Bastian shrugged off the thought. Thieves didn't have time to think about consequences.

The memory of the blush of Oriana's cheeks consumed his mind as he climbed the side of the gatehouse. She wouldn't have blushed if what he had said wasn't true. She could feel it too. Nut went right through a small gap in the gate and followed Bastian across the bridge toward the castle. They kept low, hiding behind any barrels or bushes that might provide cover.

Bastian paused at the edge of the bridge. He stared up at where the guards should have been roaming the ramparts. Maybe it was too dark. Or maybe he was too far away. But he couldn't see them. It made him feel uneasy. Knowing where danger lay was the key to not ending up on the wrong side of Arwin's Wall. He scanned the top of the castle again and squinted his eyes.

Nut squeaked from a few paces ahead of where Bastian was crouched. If Nut didn't sense danger, then it was probably safe. He glanced once more at the castle. He really wished that Logan had been fit to help him tonight. But he followed Nut, hoping that his squirrel wouldn't choose tonight to finally let him down.

As they approached Vulture Keep, Bastian was surprised to see that there really weren't any guards at their usual posts. Where were they all? Usually there was a strong force of men, just waiting for someone to sneak in. Bastian took it as a sign that he was supposed to be here. He just hoped it didn't mean they were roaming the halls of Vulture Keep.

He stayed low as he finished sneaking up to the stone wall of the castle. He looked up, scouring the windows above. Unfortunately, he had no idea which one led to Oriana's room. There were a few windows with flickering lights inside. They'd be the riskiest to look into. But Bastian had a feeling that Oriana was awake, waiting for him to arrive. The smart thing to do would be to sneak into a dark window and quietly sneak by whoever was sleeping. If he was lucky, the room would be empty. Then he'd use the key he had swiped from Oriana's pocket on every door until he found a match.

No matter which route he took, he had to climb up there first. Bastian stepped up to the castle and ran his fingers across the rough stone. There were plenty of spots to fit his hands and feet. "Come on, Nut," he whispered and tapped his shoulder.

Nut scurried up his pant leg and shirt and settled onto Bastian's shoulder, just as Bastian wrapped his fingers around a stone in the wall and lifted himself up. He looked up above him as his foot found another crevice. *This is going to take a while.*

He tried not to look down as he continued to scale the wall of the castle. But every time he glanced up, it didn't seem like he was getting any closer. Nut chirped in his ear and he slipped slightly. It felt like his heart was going to beat out of his chest as he just barely maintained his footing.

"Are you trying to get me killed?" he whispered.

Nut squeaked again.

Bastian shook his head, ignoring his squirrel as he reached up in search of another place for his fingers. The last thing he needed was a broken limb if he was going to be banished over the wall.

- CHAPTER 24 -
TERRIC

Terric squinted his eyes as he stared out the window. He could have sworn he saw someone creeping toward Vulture Keep. But on second glance, there was no one there. He stared for a moment longer. If there had been someone there, they were quite sneaky. Terric would need to channel that sneakiness if he was going to pull this off.

Earlier that day when he had seen half the guards moving from their usual posts to stand around the guest tower, Terric had been devastated. It would have been impossible to get past all of them to steal the prince's ring. But then Quentin had moved all of Rixin's things to Aldric's room, and moved Aldric down to the servant's quarters. Two of Reavus' blacksmiths had been stationed at the door, but the window was wide open.

Ever since then, he'd been waiting for Rixin to go to bed.

Terric poked his head out the window to confirm that the candle in Rixin's room had been extinguished. He was finally asleep.

Now that the time had come, Terric was tempted to back out. He had practiced pickpocketing all day and had only gotten away with it once. And it was telling that the only person he could steal from was his little sister, Nesta. The folds of her dress had been filled with all sorts of odds and ends. Needles, breadcrumbs, lots of chocolate. Even a little strap of leather that looked like a falconry hood.

He put his hand in his pocket and immediately poked himself with the needle he had swiped from her.

Ow. He put the side of his finger in his mouth to prevent it from bleeding as he stared out the window again. This would be different. Rixin was asleep. All his previous marks had been wide awake. But none of them had been wearing a ring on their finger either. How was he supposed to pull a ring off a knight's hand? And not just any knight. Rixin had the fastest reflexes of any knight in Treland.

This wasn't helping. He needed to get on with it. If he got caught, he was going to pretend to be drunk. One time Warin had gotten his hands on a bottle of fermented giraffe's milk and shared it with Terric. Could he replicate his drunken slur from that night? If he got caught, maybe his father would ban him from becoming a priest after engaging in such gluttony.

For some reason, Terric didn't feel like luck was on his side as he finally found the courage to climb out his window. It felt a lot more like he was climbing to certain death. Rixin would probably wake up and slice his throat. But then again, death would be better than becoming a priest. His life wasn't worth living the way it was heading. He had to do this.

The descent was easy. Years of practice had made him excellent at this exact thing. He had a suspicion that if he was ever banished over the wall he'd be able to climb back into Arwin's Gate. It was the only thought that gave him comfort as he climbed down toward Rixin's window.

Easy.

At least, he thought it was easy until he heard someone curse beneath him. And he lost his footing. And his hands slipped. His heart leapt into his throat as he slid down the wall. *Death isn't better than being a priest!* He grasped for safety as he fell. His fingertips bled as they scratched against rough stone but refused to make purchase. Then someone caught his arm.

Thank you, Arwin! I'll do whatever you want me to do! He immediately grabbed onto the rocks in front of him and found his footing once more.

"Are you alright, my lord?" said the man who'd caught him.

Terric glanced up at the stranger. He was perched between two of the wooden rods that Terric found so useful for climbing.

"Yes," said Terric. He tried to sound braver than he felt. Like the man had said, he was a lord, after all. "Who are you?"

"No one," said the stranger.

"Where are you going? And what is that?" Terric stared at the squirrel on the man's shoulder.

The squirrel immediately squeaked and lifted his head in the air like it was sniffing him.

"This is Nut," said the man. "And I could ask the same of you. Where are *you* going?"

It took Terric all of a few breaths to renounce his sudden interest in being a devout follower of Arwin. Because in that moment, he hatched a new plan. This stranger had surely been the one creeping up to Vulture Keep. And he was sneaky. Much sneakier than Terric. Possibly even sneaky enough to pull off the impossible pickpocketing. "I'll help you find whatever you're looking for here. As a thank you for saving my life."

The stranger hesitated. "How about you just forget you ever saw me." He winked at Terric and started to climb again.

"No, wait!" Terric quickly caught up to him. "Please, sir, I owe you my life. Just tell me your purpose here. I'll help you."

The man eyed Terric. It was as if he was studying his face. Terric looked down at the squirrel. It was studying him too.

"What's your name?" Terric asked the stranger. He assumed it was just some knight trying to eye the competition or something harmless like that. Certainly he wasn't there to do anything more sinister than what Terric was currently contemplating.

"Bastian," he finally said after a long silence. "And you must be Terric Hornbolt."

Terric's fingers had started to go numb while he'd waited for a response. He shifted his hands. It wasn't unusual for someone to know his name. But he didn't know any knights named Bastian. And Bastian didn't look like a knight, either. And knights traveled with squires, not squirrels. *Who is he?* Terric had a brief moment of uncertainty. Was it safe to allow him into the castle? He dismissed the thought. Terric needed his help. "And you're here to...?" his voice trailed off.

"I'm here to see Lady Oriana."

"Ew. My sister?"

He laughed. "Like I said. Forget you ever saw me." He started to climb again.

"Ori's room is this way." Terric nodded his head up. Ori could take care of herself. Bastian hardly seemed dangerous. He had saved Terric's life, after all. There was no way he was a threat to his family, or he would have let Terric fall to his death.

A smile spread across Bastian's face. "Ori?"

"That's what we all call her. This way, then." Terric started to climb toward the window he had nodded to. He was happy to hear the scrape of stone as Bastian followed him. "Why are you visiting my sister in the middle of the night?" whispered Terric.

"Why are you scaling the castle walls in the middle of the night?" Bastian said back.

You're about to find out, Terric thought as his fingers found the edge of the windowsill. He peered into the darkness. There wasn't a sound in the large room. "Come on," he said over his shoulder as he climbed into the room. His eyes slowly started to adjust as Bastian climbed in beside him.

"This isn't Oriana's room," whispered Bastian. They were in a sitting room adjoined to a bedroom, and the black suit of armor in the corner gave away that it probably wasn't a lady's room.

"No." Terric shook his head, trying to rid his nerves. "It's not. Before I show you the way to Ori's room, I need you to do something for me."

"I already saved your life," whispered Bastian. "You owe me, not the other way around."

"I need one more thing. I need you to steal something for me." Terric pointed towards the bedchamber.

"My lord, I'm not..."

"I'll scream." It was Terric's last idea. A threat. *Please, just do it.*

Bastian hesitated. "Are you trying to get me killed?"

"No. Of course not."

"Well, you sure have a way of showing it." Bastian raked his fingers through his hair. "What do you need me to do?"

"That man stole my ring. I want it back," Terric lied.

Nut leapt from Bastian's shoulder and onto Terric's back, squeaking relentlessly.

"Get off of me," Terric muttered as he tried to grab the squirrel off his back.

"Nut. Here," Bastian said calmly and tapped his shoulder. The squirrel immediately jumped back to its post. "You're lying," Bastian said.

"I'm not..."

"Nut can tell. Better than I can, that's for sure. Now spill the truth if you want my help."

Terric sighed. "Please, it's a life or death situation."

"Tell me the truth or *I'll* scream," said Bastian. "And I'll be out of here so fast, only you'll be caught."

Terric gulped. Bastian had used his own threat against him. "I need Prince Rixin's signet ring."

"That's Prince Rixin Talenov?" Bastian hissed. He peered into the bedchamber at the sleeping prince. "Have you gone mad?"

"Please. I need his ring in order to seal a letter about how I'm fit to be a squire. I can't take the oath of Arwin. I can't. Please, Bastian."

"I'm not..."

"I'll scream," Terric threatened a little louder.

"Would you lower your voice? You're gonna get us both killed."

Terric scrunched his face up into the desperate look that had gotten him out of trouble so many times with Isolda. "Please?"

"Fine. But you owe me directions to Oriana's room and...something else. I'll call upon you for a favor one day and I expect you to deliver. No questions asked. Otherwise I'll disappear through that window and you never see me again. That's my final offer."

"Done," Terric said, a smile crossing his face. He stuck out his hand to finalize the deal.

Bastian paused before shaking Terric's hand. "Are the rumors true? About the prince and your sister?"

"Is this the favor you requested?"

Bastian scowled. "No. Just a question. Forget I asked. Hold Nut." Bastian pulled the squirrel off his shoulder and handed him to Terric.

Nut squeaked in protest, but Bastian held his finger to his lips, immediately silencing his trusty companion. He slowly walked over to the bed. Terric cringed when he heard some birds in the ceiling chirp, but the prince didn't stir.

Terric covered his eyes and looked away, as if that might help Bastian not get caught. The sooner they were out of this room, the better.

After a few seconds, Terric opened his fingers and looked through the crack to see Bastian's progress. He had reached the bed and was slowly lowering the sheets off Rixin's torso. Rixin snored and turned away, revealing the ring on his left pinky finger.

Bastian glanced back at Terric. "This one?" he mouthed silently and pointed.

Terric eagerly nodded his head. He held his breath as Bastian touched the ring. Rixin moaned in his sleep. But he didn't open his eyes.

Bastian leaned forward again delicately grasped the ring between his thumb and index finger. Then, ever so gently, he slid the ring off Rixin's finger.

Terric didn't let out his breath until Bastian safely returned to the sitting room. "How did you do that?" he asked with wide eyes.

"Years of practice."

"Do you live on the streets or something?"

Bastian puffed out his chest. "No. I'm a member of the Thieves Guild."

Terric stared at the stranger with awe. He had heard rumors of the notorious Thieves Guild, but he had never known it actually existed. Bastian was living proof that someone could make it on their own without being a knight.

Bastian dropped the ring in Terric's hand. "Now, where is your sister's room?"

Terric slipped the ring into his pocket. Maybe he could make it on the streets, but he'd prefer to start out as a squire. "They're just rumors," Terric said.

"What?" asked Bastian.

"About my sister and the prince. Nothing is set in stone."

Bastian smiled.

"This way," Terric whispered and hopped out onto the window sill. The thought of being related to a member of the Thieves Guild was suddenly much more exciting than the prospect of being more closely related to the prince. Besides, Rixin was already his cousin. There were no thieves in his family, though. Hopefully Oriana would be excited by the idea too.

Now he had about a million questions to ask Bastian. "Does Nut come with you everywhere?"

"Not everywhere."

"Does he help you thieve?"

"Yes. Would you keep your voice down? You're going to get us caught." Bastian climbed down beside Terric.

But Terric already felt like they were in the clear. He had the prince's ring. His plan was coming together.

- CHAPTER 25 -
ORIANA

Oriana blew the candle out and sat down on the edge of her bed. She had been pacing back and forth for what seemed like an eternity. The floor was probably worn out beneath her feet, especially after she had gone through the same routine last night.

What am I doing? she thought. Bastian hadn't shown up last night. Just like Rixin had stood her up at supper yesterday. It was starting to become a pattern. But at least Rixin had apologized. Maybe Bastian would show up to apologize too.

Even though it was now dark, she stared down at the letter in her hands. She had it memorized by heart.

My lady,

A little something beautiful for the most beautiful woman in the realm.

I'll be seeing you soon,

-Bastian

His words made her stomach turn over and her heart race. She was embarrassed by her reaction. It was foolish of her to think that Bastian was going to sneak into her room. What a scandalous thing to surmise. And just because the key to her room was missing, it didn't mean that Bastian had stolen it. She had probably just dropped it in that alley that she should-n't have been anywhere near in the first place. She sighed and lay back onto her bed.

There was no fighting it. She had completely lost her mind. How could she be daydreaming of Prince Rixin one moment and then dying to see Bastian the next? The whole thing was preposterous. She should have been solely focused on winning the prince's affection.

He had given her some hope when he apologized today, but he still hadn't bothered to talk to her for very long. Oriana couldn't help but feel like that stupid doll had ruined every-thing. How could she have let him see her with Nessy? And it wasn't just any doll, either. It was worn and old and it made it look like she played with it constantly.

Oriana had locked Nessy in the chest at the bottom of her bed when she'd run around hiding anything embarrassing from sight. After getting Bastian's note, she was consumed with not ruining her chances with him either. But what chance was she even referring to? Her father would never allow her to marry Bastian. He had no title. And as far as she could tell, no mon-ey.

She assumed he had stolen the necklace, just like he had stolen the golden fabric. *Something beautiful for the most beautiful woman in the realm.* Oriana rolled her eyes. If that line was true, he'd be here right now. Maybe Rixin had stood her up once at supper, but as far as Ori was concerned, Bastian had now stood her up thrice. Even though he had slipped her the note at their first promised meeting. And even though he hadn't specified when he'd be seeing her next in said note. It still felt like she had been slighted.

Ugh. There was probably no reason to be thinking of either of them. She'd end up as an old maid sewing dolls for all eternity. Oriana pictured the doll in the locked chest. It was lying right next to the necklace Bastian had slipped into her pocket. The necklace was beautiful, but she refused to wear a stolen gem. What would people think? And besides, she couldn't exactly say where she had gotten it from. No one could know about Bastian. Her father would say no to a betrothal with him for sure. Worse yet, Garrion would probably banish Bastian just for talking to her. She didn't want that. Even if he had stood her up thrice.

She stared up at the dark ceiling. What if Bastian really hadn't stolen the key to her room? She could have simply dropped it, and anyone might have found it. She swallowed hard. Maybe she should light that candle again just in case. Her whole body froze when she heard a scraping noise on her windowsill.

Her heart leapt into her throat. What was the point of even having a key if just any old person off the street could come in through her window? She stood up, grabbed the candlestick off her nightstand, and pressed her back against the wall.

The only thing she knew for sure was that this wasn't Bastian. If he was coming, he probably had a key to her room. There was no reason to scale the walls of the castle and sneak in through her window. *Arwin, please save me*, she prayed as she slid her back along the wall, getting closer to the window. She wondered if someone would be able to hear her screams. The castle was big, but her sister's rooms were nearby. Arwin help her if only Nesta came to her rescue.

She had just raised the candlestick in the air when a hand caught her wrist. She was able to let out the "H" in help before another hand was clapped over her mouth.

"I told you I was coming, didn't I?" Bastian smiled down at her as he pressed her back against the cold wall.

Oh my. "No, you said see you soon. That could have meant anything."

"You waited up for me."

"I did no such thing." She immediately pushed him away.

The way he smiled made her heart race even faster.

"I just...I couldn't sleep. That's all."

"Because you were thinking about me."

The audacity. The...muscles. She forced her eyes back to his face. "No, Bastian. It was just chilly this evening. I awoke because I was cold." She was suddenly very aware of the fact that she was wearing nothing but her nightgown. The thin material was barely an excuse for fabric. She folded her arms across her chest.

"It's never cold in Arwin's Gate. Are you implying you need someone to keep your bed warm?"

She swallowed hard. "I didn't..." she let her voice trail off when she saw the playful smile on his face. "I thought you were an intruder."

"I can see that." He grabbed the candlestick out of her hand. "And you were going to beat an intruder over the head?" He reached around her, gently placing a hand on her hip, as he set the candlestick down on her nightstand.

She should have slapped him. Instead, she was glad when his hand lingered. Truthfully, she had been cold. And his hands were so warm. "Yes."

"Am I not an intruder?"

"It's different." She tucked a strand of hair behind her ear. "I know you."

"So you *are* glad that I'm here?" His hand was still on her hip as he stepped even closer to her.

"I'm just glad it wasn't a stranger. Why did you come in through the window when you have a key?"

He smiled. "I like to keep you on your toes."

"You shouldn't be here."

"It's a little late for that, don't you think?"

She could feel the warmth of his body. She inched closer to him and then immediately leaned back. What was she doing? She should be screaming. She should still be hitting him over the head with a candlestick.

A scratching noise made her turn her head. Nut was circling her pillow, trying to find a spot to get comfortable.

"Is he clean?" she asked.

Nut froze and stared at her. He made a low squeaking sound and sat down butt first in the middle of her pillow.

Why, that little...

"Ori." The sound of Bastian calling her by her nickname made her turn her attention back to him. He gently touched the side of her face. "You are happy that I'm here, are you not?"

His touch sent a spark through her. "I'm confused about why I'm so happy," she said.

"And why should happiness be confusing. You should be embracing that feeling, not running away from it." His fingers trailed down the side of her neck. "You're not wearing your necklace."

Oriana lifted up her hand and placed it on the front of her neck. When she had gotten home, she'd tried it on. It was the most beautiful thing she had ever worn. But it wasn't hers. Because it wasn't truly his to give in the first place. "I can't wear a piece of stolen jewelry. I'd rather not have my hand chopped off."

"I didn't steal it."

She stared into his eyes. "You didn't?"

"No. Where is it? I want to see how beautiful it looks on you."

Oriana could feel her cheeks blushing. She turned away from him and unlocked the chest at the foot of her bed. When she opened it, she silently cursed. Nessy was sitting right next to the necklace. She quickly grabbed the necklace and slammed the chest shut.

Bastian had clearly seen the doll. But unlike Rixin, he didn't say a word. He didn't make fun of her. And she was pretty sure it was because he was too busy staring at her instead of some stupid toy.

She lifted up the necklace and fumbled with the latch in the back.

"Let me," Bastian said as he stepped behind her.

She swallowed hard as his fingers brushed her loose curls to the side.

"There," he whispered in her ear.

Everything he did made goosebumps rise all over her skin. She touched the front of the necklace as he stepped back in front of her.

Bastian grabbed her hand and removed it from the necklace, interlacing his fingers with hers as their hands dropped together. "You're simply breathtaking, my lady."

She couldn't even resist smiling. "You really think so?"

He pulled her over to the mirror so she could see her reflection. "You're the most beautiful woman I've ever seen."

"Surely you say that to everyone."

He stepped in front of her, blocking her reflection. "No. Not everyone."

"Just a select few?"

"Just you."

Oriana looked up into his dark brown eyes. It seemed like he was telling the truth. *Just me.*

"I don't want you to take this off." He lightly touched the gem at the bottom of the necklace. "I want you to think of me when we're apart."

"I already think of you." She pressed her lips together. *Why did I say that out loud?*

The knot in his throat rose and fell. "Regardless, this way a piece of me will always be close to your heart."

Oh my. "People will wonder where I got it."

"Just tell them you found it." His finger fell from the gem and slowly trailed down the center of her chest, pulling slightly at the neckline of her nightgown.

"Bastian." Her words came out as barely a whisper.

"Ori." He tilted his head down.

She licked her lips in anticipation.

Nut started squeaking but it didn't break their heated stare. Bastian put a hand on the side of Oriana's face, tilting her head toward his.

A loud knock on the door made them both jump.

"Ori!" Selina said from the other side. "Ori, are you okay?"

"It's my sister," Oriana hissed. "You have to hide."

"No need. I'll be back tomorrow night, alright?"

"Isn't it safer if I just meet you in the market?"

"You told me you needed someone to keep your bed warm. I'm not about to let you down." He grabbed her hand and placed a soft kiss on it. "Until next time, my lady."

Before she could protest, Bastian ran over to the window. He winked at her before disappearing out the window. Nut leapt off the ledge after him.

Her heart was pounding in her chest as she walked to the door. Just before opening it, she pulled her hair in front of her necklace.

"Is everything okay?" Selina said. "I thought I heard voices."

"Oh, no. It's just me."

"I could have sworn I heard you talking to someone." She peered into Ori's room.

Oriana laughed. "Who would I be talking to at this time of night?"

"That's why I was worried." Selina lowered her voice to a whisper. "I thought I heard a man's voice."

Oriana shook her head and opened up the door a little more. "No. Just me in here. See?"

"I'm sorry. I was just thinking that maybe after Rixin didn't show up at supper, he wanted to make it up to you. And my mind started racing. Could you even imagine the scandal if he had snuck into your room in the middle of the night? Your good name would be in question. Your whole future could be ruined. The king would never allow you two to marry." She placed her hand on her chest. "Thank Arwin it was just my imagination."

"Mhm," said Ori. It came out squeaky and weird. Then something hit her. Navya was staying with Selina. Had she heard something too? "Where's Navya?"

"She's still asleep. I didn't want to wake her, especially since I thought Rixin might be in your room. That would have been a disaster."

Oriana nodded. "I should really get some rest. I'm exhausted."

"Of course. Good night, Ori."

"Good night, Selina." She closed the door and let out the breath that she had been holding. Her sister was right. Especially because it wasn't Rixin who had visited her. It was some man that she had met on the streets. She touched the gemstone at the bottom of her necklace.

Bastian wasn't just some man. Just thinking about him seemed to calm her down. The way he looked at her. The way his fingers had dipped between her breasts. If Selina hadn't interrupted them, she wasn't sure what would have happened. And she wasn't sure she would have wanted to stop it.

If being with Bastian would ruin her future, though, she had to end it. *Right?* She grabbed the pillow off her bed and tossed it on the floor. She didn't want to sleep with memories of Nut's butt on her pillow. She wanted to sleep with memories of the feeling of Bastian's lips on her hand. Or the feeling of his fingers on her waist and neck and chest. Or what would have happened if they'd had another second alone.

- CHAPTER 26 -
GARRION

The first few rays of morning sunlight began to peek over the horizon as Garrion and Aldric navigated the campgrounds. For the past fortnight, the grounds had been filling with pavilions of all shapes and colors that would be the temporary homes of hundreds of lords, knights, and squires. Some of those men, like the drunken, half-naked man that Garrion just had to step over, had merely come for the festivities. They were technically knights, but no one, including them, believed they had a real chance at winning the tournament. Their training varied greatly, but most of them had to spend half their time managing an estate rather than being completely devoted to martial training. A few might make it past the preliminary archery round into the contest of arms, and with some luck, one or two might make it to the joust. But there were only a handful of knights that Garrion thought had a realistic chance of walking away with the title of Arwin's Lance.

Marcus and Prince Rixin were at the top of that list. Sir Ngolo Mobek was too, and he was the primary reason Garrion and Sir Aldric had woken up well before dawn to finish their prayers early and ride down to the campgrounds.

Ngolo's pavilion was unmistakable. It was on the larger side, easily accommodating Ngolo and half a dozen of his men, but many knights had tents that size. What made it instantly recognizable was that it was covered in zebra skin. Ngolo's colors weren't black and white - his sigil was a yellow tribal mask on a field of half red and half green, and all of the colors were audaciously bright - but house Mobek was famed for their ability to tame and ride zebras into battle. Garrion would always remember fighting next to Obasi Mobek at the battle of Port Claudius and the way the Mobeks' zebra cavalry had devastated Brutus Zaberwald's soldiers with their bites and their kicks. The image of a zebra's two-footed kick crushing a man's skull was forever seared into Garrion's mind. The man had even been wearing a helmet, but it had caved in as if it was made of a bed sheet.

The guard posted at the entrance to Ngolo's pavilion removed his helmet and bowed as Garrion approached. "Good morning, me lord," he said in the thick accent of the East Shield. "Please, come in." He pulled back the zebra striped flap and gestured for Garrion and Aldric to enter.

Despite it being early, the tent was quite lively. One soldier sharpened a hunga munga, a distinctive blade with many curves and points, while a squire pulled a colorful green, red, and yellow doublet over Ngolo's dark skin.

"My lord, my friend," said Ngolo with a wide grin. "It is an honor to see you this morning. Forgive me for not being dressed. I was not aware you planned to visit." Ngolo allowed his squire to finish buckling his doublet before bowing.

Garrion hadn't seen Ngolo in nearly five years. In that time, the knight must have added at least fifty pounds of muscle, and another few pounds from his thick, black dreadlocks that reached a few inches past his shoulders. Garrion tried to determine how that would affect his performance in the tournament. Would it make him slow and vulnerable? Or would it allow him to generate a tremendous amount of power with his lance? Probably both.

"And who is this with you?" asked Ngolo.

Aldric stepped forward. "Sir Aldric Alsight, Lord of Tower Alsight and master-at-arms of Arwin's Gate."

Ngolo's face showed no sign of recognition. "A pleasure to meet you, my lord."

"I wanted to personally welcome you to Arwin's Gate," said Garrion. "And also to give you condolences for the loss of your father. He was a wonderful man. His contributions to Treland and to the good Lord Arwin will not be forgotten."

Ngolo nodded. "I thank you, my friend. He spoke of you often."

"You know, it was so hot here last summer that I had half a mind to come join you at Corongo Keep. Now I wish I had."

"Do not blame yourself," said Ngolo. "I know my father would not have. The work you do here to keep the kingdom safe from the Rashidi...that is truly the work of our Lord."

Garrion nodded. He'd always admired House Mobek for their devotion to Arwin. Of all the men who could have beaten out Garrion for the title of Arwin's Lance, he was glad that it had been Obasi. He was a faithful servant of Arwin. For the past twenty years he'd had the power to declare a holy war on Rashidi, but he had not done so.

Now Garrion had to make sure that Ngolo would follow in his father's footsteps, should he beat Marcus and Rixin to the title.

"Would you like some bread? asked Ngolo. He turned to his squire. "Idoji, bring us bread."

Idoji appeared a second later with a platter covered with a bright red cloth. Ngolo pulled the cloth off and tossed it away to reveal a few loaves of dark, nutty bread. He held it out for Garrion and Aldric.

Garrion didn't really want one, but it was polite to take it. He and Sir Aldric both grabbed a loaf. Upon taking a bite, which was more like grinding his teeth against stone than eating something fit for human consumption, he immediately regretted his decision. Even if the Mobeks embraced the word of Arwin, they certainly hadn't embraced Trelish culinary tradition. If the conversation didn't go as planned, perhaps Garrion could convince Ngolo to join his side by offering to loan him Conrad for a few months.

Ngolo took a bite and washed it down with some ale. "I am pleased to have your company this morning, but I suspect you have other reasons for being here. Have you come to scout out Marcus' competition?"

"What?" asked Garrion. "I can't come to share old war stories?"

"You can, but I don't think you did. Not at this hour. On a normal day you would just be starting your morning prayers, as I should be doing."

"I guess your father told you more about me than I realized," said Garrion. "Very well, let's sit down and I'll get to the point."

The three men sat on cushions laid on the hard ground.

"I'm worried Duke Reavus is planning something."

"Oh?" asked Ngolo. "You two are still at each other's throats, are you?"

"No. In fact, when he arrived yesterday he apologized for..."

Ngolo nodded his understanding. A few dreadlocks fell in front of his face.

"But he's not being genuine," continued Garrion. "First he sent Prince Rixin early and unannounced, and then he made his backhanded apology and pretended like we were friends. I couldn't figure out what he was getting at, but the good Lord spoke to me last night. I believe Reavus is going to try to bribe Rixin's competition."

"Why would Reavus care so much about Rixin winning?" asked Ngolo. "He is hardly the most devout Arwinian, and Rixin is already the crown prince. Why would he need the title of Arwin's Lance?"

"He wants to start a war with Rashid," said Garrion. "He's always wanted to, but up until now, King Ivan has kept him from breaking the Treaty of Islos. He can't afford to start a war on two fronts. But if Arwin's Lance declares war on Rashid, it would technically not be Treland declaring the war and thus would not break the treaty."

"Would Fjorkia and the Huntlands care about that distinction?" asked Ngolo. "If all our forces are off fighting in Rashid, it would be the perfect opportunity for them to launch an attack. That is part of why my father never declared a holy war."

"He was a wise man. I pray that whoever wins the title next shares his wisdom."

"Well you are in luck, my friend. Because I plan on both winning and keeping the peace." Ngolo gave Garrion a big grin.

"It puts my mind at ease to know that I am not alone in the pursuit of peace. Arwin willing, it will be you and Marcus in the final joust."

"That is what I shall pray for too, although I am afraid it would not end in Marcus' favor."

"We shall see," said Garrion.

The three men stood and shook hands again. The force with which Ngolo gripped Garrion's hand made Garrion worried for his son's safety should he face Ngolo in the tournament. But with Ngolo having pledged his loyalty, it was less of a concern.

Ngolo bowed as Garrion and Aldric exited.

"I can't believe it," said Aldric when they were out of earshot of the tent.

Garrion patted him on the back. "I'm sure Obasi had told Ngolo about how you killed the three Zaberwalds. He probably just forgot."

"Not that," said Aldric. "Although he is just as ignorant as the rest of these swine." They made their way past several drunk men. "I meant that Reavus beat us there."

"What?" asked Garrion.

"You didn't see it?"

"See what?"

"The bag of bloodgold by Ngolo's bed," said Aldric.

"No, I didn't see it. Are you sure?"

Aldric pointed to his golden eyes. "Do I ever miss anything? That was the reason why he offered us that terrible stale bread. He just wanted to take the cloth off of it so that he could throw it on top of the bloodgold."

Garrion clenched his fists and kicked a nearby mug. Ale spilled out of it as it flew through the air and ended up in the lap of a sleeping drunk.

"So this is his plan," said Garrion. "Bribe all the contenders. I thought he'd at least be creative about it."

"A plan doesn't have to be creative to be effective," said Aldric.

"True. But even if he has every other knight under his thumb, he won't be able to bribe Marcus into losing. Or starting a war once he wins. Right?"

"No, I don't believe Marcus would turn. He's our only hope. Which is why it's a good thing you have me training him."

- CHAPTER 27 -
RIXIN

Rixin rolled up the sleeves of his red and white checked tunic as Nigel finished buttoning it for him. It was going to be another long day of practice, and he hadn't gotten a particularly good night of sleep. Some stupid birds in the ceiling had kept chirping every time he was about to doze off.

The steward had claimed that they were moving him because a rat had been discovered in the old room, but he had a sneaking suspicion that they had moved him to try to prevent him from getting any sleep. It was a fairly petty move, but Rixin actually found it kind of amusing. He liked when his competition put up a good fight.

The move might even work in his favor if it meant he was now closer to Oriana's room. He pictured her cheeks blushing and her long blonde hair. She was every bit as beautiful as the rumors, even if she did still play with dolls.

Is she still mad at me? wondered Rixin. Their last conversation had been cut short, and he hadn't been at supper for the past two days since Marcus had refused to pause training for something so frivolous. His words, not Rixin's. He hoped that missing supper hadn't hurt his chances with Oriana. He decided to go find her first, and then he'd sit down to a much-needed feast of something other than those gross gazelle steaks that they kept serving during training.

He went to tighten his belt, but the absence of the usual clicking noise against the metal made him look down. "Nigel, have you seen my ring?" Rixin asked and glanced at the floor. *No ring.* Then behind him. *No ring.*

"No, Your Highness," Nigel replied. "When was the last time you saw it?"

"I could have sworn I went to bed with it on. I must have dropped it somewhere between then and now."

"Let me find it for you." Nigel quickly walked over to the bed and examined the nightstand, opening and shutting the drawer.

Rixin checked his pockets as Nigel shoved down the bed sheets.

"Could you possibly have dropped it outside yesterday?" Nigel said as he rummaged around in the sheets to no avail.

Rixin snapped his fingers. "You know, I must have. We practiced until after sunset. I easily could have dropped it without realizing it."

"Or it could have slipped off during the change of rooms," suggested Nigel.

"Indeed." He'd have to put off speaking to Oriana and eating his much-needed meal. His stomach growled in protest. But he wasn't going to lose another ring. He'd lost one before when he was a young boy. His father had been furious. *Someone could use it for forgery*, his father had told him. It had been the most attention he had gotten from his father in years, and he remembered how he had wished that his father had continued to think he was invisible. Rixin nervously ran his fingers through his hair as he looked around the room once more. "Nigel, you go look outside. I'll retrace my steps in the castle."

"Very good, Your Highness," Nigel said with a slight bow and then quickly left the room.

Rixin checked the bed once more, knowing very well that Nigel wouldn't have missed it if it had been there, before heading out of his bedchambers to search the halls.

He heard someone humming and turned the corner to see Nesta skipping toward him with her arms overflowing with muffins. A small peeping noise fell from little Nesta's lips and she dropped most of the muffins onto the floor. Her eyes grew big as she looked up at him approaching.

"Good morning, my lady," Rixin said with a smile and a nod.

Nesta looked relieved when he didn't scold her. "Do you want a muffin?" she asked and held out one of the ones that hadn't fallen on the floor.

"You saved my day, Lady Nesta," Rixin said as he took the muffin from the young girl. "I'm starving and these look delicious."

She giggled. "Do you want to come see what I've been making?"

"Actually, I..." his voice trailed off when Nesta slipped her hand into his and started pulling him down the hall. Her fingers were sticky from the muffins she had been carrying, and she was pulling him through the hall with surprising strength for her small frame.

Rixin glanced over his shoulder at the pile of muffins and crumbs Nesta had left on the floor. "Shouldn't we clean that up?"

"If we hurry, no one will know it was us." She giggled again as they turned a corner and came to an abrupt stop outside her door. "You wait here. Boys aren't allowed in my room." She unlocked her door and disappeared inside.

"I do apologize, but I really must be going," Rixin called through the closed door. His eyes scanned the floor. He hadn't walked this way last night. Or at least, he didn't think he had. He turned around. All the halls looked the same. Rixin tried to wipe the stickiness off one hand as he took a bite of the muffin. He stifled a sigh. It really was quite good.

When he finished the muffin and Nesta still hadn't returned, he tapped on the door. "Thank you for the muffin, my lady. I'll see you tonight at supper." *Actually, I probably won't. Stupid Marcus.*

The door immediately squeaked open. "No, look. Here it is." Nesta was pretending to drag something across the floor. "I'm working on a beautiful dress for the joust!"

Rixin just stared at her. The young girl was literally holding nothing. First he had caught Oriana playing with dolls, and now Nesta was playing make-believe. The two had more in common than just their mother's blonde hair and blue eyes.

"Don't you like it?" Nesta said and pretended to throw down whatever imaginary thing she was holding.

Rixin looked harder but couldn't see anything in her arms. "I don't see it," he said.

Nesta looked down at her imaginary dress and frowned. "Did it turn invisible again? Why does it keep doing that?"

Rixin shook his head. He was considering playing along when something caught his eye. There was a tunic lying in the middle of the floor of Nesta's room. He could have sworn Terric had been wearing that same tunic yesterday. *And* what's that? *Is that one of Marcus' arrows beside it?*

"My lady," said Rixin. "Isn't that Terric's tunic? And Marcus' arrow?"

Her eyes grew round again and she stepped to the side, trying to block Rixin's view of her room. "No," she said quietly. "Boys aren't allowed in my room."

"I didn't say any boys were in your room. I said their belongings were."

"No," Nesta said a little more firmly. "They're mine."

Rixin eyed the objects again that certainly didn't belong to Nesta. Clearly his cousin was quite the little thief. "Lady Nesta, I'm missing my ring. Have you seen it?"

"No," she said defensively.

"Are you sure?

"I'm not a thief!" She slammed the door in Rixin's face.

Rixin blinked, shocked by her actions. No one slammed the door in his face. He was the prince, for Arwin's sake. He knocked on the door. "Lady Nesta. If you've seen my signet ring, I need it back."

She opened the door a crack and peered at him and then at the floor. "I haven't seen it." She reached past him, making sure to not open her door any further, and grabbed her imaginary dress. She pulled it back into her room and pretended to throw it on the ground.

"Please, it's of dire importance," said Rixin.

"Boys aren't allowed to stand outside of my room anymore either. Even if you *are* a prince." Nesta slammed the door in his face once more.

Apparently the women in Vulture's Keep weren't raised properly. *What a little monster.* "Thanks for the muffin," he said to the door and turned around.

He heard a muffled, "You're welcome, Your Highness," from the other side.

He laughed. Well, maybe they did have some manners. He wondered if Oriana was as stubborn as her little sister as he began to retrace his steps. Rixin kept his eyes on the ground the whole time, searching for his missing ring. But he didn't think he was going to find it. Nesta clearly had sticky fingers, and not just from the muffins. He was almost certain that she had taken his ring.

- CHAPTER 28 -
TERRIC

By morning, the floor of Terric's room was covered in crumpled pieces of parchment. He had been working on letters all night, trying to get the wording just so, but the proper words escaped him. It seemed like a simple task - write a letter from Rixin recommending Terric as a squire - but striking a balance of praise and simplicity was proving to be quite difficult. To make it harder for his father to track him down, he had decided to change his name to Oleg upon escaping from Arwin's Gate.

Terric grabbed a new sheet of parchment and scrawled a letter:

My Lord,
 I recommend you take young Oleg as a squire.

Terric had barely finished writing the last word before he put the quill back in the ink and pushed the paper aside. *Not exciting enough.*

He grabbed another sheet and tried again:

My Lord,

I have traveled across Pentavia, from the frozen wastes of Fjorkia to the scorched sands of Rashid, and I have never in my life encountered as fine a man as Oleg. Master swordsman, horse whisperer, and poet. Those words only scratch the surface of this young man's ability.

I first encountered him in the savanna, surrounded by razortooth tigers. I feared he would be their next meal, but as I got closer, I heard him begin to sing to the tigers. It possessed a quality of beauty more striking than the gardens of Alqaruk. I imagine that even the good lord Arwin would find it difficult to match his voice. The tigers immediately began purring and grew quite docile. One even allowed young Oleg to jump on his back and ride him.

When he fights, it is as if the swords and his arm are one, moving with the grace of a dove but the lethality of a wooly dragon. With training, I have no doubt he shall be the greatest swordsman to ever live. He may already be. I have never had the nerve to challenge him to a duel, for fear that I might lose.

I once saw him dress a man in a full suit of armor in less time than it takes most to button a doublet. His fingers are like a nimble whirlwind, buckling clasps with a speed I never thought possible.

If you do not take Oleg as your squire, I will have no choice but to strip you of your title next time we meet, as passing on Oleg would indicate that you are a simple-minded mongrel.

His Royal Highness,

Rixin of House Talenov

Crown Prince of Treland, Duke of Arwood, Blood of Arwin, Distinguished Knight of the Order of Chains, and Defender of the Wood

Better, thought Terric. *But still not quite right.* Any lord worth squiring for would realize it was a fake. If that letter were true, why would Rixin not keep Terric as his own squire?

Terric shoved all the parchment off his desk. His brain was tired and his hand was cramping up. And the morning bell was signaling that it was time to pray. It felt like it was always time to pray. Wouldn't his time be better spent trying to solve problems than praying to some invisible god who may or may not be able to help? Terric had been praying for years that his father wouldn't force him to be a priest, and that had only gotten him... *Wait a second!* Had the praying finally worked? Now that he had Rixin's ring, his escape was within reach.

Terric decided that it couldn't hurt to thank Arwin for his good fortune. Just in case. And anyway, it was good to keep up appearances until the moment of his escape. There was no reason to arouse suspicion when it wasn't necessary to do so.

But when Terric arrived at the Vulture Keep temple, it was empty. Terric could only remember a handful of other mornings on which the temple had been unoccupied. It only happened when lots of lords were in town. To accommodate the extra bodies, Father Percival must have moved the morning prayers to the much larger temple outside of the castle. With all those people, Terric's absence would surely go unnoticed.

"Skipping prayers, are you?"

Terric looked up and froze. Duke Reavus was striding towards him. What would Reavus do to him? Based on the stories that his father had told about the duke, Terric was probably moments away from being thrown into the dungeons. Or banished over the wall. He wanted to escape, but not into the razortooth savanna. Despite the claims made in his fictitious letter, Terric had never charmed a tiger with song. His voice wasn't even very melodious.

"What?" said Terric. It came out as a whisper. "No, I was just, uh..."

"Don't worry." Reavus smiled reassuringly. "If you don't tell on me for not going to the temple, I won't tell on you. I've never understood people who pray every day. Relying on Arwin is just an excuse to not take action yourself."

Terric eyed Reavus suspiciously. "I won't tell on you, but I do need to go pray."

"Suit yourself. While you're kneeling on that hard stone floor with shackles on your wrists, I'm going to be enjoying some of Conrad's chocolate pastries. I've heard they're incredible."

"They are," said Terric. His mouth watered just thinking about them. Such delicacies were usually reserved for special occasions. The Skyfall festival two years ago had been the last time Conrad made them.

"Then I guess I should consider myself lucky to have them all to myself. Have fun praying." Reavus turned and started toward the grand hall.

If this was a trick, Terric didn't care. He didn't know if he'd ever taste one of those pastries again. "Wait!" he called and ran after Reavus.

Terric and Reavus sat on either side of the table usually occupied by knights and squires. Conrad brought out a platter covered in piping hot, golden brown pastries oozing molten chocolate. Terric had experienced a burnt tongue many times in his life, but he still always found himself unable to wait for food to cool. Eating these pastries was no exception. He stuffed half of one in his mouth. As the gooey chocolate seeped out of the pastry, he had to keep his mouth open to avoid serious burns.

"Ow," he said when the pastry had finally cooled enough for him to chew and swallow.

"Worth it?" asked Reavus. He had picked one up, but he had the sense to blow on it before attempting to eat it.

Terric nodded and grabbed another. "Definitely."

"So you're the second born, yes? Doesn't that mean you're to become a priest? Or has the devout Garrion Hornbolt finally wavered in his beliefs?"

"Yes, I'm the second born. And no, he hasn't wavered."

"Have you told him you don't want to be a priest?"

"What makes you think I don't want to be a priest?"

Reavus gestured to the pastries. "No priest I know would skip morning prayers to indulge in such worldly delights."

Terric scrunched his face up. "Fine, you're right. I hate the idea of being a priest. Sitting in Arwin's Gate for the rest of my life...it's not for me. I want to see the world. I should be out there jousting, not taking some stupid oath to give up everything I love."

"If you were my son, I'd let you joust."

"You would? Why don't you have any sons?" Terric knew he shouldn't have asked it the minute it came out of his mouth, but it was already out there. "Sorry, I shouldn't..."

"Rixin is like a son in many ways. And helping King Ivan run the kingdom keeps me quite busy." Reavus stared out the window blankly, a hollowness filling his dark eyes. "I loved a woman once. I loved her dearly. But Sultan Zand took her from me." He snapped his focus back to Terric and forced a smile. "Enough about this old man's problems, though. When do you take the oath?"

"The final day of the joust."

"Then what are you doing talking to me? You should be out enjoying your last few days of freedom. How about some jousting? Come on, I'll let you ride Midnight."

"Really?"

"Yes, let's go." Reavus picked up the platter of pastries and carried them out to the courtyard.

As usual, Warin was hard at work in the stables. His day of brushing horses and shoveling manure had started well before sunrise, and it would continue until dark. Maybe later, depending on how long Rixin and Marcus wanted to train.

Terric excitedly explained to Warin what was happening. His friend didn't believe him at first, but eventually Terric convinced him to saddle up Midnight and set up the quintain.

For the next thirty minutes, Terric had the time of his life. The lance was far too heavy for his young muscles, but if he held it just so, he was able to balance it in the crook of his arm. He spurred Rixin's horse forward time after time. He missed the target on the first few passes, but then he started to get a feel for it. He made solid contact with the target. The quintain spun around and the big bag of sand knocked Terric off Midnight.

"Are you okay?" asked Warin, rushing to his side.

Terric popped up to his feet and wiped the dirt off his trousers. He hadn't been harmed by the fall. It was actually kind of fun. He felt like he had just been part of a real joust in which he and his opponent had both knocked each other from their horses. "That was awesome!"

Warin let out a sigh of relief. "Maybe you should stop..."

"No way," said Terric.

"That was quite the strike," said Reavus. "You even broke the lance." He held up the two parts of the broken lance.

Uh oh. Now there was evidence that he'd been jousting.

"No worries," said Reavus with a wave of his hand. "I'll tell Rixin to say he broke it. Let's go find another. If we're quick, you might even have time for a few more passes before prayers are over.

Terric and Reavus hurried off to the armory. Terric had mixed feelings about seeing all the weapons and armor. On one hand, he wanted to try them all, but on the other, they were a reminder of what would be taken from him when he took the oath of Arwin. He'd never get to shoot a crossbow or try on a new suit of armor.

"Do you know where they keep the lances?" asked Reavus.

Terric nodded and led Reavus to the back wall. He expected to see the usual supply of plain wooden lances, but they'd been covered by Marcus' tournament lances. Each one was painted black with a golden spiral pattern. Unlike the completely wooden practice lances, the tourney lances had flattened metal tips. The axions of Techence had designed them specifically to minimize the chances of them piercing armor.

Reavus grabbed the tourney lances to move them out of the way, but when he did, one of them slipped out of his hand and went crashing to the floor. Reavus cursed under his breath. "Can you grab that for me?"

As Terric picked it up, he noticed that the metal tip had shattered like glass to reveal a spike beneath it. It wasn't just the way it broke, either. It was clear that someone had intentionally disguised the spike.

Was this how his father planned to make Marcus win? By killing his opponents? Terric frowned. For all of his father's faults, Terric had at least believed he was a man of principle. But now he knew better. All Garrion's talk of following the book of Arwin was just a sham. He wasn't fit for the title of knight, much less duke of the Shield.

"Everything okay?" asked Reavus.

"Yes, um..." *Should I tell him about it?* "Actually, it looks like the lance cracked. I'll go put it with the rest of the broken weapons. Maybe Roger can repurpose it." Terric rushed off with the lance and hid it under a rack of halberds in a dark corner.

He hadn't decided who he should tell yet. Should he confront Garrion? Or maybe tell Marcus? Surely Marcus wouldn't dishonor himself by jousting with a tipped lance. Doing so would automatically disqualify him, and if he used it against Prince Rixin, it could be viewed as treason.

Either way, Terric had to keep it hidden until he decided what to do with the information. If Garrion was evil enough to give Marcus tipped lances, Terric didn't know what else he'd be willing to do to keep it quiet.

- CHAPTER 29 -
ORIANA

Oriana had kept the necklace on, just like she'd promised Bastian she would. She wasn't sure she'd ever take it off. The idea of a piece of him being next to her heart made it impossible for her to stop smiling.

She should have been focusing on her prayers, but her mind kept wandering. *This is useless.* What was the point in praying when she didn't feel like she had done anything wrong? She wasn't sorry for nearly kissing Bastian. Or for accepting the stolen fabric from him. Or for wearing a gift from him when he wasn't a proper suitor.

But there was one thing that was plaguing her conscience. How could she have feelings for two men at once? It was easier when she was upset with Rixin. But he had apologized.

None of these thoughts were proper during prayer. She stood up as Selina and Navya walked in.

"Sorry, did we disturb you?" Selina asked.

"No, not at all." It would be nice for Ori to have a distraction from her nagging thoughts.

"Were you praying to Arwin?" Navya asked. She walked into the room without being invited in. Her nose was in a book and she hadn't even looked up when she'd asked the question.

"Who else would I be praying to?" said Oriana.

"There are many gods. The Rashidi…"

Selina gasped. "There are no other gods. Arwin is the one true god."

"But Axion Oswald gave me a book about…"

"The book was wrong."

Navya finally looked up from the book in her hands. "But how do you *know*? The Rashidi believe…"

Oriana turned away from their debate. The last thing Oriana wanted to do was get into a religious discussion. She wasn't feeling very devout today. She lifted up her needle and thread and sat down with her dress. There wasn't much time left to finish it.

"Oriana," Selina said and waved her hand in front of Ori's face.

It appeared that Selina had been trying to get her attention for quite a while. "Yes?"

"Where did you get that?" She pointed to the necklace Oriana was wearing.

There was no way Selina would drop the topic if Ori told her she'd found it. Selina would insist on looking for the original owner to return the necklace to them. To appease her sister, Oriana had to tell a better tale. "I got a great deal from one of the merchants when I bought the fabric to fix my dress." She lifted up the material she was working with.

"A great deal for something like that? It's beautiful."

Oriana could feel Navya's beady little eyes on her. For some reason it felt like Navya could read right through her lies. And that she was just waiting to report her wrongdoings to

Rixin. "Mhm," said Ori. Her voice came out oddly high-pitched.

"Lucky you," Selina said and turned back to Navya. "If you really study the book of Arwin, you'll see how only he could possibly be the one true god."

Oriana tuned them out again. The lie had slipped easily from her mouth. Or…lies. She hadn't bought the fabric. Or the necklace. One lie had easily tumbled into two. Oriana winced. No, it was truly three. She had lied to Selina about not having a visitor last night as well. She glanced at Selina and Navya. Fortunately, Selina was content with the stories Oriana had been weaving. And even more content in her heated debate with Navya. Ori would have more to pray to Arwin about tomorrow morning. Especially since Bastian was going to show up again tonight.

She bit the inside of her lip. Shame should have been her immediate response to the thought of a man sneaking into her bedchambers. But she felt no shame - only excitement at the idea of seeing Bastian again. What would Arwin think of that?

Oriana tried to focus on the dress she was mending. She was running out of time to fix it, but she was finding it almost impossible to concentrate. She tried to remind herself that she was sewing it to impress the prince. Oriana sighed and put her chin in her hand. And when her mind focused on Rixin, it was almost just as difficult to concentrate. But not because of the way he made her heart race. Which he did. She was focused on how genuine his apology had seemed. He truly seemed sorry for missing out on supper. And the way he'd kissed her hand made her want to melt into her chair. She wanted him to kiss her hand again and tell her that she was breathtaking.

She hastily started stitching, trying to ignore her wandering thoughts. The lack of concentration caused her needle to slip, sliding into the tip of her index finger. *For Arwin's sake.* She stuck her finger in her mouth to stop the bleeding. *Ow.* Maybe that was the punishment for her improper behavior. She smiled to herself. A few nicks were worth the feeling that Bastian gave her.

"Ori," Nesta said as she ran into the room.

Oriana glanced down at her youngest sister. Nesta's eyes were slightly red and puffy like she had been crying. Oriana pushed her dress aside and crouched down. "Nesta, what's wrong?"

"Ori, I did something bad. Really bad. Am I going to be punished?"

Oriana shook her head. Certainly whatever Nesta had done wasn't nearly as bad as what Oriana had been doing. "No, I'm sure it couldn't be that bad. What happened?"

Navya closed her book and stared at them.

Nesta looked at Navya and then back up at Oriana and blinked. She looked distraught that Navya was listening. Apparently she hadn't noticed her when she'd started the conversation. "Nevermind," Nesta said.

"Just tell me, Nesta. I'm sure it's fine." Really, what was she so worried about? Oriana glanced at Navya again. It really did seem like the girl was analyzing them. It gave Oriana a nervous chill down her spine. She turned back to her little sister and pretended the hairy little princess wasn't staring at them.

Selina walked over to them. "It depends on what you did, Nesta."

Nesta blinked up at Selina. "I..." her voice slowly trailed off.

"It's okay, Nesta," Oriana said and shot Selina a stern look. "Just tell us what happened."

"I wanted the prince to like me. I gave him a muffin. And he smiled. He said I saved his whole day. And that means he likes me. Right? So then I held his hand because..."

"What?" Oriana's heart seemed to skip a beat. It felt like Rixin had been doing everything in his power to avoid her. And now he was holding *Nesta's* hand? Oriana swallowed down the lump in her throat. "Nesta, that's fine. You're allowed to hold the prince's hand." She cringed at her own words. Why did she feel jealous of her? She had been daydreaming of Bastian all day.

"That's not what I did wrong," Nesta said. "He came to my room..."

"You're not allowed to have boys in your room, Nesta," Selina said. "You know that. You're a lady, not a viriphyte temptress."

Oriana put her hand on her chest. *Am I a viriphyte temptress? What have I done?* She'd let Bastian come into her room in the middle of the night. She'd prayed he'd come. She'd been improper. Rixin *should* have been holding Nesta's hand instead of hers. He'd never want Ori now. *Do I even want him to?*

"I didn't let him come in," Nesta said. "I just wanted him to see my dress. I made him wait outside. And then I...I yelled at him. And slammed the door in his face." Her bottom lip started trembling like she was about to cry again. "And now I'm going to be banished over the wall for yelling at the prince. The razortooth tigers are going to eat me!"

Selina laughed. "Nesta, did Rixin say he was going to banish you?"

"No. But I insulted the prince. Punishment is tigers."

"That's nonsense. Father controls who goes over the wall. You're a Hornbolt, not a commoner," Oriana said. "Now tell me, when you held his hand, did he grab yours or did you grab his?" *I sound pathetic.*

"I don't remember. I'm not going to die?"

Selina shook her head. "Of course not. But why did you yell at him? You really must learn how to control your temper."

"He pretended he couldn't see my beautiful dress. And then he called me a thief."

"Why would he accuse you of thievery?" Selina asked. "Did you take something from him?"

"No!"

"Well then, what did he think you took?"

"His ring. He was looking all over for it this morning. But I didn't take it, I swear."

"This morning?" Oriana asked. Something seemed to constrict in her chest.

Nesta nodded.

Oriana thought about how it was odd that Bastian hadn't used the key to her room. He had used the window. Had he come to Vulture Keep for some reason other than seeing her? It was a fairly odd coincidence that a thief had entered the castle last night and now the prince's ring was missing this morning. *Bastian wouldn't have. Would he?* Oriana's fingers tightened around her necklace. Did he lie about this too? Was it really stolen?

"Well he shouldn't have accused you of that," Selina said. "As if you would steal a thing."

Nesta scrunched her mouth to the side. "Yes. I would never steal a thing. That would be...death by tigers?"

"Or the loss of your hand."

Nesta yelped and tucked her hands into her skirt.

"I'm sure that Rixin wouldn't have accused you if he didn't have a proper reason," Navya said and hopped down from her seat by the window. "I'm going to finish my book in my room."

"It's *my* room," Selina muttered as Navya walked out.

Nesta stuck her tongue out at Navya's back.

"Hi, Navya…oh…" Isolda's voice died away as Navya walked by her without a greeting. Isolda cleared her throat. "Well then. Girls?" she said from the doorway. "How are your dresses coming for the joust?"

"Good," said Oriana. Hopefully their mother hadn't overheard their conversation about thievery and tigers. "We're almost done." She looked up at her mother. She wasn't sure she had ever seen her mum with that expression on her face before. Was it shock. Anger, possibly? Either way, her skin was pale like she had just seen a chalkian. "Mum, is everything okay?"

"Selina, Nesta…can you please give me a minute alone with Ori?"

"Mhm!" Nesta hurriedly ran out of the room with her hands still tucked in her skirt.

"Of course," Selina said. "I need to grab a new book anyway. Maybe I can get Navya to read the book of Arwin. I fear her teachings at Bloodstone aren't up to par."

Isolda quickly closed the door behind Selina and turned around. The odd expression remained on Isolda's face. "Oriana, where did you get that necklace?"

Oriana realized her hand was still clasped around the chain. She laughed awkwardly. "Oh, this? I found it." Her nervousness made her forget that she had just told Selina she'd bought it. "It's nothing, really."

"Found it?" Her mother approached her. "Where did you find it?"

"Just on the ground. Outside, near the archery range." *Archery range? I'm never anywhere near the archery range except when I'm spying on Rixin. At this rate, I'm going to be the one eaten by razortooth tigers.*

"Oh." Isolda sighed and sat down beside her daughter. "I was hoping someone gave it to you." She patted Oriana's knee. "I'm sorry, darling, I didn't mean to upset you."

Oriana gave her mother a tight smile. "It's okay. I know you and father were probably hoping Rixin gave it to me, but he wasn't the one. He's barely even talked to me since he arrived. I'm sorry if I've let you down. I just don't know if he likes me."

Isolda was quiet for a moment. "You said Rixin wasn't the one. Who *was* the one?"

"What now?" *What in Arwin's name have I done?*

"Oriana, do not lie to me. Who gave you that necklace?"

Oh no. "I don't..."

"Oriana, just tell me."

Maybe this is for the best. "I met someone." It felt like a weight had been lifted off her shoulders. The secret had been gnawing away at her. She breathed a little easier for a moment.

"Who?"

"His name is Bastian." She didn't want to go into further detail. What if Bastian had stolen the prince's ring? What if he had stolen this necklace? Oriana's heart felt like it was going to beat out of her chest. But for some reason, she still found herself smiling. Despite everything, she was desperate to see him again tonight. And she knew in her heart that Bastian hadn't done either of those things. He was kind. And sweet. And so handsome.

"I need to meet him," said Isolda. "Immediately."

"You can't. I mean, I don't know where he lives. I met him at the market the other day."

"Surely he's promised to see you again after giving you such a beautiful piece of jewelry. It's improper of him to approach you instead of your father, but if we don't tell, it might be okay. I assume he'll make a proper introduction this evening at the feast. The name doesn't sound familiar...from what house does this Lord Bastian hail?"

Lord? Oh, no. More and more lies. There were so many it felt like the stack was about to tip. "I don't think he'll be at the feast."

"Why wouldn't he be?"

"He's not a lord."

"Knights will be invited too," said Isolda. "And any squires who've declared their intention to compete."

Oriana stayed silent.

"Oriana, I do not know who the gentleman is that gave you this necklace. But it wasn't his to give. I need to talk to him immediately before someone else finds out what he's done. We can smooth everything over privately. Without your father finding out."

No. Bastian stole it. *He'd promised me he hadn't. How could he?* Oriana shook her head. Of course he'd stolen it. He was a thief. Stealing was what he did. She put her hand on the center of her chest. It hurt. She could forgive the thievery. But she couldn't forgive the lies. Despite everything, she had trusted him. He had saved her. He made her feel alive. *He may have lied about everything. He may have come last night just to steal Rixin's ring.*

"You need to tell me where Sir Bastian lives. Now," Isolda said.

"Mother." Oriana swallowed hard. "I'm so, so sorry. He's not even a knight. Or a squire."

Isolda smiled at her daughter. "That's alright. I knew many fine young men during my time in Icehaven. And don't tell your father, but my relationships with them weren't always entirely proper."

Oriana gasped. What was her mom confessing to? "So you're not upset?"

"No, I'm not upset. But I do need to know where I can find this Bastian fellow."

"Do you promise he won't get in trouble?"

"Yes. This will be our little secret. I'm sure the business with the necklace is just a misunderstanding. But it's very important that I talk to him about it."

"He's coming again tonight." Oriana closed her eyes. "To my chambers." The room was eerily silent. "I was falling for him. I thought... I wasn't thinking." Oriana slowly opened her eyes and looked up at her mother. She didn't look upset. In fact, she looked oddly happy.

"Then I'll meet him tonight."

She again thought her mother would yell at her. That she'd tell Father. That everyone would soon know that she was nothing more than a common trollop. "Aren't you upset with me?" Oriana asked.

"Did you do anything improper with him?"

"No. We almost kissed. But we didn't."

"I understand the pressure of an arranged marriage. I never even met your father until our union. But I fell in love with him after that. And now I love him dearly."

"Rixin isn't promised to me."

"It's the marriage your father wants. As long as Rixin isn't wed, in your father's eyes, you're promised to him. I'm sorry, Oriana. I am. But you're going to have to say goodbye to Bastian tonight. You can't risk your future."

"A future that may not unfold."

"But Bastian has no title. Even if you don't marry Rixin, you'll still be wed to another lord. Thomas Charo, perhaps. Or your cousin Golias."

"What if I love him?" Oriana lifted her hand to wipe away the stray tear that had fallen down her cheek. "No one has ever looked at me the way Bastian does. I don't want to say goodbye. Please don't make me say goodbye."

"I'm sorry." Isolda squeezed her daughter's hand. "I truly am. I want you to be happy." She reached up and unclasped the necklace. "But you're young. Love is more than a look. It's more, I promise. And you'll find it one day with whomever your father chooses for you, whether it's Rixin or Thomas or Golias." Isolda stood up with the necklace in her hand.

The necklace was supposed to remind Oriana that there was always a piece of Bastian with her. And without it, she couldn't help but feel empty. She watched her mother walk out of the room. It felt like a piece of her heart had been taken with her. Oriana placed her hand on her chest. She knew that love was more than just a look. It was a feeling too. And Bastian gave her that feeling. He did. She let her face fall into her hands.

- CHAPTER 30 -
TERRIC

Terric had never seen the grand hall so full. There were four times as many tables as usual, and every bench was packed with knights and squires and ladies shoulder to shoulder. The tables overflowed with Conrad's finest dishes: mango cakes galore on one platter, the richest beef stew Terric had ever tasted on another. Conrad was even personally carving a roasted hippopotamus in the middle of the hall, complete with a watermelon wedged into its open mouth.

Terric had always wished that Garrion would hire a court jester. Garrion still hadn't given in, but Reavus had brought one of his own. And his fool was magnificent. It seemed like he could do everything. Breathe fire. Juggle knives. Mock the temple of Arwin. And he somehow got away with all of it. He even dropped a grape into Bella's cleavage while he was juggling. Everyone laughed, and they laughed harder when he fished it out. They *laughed!* If Terric had done that, Sister Morel would have slapped him and dragged him out of the hall by his ear.

Terric felt the notes in his pocket. If fools could get away with all that, maybe Terric should have written recommendations for him and Warin to become court jesters rather than squires. Either way, it was too late now. He had already dropped the ring outside Rixin's room.

Despite it all, despite the food and the fool, despite it being the grandest feast that had ever graced the tables of Vulture Keep, Terric just couldn't seem to enjoy it.

He pushed a slab of marbled hippo meat around on his plate and looked at his family. This could be the last time he ever saw them. He looked at each of them and tried to remember their faces.

His sisters were beautiful, lovely ladies. But all his life they had mostly ignored him.

His brother was a talented warrior. He was everything Terric wanted to be. But the feelings weren't mutual. Every now and then Marcus would show Terric some attention, but mostly, Marcus was too busy training or talking to the other squires to have time for his dumb, future-priest of a little brother.

And his father... His father was the worst father in the history of fathers. Not only was he forcing Terric to become a priest, but he was a filthy hypocrite. Garrion was always acting so pious, but now that Terric discovered the tipped lances, he knew better than to believe that act.

His mother was the only one of the lot he'd miss. Her stories of the north. The way she ruffled his hair. Even the way she tickled him when he was being bad. But she didn't care about him enough to convince Garrion to let him be a knight.

None of them really cared about him.

So why is it so hard to leave?

Terric started to turn back around from looking at his parents, but as he did, Sir Aldric's golden eyes met his gaze.

How had he overlooked Sir Aldric? The old hawk saw everything. He could spot a commander across a battlefield. He could probably spot a bandit approaching the wall before the bandit could even see the wall. So there was no way he wouldn't spot Terric leaving the grand hall when Terric was literally sitting right in front of him.

Unless...

As the fool walked in front of the main table, Terric reached out and flicked one of the balls dangling from the fool's black and red hat.

The jester turned around. "Ah, look who we have here. Young Terric Hornbolt. At least, that's his name for now. In two days he's going to take the oath of Arwin, an oath of celibacy. So I guess that means he'll be Terric *Horny*-bolt."

The cheap wordplay got a few snickers from the hall. Terric didn't laugh. He could definitely make better jokes than that.

"What can I do for you, Lord Hornybolt?" asked the fool. "Or did you just want to touch my balls?" He shook his head to make the balls on his hat jump around.

More laughs at Terric's expense. Even Princess Navya was laughing, with her hideous horse face and her hairy arms. What a disappointment she had turned out to be. In his dreams, she had been even more beautiful than Bella. In reality, she was a hideous monster.

But that didn't matter. Terric was going to run away. He was done with his stupid family and the stupid ugly princess. He just had to distract Aldric first.

"I was hoping you could tell us a story about Sir Aldric," said Terric.

"Sir Aldric?" asked the jester.

"Yes, from his time in the Wizard's War. I want to hear of his great feats."

Terric glanced back at Sir Aldric. He had never seen the grumpy old knight look so excited. *It's working!*

"I only have limited room in my foolish fool's brain. I don't have space in there for stories of old gargoyles."

Terric was glad that this round of laughs was at Aldric's expense rather than his own. But he wasn't glad that his plan to distract Aldric had failed miserably. Aldric had stopped grinning and was now giving the fool a death stare.

"How about..." started the jester.

"How about you let a real storyteller weave some tales?" said a booming voice from across the grand hall.

Terric looked up. The man standing by the door had aged since Terric had last seen him. His sandy blonde beard now had specks of white. And the number of scars on his face had doubled. And the sigil on his shield had changed from a chained rhinoceros to an unchained gorilla. The tunic that the man was wearing might have once been normal, but it had now been patched with every imaginable fabric and color and pattern. Daggers and flasks hung from every belt and strap, and dozens more must have been hidden within the multicolored packs slung over his broad shoulders. Terric had only been four when he last saw the man, but he still recognized him immediately.

"Uncle Jax!" yelled Terric. In a flash he had leapt from his seat and pushed through the masses of guests to give his uncle a big hug. Jax picked him up and spun him around.

"Terric, my boy. My how you've grown. At first I thought you were Marcus."

"Where have you been?" asked Terric. "Were you really in Tujira? Where did those scars come from? What's your new sigil?" Terric could have asked a dozen more questions, but Garrion clearing his throat cut him off.

- CHAPTER 31 -
GARRION

Garrion couldn't help the smile that spread across his face. He hadn't seen or heard from his little brother in eight years. He'd thought Jax was dead. And yet, here he was.

"You're alive," said Garrion.

"Of course I'm alive," said Jax. "What, you think I'm stupid enough to go get myself killed?"

"Yes."

Jax nodded. "I suppose I am. But for now, I'm still kicking."

"You almost died?" asked Terric.

"I'm sure there will be time for such stories later," said Garrion. "But first I need to find Uncle Jax a room."

"But the boy..." started Jax as Garrion grabbed his arm and yanked him out into the hall. Jax turned back to Terric and yelled, "I'll tell you later!"

"Jax," said Garrion once they were out of the grand hall. He could still hear the dull roar of the feast, but he was sure no one in there would be able to hear him. "We need to talk."

"I thought you were going to find me a room?" asked Jax.

"No."

"Then why'd you drag me away from the feast? That hippo meat was really calling to me."

"I need your help." It felt weird saying those words to his little brother. He had always viewed Jax as the one who needed *his* help.

"You do?" asked Jax. His eyes twinkled with amusement.

"Yes, the tournament starts tomorrow, and I think Reavus has been bribing knights. Actually, I'm almost positive of it."

"What for?" asked Jax.

"I'm not sure, but I assume it's so he can start a war with the Rashid. I doubt he's forgiven Zand for stealing Tarini."

"Well he's certainly not bribing them to win," said Jax. "So that means he's bribing them to lose."

"That's the obvious conclusion, yes. But I think there may be more to it than that. I think he's..." Garrion cut his sentence short as the door to the grand hall opened. He was relieved when it was just Sir Aldric.

"What'd I miss?" asked Aldric.

"Not much," said Jax. "But I sure am missing some of that hippo meat. Can you grab me a slice?"

Aldric frowned.

"As I was saying," said Garrion, "I think Reavus might be trying to have Marcus killed."

"I've been away for some time, but if the sailors I've talked to can be trusted, Rixin is undefeated in tournaments. Why would Reavus risk murdering Marcus?"

"Someone decided Marcus is the second coming of Arwin. Apparently all the bookies have him as the favorite."

"Which is mad," said Sir Aldric.

Jax raised an eyebrow. "It might not be that crazy. I haven't been in town long enough to look for all the signs of the prophecy..."

Garrion put his hand on Jax's shoulder. "Forgive me, but I'm not sure you're the best authority on the subject of prophecies." *After you went to Techence rather than taking the oath of Arwin.*

"I've seen both men train," said Aldric. "There's no way Marcus is going to beat the prince. If anything, I think the room change we arranged had the opposite effect of what we wanted. Rixin was flawless in training today."

Jax laughed. "You tried to razz Prince Rixin by making him change rooms? You really do need my help."

"Gloating makes you ugly," said Garrion.

"At least I'm not naturally ugly," replied Jax with a grin as he patted his brother's cheek. "So how can I help? You want me to mix up a mindbend potion to force Reavus to confess? While I'm at it, I could force him to do a silly little dance."

"You can do that?" asked Garrion.

Jax shrugged. "With the proper ingredients, perhaps. But I doubt you have what I'd need. Anyway, I find it much easier to use my irresistible charm." He licked his fingers and smoothed his thick eyebrows. "What exactly do you want me to find out?"

"If Reavus is paying to have Marcus killed," said Aldric. "We're almost positive that Ngolo Mobek received one of his bribes. Maybe start there."

"And if you can," added Garrion, "find out if Rixin plans to declare war on Rashid if he wins the tournament."

"As you wish," said Jax. "But I have one condition."

"Name it."

"I want you to wrap up some of the hippo meat for me to take with me."

"Take with you?"

"Unfortunately, yes," said Jax. "I wish I was in town for the tournament, but alas, other business requires my attention. I'll be gone by sunrise."

"Then we'll have a hippo leg waiting for you by the gate," said Garrion.

"Deal. Be back in a few." Jax turned and went back into the grand hall.

"Think he'll find anything useful?" asked Aldric.

Garrion nodded. "Maybe. Or he'll run off with the first serving girl he sees. Could go either way."

Upon re-entering the grand hall, Garrion was immediately swarmed by a group of men wanting his attention. Some had gifts. Others wanted to marry their daughters off to Marcus. Some just had complaints.

Garrion found it impossible to focus on any of their requests. He was too preoccupied with the sight of Reavus smiling. Next to him, Arwin's Voice was stuffing his oversized face with mango cakes. If he wasn't careful, his head might get so large that he'd need to commission a brand new crown. *What a disgrace.* Garrion felt the blood rushing to his hands. He had to look away before the anger consumed him.

On the opposite side of the dais, Isolda and Tobias were deep in discussion. It was odd to see Tobias so talkative, but Isolda had that effect on him. She had that effect on everyone. Garrion decided to go sit with her and relax until Jax had news for him. This feast had cost him ten thousand golden drachmas that he couldn't really afford to spend, he might as well enjoy it.

Just as Garrion was about to sit down with a piping hot bowl of ostrich stew, Tobias stood up and waved him over.

What now? thought Garrion.

"My lord," said Tobias. "Forgive me for interrupting your meal, but this is of great importance."

"Garrion nodded. "Out with it then."

"I found an old copy of Axion William Willerby's book 'The Path of Storms'..."

What a heretical title.

"In it, he outlines three simple ways for predicting the trajectory and speed of extreme weather cells. So I asked Aldric's rangers to collect some data using some makeshift devices I built. Did you know you can make a barometer out of a goat's bladder, acacia sap…"

Garrion sighed. "Please get to the point."

"Yes, yes. Of course. As I was saying, the method is only 86.29% accurate, and a lot of things can affect the speed of a storm, but I think that the storm Brother Savaric told us about is going to hit the city within the next few days. Although I should note, the data collected by the rangers was scattered at best. The storm isn't behaving as a normal storm. The speed keeps changing."

"Odd," said Garrion. "It's much too early for the summer rains."

"I agree. I'll keep monitoring it, but perhaps we should consider creating a contingency plan in case the weather disrupts the tournament."

Garrion took a moment to consider this new development. It seemed obvious to him what was happening. Reavus' bribing had gone against the will of Arwin, and now Arwin had sent a storm to set things right.

"No need for a contingency plan," said Garrion. "We already have the alarm horn being manned at all times on the wall. And anyway, the weather is the work of Arwin. If the storm comes early, it comes for a reason."

"Storm?" asked Jax. He had just appeared at Garrion's side.

"Nothing to worry about." He pulled Jax back into the hall, away from prying eyes and ears. Aldric followed. "What did you find?" asked Garrion.

"You're right. Reavus has definitely been bribing knights. I can't figure out why, though. Maybe I've lost my touch." Jax paused. "I wasn't a complete failure, though. I can confirm that Rixin is going to start a war on Rashid if he wins the title. He was more than happy to ask me all sorts of questions about possible routes through Tujira."

Garrion slammed his fist against the wall. "I knew it."

"How are you going to stop him? Maybe you need to get more aggressive with the room moving. Instead of moving him before bed, try moving him once he's asleep. Waking up on the roof of Vulture Keep would give him quite a shock."

Garrion ignored Jax's terrible idea. "Aldric, what've you found about Rixin's weaknesses?"

"I believe my original guess was correct," said Aldric. "Oriana is his weakness."

"Then I guess that's our only choice." As much as he didn't want to use his daughter as leverage.

"During my travels, I once came across a tribe with a most peculiar custom," said Jax.

"Not now," muttered Garrion.

"It's relevant, I promise."

"Okay, but make it quick."

"In this tribe, whenever a suitor asked for a woman's hand in marriage, the man would have to strip down to his loincloth and let the woman beat him to within an inch of his life in front of the whole tribe. It showed that he was devoted to the union, and also that he trusted her with his life."

"You want to have Oriana beat the snot out of Rixin?" asked Garrion. It was rather entertaining to picture, but it hardly seemed like a viable option.

Jax laughed. "No, you idiot. I want you to make Rixin prove that he's devoted to Oriana by losing the tournament."

"That's rather dishonorable," said Garrion.

Jax shrugged. "All is fair in love and jousts."

"You can't just replace a word in an idiom with 'joust' and have it make sense," replied Aldric.

"Sure you can. Jousts speak louder than words. Don't count your chickens before they joust. It takes two to joust. Kill two knights with one joust. Be careful what you joust for..."

"Fine," conceded Aldric. "Maybe you can."

"But back to the original point," said Garrion. "It doesn't feel right to gamble Oriana's future like this."

"Wouldn't you feel more comfortable with the marriage if you knew that Rixin was willing to lose a joust for her?" asked Jax. "He *never* loses."

"Yes, I suppose I would," said Garrion.

"Then there you have it. It's not gambling. It's just doing your due diligence as a father. And speaking of gambling...if you do give Rixin this ultimatum, let me know. It's possible I might have made a few bets..."

"You actually have a good point. I guess it's not gambling."

"Don't sound so shocked. I've grown wise in my travels."

"Enjoy the rest of the feast. And make sure you come to see me before you leave. I believe I owe you some hippo meat." Garrion walked back into the grand hall, and before he could change his mind, he put a hand on Rixin's shoulder. "Can I speak with you in private, Your Highness?"

"Of course. What is it about?" Rixin followed Garrion behind one of the rhino statues, away from the other guests.

"It's about Oriana." Garrion tried to keep the smile off his face. He saw the prince light up at the mention of his daughter. If he hadn't been certain before, he certainly was now. Rixin was falling for Oriana. Which meant his plan was going to work perfectly. "I think the two of you would make a handsome pair, don't you?"

Rixin smiled as he spotted Oriana across the grand hall. "Your daughter is indeed very lovely."

He needed Rixin to say the words if this was going to work. "Do you want her hand?"

Rixin turned his gaze to Garrion. His smile was gone, and a curious expression had replaced it. "We both know it's not my decision."

Garrion laughed. "Don't give me that. Because we also both know that you have no desire to marry *that*." He gestured to Navya who was sitting with her nose in a book. With only her frizzy hair visible, she looked like a big furry greeplesnart.

"Careful, Uncle. Princess Navya is like a sister to me, and I'll not stand for you insulting her. She has many wonderful qualities."

"Apologies, Your Highness. But I'm afraid you've just proved my point. You view Navya as a sister, not as a potential bride. So I ask you again: do you want to marry my daughter?"

"That's up to you and my father, isn't it?" asked Rixin.

"It is. And I believe I could convince King Ivan to agree to the match. You've heard about how I saved his life at the end of the war, yes?"

"I have."

Garrion looked Rixin square in the eyes. "Then tell me: do you want to marry my daughter?"

"Yes, I'd be honored to marry Oriana."

Garrion smiled. Prince Rixin seemed wistful. He had him right where he wanted him. "Then you have my permission." Garrion put his hand out for Rixin to shake. "And I'll make it my personal mission to convince your father of the match."

Rixin reached to shake it, but Garrion pulled his hand away.

"Under one condition," Garrion said.

"Name it."

"Throw the joust."

Rixin let his hand fall back to his side. "Excuse me?"

"You can marry Oriana if you purposely lose the joust. I want you to show me that you'll be devoted to this union. This is how you'll prove it to me. Otherwise I'll see to it that you never come within ten feet of my daughter. *Any* of my daughters."

"I guarantee you, I only have eyes for Oriana."

"So do we have a deal?" Garrion extended his hand again.

Rixin stared at him.

"Talenovs and Hornbolts make good matches. Look at me and your aunt. Five healthy children. A happy marriage. What would your life be like if you wed Princess Navya?" *Besides...hairy.*

"Lord Garrion, I would love to marry your daughter. But under no circumstances would I throw a tournament with such high stakes. And I don't think you'd really want a man to marry your daughter who would be willing to do such a thing."

He was right.

"Wait, is this a trick? You'll try to get me to throw the tournament three times, and on the third time you'll smile and tell me I'm a good man and that I can marry your daughter after all? Then I say three times. No, no, and no."

"This is not a trick. You have my word. Throw the joust, and Oriana shall be your wife."

Rixin shook his head. "You can't blackmail me. I'm the prince of Treland, for Arwin's sake. Have you lost your head?"

"If we don't have a deal, then I expect you'll stay away from Oriana. I will never give your union my blessing. And I'll do everything in my power to convince your father to make you marry Navya."

"Well good luck convincing him of anything. He never leaves his bloody castle to talk to anyone. He doesn't care for my happiness anyway. Just like it appears you don't care for Oriana's." Rixin walked away without another word.

Garrion turned toward Oriana. She was laughing with her handmaiden. Of course he cared about Oriana's happiness. That's why he was hoping Rixin would accept his offer. He truly believed they'd make a great match.

"How did it go?" asked Aldric, filling Rixin's spot beside him.

"It certainly made him angry. In that respect, I'd say it went fairly well. He's clearly smitten with Oriana, just like you said." He continued to stare at his daughter. "But he didn't agree to it."

"Give it time," Aldric said. "You'd be surprised what a young man would be willing to do for a pretty lady."

"I'm hoping I know exactly what one would do."

- CHAPTER 32 -
TERRIC

Terric spent the rest of the feast watching Jax. Every person within earshot of the adventurer was transfixed by his stories. One minute the table would erupt in laughter, then the next minute Jax would produce a trinket from his overstuffed pack and his audience would gasp. But Terric was too far away to hear or see any of it.

Garrion and Sir Aldric had left the grand hall on a few occasions, but it had never seemed like a good opportunity to make his escape. Actually, if he was being completely honest, he was procrastinating so that he'd get to talk to Jax. If he was lucky, Jax might tell him about the perfect destination.

But he wasn't allowed to talk to Jax yet. Feasting with the common lords and knights would have been unbefitting of the duke's son.

Eventually, when the sun had set and the roasted hippo had been picked to the bone, the feast began to come to a close. Lords and ladies trickled out of the grand hall. Actually, it would be more accurate to say that many of them stumbled out of the grand hall. They must have gone through an entire cellar's worth of wine and ale.

Isolda tapped Terric on the shoulder. "Thank you for being so patient," she said. "It looks like there's an open seat next to Jax with your name on it."

Terric's eyes lit up. "Really?" he asked.

Isolda nodded.

Terric didn't need to ask twice. He climbed over the table and ran towards Jax. Isolda and his siblings all followed.

"Now this is the audience I was hoping for all night," said Jax. "Let's see what we have here." He looked at the children. "You've all gotten so big. Marcus, I see you've finally grown some muscle. And Oriana, you've blossomed into quite a beautiful young woman. And Selina..." He paused for a second. "Uh, you have too. Terric, I saw earlier that you haven't lost a bit of your curiosity."

Nesta pulled on Jax's pant leg.

He looked down.

"Who are you?" she asked. "And why is your beard so weird?"

"You must be Nesta," said Jax. He lifted her onto his lap. "When I was last here, you didn't exist yet."

"What was I then?" asked Nesta.

"Good question. An axion could probably give a better answer than me, but basically, until your mother and father..."

"I think that's a discussion better left to another time," said Isolda, shooting Jax a harsh glance.

Terric sighed. He had been able to work out most of how babies were created based on conversations he overheard from Marcus and the knights, but he wouldn't have minded a quick refresher course.

"Oh right, right," said Jax. "How would you like some presents?" He shoved some empty plates and mugs to the side and hoisted his pack over Nesta's head onto the table.

Terric could hear a hundred different noises of trinkets shifting in the pack. Metal and glass and wool. He held his breath as Jax started to untie the pack. But then Jax paused.

"So where shall I begin?"

"With the presents!" said Terric.

Jax laughed. "I meant, where shall I begin the story."

"From the beginning," suggested Selina.

Nesta reached into Jax's pack and pulled out a round tin container the size of her fist. "What's this?"

Jax grabbed the container. "That, dear girl, is where our story shall begin. When I left here eight years ago, I set sail for New Barcova, and from there we planned to go on to Tujira. But when you're sailing on the high seas, sometimes the gods have other plans for you. The storm that hit our ship was like nothing I've ever seen. Clouds as dark as night. Waves as tall as Vulture Keep." Jax started bouncing Nesta on his knee to simulate the waves. "Our ship was nothing to that storm. Just a tiny speck on Krakos' seas. The last thing I remember was one of the sails cracking. It whacked me right in the head. Then everything went dark." He put his hand over Nesta's eyes.

Nesta let out a frightened squeal.

"When I woke up, I was lying on a beach with a mouthful of sand and seaweed. I thanked the gods that I had been delivered safely to land...until I opened my eyes." He moved his hand off Nesta's eyes. "To my left and right, all around me, I saw birds feasting on my fellow sailors. The captain was screaming as a bird tore into his stomach and pulled out his intestines. The first mate..."

"It might be best to skip some of these details," said Isolda.

"But I'm just getting to the good part. The part when one of the birds stands up, and I realize that it's not a bird at all, but a man with wings. My body was beat up, but let me tell you, seeing a winged man with intestines hanging from his mouth will get you moving. I don't think I've ever run as fast as I did. Soon a whole flock of them were chasing me, swooping down and taking swipes at me."

"Come on," scoffed Marcus. "Winged men?"

"Oh, you don't believe me?" Jax pushed his beard aside and yanked at the collar of his tunic to reveal a scar of three parallel talon marks. "How about now?"

"I believe you!" said Terric. "How'd you escape?"

"I didn't. They caught me and put me in a great labyrinth."

"What's that?" asked Nesta.

"A giant maze," said Selina.

"Exactly. A giant maze. And to make it worse, the labyrinth was home to a fearsome beast. I only saw it once, but I'll never forget it. It stood upright and had the torso of a man, but its legs and head were that of a bull. And the red eyes..." Jax paused and shook as if a chill had gone down his spine.

Terric was totally entranced by the story.

"It charged at me, but I dove into a crack too small for it to fit in. And I found myself on top of a corpse. A woman's corpse, by the look of the clothes. And that's where I found this." Jax held up the tin and pointed to the symbol on the front: a sword piercing a shining sun. "Old Barcovan face powder. My present to you, Oriana." Jax handed the tin to Oriana.

Oriana took it from him, opened it up, and dabbed a bit on her cheeks. "Thank you, Uncle. How does it look?"

"Quite stunning. But you should save it for special occasions. Powder like that isn't easy to come by."

"So where were these birdmen?" asked Terric. "Were you past Edge Island?"

"Oh no. I haven't been out there...not yet. This was on the other side of the world, in ancient Marinth. I can't be sure, but I believe it was the ancient city of Arginth. You should have seen it. The entire city is made of black marble with red clay roofs. Black columns and statues everywhere. And the temple to Chalkos, the Marinthian god of death. It was the size of this castle, with columns holding up the domed roof. The statue of Chalkos was ten times the size of these rhino statues, and just as the stories describe, he had flaming hair, a metal leg, and a three-headed crow perched on his shoulder. Let me tell you - talons digging into your back is never a pleasant experience, but it was worth getting a bird's eye view of Arginth."

Terric nodded. While the city did sound impressive, Terric was happy to hear that the birdmen were nowhere near his intended destination of the Huntlands. "Do you have any stories of the Huntlands?"

"Why do you want to hear about the Huntlands? When you can hear about..."

"What are these?" asked Nesta. She had pulled out a whole pile of trinkets from Jax's pack.

"Well now you've gone and spoiled the surprise dear girl. Let's see what we have..." Jax picked up a hand mirror with a grotesque red and white face sculpted on the back. Terric had never seen a drawing of a chalkian, but he imagined that was how they looked. "This, Nesta, is your gift. I got it from a courtesan in Meitong. Beautiful woman she was. Skin like gold, hair smooth and black and straight as an arrow. Eyes shaped like almonds. And the way her silk dresses plunged between her breasts..."

Terric shifted to the edge of his seat to make sure he didn't miss whatever Jax was going to say next. But Isolda clearing her throat sent Jax's story in a different direction.

"She gave me this mirror. As her story went, when you look into it, it reveals your true self."

Nesta picked it up and stared into it. "I see myself."

"Then it worked," said Jax, patting Nesta's head.

Nesta immediately stuck the mirror into the folds of her dress.

Jax picked up the next gift, a green and purple tunic with wild floral patterns. The way the fabric shimmered in the candlelight reminded Terric of the sun reflecting off Katra's Crossing at dusk. "This, Marcus, is a tunic from the Aipan Islands. I never made it to their shores, but an Aipanese merchant in Meitong sold it to me. He claimed it was made from the silk of a worm the size of..." Jax looked around for something to compare it to. "The size of this table. He told me it couldn't be torn, so I asked if he wanted to bet on it. Our wager was that I'd buy it for twice the price if I was wrong, but if I could create even the smallest tear, I'd get it for free. I thought I'd be clever and just cut it with a knife. Worst wager I ever made." Jax tossed the tunic to Marcus.

Marcus unfolded it and held it at arm's length to inspect it. The patterns were odd and the wrapped style of the collar looked like the few drawings Terric had seen of what the Rashidi wore. Marcus frowned. "Thanks. Listen, I have to get up early for the tournament tomorrow. I should really be heading to bed."

"Me too," said Oriana.

"And me," said Isolda quickly.

"Don't make me go to bed yet," said Terric. "I haven't even gotten my present yet!"

"Who says he has a present for you?" teased Isolda.

Terric frowned. "But... Why would he not bring me a present?"

Isolda smiled. "Of course Uncle Jax didn't leave you out. Enjoy the stories, but don't stay up too late." She ruffled Terric's hair and followed Oriana and Marcus out of the grand hall.

"Now, where were we?" asked Jax. "Ah yes, presents." Jax picked up a thick book bound in scaly black leather.

A book!

"This," said Jax, "is my journal from the past eight years. It isn't organized, and it doesn't include every last detail, but all the best bits are there. I even tried to illustrate some of what I saw, although I'm the first to admit that I'm not a great artist."

Yes! This is the best gift ever!

"Did you draw the girl from Meitong?" asked Terric. He had an idea of how she might have looked, but a sketch would still be much appreciated.

Jax laughed. "Ah, I wish I had. Alas, my time with her was cut short when the Ukhol hoard came."

"That's okay." Terric started to reach for the book.

"Anyway, Selina, I hope this book gives you a bit more entertainment than those boring books in the library here."

"Wait," said Terric. Had he heard his uncle wrong? "Why does Selina get the book?"

"Thank you, uncle," said Selina. She took the book and hugged it to her chest. "I can't wait to start reading it."

"But..." muttered Terric.

Jax smiled at Terric. "Don't worry, my boy. I've saved my favorite present of all for you."

"You have?" That sounded promising, but what could be better than a book of adventures?

"Yes, I have." Jax held up a thick reed of red grass. "Bloodgrass!"

"Bloodgrass?" Terric was less than enthused.

"You heard me. Straight from the Bloodplains of Uhkolia. Home to the fiercest warriors I've ever encountered. They're hairier than a bear, and as strong as one too. In Meitong I had always heard rumors of them, how they rode on wooly rhinos twice the size of a horse and could snap a man in two with their bare hands. But I didn't fully understand it until the morning they sacked Wuyang. Dragged the Meitongese emperor into the city square and ripped his head clean from his body."

Nesta let out a frightened peep. "Are they going to come here?"

"No, sweet girl. The Uhkols are thousands of miles away. There are mountain ranges and jungles and oceans between them and Arwin's Gate."

"So how'd you get the grass?" asked Terric.

"The Ukhol warlord, Qarajin. For whatever reason, he liked me. So he took me with his band of raiders when they went back to the Bloodplains. I was their captive for over a year, but finally, I was able to escape. And when I did, I took some bloodgrass with me. And seeds." Jax tossed a bag of tan seeds to Terric and handed him the reed of dried grass.

"Oh, thanks," muttered Terric. On a different day, he would have loved to hear more about wooly rhinos and men who can tear each other in half, but he was distracted by getting the worst gift ever. It was stupid, but he could feel tears welling up in his eyes. He didn't want to see Jax anymore. Not tonight. "Well, I guess I better get to bed. You heard Mum, I'm not to stay up too late."

"Don't you have time to hear one more story? I still have a final gift - one for the whole family."

Terric scrunched up his face and thought about it. "I'm not sure..."

"But don't you want to know how I got this scar?" asked Jax. He rolled up his sleeve to reveal a nasty scar carved deep into his bicep.

And that was enough to pique Terric's curiosity. The promise of another present didn't hurt either. Maybe *this* would be the great gift he was waiting for. Even if it was for the whole family. "Okay, I have time."

"Great! So it had been many months since my escape from Ukhol. Maybe even years. I lost count working my way back north, bouncing between various tribes. But one tribe stood out among the rest. I had heard rumors of them during my journey. Some tribes feared them, others mocked them. Some even worshiped them. I knew I had to find them before I left the jungle. I was too curious. But they always seemed to be one step ahead of me. Over and over again, I would come across their camp just after the fire had been extinguished. I could never catch them, but eventually, they caught me. I fell right into one of their spike traps. Sliced my arm clean open. The spike must have been laced with something, because I was unconscious within seconds. A few hours later I woke up with a shooting pain in my arm. It was like nothing I had ever felt before. The bleeding had stopped, but there were four ants the size of my fists latched onto my arm. Their pincers kept the wound shut, but by the gods, it hurt something fierce."

Nesta balled her hand into a fist. "Ants...this big?"

"More like this," said Jax. He held up his own fist, which was at least triple the size of Nesta's.

Her eyes got big.

"I felt the same way. So I passed out again. And the next time I woke up, there were three men standing over me. They were practically naked, with skin spotted like cows. Brown and white. And their eyes...their eyes were a milky white. I had finally met the Isi."

"Cow men!" said Nesta. "Did they moo?"

"Shh," said Terric. "Let him finish the story."

Jax laughed. "No, they didn't moo. But as soon as I talked, they did hold spears to my chest. I thought they were going to kill me. I tried every language I knew. They reacted differently to each one. Some tribes' languages they liked, others they hated. When I spoke Pentavian, they nearly ran me through with a spear."

"Do the women go naked too?" asked Terric.

"I said *practically* naked. Most of them wore loincloths, but other than that, they have little need for clothes. They're all blind, so they can't see each other. And the weather there is hot and sticky - even hotter and stickier than the summers here. Clothes would be little more than a nuisance."

"How did they survive if they were blind?" asked Selina.

"They relied on their other senses. They could hear and smell animals much faster than I could see them, especially with how dark it was deep in the jungle. And you should hear them sing." Jax shook his head in amazement. "I'm not even sure if I can call it singing, as that implies that what we know as singing is somehow comparable to theirs. In truth, it is not. Theirs is a far superior art form. Just as the elegant architecture of Marinth puts our castles to shame, so too do the songs of the Isi when compared to our crude forms of music.

"Can you sing us one?" asked Nesta.

"No, no. I wouldn't dare butcher one of their beautiful songs. But I suppose it wouldn't hurt to recite one of the translations." Jax licked his fingers and extinguished the candles on the table. The candles left on other tables flickered in the breeze blowing through the open windows, casting odd shadows in the hall. A chill went down Terric's spine. Jax cleared his throat and began: "In the days when men take to the skies..."

"Now, now," said Brother Savaric. Terric didn't realize when he had joined them at the table. "The children don't need to hear heretical prophecies."

"Do my eyes deceive me, or am I in the presence of the great Captain Savaric?" asked Jax.

Captain? Are the pirate stories true?!

Saravic shook his head. "I'm not a captain. I'm merely a humble servant of the good lord Arwin."

"He's father's master of coin," said Selina. "But he's also the master of expansion. He's helping father spread the word of Arwin to the far corners of Pentavia and beyond. Maybe someday he can even find the Isi and show them the path of Arwin."

"That's quite the change from your days as a pirate. And not just any pirate - you were the most feared captain in the Tujiran Sea."

"I knew you were a pirate!" said Terric. "Why wouldn't you tell me the stories?"

Savaric sighed. "I prefer to keep those dark days in my past. I'm not that man anymore."

Nesta spit something onto the floor. "Yuck!"

Jax laughed. "Ah, I see Nesta has found the final present: cocoa beans. Those really aren't meant to be eaten by themselves. You have to add milk and sugar."

"It tastes like someone pooed in Conrad's chocolate."

"You already have chocolate?" asked Jax.

"Yes," said Nesta. "Brother Savaric's boats bring it."

Jax turned to Savaric. "You've met the Isi then?"

"Never heard of them. We get it from a different tribe," said Savaric. "Isn't that enough stories for one night, Jax? The children should be getting to bed. If you have a few minutes, I was hoping you could accompany me to the dovecote. While I've been cleaning up Father Percival's mess I found a few birds that need to be taken to other cities. Depending on where you're traveling next..."

Terric's heart sank when he processed that chocolate was the final gift. It wasn't that it was bad - he loved Conrad's chocolate pastries - but it wasn't awesome either. He grabbed the bloodgrass and seeds off the table and sulked out of the grand hall.

On his way up to his room, he passed Bella standing at the end of a long line of servants waiting to bathe. Usually they bathed during the day, but with so many guests, they were forced to all wait until night.

Maybe watching Bella bathe was just what he needed to lighten his mood.

- CHAPTER 33 -
ISOLDA

Any minute now, Isolda would finally have some answers. If this Bastian fellow had the necklace, he must have stolen the entire suit of armor. And she fully intended to get it from him.

Isolda tried to push the dresses to the side, but it was no use. Since when had her daughter owned so many dresses? Maybe hiding in the dresser had been a bad idea. She didn't want to scare the poor man when she popped out. But she needed to make sure he came in, and there was no way he would have come if he saw Isolda in the room.

She heard a sniffle from outside the dresser and winced. All day Oriana hadn't seemed quite like herself. Every fiber of Isolda was screaming at her to talk to Garrion about this man that Oriana apparently loved. Would it be the worst thing if their daughter married someone without a title? She sighed. She already knew what Garrion would say. Garrion didn't want his eldest daughter to marry an average lord. He wanted his eldest daughter to marry the crown prince. He wanted his daughter to be the queen of Treland one day. And it was still a possibility that she would be. King Ivan had yet to announce a match for Prince Rixin. Oriana was beautiful and kind-hearted. Surely Rixin would fall for her.

"Ori!" Nesta yelled.

No. Why was Nesta in the room? Her presence would scare Bastian away. This was all going terribly wrong. Isolda peered through a crack in the dresser.

"Nesta, what are you doing up so late? You need to get to bed," said Oriana.

"I know. But I had to tell you something important."

"Very well. Make it quick, we don't want Mum to find us up so late."

Isolda stifled a laugh. As if she'd ever yell at her children for staying up past their bedtime. That's what childhood was all about. Breaking the rules.

"Prince Rixin found his ring!" said Nesta.

"Really?" asked Ori. "When? Where? Are you certain?"

"Yes! Just a minute ago he showed it to me and apologized. He said he found it right outside his room before the feast. I don't have to be eaten by tigers! And now he likes me again!"

"That's wonderful news," said Oriana. "Now get to bed. You'll want plenty of rest before the start of the tournament."

Nesta turned and walked towards the door. "He's going to win!" she yelled.

"What about Marcus?" Oriana called after her sister, but the door had already slammed shut.

Isolda was relieved to see Oriana walk over and lock the door. Isolda pushed the dresses to the side again. How much longer would she have to wait in this overstuffed dresser? The temperature inside was becoming unbearable.

"So much for family loyalty," Oriana said with a sigh.

The words cut through Isolda. She put her hand to her chest. Was her daughter that unhappy about Nesta rooting for

Rixin? For weeks all Oriana could do was talk about the prince coming. And now that he was here, she was suddenly not interested? What could Bastian possibly have that the crown prince of Treland did not? Isolda smoothed the end of one of her braids. Maybe it was just that Oriana felt like Bastian could be hers. Maybe there were no other women vying for his attention.

Isolda closed her eyes and rested her head against the back of the dresser. Tomorrow she could focus on Oriana's happiness. But tonight she had to put all her energy into making Bastian hand over the body of Arwin and tell her everything he knew. She hadn't come this far to still be left without answers. She had been waiting far too long to get justice for her father's murder.

"Your sister is very cute," said a deep voice.

Isolda's eyes flew open.

"I'm sorry, Bastian," said Oriana with a sob. "I can't..."

"Why are you crying, Ori?"

"I'm so, so sorry."

Isolda couldn't stand to hear another second of her daughter in pain. She pushed the dresser doors open to see Oriana's arms wrapped around the man's neck. Her face was nuzzled into his tunic like she belonged in his arms. He pressed his hands against her lower back and pulled her closer.

"Talk to me," he said and pushed a strand of hair away from her face. "Please talk to me."

Isolda stood frozen in place, feeling very much like the intruder she was. Finally, she cleared her throat.

Bastian immediately released Oriana from his embrace and took a step back. "My lady," he said and bowed his head.

"No need for formalities," said Isolda.

He opened his mouth like he was about to say something, but Isolda held up her hand.

"Oriana's told me everything." She glanced at her daughter's red eyes. There was no reason to make this take any longer than necessary. "We'll discuss your relationship in a moment. But first we need to discuss this." Isolda pulled the necklace out of her pocket.

Bastian looked at the necklace and then back at Oriana. "That was a gift for Ori."

"That's very thoughtful. But we both know this wasn't yours to give. How did you come into possession of this necklace?"

"I found it."

"You found it? Really?" Isolda jumped when a squirrel darted past her feet.

Bastian leaned down and patted the rodent's head. "You're right. I didn't find it. Nut did."

Isolda glanced down at the squirrel. "The squirrel found it? And what? Picked it up and brought it to you? It's a squirrel." Was Oriana falling for a madman?

"I'm not lying." He sounded defensive. "Nut can do more than you'd expect. Show 'em, Nut." Bastian pulled a grape out of his pack and tossed it to the squirrel. Nut flipped into the air and caught it. "See?"

"Okay, so the squirrel found it. Where'd he find it?"

"On the ground."

Isolda glared at him. "If I call for the guards, you and your squirrel are going to be doing tricks on the other side of Arwin's Wall. And don't think you can just climb out the window and disappear. I knew you were coming - I have guards stationed all over." It was a bluff. But Bastian had no way of knowing that.

"Okay, okay," said Bastian. "But what's to keep you from doing that after I tell you what I know?"

"You have my word. Tell me everything you know and I won't call for the guards."

"Or have me arrested later?"

"Not for this, no."

"And I'll still be able to see Oriana?"

"We'll discuss that after. Now, tell me about the necklace."

Bastian took a deep breath. "A few nights ago, my friend and I were scouting out the Razortooth Tavern. We were waiting for some drunks to stumble out so we could pickpocket them. But then we saw something better. Two men walked out carrying a suit of golden armor. We tried to fight them for it, but they were talented swordsmen. Nearly cut my friend's arm off. Anyway, they got away with most of the armor. But a gauntlet fell off in the process. And so did the necklace. I would have missed it, but Nut found it."

Isolda thought about it. If the story was true, Bastian didn't have anything to do with her father's murder. He was just in the right place at the right time to see the men stealing it from the brothel. The men...they were the ones she wanted. "Tell me about the men."

"The ones with the armor?" asked Bastian.

"What other men would I be talking about?"

"I don't remember much about them. They were wearing brown cloaks. Or black cloaks? Definitely had hoods."

"Anything else?"

Bastian stroked his chin and then snapped his fingers. "Ah, that's right. One had red hair."

"And the other?"

"Brown, I think."

That might be enough. Isolda would have Tobias check with the mistress of the Viriphyte Palace to see if the girls had seen men matching that description. But finding the men was only half of the equation. They could just be thieves like Bastian.

Or they could be working for the man who killed her father. The appraisal of the armor would give her some hint as to which it was. But in order for the appraisal to happen, she had to get Bastian to hand over that gauntlet. "I need you to bring me the gauntlet."

"Of course," said Bastian.

That was easy.

Bastian glanced at Oriana. "All I ask in return is Oriana's hand in marriage."

"I'm sorry," said Isolda. "I'm not sure I heard you right. Did you say you wanted me to call the guards?"

"You can call the guards if you want, but I'm not giving up that gauntlet without getting your blessing to marry your daughter."

Isolda had overplayed her hand. Bastian knew she wanted the gauntlet, and he was going to take full advantage of it. "Do I have your word?" she asked.

"Yes."

Isolda glanced at Oriana, who was staring at her eagerly, as if a small part of her believed that Isolda held the power to make her happy. "As long as it makes Ori happy, you have my blessing."

"Really?" asked Bastian. He looked stunned. Ori's expression was a mix of excitement and bewilderment.

"Yes, really," said Isolda. She quickly looked away from Ori. She didn't want to watch her eldest daughter's heartbreaking. "You seem like an intelligent young man. And it seems like you care for my daughter. She certainly cares for you. Unfortunately, the blessing that matters is my husband's. And unless you magically get a title, my husband will never even consider the thought of you two marrying. Never. I'm sorry, Bastian. I truly am. Meet me outside the Razorooth

Tavern tomorrow at noon with the gauntlet and no one has to know you were here."

"Wait," said Bastian. "That doesn't count. I meant..."

"You gave me your word. My blessing for the gauntlet."

"It's worth a fortune," said Bastian. "If it's so valuable, I'll just take the gauntlet to someone else and make a name for myself. Then I'll prove to your husband that I'm a proper suitor."

"That's a great plan. But you forgot the part where I tell Garrion that you're nothing more than a thief who snuck into his daughter's bedchambers. You'd be banished forever. Actually, he'd probably make an exception and reinstate capital punishment just for you."

"Mother!" Oriana said. "You promised me he wouldn't get in trouble! You promised."

"And he won't if he does what he's told. Now say goodbye. This will be the last time you see each other."

- CHAPTER 34 -
BASTIAN

Bastian thought Isolda might walk away. But she stood there, staring at them, waiting for them to part forever. He knew his time with Oriana was limited. He had known that all along. Now that the end was there though, he refused to believe it. He turned toward Oriana.

"I'm sorry," she said.

They seemed to be the only two words she was capable of saying. She had set him up. But he could tell from the tears rolling down her cheeks that she meant what she said. Her mother had forced her into this ambush. He leaned forward and tried to ignore Isolda staring at them.

"Run away with me," he whispered into her ear.

"What?" She looked up at him with her big blue eyes.

"You heard me, Ori. I'll sell the gauntlet. It'll be enough to send us across Pentavia. I'll take care of you. I'll protect you." He grabbed her hand. "I'll be the proper suitor you deserve."

Tears rolled down her cheeks. "I don't deserve you, Bastian. I doubted you. I thought...I thought you came last night just so you could steal Prince Rixin's ring. I thought you were using me. But I realized I was wrong when Rixin found his ring. I don't deserve your care or protection. But that doesn't mean I don't want it. I love you."

Bastian didn't know what part of her confession to focus on first. The fact that she loved him? Or the fact that she had figured out he stole the prince's ring. *How did she find out about the ring?* "I came to see you last night. I had no intention of stealing anything, I swear to you. Terric forced me to break into the prince's bedchambers and take the ring. But I was under the impression that he was going to give it back, so I didn't think it really mattered."

Oriana immediately pulled her hand away. "What? You *did* steal it?"

"Yes. But like I said, your brother..."

"Terric is taking the oath of Arwin in just a few days time. He would never steal anything. He's practically a priest already. How dare you accuse him of that!"

That little rhino's rump completely set me up. "Forget about the ring. It doesn't matter."

"Of course it matters."

"Oriana, I love you." Bastian put his hand on the side of Ori's face. "Nothing else matters. Just say yes and we can go wherever you want to go. We can see the whole world. We can travel to every city in Pentavia."

"I can't." But her actions betrayed her words as she leaned into his touch.

"Why?" Bastian wanted to shake her. "Isn't my love enough?"

She moved her face away from his hand. "How am I ever supposed to trust you? You used me. You used me to get close to the prince. And you probably just gave the ring back because you knew I suspected you."

"I didn't..."

"You heard my mother, Bastian. You have to go. I can't see you anymore."

"I'm not going anywhere without you. I love you." He grabbed her hand again. "And you love me."

She immediately pulled away. "If you love me then you'll do what my mother asked. So that you won't be banished. Maybe you'll find me someday when you're done stealing. And lying. And breaking hearts." She turned away from him.

"It's late, Bastian," Isolda said. "It's time for you to go."

"Ori," he said one last time. "I'll make it right."

His words were greeted with a sob. How had everything gone so wrong? He came for a kiss. And he left with his life in Isolda's hands. But he didn't care. The only thing he could focus on was the sound of Ori crying. And how it was his fault that she was shedding tears. He had broken her heart before he even realized that he had it. He climbed out the window with Nut.

The farther away he climbed, the more he realized that the sound was in his head. But the echo of her sobs wouldn't seem to fade. He needed to win her back. He needed her. There had to be a way. But all he could focus on was the fact that her father would never accept him.

His escape from the castle was a blur. He almost got caught twice, but eventually he made it safely across the bridge and over the gatehouse. He leapt down when he was close enough to the ground.

"Judging by your face, I guess you still haven't shagged the princess."

Bastian jumped at the sound of his friend's voice. "Stop sneaking up on me, Logan. What are you even doing here?"

"I thought you might be going to get some scorpium. Why won't you just tell me who your contact is?"

Bastian brushed past his friend.

"You spend a few minutes in the castle and you're acting like there's a rhino horn shoved all the way up your back door." Logan scratched his arm. "What gives?"

Suddenly Bastian felt like he had no energy left. Like Oriana's love had been keeping his heart beating. He stopped walking and sat down in the grass. "I need to get her back."

"Get her back? Did you ever have the princess in the first place?"

Bastian tilted his head back and look up at the stars. For a few brief moments, he did have her. He had everything. He leaned back until he was lying in the grass. Now he wasn't sure if he could keep going without her. Even the stars seemed dim.

He hadn't looked at the stars in years. Not since his mother had died. Not since his father had thrown it all away.

Wait a second!

"That's it!" said Bastian.

"What?" asked Logan.

"My father. He's the key. Before the war, my family meant something. My family had a title. I wasn't a prince, but my father was still a count. I have to reclaim my title."

"How ya gonna do that? You can't just go steal it."

"I don't know. But I'll have plenty of time to make a plan on the long road north to the Huntlands. And when I come back as a count, I'll get Oriana's hand in marriage."

TERRIC - CHAPTER 35 -

Bloodgrass? Really? Terric twirled the thick reed around his hands. It just looked like red hay. It wasn't anything special. And the bag of seeds wasn't either. Did Jax get confused and think that Terric liked gardening for some reason? Even if Terric did like gardening, the gift still would have been awful. No self- respecting gardener would want to plant a bunch of red grass.

Why couldn't Jax have given *him* the book of tales? Why had he given that to Selina? Even Marcus' tunic or Nesta's mirror would have been better than grass. At least the mirror had an interesting face carved into the back.

Then an idea struck Terric. What if Jax did it on purpose? What if he gave the book to Selina so that Terric would have to steal it? What if this was all just a test to see if Terric would be a worthy travel companion, or if he was a boring little boy who deserved to spend the rest of his days locked up in a temple keeping records and making copies of the Book of Arwin?

It seemed a bit farfetched, but Terric decided it was the truth. This was a test.

He didn't hesitate to climb out the window and begin scaling the walls.

But instead of going to Selina's room, he soon found himself at the steam vent above the bathhouse. He had seen Bella in line to bathe on his way up to bed. This was Terric's chance to see her one last time.

He held his breath as he slowly peered into the vent.

And there she was. Bella. Sitting in the bath completely naked. The water obscured her figure, but the tops of her breasts were visible just over the waterline. She reached up and ran her hand through her long dark hair, then she lifted one of her smooth legs out of the water and leaned forward to scrub it.

Yes!

But then there was a light knock on the door. Bella jumped back and covered her breasts. "Who is it?"

The door creaked open.

"Excuse me, Bella," said a familiar voice. "Can I please have the bathhouse to myself for a bit?"

This is it! Bella was finally going to get out of the water.

"Yes, m'lady," said Bella. "Just one moment." Bella leaned back to wet her hair once more. As she leaned back, her breasts were almost visible. But not quite.

Come on. Come on!

Finally, Bella stood.

Terric wished he could freeze time. He wished he could look at her forever. At her beautiful face. At her long dark hair. At the water dripping down the contours of her body. And especially at her full breasts and the little droplets of water on them that shimmered in the candlelight. She was magnificent. It was even better than Terric had remembered.

For one moment, everything was perfect in Terric's life. And then Bella wrapped a towel around her body and walked out of sight.

Terric tried to hang onto the feeling he felt when he saw Bella, but it was fleeting. Was this the last time he'd ever see her? Would it be possible to find a woman who could match her beauty? If only he had more time. If his stupid father hadn't moved up his vows, maybe he would have been able to convince her to run away with him.

But there was no more time. There was only a day and a half until his vows. He had already missed an opportunity to escape today because he wanted to hear Jax's stories. But tomorrow had to be the day. It didn't matter if he could convince Jax to take him away on an adventure or if Warin would come or if he had to go alone. One way or another, he had to escape.

Maybe in the meantime he should watch this other woman bathe, though... He'd recognized her voice. Who had it been? One of the scullery maids, perhaps. None of them were even close to being as beautiful as Bella, but a few of them weren't half bad.

Terric circled around the vent to get a better view of the door. But when his mother entered, he ducked away from the window so fast that he lost his footing. He just barely caught himself before he would have slid off the roof entirely.

Gross! Terric said a quick prayer to Arwin to thank him for the fact that Isolda had still been fully clothed. Seeing his mother naked might have ruined the female form for him forever. At the end of the prayer, he asked for forgiveness for spying on Bella:

"I'm sorry, Lord Arwin, for spying on Bella. But you're a man, right? You must understand the urge to look at beautiful women. Or are you like your priests? Do you not like women?" Terric shook his head. His prayer was getting off topic. "Please, Lord Arwin. Don't make me fall to my death. And please help me escape tomorrow. With Jax, if possible. But I guess you know the best path for me. Or something like that."

Terric opened his eyes and started to climb away from the bathhouse. But then he heard another voice. This time it wasn't Isolda's. It was high, but not quite a woman's voice. *Tobias! Wait. What is Tobias doing talking to my mother in the bathhouse?*

Terric didn't dare crawl back to the vent out of fear of what he might witness. Instead, he pressed his ear to the roof.

"Foreman Owen was found dead," said Axion Tobias. "Killed in his own bed." Tobias began giving more details, but vultures squawking on a nearby tower drowned out his voice. Terric quickly found a rock to throw at the birds. They squawked again and flew off.

Terric crawled a bit closer to the vent and pressed his ear to the roof again.

"And what of the men I described?" asked Isolda.

"I don't know if you're going to like the answer," said Tobias.

"They didn't recognize them?"

"No...the opposite, actually. The girls knew exactly who I was talking about. They remembered them perfectly. Two of Garrion's soldiers."

"You're certain?" asked Isolda. Terric had never heard her take such a serious tone.

"Yes. I made sure of it. I asked them again and again for details. The girls even saw their patches."

"No," muttered Isolda. Terric heard a retching noise and then a big splash. Had Isolda just thrown up in the bath? That would be an awfully rude surprise for the next bather.

"I'm afraid so, my lady," said Tobias. "The girls were sure."

"So that's it then," said Isolda. She sounded broken. "Garrion...Garrion murdered my father."

Terric gasped and clapped his hand over his mouth. He shouldn't have been surprised, though. It all made sense. The tipped lances were already proof that Garrion was willing to take a life to get what he wanted. It seemed like Terric was learning some new horrible secret about his father every day, but this was surely the worst.

"What should we do, my lady?" asked Tobias. "Reavus is here. If we tell him everything, surely he'll arrest him for treason. Garrion wouldn't dare fight back. Not when the Blacksmiths are here."

"We don't do anything yet. Not until the appraiser confirms it's real. And even then, we'll have to take steps to protect the children. I pray that Reavus has changed, but we would be fools to not remember what he did to the Hyposas - to their entire city - when Julian was charged with treason."

"Perhaps I should leave the city before you bring any charges," said Tobias. "Just in case."

"That might be wise. But we should make no plans until the appraisers confirm our suspicions. Until then, we must act natural."

Terric could hear footsteps on the stone floor and then the bathhouse door opened and closed. Isolda and Tobias were gone. Terric was still trying to process what they had said.

Garrion had murdered Isolda's father. Garrion had murdered King Bogdan!

Maybe this was Terric's punishment for spying on Bella. Arwin had cursed him with the worst father imaginable.

Terric suddenly felt exhausted. It was too much to process. He didn't have the energy to steal Selina's book. He didn't have the energy to do anything. He just wanted to sleep. And in the morning, he'd escape and never see his wretched father again.

- CHAPTER 36 -
RIXIN

Rixin waved to the adoring crowd as the Blacksmiths escorted him to the arena. The spectators were all screaming his name. A number of them waved red and white checked banners. A few particularly enthusiastic fans had even made leather bat masks to wear in his honor.

Eighteen wins. Zero losses.

That was Rixin's record in tournaments since he had begun jousting three years ago.

Yes, there had been a few close calls. He'd even almost been unhorsed once. But he overcame it all. He simply didn't lose.

Would this tournament be any different?

It was already a little different. It was the first time since his first tournament that he wasn't heading into it as the favorite. The fools at the gambling houses thought Marcus was the second coming of Arwin. Rixin laughed at the thought. Marcus was decent, but he was no match for Rixin. And Ngolo Mobek, the projected third-place finisher, was talented, but Rixin had already beaten him in the previous two jousts.

If Rixin wanted to, he was confident he could win the tournament.

But did he want to?

For the glory, yes. For the title, yes. For the ability to conquer Rashid once and for all, yes.

There was more to it than that, though. Uncle Garrion had made sure of that. His offer was simple, really. In a way, it was the simplest thing he could have asked for. All he had to do was lose the tournament, and Oriana would be his. It required no skill of any kind. And yet, it was the most difficult decision he'd ever made. So difficult, in fact, that he had yet to make up his mind.

Before he knew it, Rixin had arrived at the tourney grounds. His fans shouted a few final words of encouragement as he slipped into the underbelly of the gigantic stone arena. It was bigger than any arena he'd competed in before.

As per his usual pre-tournament ritual, Rixin methodically checked his bowstrings, selected the straightest arrows, and personally polished his armor. Nigel could have done all of that, of course, but the routine helped Rixin focus. It helped him shut out all the noise and the excitement. Only today, it didn't work. He couldn't banish the thoughts of Ori from his mind.

Rixin threw the bow down and paced around the room. He considered running up to the stands above to talk to Oriana. He needed more time with her in order to make the right decision. Maybe that would clear his mind.

"My lord," said Nigel. "You're next. Are you all set?" He looked past Rixin into the room. The armor was half polished and all the arrows were scattered on the floor.

"Yeah, almost. Help me grab some arrows."

Rixin and his squire quickly gathered some arrows into a quiver and then headed for the arena entrance. The noise of the crowd coming through the gate ahead was like nothing Rixin had ever experienced. Even the battles where he'd fought at Reavus' side hadn't been *this* loud.

"Lords and ladies," began the bard in the center of the arena. "It is my distinct pleasure to introduce to you... the Crown Prince of Treland, Duke of Arwood, Blood of Arwin, Distinguished Knight of the Order of Chains, Defender of the Wood, the undefeated, the Shadow Prince. His Royal Highness, Rixin of House Talenov!"

Rixin burst through the gate and the cheers grew even louder. All around him, thousands of people stood cheering. But Rixin only had eyes for one person in the crowd. Oriana.

She was easy to spot near Arwin's Voice, Reavus, Garrion, and the other Hornbolts. Her bright golden hair stood out like the sun in the sky, but what really made her stand out was the fact that she was hardly clapping. Nesta was jumping up and down on the chair next to her. Why wasn't Ori as excited to see him?

He'd have to deal with that later. For now, he needed to focus on archery. It would have been easy to just miss the target with all ten shots and then go tell Ori that they were to be married, but he couldn't do it. Not yet. Not after she hardly clapped for him. Not until he had more time to figure out what he truly wanted.

If he was going to lose, he was at least going to make it to the joust.

He pulled back the bowstring and let his first arrow fly. Bulls-eye. Then another, and another. Nine in total. One arrow left.

And still no reaction from Oriana.

To have a little fun, he tore off part of his tunic and tied it over his eyes before firing the final arrow. By the eruption of cheers, he was sure he'd hit the tenth and final bulls-eye. Or accidentally killed someone in the stands.

He untied the blindfold to confirm that he'd hit a bulls-eye rather than committed murder. Sure enough, the arrow had stuck right in the middle of the target.

How's that, Ori?

He glanced up to see her reaction, but she wasn't there. She had disappeared from her seat. He scanned the crowd to see her making her way through the stands.

"Where's Oriana going?" Rixin asked Nigel.

"It appears she's leaving," said the squire. "Perhaps she's feeling ill again. Shall I fetch her for you?"

"No, that won't be necessary." Rixin handed his bow to Nigel and ran towards her. There were no stairs up from the arena grounds, so he had to go through a set of arches to the hallways under the stands. He bumped into her near an exit.

She fell into his waiting arms, much like she had in the stairwell. But this time he had collided with her on purpose. He needed to feel their chemistry. He needed to know if it was more than just attraction. And what better way than to have her in his arms?

He did feel it. His heart rate accelerated. His fingers itched to slide down her curves. All he could focus on was how his body was reacting to hers being so close. He had never felt such an instant connection with anyone before.

"I'm so sorry," she stammered. "I…" her voice died away when she realized it was him. She cleared her throat and pulled away far too soon, smoothing out the skirt of her dress. "Your Highness," she said with a bow. "If you'll excuse me."

"Rixin," he corrected. He had asked her once before. And right now, he needed to get past formalities. She didn't realize it, but he was running out of time to make up his mind.

"Right. Rixin. I really must be going." She started to walk away.

Had she really not felt what he just had? "Oriana," Rixin said as he caught her wrist in his hand.

She looked down at his hand like it offended her.

Rixin immediately released her from his grip. *She still seems cross with me. Is she still upset because I missed supper?* He needed to clear the air so they could have a real conversation. "I truly am sorry about the other day, Oriana. Your brother refused to stop practicing to attend supper. It wasn't my intention to stand you up. Trust me, I would have rather been with you than with him. I've been looking forward to nothing else since I arrived." Rixin glanced over his shoulder. Through the columns, he could see that Marcus was next in the archery portion of the competition. And he was currently staring daggers at Rixin and Oriana. Rixin frowned and turned back to Oriana. She was almost giving him the same expression. What was wrong with the Hornbolts? It was like every one of them had forgotten he was their prince.

"Rixin, I've already forgiven you. Really, it doesn't matter."

"Then tell me what's bothering you."

She finally made eye contact with him. "It doesn't concern you."

"It does concern me." He was surprised when the words tumbled out of his mouth. Because he cared. He didn't want to see her upset. He loved her smiles, not her frowns. "Tell me. Maybe I can help."

She opened her mouth but then immediately closed it again. "I'm sorry for cutting this conversation short, but I'm feeling ill. Congratulations on taking the lead in the tournament. But my brother is certainly about to surpass you."

He was trying to be nice and *that* was the reaction he got? *What happened to the girl who blushed at everything I said?* He remembered Oriana being sweet as a child. And completely smitten with him. She seemed to be exactly the same the other day when he ran into her. So he hadn't been anticipating Oriana stomping on his advances. For some reason, it made him want her even more. "Please stay," said Rixin. What was he, a common beggar? "The tournament has barely begun. And…I want you to stay."

Oriana turned her face back to his. "Like I said, I'm just not feeling well. And I'm sure there are plenty of other women here that would love to spend the rest of the day celebrating your perfect score."

Yes, he definitely liked this bolder side of her. His whole life everyone had always catered to him. He wasn't used to being denied what he wanted. And he wasn't going to lose her. Besides, now he at least knew that she had been watching him. He had landed all of his arrows directly in the bulls-eye. "You look absolutely stunning," he said. "Especially for someone who doesn't feel well." He gave her his most seductive smile and lightly touched her collarbone.

Oriana looked down. The expression on her face changed from a frown to one of pain. "I really must be going. Good luck in the rest of the tournament." Oriana turned away from him.

"Are you not planning on watching?"

"Maybe if I feel better. Good day." She started walking away again.

"I'm declaring you in the joust," Rixin said from behind her.

She slowly turned around. "And why in Arwin's name would you do that? I'm not a fool, Rixin." She stepped back toward him. "You're practically betrothed to Navya. Do you really think I haven't heard the rumors?"

"I'm not betrothed to anyone." But the longer he spoke to her, the clearer it was to him that he wanted to be betrothed to her.

"Fine. Which means you're not betrothed to me either." She poked Rixin in the middle of the chest. "And I'm not going to stand here and pretend..."

Rixin grabbed her waist and pulled her in close.

"What are you doing?" The sultry tone of Oriana's voice was gone. And Rixin was very aware of the fact that her chest was rising and falling rapidly with her breath, as it pushed her breasts against him.

"Showing you that it's not pretend." Rixin tilted his head down and placed his lips against hers.

She immediately put her hands on his chest like she was going to push him off. And for just a moment, he thought she might pull away. But then her fingers slowly ran up his shoulder and behind his neck.

Rixin pressed his hand firmly against her lower back as he deepened the kiss. He smiled at the soft moan that escaped her lips. He wanted to hear that sound over and over again. He didn't care what her father had said. He didn't care what his father wanted. Because this? This feeling was worth fighting for. He relished the feeling of her body melting into his. And the taste of her lips. The smell of her skin. She felt it too. He knew she did. Whatever this was between them was real.

She pulled away far too soon, panting, with stars in her eyes. "Rixin."

"Oriana." He wanted to kiss her again. Out of the corner of his eye, he saw Marcus' arrow land nowhere near the bullseye. Clearly Rixin kissing Oriana was upsetting Marcus. Two pros and no cons in sight. He leaned forward again.

She blushed and looked down at their connected bodies, leaving Rixin to kiss her forehead. But he didn't mind. For just a moment, they stayed perfectly still.

"We can't." She slowly removed her hand from the back of his neck. "That doesn't...this doesn't..." her voice trailed off. "You shouldn't have done that. It changes nothing."

Her breaths were sweet. Her protests completely lost on him. In his mind, she was already his. "It changes everything."

She shook her head. "Declare me in the joust if you want. If you even make it."

In Arwin's name, I'm going to marry this girl. "I'm going to make it."

"We'll see. But as for you and me beyond this moment? Your father wants you to marry Princess Navya. And I'm not interested in being a consolation prize. I deserve more than that. I want someone to look at me like I'm the only woman in the room." Her eyes had suddenly gotten teary. "So this," she said and gestured back and forth between them, "isn't going to happen again. This is the end of our story. Now would you please remove your hands from me?"

"I don't accept that." He let his hand slip down her waist, leaving it dangerously close to being quite inappropriate.

"Rixin, ever since we were children, you haven't liked me. You don't think I saw how you looked at everyone else besides me? With my chubby cheeks. And my dolls." She rolled her eyes at herself. "I had the biggest crush on you. But we're not kids anymore. Besides, it's not like you're the only one trying to win my heart. I'm not some pathetic girl anymore. I have hopes and dreams outside of you. And I just really need you to remove your hands because I can't think when you're doing that."

Who else is trying to win her over? Rixin tried to focus on what she had said. Her rambling was back. The cute side of her. The one that he always liked in the first place. She was everything he wanted. The whole package. And he wasn't about to lose her to someone else when it was so clear that they belonged together.

But he didn't want to have to throw the joust. There had to be another way.

She somehow managed to slide out of his arms. "Good day, Rixin."

This time he let her go, because his mind couldn't be any more clear about her. He was vaguely aware of the fact that his heart was beating faster than it ever did during a sword fight or a joust. He watched her disappear out of the arena.

He was going to propose to Oriana Hornbolt. Right after he figured out what to do about the tournament.

And he didn't just want her to say yes. He needed her to say yes.

RAZORTOOTH
TIGER

- CHAPTER 37 -
TERRIC

The tournament was even better than Terric had imagined. He was accustomed to seeing swordfights in the courtyard between Marcus and the other squires, but this was different. These were real knights, fighting with real swords and axes and spears. Prince Rixin had scored highest in the archery competition that morning, so the first fight of the afternoon featured him against Sir Bertram, a lowly knight from Port Claudius dressed in dull armor that looked more like it belonged in a reliquary than on a tourney ground. The fight could not have been any more mismatched, and Terric immediately understood how Prince Rixin had earned the nickname the Shadow Prince. It was as if Rixin knew every move Sir Bertram's would make a full second before it occurred. Sir Bertram would put all of his strength into a lunge, but his sword would find only air. No matter what he tried, it failed. Eventually Rixin grew tired of dancing and brought the knight to his knees with a single blow. Arwin's Voice immediately raised his jewel covered hands to put an end to the fight.

Rixin raised his visor and waved at the adoring crowd. The prince's gaze seemed to linger on one particular person in the stands. Terric turned to see who it was. It appeared to either be Oriana or Navya. He couldn't imagine why Rixin would be interested in either of them, though. Oriana was gross, and Navya was definitely worse.

Terric also couldn't help but notice that Sir Aldric was still not present at the arena. He had been missing all morning. During the break between the archery and hand-to-hand combat portions of the tournament, Terric had tried to eavesdrop to determine the nature of Aldric's absence, but nothing had been said. Most of the conversation he heard was focused on the tournament. There was talk of Rixin's perfect score in archery, and how he had even taken a shot blindfolded, but most of the discussion was focused on who would win their hand-to-hand combat bouts to advance to the joust. Only four knights could advance. Three spots were expected to belong to Prince Rixin, Marcus, and Sir Ngolo Mobek, but there was no clear favorite for the fourth.

The only thing he heard that could have possibly related to Aldric's absence was a brief mention about how the number of men patrolling the savanna had been tripled for the tournament. He hoped that meant Sir Aldric was in the savanna too, but either way, Terric was prepared to go ahead with his plan. He just had to wait for Marcus to be introduced to ensure that his whole family would be focused on the tournament rather than Terric's sudden disappearance.

Or maybe he was just procrastinating so that he'd get to watch more fights.

"Fresh turkey legs!" called a nearby vendor walking up and down the stands.

Terric waved him over and purchased two. Then he leaned back and enjoyed the action unfolding below.

The other fights of the afternoon turned out to be even better than Rixin's, as they were at least competitive. One man lost a hand due to a faulty gauntlet, and another was almost killed when his opponent ignored Arwin's Voice. It took four knights to stop him. He was disqualified for his unchivalrous behavior.

Then it was time for Marcus' introduction. The crowd cheered wildly for the city's favorite son, but not quite as loud as they had cheered for the shadow prince.

Terric couldn't help but wish that it was him out there instead of Marcus. He wanted to have the crowd cheering for him. He wanted to feel the thrill of a real swordfight. And he would soon, but first he had to get as far away from his cursed father as possible.

The matchups for the hand-to-hand combat were determined by archery scores, and as fate would have it, that meant that Marcus was set to fight his best friend, Peter Harlow. Marcus pressed hard early in the fight, raining heavy blows down on Peter. His problem was that he was too predictable, especially after the two had practiced together so frequently. Peter appeared quite prepared for the onslaught. It didn't matter, though, Terric suspected. He had seen Marcus' tipped lances in the armory. He had to assume that his brother had some other trick up his sleeve to ensure that he'd make it to the joust, even if it was at the expense of Peter.

Either way, Terric didn't care to stick around to see what it was. Garrion and Isolda and everyone else in their section of the stands had their eyes fixed on Marcus, which gave Terric the perfect opportunity to slip out undetected.

Before he stepped out of the stands, he glanced back one last time at his family. Would he ever see them again? He could do without Oriana and her stupid dresses, and Selina always tattling on him, but he would miss little Nesta. And he would miss his mum, even if she didn't care enough about him to keep him from being a priest. But he would certainly not miss his cheating, lying, murderous father. Maybe someday, once he was the greatest knight in the realm, he could come back and save his mum and Nesta from the rest of his miserable family.

He turned away and pushed through the throng of people trying to get past the guards into the arena. He didn't stop walking until he was at the East Gate.

"Terric," whispered someone behind him.

He turned and saw Warin with a cloak pulled down over his eyes. Warin handed him a cloak of his own and the big leather sack that he had packed early that morning.

"You sure you want to do this with me?" Terric asked.

Warin hesitated for a second and then nodded. "I'll miss my mum," he said.

"I know," said Terric. "But just think how proud she'll be of you. You're going to be a knight!"

Warin mustered a half smile. "Yeah, you're right. Can I come back for her one day?"

"Of course. We can plan it all out. But first we should get going. Have you seen Sir Aldric?"

"This morning. He and a dozen guards took horses. Had them saddled up for the savanna. Going on a patrol, I reckon."

Terric smiled. He couldn't have asked for better luck.

They walked for hours, but Terric's legs didn't feel the least bit tired. He seemed to get more energy the further they got from Arwin's Gate, as if the chains of Arwin were being lifted from his shoulders.

"Are you sure this is a good idea?" asked Warin.

"Yes," replied Terric. "With our sealed letters from Prince Rixin, no knight in the realm will refuse to take us as squires. We can take our pick."

"I don't mean that part of it. I mean...it's starting to get dark. I've never been this far from Arwin's Gate before. Have you?"

Terric looked around. At first everything had been so familiar. He had been to the manor houses and temples surrounding Arwin's Gate many times with his father. But now they had been walking the better part of the day, and he was far from home. The familiar farms had been replaced by untamed savanna grass. It seemed to get longer with every step they took. In fact, it had gotten so long that Terric would have had to sit on Warin's shoulders to see anything off the path. A few hours ago they had hidden every time someone passed out of fear that they'd be recognized and sent back to the castle. But now Terric longed to see another face on the path. Or did he? They could easily encounter a robber. Sir Aldric's patrols kept the road safe near the city, but this far out...did the patrols go this far out?

"Of course I've been this far," said Terric. He pulled out the map and squinted to make out the writing in the fading light. He tried to find landmarks he recognized, but the only thing marked on the Grass Road anywhere close to Arwin's Gate was Fort Orenga. He held his finger up to the map and calculated the fort was three hours travel away from the city. And they had been walking for about that long. *Thank you, Axion Tobias.*

"Why are you looking at your map if you've been this far?"

"Just wanted to check to see exactly how far Fort..." Terric glanced back at the map to get the name right, "...Fort Orenga is from the city."

"And?" asked Warin.

"It should be just up ahead."

"Then why aren't we seeing anyone on the path?"

"Who would waste their time at Fort Orenga when they could travel half a day and see the biggest tournament of the last decade?"

"Us, I guess," said Warin.

"You'd rather go back to Arwin's Gate and see me become a priest? I wouldn't want to go back even if I didn't have to take that oath. I never want to see my father again."

"You really think he killed King Bogdan?"

"I heard my mum say that he did. And you saw the tipped lances. Killing King Bogdan wasn't enough. Now he wants Marcus to kill Prince Rixin too."

"Maybe we should go back and tell someone."

Terric shook his head. "I can't go back there. Not until I'm a knight."

"I think we made a mistake. If we go back now, no one might have even noticed that we left. We'll wake up in the morning and everything will be normal."

"Except it won't. I'll be forced to take the oath of Arwin."

"Can't you just refuse? To take an oath, you have to say the words."

It was an interesting point. But Terric quickly rejected the idea. His father would probably just have him beheaded if he wouldn't take the oath. "Someday when you're a knight, you'll thank me for this."

"If we survive the night," said Warin. A rustling in the grass made him jump. "What was that?"

"Must have been the wind. Either way, an aspiring knight shouldn't be unmanned by a sound in the dark. No beast or highwayman would dare attack Sir Wilmarc and Sir Oleg." Terric made a point to not even look at where the sound had come from.

"No, they wouldn't. But we're not them. We're just Warin and Terric. We're not even sirs yet!"

The two boys continued in silence for some time. The shadows of the tall grasses grew longer until the sun had disappeared completely and darkness settled on the endless fields. Warin kept looking over his shoulder, but Terric stayed focused on the path ahead.

Suddenly Warin stopped and gripped his sword. Terric could see pure fear in his eyes.

"What?" whispered Terric. His eyes followed Warin's stare. For a split second, he thought he saw something slinking through the grass, but then it was gone.

"Did you see that?" asked Warin.

"Probably just a trick of the light," said Terric. He tried to sound brave, but his voice cracked halfway through. "We should keep moving."

Terric's hand didn't leave the hilt of his sword the rest of the walk.

***

Fort Orenga wasn't at all what Terric had expected. He'd thought he'd hear and see and smell it from a mile away...candlelight in the windows, the smell of freshly baked bread from the kitchen. But none of that was present. In fact, they might have walked right by it if Warin hadn't run off the path screaming because he thought he saw a razortooth tiger. They didn't bother to knock on the gate. Terric just started climbing the dilapidated stone of the curtain wall and beckoned for Warin to follow.

Warin was entirely out of breath by the time they reached the top of the wall, so Terric offered to take first watch. He sat on the edge and looked out at the courtyard while Warin curled up on some foliage that had taken root in the cracked stone.

My first night of freedom, thought Terric. He had really done it. He had really run away. This was the start of his first great adventure. He began to imagine where the path - his own path, not Arwin's - might take him. Maybe they'd meet up with a group of traveling actors. Maybe he'd rescue a beautiful damsel in distress. Maybe they'd narrowly escape death like his Uncle Jax had done so many times. *Uncle Jax.* Why had he given such wonderful gifts to Terric's siblings and only given Terric some dried grass and a bag of seeds?

Terric rummaged through his pack and found the seeds. Maybe there was more to them than met the eye. But what? Terric poured a few out and pushed them around his palm. As he did, his imagination started to run wild and his eyelids grew heavy.

- CHAPTER 38 -
BASTIAN

"Would you stop fidgeting?" whispered Bastian and punched Logan's arm to silence him.

Logan rubbed his arm. "Eh, then stop pushing me off the path."

"You're the one that said you wanted to come, so stop complaining. We've barely even made a dent in the journey." Bastian pushed aside some of the tall grasses and peered back out at the path. The shadows of the two boys had disappeared.

Nut jumped off his shoulder and walked back onto the path.

"Yeah, we've barely walked at all. So what are we doing taking a break already? Maybe some scorpium would give us more energy." Logan scratched the inside of his wrist.

So that was why Logan was still with him. He just wanted more scorpium. Bastian had thought Logan was being a good friend. "We're not taking a break. I just...I swear I saw Lord Terric up ahead."

Logan laughed. "And I swear it couldn't possibly be him. What would the little prince be doing out here in the middle of the night?" He brushed past Bastian and stepped back onto the path.

"He's not a prince." Maybe Bastian could get his title back and become a count himself. *Maybe.* But he'd never be a prince. If that's what it would take to win Oriana's father's blessing, then there was no hope. He tried to shake away the thought as he rejoined Logan on the dirt path.

"Practically a prince then," Logan said. "Besides, it's not him. He wasn't traveling with any guards." He scratched his arm again. "Actually, I don't see him anymore at all. Maybe it was just a trick of the light."

"It was definitely him." Bastian squinted his eyes, trying to see in the darkness. The outline of a castle in the distance caught his attention. "Maybe they went in there," Bastian said and pointed at the structure.

"What? I don't see anything," said Logan as he started to follow Bastian.

Nut started squeaking at the castle, confirming Bastian's suspicions.

"Where else would they have disappeared to?" Bastian whispered as he stopped in front of the castle.

"Maybe they got eaten by a razortooth tiger." Logan chuckled to himself.

The thought of razortooth tigers made Bastian swallow hard. Suddenly the gauntlet felt heavy in his bag. He had skipped the meeting with Isolda. He didn't believe her threats, and he wasn't about to give up something that was worth so much for nothing in return. But what if Isolda had been serious? What if they caught him and threw him over the wall? He'd be at the mercy of the tigers.

And it wasn't just the thought of tigers that gave him pause. Ori was upset at him because she thought he was a liar.

Would Ori really want him even if he got his title back? Would it make any difference in her eyes or her father's?

He had to hope so. It was his only option.

Unless... What if he really had stumbled upon Terric trying to escape. If he caught him and brought him back, along with the gauntlet, would that be enough? It would certainly be simpler than going all the way to the Huntlands to regain his title. And the thought of being away from Ori for that long made the decision easy.

"They're going to make him take the oath of Arwin," Bastian whispered into the silent night.

"Who?" Logan asked. "The tigers?"

"No, not the tigers. Lord Terric."

Logan shook his head. "The oath of celibacy I call it. Could you even imagine that? Poor little prince."

Bastian raked his fingers through his hair instead of pointing out the fact that Terric wasn't a prince once again. "But if that was forced on you, wouldn't you run away?"

"Hm." Logan rubbed his chin with his fingers. "Now that you mention it, I probably would. So you really think it's him sneaking off?"

Bastian thought about the ring he had stolen for Terric. Terric had claimed it would help him be a squire. Maybe his plan had backfired and this was the only way out of becoming a priest. "It looked just like him. At least, as best I could see him in the dark."

"And without any guards," said Logan. "I bet the little prince is traveling with all sorts of valuables." Logan took a step toward the castle.

"We're not going to rob him," Bastian said and caught Logan's arm.

"What? Why not? I thought that's what you were contemplating this whole time. How to best sneak up on them and take their loot. That's why you kept pushing me off the path."

"No." Bastian shook his head. "I was thinking of something else." Bastian stared at the castle. There were no signs of life. No fires flickering. No sounds at all. Which wasn't surprising. Now that they were closer, he could see that the stone walls were crumbling. It looked like it hadn't been inhabited in decades.

Before Bastian had joined the Thieves Guild, he had spent many nights in old abandoned castles such as this. Of course Terric would do the same.

"Follow me," Bastian said and started toward the castle wall.

"I knew you'd change your mind."

"I'm not changing my mind. I'm going to try and convince Lord Terric to come back to Vulture Keep with me."

"But what about the gold?"

"He's just a kid. He's probably not traveling with any gold." Bastian ran his fingers along the stone, trying to see if it was possible to scale the wall.

"What prince doesn't travel with any gold?"

"For the last time, he's not a prince. Just stay here until I come back down." Nut hopped onto his shoulder right before Bastian began his ascent.

As Bastian climbed higher and higher, the sound of light snoring made him smile. There was definitely someone inside. He slowly lifted his head above the ledge.

Lord Terric was perched along the ledge with a bag in his lap. His head was drooped forward and it rose and fell with his chest. It was as if he was perched there as a lookout. But he had clearly fallen asleep.

"My lord," Bastian whispered as he sat down on the opposite end of the ledge.

Terric's eyes flew open as he jolted awake. The bag that had been on his lap tumbled over the edge of the castle, landing in the overgrown grasses below. For a moment Terric looked upset, but then he just shook his head and glanced down at something in his hand. "What are you doing here?" he finally asked.

"You owe me a favor."

Terric looked up at him. "No, I don't." He tossed whatever was in his hand out into the night air. "I don't owe anyone anything. I'm making my own decisions now." He puffed out his chest slightly.

"I saved your life, my lord. And then I stole the prince's ring for you. All you did was show me Ori's room, which I could have found on my own. That's two for one. Not two for two."

"I helped you break into Vulture Keep, the most secure castle for miles. That should count for more than one."

"Then stealing the prince's ring should count as ten."

Terric laughed. "That was pretty awesome."

Bastian didn't find this conversation funny. "I'm cashing in on the favor you owe me. I need you to come back with me to Vulture Keep."

"What? No." Terric hopped off the ledge, moving away from Bastian. "I can't go back, Bastian. I can't be a priest. I have a letter with Prince Rixin's seal saying I should be taken on as a squire. If I go back, I'll never get to be a knight."

So that's what he did with the prince's ring. "It's not very knightly of you to go back on your word." Besides, stealing the prince's ring was part of the reason Ori didn't trust Bastian. Terric owed him this.

Terric pressed his lips together. "I'm not a knight yet. Once I am, I'll grant you anything you want. Maybe you can even be my master of spies."

"I don't have time to wait for that. And what's so great about being a knight anyway? Riding into battle to die for a cause you don't believe in? Playing with swords?"

"And being a member of the Thieves Guild is so great?"

Not if it's what's keeping me from having Ori. "Yes. Maybe being a knight sounds prestigious to you. But it's not so different from my own life. Knights train. I trained. Knights perfect their skills. So did I. Knights have horses. I have a squirrel."

That got a smile from Terric.

Nut hopped off Bastian's shoulder and approached him. Terric lightly patted his back.

"It's the life I chose," Bastian added. *It's the life that was forced upon me.*

Terric stopped petting Nut. "And I'm choosing to be a knight."

"Okay. If being a knight is the life you want, I'll help you escape again. You have my word. But I need you to come back with me now." He tried to hide the desperation in his voice.

Terric didn't respond.

"I'm going to be banished."

Terric took a step back. "Why?"

"Because I'm a thief. I have no title. My word means nothing. But your word? You're practically a prince." The words Logan had been saying all evening left a bad taste in his mouth. "You can get your father to see me in better favor. You can get the charges reversed." *You can help me get Ori's hand in marriage.* The plan started to solidify in Bastian's head. "You'll tell your parents that you were kidnapped and I saved your life."

Terric stared at Bastian. "My father is a disgusting, vile, horrible, rhino's rump." Terric immediately nodded his head, agreeing with his own statement wholeheartedly. "I can't go back. I'm sorry, but I just can't. I can't be a priest."

"I'm not asking you to be. You have my word, Terric. I'll help you escape again." Terric had taken another step back, so Bastian took a step closer. "Please, Terric."

"You just said your word means nothing."

"And *you* just said I'd make a great master of spies. If I can steal a ring off Prince Rixin's finger, surely I can smuggle you out of the city. Hell, you already did it once without my help."

Terric's eyes glanced to the right of Bastian. At the exact same time, Nut started chirping like mad. Before Bastian could turn to see what they were both looking at, he felt something hard hit the back of his head.

Bastian stumbled forward slightly. "What in the name of..." Bastian put his hand on the back of his head and looked down at the child beside him.

The boy was holding a huge piece of lumber. He lifted it up again like he was going to strike Bastian with it a second time.

"Don't even think about it," Bastian said and continued to rub the back of his head.

The boy shrugged his shoulders and dropped the lumber back on the floor. "I'm no good at this sneaking away thing, Terric. I couldn't even knock out this intruder."

"Warin, you only tried one time!" Terric protested. "If you swung it again, you'd surely knock him out."

Warin looked down at the piece of wood. "No, I don't think so. Besides, he doesn't seem dangerous."

Bastian would have been insulted, but he was just relieved the boy wasn't hitting him again.

"He even has a cute pet," said Warin. Nut had hopped back onto Bastian's shoulder. He put his little paws on the back of Bastian's head like he was inspecting it for damage.

"He's a member of the Thieves Guild!" said Terric. "He's very dangerous. Hit him again, Warin!"

Nut looked at Terric and squeaked angrily.

"But he said he'd take us back to Vulture Keep," said Warin. "That doesn't sound very dangerous. It sounds like a good plan if I ever heard one. He's not trying to murder us. He's trying to help us."

Bastian opened his mouth and then closed it again. This kid was making his argument for him.

"I can't go back, I'll..."

"Terric," Warin said, cutting him off. "I miss my mum. I just want to go home."

Terric looked back and forth between Warin and Bastian. "If he takes us back to Vulture Keep, you'll get in trouble, Warin."

"Oh. Right." He looked up at Bastian. "Could you maybe just take me to the outskirts of the castle? I just want to go home," he repeated. "I don't want to be...banished."

Bastian smiled and stuck out his hand. "You have my word, Warin. No one will know what happened tonight."

Warin immediately shook his hand.

"It's the word of a thief, Warin," Terric said. "You can't trust him."

"I've never lied to you," Bastian said. "But you've lied to me. You said you were taking me to Ori's room when really you led me right to Prince Rixin's."

Terric sighed. "If I come back with you, you swear you'll help me escape again?"

"I swear it."

"On your mother's life?"

Bastian lowered his eyebrows. "My mother is dead."

"On your father's life?"

He swallowed hard. "My father is dead."

Terric stared right at him. "On Ori's life then?"

Bastian stuck out his hand. "I swear it on Ori's life."

"Okay, let's go then." Terric walked back over to the ledge and hopped up while Warin scrambled to gather their belongings.

"Just like that?" Bastian asked. After all the arguing, he thought for sure Terric would ask for more than an escape. He'd expected to be bartering until dawn.

"Well, if I went against my word I wouldn't be very knightly." He gave Bastian a small smile. "And you heard Warin. He's scared. He misses his mum. And he just wants to go home. What kind of friend would I be if I didn't help him go back?"

Bastian smiled. "It has nothing to do with the fact that it's actually scary out here at night? Or that you miss *your* mum? Or that you want to go home?"

"No, I'm a grown up just like you. Why? Do *you* think it's scary?" Terric asked.

"Of course. Anyone could sneak up on you in the night without you seeing. You're lucky it was me and not someone else."

"Oh. Now that you mention it, I guess it is a little scary out here at night. Just a little. A very little. I definitely hadn't noticed it before, though."

ISOLDA
- CHAPTER 39 -

Where are you? thought Isolda as she looked under Terric's bed. He wasn't there, though. He wasn't anywhere. She had been looking for hours. The guards had been looking for almost as long. Garrion had spent much of the night searching outside the city walls. But Terric was nowhere to be found.

For the first time in her life, Isolda found herself wishing that Sir Aldric were there. Maybe his creepy, watchful eyes were more useful than she had realized. Surely Aldric would have been able to find Terric, but alas, he was still on duty patrolling the savanna. He would likely be out there until the tournament was over and all the lords were headed safely back to their castles.

If only her Terric were safe. *Of course he's safe,* she told herself. He was the son of a duke. People didn't kill sons of dukes. They kidnapped them and asked for ransom.

So why had no ransom note come?

Earlier today when Bastian hadn't shown up for their meeting, she'd wondered how her day could possibly get any worse. Now she had that answer: Terric could go missing.

But she'd find him, wouldn't she? There had to be a clue around here somewhere. She looked under the bed again and started pulling out all the toys - the building blocks, the wooden swords. Even a toy bow. *Or is that a real bow?* And then a crumpled piece of paper caught her eye.

She opened it up and read the letter.

My Lord,

I have traveled across Pentavia, from the frozen wastes of Fjorkia to the scorched sands of Rashid, and I have never in my life encountered as fine a man as Oleg. Master swordsman, horse whisperer, and poet. Those words only scratch the surface of this young man's ability...

What is this? thought Isolda. She quickly scanned to the bottom. In her worry for Terric, she took it at face value. It was a letter of recommendation from Prince Rixin for Terric to become a squire.

But then, even in her hysterics at the loss of her son, Isolda saw the truth of it. It was clearly written by Terric himself.

Suddenly, it all made sense.

Isolda thought back to Rixin's missing signet ring. *Of course.* Terric had stolen the ring, forged a letter of recommendation, and then, the day before Garrion was going to force him to take the oath of Arwin, Terric ran away.

It was all Garrion's fault. Just like her father's murder. Thinking about Garrion made her feel nauseous. She gripped the side of the bed. Was Garrion trying to take everything from her? Were her other children in danger too? She shook the thought away. *No.* Despite the growing evidence that he had killed her father, she had no reason to think he'd harm their children. He was a great father. *But I thought he was an honest husband too.*

She swallowed down the lump in her throat. She was partially responsible too. Couldn't she have tried harder to convince Garrion to delay the oath? Maybe she would have if she hadn't been so focused on finding the body of Arwin.

Now the body and her son had both slipped through her fingers.

"My lady," said Tobias from the door. The expression on his face was the same as when he had delivered the news about Garrion's men being the ones who took the body.

"You couldn't find him?" asked Isolda.

Tobias looked down and shook his head. "No. None of your girls had heard anything about him."

Isolda gripped a chair to steady herself. She hadn't realized until just now how much she had been relying on the thought that her girls would have seen something.

"But Terric did just arrive at the front gate," Tobias smiled behind his thick spectacles as if he had just played a great prank on her.

Tears of relief pooled in Isolda's eyes. "Really? He's back? He's safe?"

Tobias nodded.

"What's wrong with you? Why would you not lead with that information? And that distressed look on your face...You almost made me faint!"

"I'm sorry...I thought it would be more exciting if I told you that way. I've always wanted to have a big dramatic moment like that."

Isolda ignored him. "Where is he?"

"He's waiting at the gate for you. Along with the man who brought him back."

"Man who brought him back?" asked Isolda. She didn't wait for Tobias to answer. She was already halfway to the front gate by the time he could start to respond.

***

Isolda rushed over to Terric and scooped him up in her arms. Tears streamed down her cheeks as she hugged him. And hugged him. And hugged him some more. She never wanted to let go.

"I'm sorry," she said. "I'm so so sorry. We should never have made you feel like you needed to run away..."

"What?" asked Terric. "I didn't run away, mum. I was kidnapped."

"Kidnapped?" gasped Isolda. She released her hug and stood back to get a good look at him. "Were you hurt?"

"No. No, I wasn't hurt. Bastian saved me."

"*Bastian?*" asked Isolda.

"Yeah. You should have seen him. He killed all the kidnappers and brought me back safely."

"How many were there?"

"Uh..." started Terric. "I didn't really see them all. It was dark. A bunch, I guess."

"A bunch? How did Bastian overpower a bunch of kidnappers?"

"Maybe it was only like, four."

"Sure it was," said Isolda. She eyed her son suspiciously.

"It was! You should have seen them. They all had swords and dreadlocks. But Bastian killed them all."

Isolda stifled a laugh. The more Terric talked, the more obvious it was that he was lying. But he could lie all he wanted as long as he didn't run away again.

"I see," said Isolda. I better go talk to our hero, then. I believe a reward is in order."

"Yeah. He definitely deserves a reward. We should probably let him marry Oriana. It only seems fair. I mean, she's gross and all, but if he's into that..."

"I'll make sure he's properly rewarded. While I do that, Tobias will take you to bed. You must be exhausted after this whole kidnapping ordeal." Isolda ruffled his shaggy blonde hair. "Before you go to bed though, know that I'll make sure you don't have to take the oath."

Terric's eyes lit up. "Really?" Then he frowned. "How can you say that, though? I thought it was up to Father."

"It is, ultimately. But I'll talk to him. I'll do everything I can to convince him."

Terric hugged Isolda harder than he'd ever hugged her before. "I love you, Mum."

Isolda hugged him back. "I love you too, sweet boy." *I just hope I can actually convince Garrion.* "Now get some rest."

Isolda turned her attention to Bastian. He was surrounded by a ring of guards, all pointing halberds at him.

"Lower your weapons," demanded Isolda. "This man saved Terric's life."

"See?" said Bastian to the guards. "Told you so."

The captain grunted but followed Isolda's command.

"Thank you for saving my son, sir," said Isolda. She had to be careful what she said in front of Garrion's men. "Would you please accompany me to the castle so that we may discuss your reward?"

"Of course, my lady," said Bastian with a bow and his charming smile.

They didn't speak again until they were through the gate and away from the guards.

"We need to talk somewhere private," whispered Isolda. "You have a lot of explaining to do." The first building that they came to was the dovecote. She hadn't really thought of it before, but it was a pretty decent place for a private meeting. Except for her and Garrion, only Father Percival and Brother Savaric had keys.

Isolda unlocked the door and went inside. She hadn't been in the dovecote for quite some time, but it was much better organized than she remembered. Each cage was perfectly labeled with the city to which the birds inside would fly. The cage labeled Icehaven caught her eye, and suddenly she remembered that with all the excitement of the tournament and the body of Arwin, she had never written back to her sister's last letter.

And then her path became so clear. She couldn't reveal Garrion's treachery to Reavus. It was too dangerous. He might end up slaughtering her entire family. Maybe even the entire city. Instead, she would take Terric and her other children north to live in Icehaven with her sister. She would take everything Garrion had ever loved, just as he had taken her father from her.

But first she had to deal with Bastian.

She pulled the ironwood pin out of her braids and jammed it into the lock. No one would disturb them until she had the answers she needed.

"So," she began. "Where were you this morning?"

"That's what you're going to start with?" asked Bastian. "You're not going to thank me for saving Terric?"

"We'll get to that. But first I want to hear about this morning."

"I was going to come. Really, I was. But then I got wind of a plot to kidnap Terric. I thought you'd be more concerned with your son's safety than some piece of armor."

"How very noble of you. Tell me, Bastian. How many men kidnapped Terric?" She raised an eyebrow, daring him to lie to her.

"There were..." began Bastian. "Fine. There were no kidnappers. I caught him running away."

"Ah, now we're getting somewhere. What else have you lied about? Are you even interested in my daughter? Do you even have the gauntlet?"

"Of course I care about Ori. And yes, I have the gauntlet."

"Can I see it?" asked Isolda.

Bastian reached into his satchel and handed Isolda the golden gauntlet. She turned it over in her hand. It was definitely a part of the body of Arwin. There were even a few small bloodstains, and...

What's that?

Isolda tugged on a little swatch of red fabric jammed between two of the metal plates. The night of her father's murder, Katrina had seen a man in a red cloak standing over her bed for a moment before she went and found the dead body. Was this a part of that cloak?

She considered tearing off the fabric so that she could attempt to match it to the murderer's cloak, but then she thought better of it. She didn't want to do anything that might interfere with Wymund's inspection.

"Is that what you wanted?" asked Bastian.

"It is," said Isolda.

Bastian nodded. "Then I have your blessing to marry Oriana?"

"The deal was for you to come this morning. You didn't."

"I know. I wanted to, but I couldn't. You said it yourself - it's not your approval that matters, it's your husband's. So I was going to go to the Huntlands to reclaim my father's title. I *was* a lord once. Until my father destroyed his castle and disgraced our name." The thought of his father made Bastian's blood boil. "With that title, I thought your husband might view me as a worthy suitor."

"You were going to travel all the way to the Huntlands? Just to win Garrion's approval?"

"Yeah. It sounds like a stupid plan now that I say it out loud..."

"It's not stupid at all. It's the sweetest thing I've ever heard."

"Maybe. But I didn't go through with it. When I saw Terric on the path, I figured I could just bring him home safely and pretend like I saved him from a kidnapping. I thought maybe Garrion would award me a title for saving his son. Then I'd be a proper suitor."

"That's not a bad idea either. But it wouldn't have worked. I doubt Garrion will let Ori marry anyone less than a count, and only King Ivan can award such a title."

Bastian looked down at the ground.

"It's a good thing, then," said Isolda, "that I'm the king's sister. If I told him of the heroic man that saved his nephew from vile kidnappers, he might be moved to make you a count."

"Really? You'd do that?"

"Yes. I would." Isolda smiled. She had Bastian just where she wanted him.

"I don't know how I can ever repay you, my lady."

"I do. Tomorrow morning, a man will be waiting for you at the Last Oasis. You'll need to show him the gauntlet, and give him fifty gold drachmas."

"*Fifty*?" asked Bastian. "I love your daughter, but I can't just come up with that sort of money in one night. Not unless I sell that gauntlet."

"I'll give you the gold," said Isolda. "And a letter of safe passage in case you encounter any rangers."

Bastian grinned. She couldn't tell if it was because he thought he had a chance to marry Ori, or if he was super excited to steal the gold and run.

Now that she thought about it, it was kind of crazy to trust this thief with so much gold. And with the gauntlet. And with her only opportunity to know if it's real.

But what else could she do? She couldn't very well send Tobias. He'd die of fright the minute he stepped foot in the savanna.

Bastian was her only hope.

LADY ORIANA

- CHAPTER 40 -
ORIANA

Oriana sucked in her stomach as Bella tied her dress.

"Can you make it any tighter?" asked Ori for the third time.

"Not if you want to be able to breathe," replied Bella. "You look stunning. Don't you want to see?"

No. She was terrified to look in the mirror. What if it was awful? What if she had ruined it? She had been up all night making adjustments. The last time she tried it on was before Nesta had torn it in half, but it hardly even looked like the same dress anymore. Ori had cut out the shoulders entirely where the fabric had torn, and then she'd completely redesigned the neckline to have a high collar and plunging neckline like the ones all the ladies in Reavus' court had arrived in. But she had never done a neckline like that before. *Hopefully it's not too low.*

Oriana took a deep breath. As much as she wanted to, she couldn't delay any longer. She had to look. "Okay, I'm ready." She slowly spun around. As she did, the delicate black fabric of her skirt caught the air and puffed out around her, revealing the golden fabric - the fabric Bastian had stolen for her - underneath. The morning sunlight streaming in through the window caught the fabric just so. It looked like she had captured the sun and hidden it in the folds of her dress.

Bella gasped. "It's beautiful!"

She was right. It was. But the neckline... *Oh no.* Oriana stared in horror at how much cleavage she was showing. She had made the neckline way too low. "What have I done?"

"What's wrong?" asked Bella.

Oriana tugged on the collar to try to cover more of herself, but as soon as she let go, it sprung right back to where it had begun. "Everything," she said. "I can't wear this. Look at it!" She pointed to her chest. "It plunges almost to my belly button!"

Bella laughed. "My lady, that's a bit of an exaggeration. And anyway, I think the prince will very much enjoy this dress. You have nothing to fret over."

"Really?"

"Yes, really."

"I don't know. Are you sure there's no time for me to fix it?"

"I think you'd only risk ruining it. Here..." Bella grabbed a few gold bracelets off the vanity and slid them onto Ori's wrists. "Now it's complete."

Selina knocked on the door once and walked in. "Are you ready?" she asked.

"Yes, almost," said Ori. "But I'm worried that my dress..." She spun so that Selina could see it in all its glory.

Selina gasped in amazement at the sight of the golden fabric in the skirt and then gasped in horror at the sight of Oriana's cleavage.

"It's that bad?" asked Ori.

"No. It's um...interesting. Don't worry, we can fix it right up." She gave Ori a half smile. "Let me go grab some black silk and some thread."

As Selina turned to go, Ori realized something. She hadn't even noticed what Selina was wearing. Yes, it was partially because she was so worried about her own dress, and it was partially because Selina wasn't exactly the most beautiful model, but there was more. Selina's dress was masterfully made. The design was timeless - with capped sleeves, a square neckline, and a draping skirt - and the stitching was flawless. It was the embodiment of everything Sister Morel had taught them. But it was so...boring.

A dress like that would never get the attention of Prince Rixin. But Ori's would.

"On second thought," said Oriana, "I think I'll keep it how it is."

Princess Navya walked in the room. "What's taking so long?" she asked.

"We were just discussing Ori's dress," said Selina.

Navya inspected it and nodded. "The seams are well done. And the design is a clever blend of 1st century Barcovan and contemporary Shadowlandish. If I looked the way you did, I'd be delighted to wear such a dress."

For a moment, Oriana thought she saw a glimpse of sadness in Navya's usually stoic eyes.

"If I was going to be working at a brothel," added Navya quickly. The hard exterior had returned.

Oriana's thanks had been on the tip of her tongue, but she easily swallowed it back down with that comment. "Well, no time to change it now," she said. "Where's Nesta?"

"She wasn't in her room," said Selina. "I think she must have gone down early. You know how eager she is to see Prince Rixin win the joust."

Rixin. The sound of his name made Oriana's stomach do flips. Their last conversation had been so confusing. First she'd been rude, then they'd kissed. Then she'd been rude again. Would he declare her in the joust, or would he never speak to her? Neither would surprise her.

And then there was Bastian. His final words to her had been stuck in her head. *I'll make it right.* What did that mean? Was he going to repay whoever he had stolen that necklace from? Or did he mean he'd do something to win the approval of her parents?

A little part of Oriana hoped Bastian and a band of thieves would waylay her on the way to the tourney grounds and take her away. Even if she wasn't sure if Rixin would approve of her dress, she knew Bastian would love it.

"So are we ready, or are you planning on removing more material?" Navya asked.

I can't believe I almost thanked her. "I'm ready." Oriana followed Selina and Navya out of the room and down to the waiting carriages.

The cheers from the crowds at the tourney grounds could be heard all the way from Vulture Keep. The whole city and everyone from miles around would be there. Surely Bastian would be there too.

What was she thinking? *I should be angry at both of them.* Rixin had kissed her without permission. And Bastian had stolen Rixin's ring and blamed it on her little brother.

But Oriana had appreciated the prince's kiss. She hadn't appreciated Bastian's lies. There was no reason to think any further about Bastian. He had no title and no honor. Her father would never approve of him. And she'd never trust him again. Ever.

Rixin, on the other hand, was her father's first choice. And he finally seemed interested in her. If Rixin really declared her in the joust, she'd know for sure if his intentions were true. She bit her bottom lip, remembering how it had felt to kiss him.

A kiss that should never have happened. When had she turned so improper? She tried to push thoughts of Rixin and Bastian aside. Really, they should both be banished over the wall.

- CHAPTER 41 -
BASTIAN

Bastian yanked on the rope to see if it was secure. It was, but it still gave him little comfort when he looked off the edge of the Shield. His boot hit a stray rock and sent it plummeting down 150 feet of sheer, sandy rock. It smashed into a million bits on the rocky savanna below. Nut chirped and backed away from the cliff.

"It's okay, boy," said Bastian. "We're not going to fall." He scooped up his pet and put him in his satchel, right next to the gauntlet. He double checked to make sure he had everything Isolda had given him: a map, a sealed letter of passage, and fifty golden drachmas.

For a split second he considered turning around and disappearing with the drachmas, but he couldn't do it. He gripped the rope and eased himself over the edge.

This is for Ori, he told himself with every step of the descent. His hands were screaming by the time he reached the bottom. The climb back up would surely be much more difficult, but he had plenty of other problems to deal with before he could worry about that. He had to find the Last Oasis, and along the way he had to avoid guards, bandits, and tigers.

The guards had been easy to avoid thus far. They didn't seem to be terribly concerned with preventing citizens of Arwin's Gate from scaling the cliff into the savanna. Why would they be? That would be like guarding the gallows to make sure criminals didn't hang themselves. As far as the guards were concerned, madmen were welcome to die in the savanna. Bastian hoped he hadn't just condemned himself to such a fate.

Nut jumped out of Bastian's satchel with the map in his mouth. The first landmark shown was an oasis with twin trees about four miles south of the city, so that was the direction in which Bastian headed.

"The savanna doesn't seem so bad," said Bastian to Nut. As far as he could tell, the place was deserted. They hadn't seen any rangers or bandits or tigers. The closest he had come to a living creature had been a near miss with a pile of dried, crusty elephant dung. His boot would never have smelled the same if he had stepped in it, but it was hardly the life-threatening incident he had expected from the terrifying way people in Arwin's Gate always spoke of the savanna.

Bastian was scanning the ground for more elephant dung when Nut chirped softly.

"What is it, boy?" asked Bastian. He looked up and saw that the oasis with the twin trees was off to their left. They were slightly off course, but overall he was pleased with his navigating. At worst they had added a quarter of an hour to the trip. He patted Nut on the head and fed him a grape. "Good find."

Nut spit the grape out and chirped again, even more quietly than before. And that was when Bastian realized that something was very wrong. Bastian followed Nut's stare. He missed it the first time he looked at it - its sandy fur and burnt orange stripes camouflaged it amongst the tall grasses and dusty rocks - but on his second glance, the razortooth tiger's bloodstained fangs gave it away. Its fangs were massive, twice the length of Bastian's daggers, and the rest of the beast was even bigger than Bastian had expected. He had thought that the sculptor responsible for the razortooth tiger statue outside the tavern had taken artistic license with the creature's size. Unfortunately for Bastian, that was not the case.

Before he could reach for his daggers, the tiger pounced, easily clearing twenty feet in a single leap to bring it face to face with Bastian. It opened its enormous mouth and roared. Bastian could feel the wind from the roar, and he could certainly feel the droplets of thick saliva that flew onto his tunic. And the stench... Bastian couldn't recall ever smelling something so foul. It stank like rotten eggs and elephant dung and death all rolled into one.

The tiger studied Bastian and licked its lips.

Bastian tried to back away slowly. He had been so close to having everything he'd ever wanted. *Oriana*. He didn't care about reclaiming his title, or having a fortune, or any of it. He only cared about her. And she'd never know how he died. She'd never know he had risked his life to win her back.

The tiger growled.

"Well Nut, it looks like this is where it ends," he whispered. But Nut wasn't on his shoulder anymore. "Nut?" Bastian only made it a few steps before the tiger swiped one of its massive paws into his arm and sent him sprawling into a short, thorny shrub. He looked back at the tiger. It was crouched on the ground, tail wagging, ready to pounce and enjoy its feast. But just when it was about to pounce, Bastian heard an angry, high pitched chirp. The tiger stopped and looked to see what had created such an awful noise. Nut was snarling at the tiger with his claws in the air and his tail all fluffed out. Bastian used the momentary distraction to throw one of his daggers at the tiger. He'd aimed for the neck, but it missed the mark slightly and lodged between two ribs. The tiger roared in pain. Its rancid breath knocked Nut over.

And then the tiger pounced. Bastian closed his eyes and braced himself for the impact. He pictured Oriana in her nightgown. His fingers pulling down the fabric on the center of her chest. Their lips a moment away from meeting. *So close.*

The impact, however, never came. Instead, Bastian heard a squishing sound, like a knife piercing a grape, and then a loud thud.

The visions of Oriana dispersed. Bastian opened his eyes and saw the tiger laying a few feet in front of him. An arrow with blue and silver fletching stuck out of the center of one of the beast's eyes.

Nut cautiously approached the tiger and sniffed it. When he was sure it was dead, he jumped up on top of it and chirped triumphantly.

"Did you do that?" asked Bastian. He shook his head. He wasn't thinking straight after nearly being mauled by a razor-tooth tiger. Of course Nut hadn't shot the arrow. But that meant... *Bandits!*

He drew his second dagger and spun around in one fluid motion. No one was there. All he saw were two hawks circling overhead.

"Who goes there?" asked Bastian. There was no answer. Whoever it was clearly had Bastian at a disadvantage. He was armed with only a dagger, while his opponent was armed with a bow. And based on the accuracy of their last shot, they definitely knew how to use it. He decided to take a different approach. He let the dagger fall limp between his thumb and forefinger as he slowly bent to put it on the ground. "I mean you no harm, friend," he called into the seemingly empty expanse of dried grass and dirt.

The second his dagger hit the ground, an archer emerged from behind a rock with his bow pulled taut and aimed directly at Bastian's chest. Two men followed him, also holding bows.

Bastian recognized the first man immediately from his hawk head helm. It was the man every thief in the city feared most. Sir Aldric Alsight.

"My lord," said Bastian with a bow. "I owe you my life."

"You do, and I might yet take it," said Sir Aldric. "Identify yourself."

"The name's Bastian, my lord."

"Well, Bastian. This can go one of two ways. Either you tell me where your camp is and I'll end your life painlessly with an arrow through your neck, or I can let my birds feast on your flesh. Quarry has been hard to come by today - my hawks must be famished."

Bastian carefully considered his next words. He was supposed to avoid telling any guards his business, but Isolda *had* given him a sealed letter of passage to be used as a last resort. And this felt like a good time for a last resort. "My lord, I'm on official business of Lady Isolda Hornbolt."

"And I'm King Ivan," scoffed one of the rangers. He was a thin man with a confident grin, and he was clad in heavy metal armor.

"I must admit," said Sir Aldric. "Of all the pleas I've heard, that's the most creative."

"No, truly. I have a sealed letter to prove it. If you'll allow Nut..."

"Nut? Whose Nut? I thought you were alone." Aldric's golden eyes scanned the savanna.

"My squirrel."

"Squirrel, eh? He'll make a lovely appetizer for my hawks."

"Nut, get the letter," called Bastian.

A second later, Nut appeared with the letter in his mouth. He kept his eyes fixed on the hawks as he scurried up and dropped it in front of Sir Aldric.

"Make sure he doesn't try anything stupid," said Aldric to his rangers as he lowered his bow and picked up the letter. Aldric's hawks circled closer overhead and the rangers kept their bows trained on Bastian. The thin, armored one looked a little too eager to loose an arrow. Sir Aldric's eyes narrowed at the sight of the golden wax pressed with the rhino sigil of House Hornbolt. He broke the seal and read the letter. When he was done, he folded it up and tucked it in his belt. "Lower your bows, men. This man rides on direct order of Lady Isolda." He turned to Bastian. "I pray your forgiveness, my lord."

"No forgiveness required, sir," said Bastian. "I'm fortunate that you came across me when you did."

"The good Lord Arwin works in mysterious ways. It seems he's brought you and me together for a reason. I should like for my men and me to accompany you and see to it that you make it to your destination unmolested."

Bastian shook his head. "I hate to impose on you. Frivolous tasks such as mine are of secondary importance to the protection of the savanna."

"It would be no imposition. These ripe young recruits would do well to range a bit further from the Shield. And you can never have too many companions in these parts. Bandits would kill for that golden gauntlet, I reckon."

Bastian turned to see that the gauntlet had spilled out of his sack when the tiger had swiped at him. *Not good.* Isolda had given him strict instructions to not let anyone see it, even if he had to show someone the letter. "This old thing?" asked Bastian. He picked up the gauntlet and waved it in the air nonchalantly. The little swatch of red fabric that was wedged between two of the golden plates fluttered around. "This is just a uh...good luck charm. From my grandfather. Figured a little extra luck couldn't hurt when I'm out here in the savanna. I'm not even sure it's made of gold. Either way, I guess it's actually good luck. Maybe it's the reason why you showed up when you did."

Sir Aldric walked up to the tiger's body and pulled his arrow free. "This arrow is my good luck charm." He wiped the end of it clean on his tunic and put it back in his quiver. "Ended the entire Zaberwald bloodline with it. Count Erasmus Stone was so scared of it that he blew up his whole castle just to prevent it from finding a home in his heart."

Bastian winced at the name. His father's name.

Nut chirped angrily. It was sweet of him to be defensive of Bastian's dead father, but it was unwise of him to draw attention to himself. The last thing Bastian needed was for a hawk to swoop down and take Nut from him too. He lifted up Nut and stuffed him back into his satchel.

"Some say it never misses," said Aldric. "I don't know if that's true, but I've never seen evidence to the contrary."

"He tells the truth," added the thin man. "Never misses."

"Quit talking and prepare the horses," said Aldric. He whistled and three steeds appeared from a patch of particularly tall grass. "We have a lot of ground to cover. If we hurry, we might even get back in time for the final joust."

SKYFALL
MUMMER

- CHAPTER 42 -
GARRION

Skyfall was one of Garrion's favorite days of the year. It was a beautiful thing to watch everyone in the city gather to celebrate when Arwin sacrificed himself to defend his people from the evil Voltanis. He'd hired the best mummers around to play the parts of the evil Sky Islanders, and Aldric had been training the guards throughout the year to ensure that their part was properly choreographed.

This year, with the joust falling on the same day as Skyfall, Garrion had spent even more drachmas to ensure this parade would be one for the ages.

But for some reason, he couldn't seem to enjoy it. Not after what Isolda had said to him about Terric last night.

It was as if his horse could sense his irritation. He had to pull back on the reins to prevent the horse from cantering ahead in the parade.

Why did Isolda keep saying that Terric wanted *more*?

She had been saying it for weeks now, but she'd brought it up again last night when Garrion got back from searching for

Terric. She'd insisted that Terric didn't want to take the vows. Rather forcefully, too.

"Why are you trying to take everything from me?!" she'd demanded. Garrion thought it was a bit dramatic, but it *did* get her point across. It made Garrion rethink everything. He wondered if he had misread the situation so badly, if he had totally missed that Terric really did not want to take the oath.

The thought of it had kept him up all night. He'd prayed to Arwin for guidance, but he received no response.

A winged man dressed in black rags and a bird mask swooped down at Garrion from a nearby roof as the parade entered the new market. Garrion dodged to the side and then watched as his guards surrounded the attacker.

Worth every drachma, thought Garrion approvingly. He didn't know of any other city that had ever had *flying* mummers for the Skyfall Festival. They couldn't really fly, of course. They were just wearing fake wings and using ropes, but it still created an impressive illusion.

Up ahead, more winged mummers swooped down as if they were real thunderkin descending from the Sky Islands. The knights leading the parade - all of the competitors who had already been defeated - engaged in mock battles with the mummers. The crowd cheered louder with each thunderkin that fell.

In the center of the knights, the four remaining finalists rode their mounts in full jousting armor. They all looked impressive - Prince Rixin in his red and white checked cloak on top of pitch black armor, Ngolo Mobek on his powerful zebra, and Thomas Charo with his fishnet cloak and dual swords strapped on his back. But Marcus stole the show. He cut a striking figure in his new golden armor. Sir Aldric had done an excellent job with the additions he had requested from Roger. The bulky horn-shaped pauldrons were enough to intimidate any opponent. Even Ngolo Mobek, Garrion hoped, as that was who Marcus was facing in the second joust of the day.

"Beautiful day for a joust, isn't it?" said Reavus, riding up beside Garrion.

"It is indeed," agreed Garrion. "I couldn't have imagined a finer day to watch Marcus be crowned in the winged wreath and lift Arwin's Lance."

"I must say, you've done an impressive job of hosting this tournament. The thunderkin flying off buildings is an especially nice touch."

Garrion suddenly realized that he had missed a great opportunity to have a mummer swoop down and tackle Reavus off his horse. Now *that* would have been a nice touch.

"But," continued Reavus, "I think you might need to re-read the story of Arwin's sacrifice."

"And why is that?" asked Garrion.

"Well, I see that you dressed Marcus in golden armor, similar to what Arwin wore."

"I did."

"Won't the crowd be confused, then, when Marcus is lying on the ground while Rixin gets doused in red paint and then rises with the winged wreath?"

"That might be confusing, yes. So it's a good thing it's not going to happen. Marcus is going to win the tournament."

"You seem awfully confident," said Reavus. "Does that mean you've bought into the rumors that Marcus is the second coming of Arwin?"

"I believe that Arwin will reveal the truth to us when he deems it appropriate. Until then, speculation does us no good."

"Suit yourself. I personally think the rumors might be true. Look around...the mummers have taken to the sky, just like the prophecy predicted. What's that one line in the middle?"

"A king will fall?" suggested Garrion. "I certainly hope that's not referring to our dear Prince Rixin."

"No, no. Not that line. The one about gold."

"He shall bathe himself in gold and drain himself of blood."

"Yes, that's the one. It seems you've already fulfilled the first half of it by giving him that golden armor. I hate to think about what the second part might mean." Reavus' mouth curled into a wicked grin.

"Prophecies rarely mean what we think they do," said Garrion.

"We'll see," said Reavus. "You know, we never did finish our conversation from the other day. Shall we make a wager on the outcome?"

"No, we shall not."

"Does that mean you don't really believe that Marcus will win?"

"If we begin wagering, where would we draw the line?" asked Garrion. "Would it be okay to start bribing too?"

Reavus feigned shock. "Duke Garrion, are you accusing me of bribery?"

"Should I be?"

"Not unless you have some evidence to back it up."

"I saw the bloodgold drachmas you gave Ngolo," said Garrion.

Reavus laughed. "That wasn't a bribe."

"So you admit to paying him?"

"Of course. As General-of-Arms of Treland, it is my responsibility to see to it that the kingdom is well fortified at all times. That payment to Ngolo was necessary to ensure that the troops at Corongo Keep are prepared for whatever the Sultan might throw at them in the coming months. Who knows...we could be at war with Rashid by the end of the day if the new Arwin's Lance is so inclined."

"I hate to spoil your fun, but Marcus is going to win. And he's going to keep the peace."

"Maybe so. He is a talented boy, I'll give you that. But after staying up so late last night looking for Terric, I suspect Marcus will be exhausted today." Reavus shook his head dramatically. "Horrible business, that kidnapping. And the timing couldn't have been any worse."

Was Reavus behind Terric's kidnapping?

Bribing Ngolo was one thing, but kidnapping Terric crossed the line. Garrion felt the blood start to rush to his hands. He gripped his sword, but Isolda's words replayed in his head. *You are Arwin's Rhino.* Garrion took a deep breath. He couldn't allow Reavus to bait him into doing anything foolish and spoiling the joust.

"I trust that Marcus will be fine," said Garrion. "If anything, the realization that our enemies would go so low as to kidnap an innocent child will strengthen Marcus' resolve to win."

"I didn't kidnap Terric, if that's what you're saying."

"Speaking of competitors being distracted...it seems that Prince Rixin is quite fond of Oriana. I do hope that doesn't impact his performance."

"I don't think it will. And I'm confident enough in that to back it up with a sizable wager. Judging by the look of your guards," Reavus paused and made a show of eyeing the Hornbolt guards on either side of the parade, "you could use a little boost to your treasury. I'll put a thousand bloodgold drachmas on Rixin's victory. You don't even have to wager on Marcus if you don't want to. Ngolo seems a better option."

A thousand bloodgold drachmas? That was a fortune. With that kind of money he could repair every crack in Arwin's Wall and buy new siege engines from Techence. From the tests they had run, it seemed like Tobias had been true to his word about providing Marcus with the best equipment money could buy. And if Rixin accepted his offer and threw the tournament... *Stop!* Garrion told himself. *Don't let him tempt you.*

"Gambling is illegal in Arwin's Gate," said Garrion.

"Why? Are you worried that Arwin's Voice is going to excommunicate you? Look at him. He doesn't care about gambling."

Garrion looked back at Arwin's Voice.

The delicate, golden chains connecting the headband and bracelets of Arwin's Voice gently clinked together as he waved to the adoring crowds. He rode in a carriage that looked like it belonged to an old woman overcompensating for her deteriorating beauty. Garrion could hardly fathom how many hungry mouths the temple could have fed if they had spent that money on food rather than on commissioning such a carriage.

It was a disgrace. And Garrion, in his position as the Duke of the Shield, could do nothing about it.

But Terric could.

After taking the oath and becoming a priest, Terric could rise in the ranks. He could show everyone how a priest should act. And if all went according to plan, he could be elected as the next Arwin's Voice. With that title and the power that comes with it, Terric could make the world a better place. But if his heart wasn't in it, he would do more harm than good.

And suddenly, Garrion realized he'd received his answer from Arwin.

Garrion would let Terric watch the joust. He'd let him see that knocking other men off horses does nothing to better the world. Garrion never wished for death, but one of the remaining competitors getting injured might be just what Terric needed. Bards always made cutting down faceless enemies on a battlefield sounds so wonderful and heroic. If Terric got such an up-close view of death, maybe he'd realize how awful it really was.

Either way, he'd talk to Terric after the joust to find out once and for all what the boy wanted. If he wanted to be a priest, he'd have him take the oath. If not, he'd postpone it. Maybe he'd even try to find a suitable lord to take Terric on as a squire. The last thing Treland needed was an Arwin's Voice that wanted to be a warrior. They'd had plenty of those in their history, and every time it had ended in war.

Arwin would show Terric his path, even if it wasn't the path Garrion had imagined for him.

Was it possible that Reavus' wickedness was part of Arwin's path, too? He certainly didn't live his life according to the book of Arwin, but perhaps he was a necessary evil. If not for his actions, if not for what he did to Julian and Dory, Garrion's life would have been entirely different. He would never have married Isolda. He would never have had Marcus and Terric and his three beautiful daughters.

Maybe everything was turning out just as it should. He just had to trust in Arwin. The thought was comforting.

Garrion turned back to Reavus. "I won't gamble with you, Reavus. If Arwin would have Prince Rixin represent him as Arwin's Lance, then so be it. I will follow him. But I don't think that's going to happen. Arwin teaches peace, not war. And Marcus will keep that peace."

"Arwin may be powerful," said Reavus. "But so am I." His black eyes twinkled with amusement and the grin on his face chilled Garrion's bones.

Garrion had seen that cocky look once before: right after Reavus had told him to kill Dory.

Was it possible that Reavus was up to something more than bribes and kidnapping?

LADY
NESTA

- CHAPTER 43 -
ORIANA

The opening ceremonies of the joust seemed to go on *forever*.

All Oriana wanted was for the bard to introduce Prince Rixin. But first he had to introduce Arwin's Voice. And then Arwin's Voice had to tell the story of Arwin's sacrifice. And then the bard had to read the rules.

The joust would consist of three separate events. Prince Rixin would be jousting first against Thomas Charo, and then Marcus would face Ngolo Mobek. And then there would be a brief intermission before the two winners squared off for the title of Arwin's Lance.

The goal of the joust was to unhorse your opponent; doing so resulted in an automatic victory. But if neither opponent was unhorsed after five passes, then the victor would be determined by how many lances they broke on their opponent during the joust. Breaking a lance on your opponent's torso was one point, while breaking a lance on their head was three points.

Oriana's mind began to wander as the bard explained the more intricate rules of the joust.

In a matter of minutes, Oriana would hear who Rixin was jousting for. She assumed it would be either her or Princess Navya. If it was her, it would mean that he meant every word he said the other day. It would mean that he was falling for her. But if he was jousting for Navya...

The thought made Ori feel like she was going to vomit up the roasted ostrich foot she'd eaten for breakfast.

If he declared Navya, Ori's life would be over. She'd be married off to Thomas Charo, with his scraggly beard and twisted, scarred face.

Or maybe she'd be wed to her cousin, Golias Frostborn, and live out her days in the frozen, depressing tundra of Fjork-ia.

Or maybe she'd run away with Bastian...

No! she scolded herself. *Don't think that! Prince Rixin is going to choose you.*

He had even told her that he would. But Ori didn't entirely trust his word. He had stood her up just days ago. And when they were little, he had borrowed a quill from her once, promising to return it. She had never gotten it back. So maybe his word didn't mean as much as she hoped it did.

"Lords and Ladies," began the bard standing in the center of the arena. "Good people of Arwin's Gate. It is with great pleasure that I present to you: the heir of Barcova..."

Ori tuned the bard out again. He was introducing Thomas Charo, not Prince Rixin. She didn't even want to look at Thomas. All she could think about when she looked at him was how his face had gotten so scarred. As far as Ori knew, all they did in the Trade Coast was go fishing. Had he been mauled by a school of vicious flounders?

The crowd's greeting for Thomas was mainly angry boos and whistling. Oriana felt the same way, although it would have been unladylike of her to express it in that manner.

Ori bit the inside of her lip as the bard prepared to introduce Prince Rixin. Would he declare her? Would he like her dress? She looked down to make sure her breasts hadn't fallen out. *For Arwin's sake, what am I wearing?*

"And now," began the bard, "the Crown Prince of Treland, Duke of Arwood, Blood of Arwin, Distinguished Knight of the Order of Chains, Defender of the Wood, the undefeated, the Shadow Prince..."

Oriana closed her eyes. She felt like she was going to explode from the anticipation.

"Jousting for Lady Oriana of House Hornbolt: His Royal Highness, Rixin of House Talenov!"

Oriana's eyes flew open. The breath she had been holding escaped her lips. The cheers of the crowd were deafening. She knew they weren't for her. They were for their prince. But it was easy to get caught up in the roar of excitement. Rixin had declared her in the joust. Maybe that meant his intentions were true. Maybe he would talk to his father. Maybe she was going to be the future queen of Treland.

She looked down at Rixin. The rubies inlaid in his pitch black armor shimmered magnificently in the sun as his red and white checked cape billowed behind him. More importantly, his visor was raised, and he was staring directly at Ori.

Rixin nodded at her, as if he could read her thoughts.

It felt like her heart was beating in her throat.

Then his perfect smile disappeared as he lowered his visor. He trotted Midnight to the starting position.

"Ori," Nesta said and tugged on the skirt of her dress.

It was hard to pull her eyes away from the prince, but Oriana reluctantly looked down at her sister. She tried to hide her gasp. Nesta was dressed in the most hideous dress Oriana had ever seen. It was a poorly stitched together jumble of mismatched fabric. Ori had so many questions. Had Nesta been mauled by a razortooth, or was the skirt intentionally hacked up? Where did all that wrinkled red fabric come from? Why was it long sleeved on the left side, and sleeveless on the right? Why were there so many ruffles everywhere? And why, for the sake of Arwin, was Nesta's stomach exposed?

Oriana hoped her mum hadn't seen it yet. Surely Oriana would be partially to blame for this monstrosity. She'd been supposed to help watch over Nesta's sewing progress. But she'd been too preoccupied gallivanting around with Bastian and fretting over Rixin.

"What are you wearing?" asked Ori, stepping forward slightly in hopes of blocking Nesta from their mother's view.

"Prince Rixin is fighting for you?" Nesta sounded so disappointed, completely ignoring her sister's question. "I thought that maybe he'd say my name." She looked down at the ground.

Oriana glanced back at their mother again. As far as she could tell, no one else had noticed Nesta's monster dress. She turned back to Nesta and again tried to hold back a gasp. For a second, it almost looked like the horrid dress flickered. Surely an odd trick of the light against the horrible design. She needed to get Nesta out of the stands.

"Nesta, you have to go change."

"Why?" asked Nesta. "Do you want to wear it? I guess you can if you really want to. Look, it even has elbow pads so I won't hurt myself if I fall." Nesta held up both arms. A triple layer of golden fabric was sewn onto the left sleeve, and since it had no right sleeve, the other elbow pad had just been tied around her arm.

A sudden clanking noise drew Ori's attention to the joust. She turned and looked out at the tournament just as the dust settled from the first pass. Thomas Charo's squire was handing him a brand new lance, while Nigel was quickly checking the straps on Rixin's armor. The bard raised a blue and orange striped flag - the colors of House Charo - to indicate that Thomas had earned a point.

One to nothing.

That's okay, thought Oriana. *Rixin will still win.*

Both knights turned to face each other and then spurred their horses forward. In an instant, there was an explosion of blue and orange splinters and a horrible clanging sound. Rixin's head swung back violently from the impact, but he stayed on his horse.

Ori let out a gasp.

Three points to Thomas.

The next pass had the same result. Rixin was starting to look woozy in the saddle.

Three more points to Thomas.

What is he doing? Ori wondered. Everyone said he was the best knight in the realm. Why was he getting beaten so badly? If she didn't know any better, she would have thought that he was intentionally losing.

She suddenly wished that he hadn't declared that he was jousting for her. She would have preferred that such a poor display be dedicated to Princess Navya.

Surely everything would change on the next pass...

The knights charged forward, and there was the all-too-familiar explosion of blue and orange splinters. For a second she thought she saw some red in there too, but then she realized that the blow had knocked some of the rubies loose from Rixin's armor.

The score was eight to nothing, with one pass left. The only way Rixin could win was by dismounting Thomas. Oriana didn't know how he could possibly do that, though. It looked to her like he was struggling to even stay on his horse.

She looked away, and when she did, her father caught her eye and gave her a confident wink. Oriana had thought her father at least approved of the match, but judging by the grin on his face, he actually preferred for Prince Rixin to get killed.

Ori turned back. She covered her face, but she couldn't bring herself to not watch. She spread her fingers to create little slits to watch through, as if not seeing it fully would make it any less awful.

All the spectators collectively held their breath as the men charged toward each other for one final pass.

There were thirty feet between them. Then twenty feet. Dust flew in the air behind their powerful horses. They were going faster than she had ever seen a man ride before. Ten feet. They lowered their lances. Five feet. Impact.

The horrible clang of metal on metal rang through the air as Rixin's lance caught Thomas square in the chest. Amongst an explosion of red and white splinters, Thomas flipped backward out of his saddle, bounced twice, and then came to rest with his arms splayed unnaturally.

The crowd burst into cheers. Rixin had won!

He pushed up his visor again and made eye contact with Ori. His smile had returned. And somehow, he made it seem like it was just them. That everyone in the crowd had disappeared.

For a second Oriana considered running down to congratulate him for his victory, but that thought quickly dissipated. He had only won the semi-final. Marcus still had to joust against Ngolo, and then Rixin would face the winner to determine the champion. Maybe after that she would run to him...

"Do you love him?" Nesta asked and tugged on Oriana's skirt.

"I...I'm not sure yet." She suddenly felt too hot in her dress. The fabric Bastian had stolen for her felt stifling.

"Well, I definitely love him," Nesta said. "I made this beautiful dress just for him." She twirled around in a circle, making the fabric flicker again in the sun. "And then he pretended not to be able to see it. And I hated him for a few moments. But I love him again now. I want to marry him and have lots of babies. Do you think they have chocolate in Thalencia? Maybe I won't go if they don't have chocolate."

Nesta was so sure of her feelings. Didn't the prince deserve someone who was sure? Didn't Bastian? Oriana felt like she might faint. She swallowed hard and began to blink faster. For a moment, it almost looked like the bottom of Nesta's dress disappeared and then reappeared. Yes, Ori was definitely going to faint.

"Ori, are you okay?" Nesta asked. "You look horrible."

The laugh that escaped Oriana's throat sounded forced. Nesta was the one who looked horrible in her dress. But Oriana did *feel* horrible. She needed to speak to both Bastian and Rixin to sort through her feelings.

Her stomach twisted in knots. But what did it really matter? Her opinions meant nothing. The decision wasn't hers to make.

"We have to go," Oriana said and grabbed Nesta's hand.

"But Marcus will be up soon. We have to see him lose."

"Nesta, would you stop saying things like that? You should be cheering for Marcus, not hoping he'll lose."

"But I want Rixin to win."

"Doesn't family loyalty mean anything to you?" Oriana pulled Nesta in the opposite direction from where Rixin was celebrating.

"No."

"Nesta!"

"Ori!"

They had almost reached the exit when Nesta pulled her hand free from Ori's.

"We need to go change, Nesta. Please."

"But I don't want to change! I made this dress for the prince. He hasn't even gotten to see it." She stomped her foot.

"Please come with me."

"After he sees it." She smiled up at Oriana and then started running.

Ori tried to catch her hand, but it was too late. The monster dress shimmered and flickered in the sun as Nesta ran down the stairs and out into the center of the arena. There was no way her mother hadn't seen the horrible creation now.

Nesta came screeching to a halt right in front of Rixin. He smiled down at her as she spun in a circle.

"You look beautiful, my lady," he said. He held his helmet under one arm as he bent down and kissed the back of her hand.

Nesta beamed at him and then grabbed his hand, pulling him over to Oriana.

"See? He loves my dress, Ori. I told you he'd like it."

"You both look breathtaking," Rixin said, locking eyes with Oriana. The fire in his gaze made her feel even more faint. He slowly lifted her hand and brushed his lips against the back of it.

But it wasn't anything like he had done to Nesta. The kiss was slow and soft. The pad of his thumb traced up the inside of her wrist, sending shivers through her whole body. And after the kiss ended, he kept her hand in his.

"You declared me," said Oriana.

"I said I would. Did you not believe me?" He continued to trace this thumb along the inside of her wrist.

Oriana looked down at their intertwined hands. "Part of me thought you might be playing games."

"I tend to leave the games to the tournament."

She bit the inside of her lip. "Look, Rixin…"

"Ori, you've told me what you thought. Now listen to what I have to say."

She locked eyes with him. This was what she wanted. To talk to him and Bastian. To sort through her feelings. "Okay," she said. Maybe what he said would help her figure out what she wanted.

"All those years ago, you thought that all I noticed was your chubby cheeks and your dolls. Well, that's just not true." He cupped the side of her face in his hand. "I saw a girl that was beautiful and sweet and kind-hearted."

Oriana laughed. "You expect me to believe that? You should be with some chesty brunette who dotes on you with..."

Rixin pressed his finger against her lips to silence her. "Oriana, I love you. I think I've always loved you."

What? That wasn't possible. He'd never liked her as much as she liked him.

He traced her bottom lip with his thumb. "I love that I can make you blush. And that you can put me in my place. I love that you're not afraid to tell me how you feel. And I don't know if you've looked in a mirror recently, but you're the most beautiful woman I've ever met. I meant what I said the other day when we ran into each other on the stairs. You're absolutely breathtaking, Oriana. And right now, I don't see anyone but you. I don't even care about the tournament. I want to win you. Your heart. Marry me, Oriana."

She was having trouble breathing. Part of her thought she had just imagined that confession. *Prince Rixin loving me?* No. She just blinked at him.

"Say yes. Let me convince my father that you're the right choice. We can rule Treland together. And I promise you, I won't for one second be looking at some stupid busty brunette when I can look at you instead."

She finally found her voice. "That's not your decision. This whole conversation is ridiculous. You must be confused from all those blows you took to the head."

He smiled. "I'll convince my father. Just say yes."

She parted her lips and then closed them again. It was everything she had ever dreamed of. So why did the thought of Bastian cross her mind? She tried to shake it away. Rixin was proposing to her. Rixin wanted her. And if that was true, if she wasn't dreaming of this moment, then the decision was already made. It's the only thing her father would approve of anyway.

"Say yes." He wiped away a tear that she hadn't even realized she'd shed.

"Um...well, I...I guess."

Rixin smiled. "You guess?"

"No, I mean..." her voice trailed off. "I think I've been dreaming of this moment since I was five. I just never thought it would actually happen. This doesn't even feel real."

He laughed. "I'm sorry it took me so long to catch up. So, is that a yes?"

"Prince Rixin Talenov, if you actually meant every word you said..."

"I meant it." He tucked a loose strand of hair behind her ear. "Ori, you have no idea how much I meant it. I'd give up everything to be with you. I swear that I would."

And she believed him. She looked into his eyes, searching for the one thing she needed to see. She was aware of her tears now. "You're looking at me like I'm the only one you see."

He wiped her tears away with his thumbs. "Haven't you been listening to anything I've said?"

"Then ask my father for my hand. Not me. This isn't how these things work."

"We've already come to an agreement."

She swallowed hard. "You have?"

"All I need is for you to give me a proper answer." He pulled her closer.

Oriana could never think straight when she was this close to him. "I don't know what you want me to say. It's up to our fathers."

"I need to hear you say yes to *me*. Not maybe. Not that the decision is out of our hands. Say yes, Ori. I need to know that you want this too."

"Say yes to what?" Nesta asked.

"I asked her to marry me."

Nesta sighed and plopped down onto the dusty tournament ground.

Oriana's throat felt dry. Maybe it was her decision after all. If she said no, Rixin would never ask his father. He'd marry Navya. He'd continue his life without her. Or she could say yes to him. She could have the life she'd dreamed about since she was a child. Her whole life she thought the decision was out of her hands. And now that it wasn't, she didn't know what to do.

"As soon as the tournament is over, I'll ride to Bloodstone to get my father's blessing. All I need is for you to say yes."

"I do love you," Oriana whispered.

He wiped another tear from her cheek. "And that pains you?" The smile was gone from his face.

Her stomach twisted in knots again. It was in that moment, the moment when his smile turned to a frown, that she knew her answer. She realized that she never wanted to put a frown on his face. Never again.

"Yes," she said.

"What?" His smile was back. "Yes?"

"Yes. I want to marry you, Prince Rixin Talenov."

"Ori." He leaned in and kissed her. Some people in the crowd cheered. Some gasped. It was horribly improper for them to kiss in public. Oriana should have been horrified. She should have pushed him off and slapped him to save whatever shred of dignity she had left. But she didn't care. All she cared about was the feeling of his lips on hers. It didn't feel improper. It felt perfectly right. It felt like the beginning of their whole future.

"This feeling is so much better than winning some stupid tournament," he laughed as he pulled away.

Oriana smiled. That meant more to her than he could possibly know. She knew how much this tournament meant to everyone. Especially her brother. He had been training his whole life for it.

Nesta knocked on Rixin's leg armor. "I love you too. Can't I have a kiss?"

Rixin laughed and got down on one knee. "Of course, my lady. Today is one to celebrate." He placed a kiss on her forehead.

The smile on Nesta's face could have lit the sky.

Oriana hoped that she truly was as excited about this marriage as Nesta was about that kiss. Her whole future had just been decided by a smile. She glanced back at Rixin. *But what a smile.*

LORD
MARCUS

- CHAPTER 44 -
MARCUS

Marcus readjusted his armor yet again. The additions had set it off balance. He would have preferred they'd done nothing to it at all. No, it hadn't looked like much. But it was lightweight and easy to move in. Now? He looked down at the armor. Yes, it was intimidating. But it was heavy. He readjusted his gauntlets. Heavy and definitely unbalanced.

And where was Sir Aldric? Marcus had been training with him for this moment since as long as he could remember. He needed some final words of encouragement from his mentor. He needed the sense of familiarity. Sir Aldric hadn't been by all morning, not even to wish him luck.

"This doesn't feel right," said Marcus.

"Yeah," agreed Peter. "He really shouldn't have kissed her in front of everyone."

Marcus looked out at the tournament grounds. From their current position in the arena stables, they had a clear view of all the action. They'd seen Rixin rally in the fifth pass to dismount Thomas, and then they'd seen him kiss Oriana. "What? No. Not that. I mean, yes. I would prefer for him to keep his hands off my sister. But I was talking about my armor. It doesn't fit right."

Peter looked at him. "Where?"

Marcus wiggled his shoulders and tried to get comfortable. "The shoulders feel too big."

"Hmm." Peter walked behind Marcus and tightened a few straps. "Better?"

"Not really."

"Alright, we're gonna have to take it off and add some padding then."

"Is there time?"

"If we're quick about it." Peter worked as fast as he could to remove Marcus' right pauldron. Just as he got it off, they heard the blare of trumpets.

"Lords and ladies, good people of Arwin's Gate," began the bard standing in the center of the arena. "Introducing the Baron of Corongo Keep, distinguished knight..."

Thank Arwin they're introducing Ngolo first, thought Marcus.

"Okay, maybe there's not as much time as I thought," said Peter.

"Just put it back on," said Marcus. If he wasn't ready for his introduction, he'd be disqualified.

"Hold on, I might have something." Peter rummaged around in his satchel. "Ah, here we go." He pulled out the silk tunic Jax had given Marcus a few nights ago.

"What good will that do? And why do you have that?"

"As your honorary squire, I wanted to bring anything you might need. And I thought you might need this. Now shut up and help me get this pauldron back on." Peter stuffed part of the tunic under the side of Marcus' breastplate and then strapped the pauldron on top of it. "How's that?"

Marcus rolled his shoulders around. It wasn't perfect, but the extra bulk of the balled up silk did make the armor fit a little better. "It'll have to do."

"And now," continued the bard. "The heir of Arwin's Gate, Squire to Sir Aldric Alsight. Jousting for Lady Ajana Alsight. The honorable Marcus of House Hornbolt!"

Marcus quickly mounted his horse and rode out to a roaring ovation. But he couldn't help but notice that the applause for him was quieter than it had been for Rixin. *Probably because I don't have an awesome nickname.* Rixin had like eight titles. *Blood of Arwin. The Undefeated. The Shadow Prince.* And Marcus' biggest claim to fame was being Aldric's squire.

That would all change soon, though. He'd beat Ngolo, and then he'd beat Prince Rixin in the final.

He had to. It was the only way to keep the peace.

He looked across the arena at his opponent, Ngolo. The giant of a man was dressed in heavy steel armor painted with bright zigzags of red, green, and yellow. Three-foot-long dyed ostrich feathers extended from the top of his helmet, which had a visor designed to look like that creepy tribal mask on his sigil. And to top it all off, he was riding on a zebra far bigger than any zebra Marcus had ever seen before.

Marcus turned to Peter, who had run out beside him. "Is he even allowed to ride a zebra?"

Peter shrugged. "Apparently so."

"And why didn't the bard do a better job introducing me?"

"He gave your official title. What else did you want him to add?"

"I don't know."

"Maybe after this you can earn a nickname," suggested Peter.

Yes. "Marcus the giant slayer does have a nice ring to it."

"Too generic," said Peter.

"Marcus the zebra pounder?"

Peter stifled a laugh. "Um..."

"Yup. I heard it as soon as I said it. Definitely not that."
Marcus was suddenly very thankful that this tournament was
based on jousting rather than rhetoric.

"How about Marcus the shadow slayer?" suggested Peter.

"Perfect!" He could imagine the bards singing the songs of
Marcus the shadow slayer, the squire who defeated the unbeat-
able prince and prevented a war with Rashid. But to earn that
title, he'd have to dismount Prince Rixin. During practice, that
had seemed almost impossible. After seeing Thomas Charo get
four clean strikes on him in a row, though, Marcus felt like he
had a good chance.

"First you have to beat Ngolo." Peter hoisted a black and
gold striped lance up to Marcus. "My advice: try to dodge him
for the first few passes and then steal it with a point at the
end."

The bard blew three blasts on his trumpet. *Here we go.*

Marcus pulled his visor down and spurred his horse forward. He eyed Ngolo charging towards him. The flat surface
of Ngolo's visor would make a nice target...

But as Ngolo got closer, Marcus realized that Peter had
given him good advice. Ngolo was huge, and his zebra was
much faster than the average destrier. If Ngolo got a solid hit
on him, he would be obliterated.

Marcus lowered his lance. Ngolo did the same. A split
second before they were going to make contact, Marcus leaned
left to dodge the strike. But his armor was heavy and unbalanced, and he nearly fell off his horse. He quickly had to adjust
his weight the opposite direction and...

Pain seared through Marcus' shoulder as Ngolo's lance just
barely caught the rhino horn ornamentation that Aldric had
added to his pauldron. Ngolo's lance didn't break, but Marcus

wished it had. The lance breaking would have dampened the force a bit. Instead, the full momentum of Ngolo's charge was transferred into Marcus' pauldron. If not for the incredible armor underneath, the impact probably would have broken his shoulder.

He brought his horse around back to his start position.

"You okay?" asked Peter.

Marcus nodded.

"Good. No harm done then. It's still zero zero. You're right where you want to be."

"I can't dodge him," said Marcus. "The armor is too unbalanced. I almost fell off."

"Change of plans, then. Try to hit that big ugly visor of his. If you can catch the tip of your lance in the mouth detailing, you'll unhorse him for sure."

"Just what I was thinking," agreed Marcus. He took a deep breath and closed his eyes. It was a technique that Aldric had taught him. The chanting grew distant and all he could hear was the beating of his own heart. He could taste the victory. He could see himself being awarded the title of Arwin's Lance. He could see his father's proud face. His mother's smile. Terric's cheers.

The trumpet blew.

He opened his eyes and flew forward. His heartbeats matched the rhythm of the horses' hooves. His whole body pulsed with anticipated. This was his moment.

Hitting Ngolo's visor would be tough. If Ngolo realized Marcus was going for a headshot, he'd be able to dodge it easily. So Marcus had to feign like he was going for a body shot, and then at the last second jerk the lance up.

It was a difficult technique, but not impossible.

It'll have to work, thought Marcus. There was no way he could withstand another four rounds of punishment from Ngolo.

Marcus lowered his lance early and aimed it directly at Ngolo's chest.

Wait for it...wait for it.

Just before they collided, panic swept over Marcus. The headshot might work, but he wasn't going to be able to dodge at all. Ngolo would basically get a free strike on him.

He thought about changing his tactic, but it was too late.

Ngolo's lance struck him square in the chest, but he hardly felt it. The armor absorbed almost all of the strike.

But then the lance slid to the right and lodged between his chest plate and his pauldron. He felt a searing, blinding pain in his shoulder as he was thrown out of his saddle. All he could see was the tip of the lance buried deep in his shoulder as he fell backward.

A silence settled over the crowd as Marcus clanged onto the ground, diminished to a twisted pile of armor and flesh.

His head slammed against the back of his helmet. And the last thing he saw was his blood seeping into the dirt of the tournament grounds before everything went black.

- CHAPTER 45 -
ISOLDA

It felt like all the air left Isolda's lungs as she watched the lance pierce her eldest child's shoulder. And the scream. That blood-curdling cry of agony. *No.* She gripped Garrion's arm. Her own hands were trembling.

She cringed as Marcus' armor clanged against the hard ground. His leg was twisted awkwardly underneath his limp body. *My baby.* Tears started to form in her eyes. She swore she was probably hurting Garrion with how hard she was gripping his arm. All Isolda wanted to do was run to her son. To kiss his wounds away. But this wasn't some bruise or scrape. He wasn't a child anymore.

Isolda watched in horror as the blood began to pool around Marcus' leg. He wasn't moving. *My baby isn't moving.* It was as if she was as frozen in place as Marcus was.

"Get up, son," Garrion said from beside her. "Get up." He placed his hand on top of Isolda's.

Not many people would have heard the agony in his voice. But she did. The pain in his words made her snap out of her trance. *Marcus needs me.* She stood up, grabbing her huge skirt, and ran down the stands.

"Marcus!" She didn't even realize she was screaming. "Marcus!"

The crowd hushed around her.

The silence was unnerving. *Please be okay.* She tried to blink away her tears. *Oh, Marcus.* Her feet hit the dirt and she kept running, not caring at all about the tournament or its rules. Her son needed her.

Tobias was already trying to pull away Marcus' armor by the time she reached him. But he wasn't strong enough.

"Someone help us!" she screamed. "Help him!" She pulled off Marcus' helmet. His face was pale. So pale. *No.*

Rixin knelt down beside Marcus and began removing his pauldron.

"Start with the leg," said Tobias. "We have to stop that bleeding." He turned to Peter. "I need a stretcher and a hot blade."

Isolda had to look away as Rixin pulled off her son's greaves. The leg underneath was mangled horribly and the pool of blood beneath it was growing rapidly. She put her hand underneath his nose. "I don't think he's breathing. Is he breathing?"

Tobias ignored her. He tore off a part of his sleeve and grabbed a piece of the shattered lance to create a makeshift tourniquet for Marcus' leg, but as he twisted the wood to tighten it, the wood snapped. He tried another piece. Same result.

He needed something stronger than the soft wood of the lance. And Isolda had exactly the thing. She yanked the iron-wood pin out of her braids and handed it to Tobias. With it, he was able to secure the tourniquet and slow the bleeding.

"Baby, wake up," Isolda said and ran her fingers through Marcus' damp hair. *Please, Marcus.*

Tobias turned his attention to Marcus' shoulder.

As Rixin and Tobias removed the pauldron, the lance fragment fell away freely. Beneath it, rather than a horrific wound, there was a wad of bright silk. Tobias pulled away the fabric and then tore at the seam of Marcus' shirt. The skin beneath was badly bruised, but there didn't appear to be any cuts. Tobias poked at it gingerly.

Isolda continued to stroke her son's hair. "His face is so pale. Tobias, please do something."

"He needs room," Tobias said.

"Lady Isolda," Rixin said and lightly tugged her away from Marcus' body. "He needs room to breathe. Let the axion do his work."

"But is he going to be okay?" She searched Rixin's face, even though she knew he didn't have the answers.

Rixin paused. That was all the confirmation she needed. She shook her head and put her hand over her mouth. She couldn't stop the tears from falling now.

Peter appeared a moment later with a stretcher.

"Help me get him on," said Tobias.

Rixin and Peter lifted Marcus onto the stretcher and started carrying him away. Isolda and Tobias ran alongside them.

"Is he going to be okay?" she asked.

Tobias shook his head. "His shoulder wasn't bad thanks to that silk tunic, but his leg... I'll do my best."

They lay the stretcher down in the center of a small room under the stands. Peter held a knife in the flame of a lantern.

"My lady," said Rixin. "It would be best if you waited outside."

"But Marcus needs me."

"You can't do anything to help him, but you can help Nesta. She shouldn't watch this." He pointed at Nesta standing in the doorway.

Isolda took one last look at Marcus. He was so pale. So lifeless...

Rixin guided her out of the room and closed the door behind her.

"Mama!" Nesta said and hugged her leg. "Is Marcus going to be okay?"

Isolda knelt down and pulled her youngest child against her chest. *I don't know, baby.* "He's going to be fine," she said as firmly as she could.

She ran her hand across the fabric of Nesta's dress. The soft red fabric seemed worn with age. And the faint pattern was so familiar. Like she had seen it somewhere. She had seen Nesta come to the tournament grounds dressed in the ridiculous dress and had tried not to laugh. But the material had been bothering her. Especially the way it shimmered in the light. Why couldn't she place that nagging feeling?

"I knew he was going to lose. I didn't think he'd die," Nesta sobbed into her shoulder. "I wanted him to lose. I'm bad! It's all my fault!"

"You're not bad. You're brother's going to be okay," Isolda said and put her hands on both of Nesta's shoulders so she could look her in the face. It was easier to console Nesta than it was to look at Marcus' motionless body.

But instead of comforting Nesta, words seemed to tumble out of her mouth: "Nesta, where did you get this dress?" She wasn't sure why she couldn't forget about the fabric.

Nesta smiled through her tears. "I made it out of a cloak. Don't you like it?" She gave her mother a half-hearted twirl. The dress flickered in the light. Almost as if it went out of view and then back again.

"It's beautiful," Isolda said with a straight face. It was easy not to laugh when her heart felt like it was in a million pieces. "But where did you get the fabric?"

"Oh." Nesta scrunched her mouth to the side. "I found it."

Isolda stared at the dress again. And suddenly, it came to her. She had seen the fabric the night before: the little swatch stuck in the golden gauntlet. Was this the clue to her father's murder she had been searching for all these years?

"Where did you find it?" Isolda lightly touched the bottom of Nesta's chin, hoping to not seem upset.

"I didn't do anything bad, Mama." A big fat tear ran down Nesta's cheek and fell on her dress. And for just a moment, the lower half of her daughter completely disappeared. Part of the dress had definitely shimmered, disappeared, and then reappeared. Isolda was in shock from what had just happened to Marcus. But she didn't think she had imagined it.

An invisibility cloak. That would explain everything. They never understood how the assassin had disappeared so quickly.

"I know you didn't do anything bad," Isolda said. "I'm upset about Marcus, not your dress. I just want to know where you found such a lovely material."

"Well, I really just found it in the castle."

"But where exactly, sweetie?"

Nesta scrunched her mouth to the side again. "I'm not in trouble?"

"No, of course not."

She looked down at the ground. "I found it in Sir Aldric's room."

Sir Aldric? Isolda's whole body felt cold. *No. It can't be.* He was her husband's most trusted advisor. Her heart thumped against her chest.

The pieces all started to fall in place. How had she not seen it sooner? Of course Aldric had been with Garrion in Bloodstone right before the murder. All that time she'd been looking for the killer, and he was right under her nose. Watching her. Making sure she didn't get too close.

The guards that were always following her, the guards who had tried to take the body...they must have been acting on Aldric's orders rather than Garrion's. Or was Garrion involved too?

Suddenly a horrible realization swept over her.

Aldric had caused Marcus' injury. He was the one who had trained him. He was the one who had designed the changes for the armor. He must have intentionally made it so that the lance would get stuck between the pauldron and chest plate.

This is all my fault. If I had never found the body, Aldric wouldn't have struck. No. She shook the thought away. She couldn't stand to think that she was responsible for Marcus' injury.

"I'm sorry," said Nesta. "Please don't be mad, Mama."

"What?" Isolda looked down at her sweet daughter. Tears were welling up in her eyes. "No, no, sweetie. I'm not mad at you. It's something else." *It's Aldric.* "Wait here."

Isolda ran outside and looked up into the stands. Aldric was nowhere to be seen. She looked to the sky. No sign of his hawks, either.

Where was he? Was he watching her now? Spying on her family? Trying to figure out whose life to take next? All she could hear was her heartbeat thudding in her ears.

They were all in danger. She looked at Garrion, sitting pale-faced and stoic in the stands. Would he even believe her? Would he think she was mad? Was he part of it? The only proof was Nesta's dress and the piece of fabric on the gauntlet. But she didn't have the gauntlet. Bastian did. And anyway, she wasn't entirely sure that Garrion wasn't Aldric's accomplice.

He wouldn't do that, she told herself. *Garrion is a good man. You have to trust him.*

She was just about to run to him when a loud, awful sound pierced the air. She immediately recognized it as the alarm horn on the wall. There were only two reasons why the horn would be blown: the arrival of the summer storms, or Rashidi invaders.

Within seconds, the stadium erupted into chaos. A flood of people emptying the stands blocked her only path to Garrion.

She had to reach him. She had to warn him about Aldric's treachery. But it was impossible.

The stampede reached her faster than she'd anticipated. She had no choice but to turn and run with them towards the exits.

A new plan began to form in her mind. She'd get out of the arena and head back to the castle. That was what they always did when the alarm sounded. Garrion had repeated it a thousand times to their children: *If you hear the alarm, drop everything and get back to the castle.* Once she was there, she could warn Garrion about Aldric. Her father's killer would finally be brought to justice. They'd all be safe.

But first they all had to make it to the castle alive. Aldric was out there somewhere, and he'd already proven he wasn't afraid to kill.

- CHAPTER 46 -
BASTIAN

Sir Aldric pulled back on the reins and brought his horse to a halt. "Do you hear that?" he asked.

Bastian and the two rangers stopped. He listened for a moment but heard nothing. "Hear what, my lord?"

"The silence," said Aldric. "The savanna has been deserted since sunrise. Save for you and the tiger, I haven't encountered a single living creature all day."

Nut jumped to Bastian's shoulder and chirped angrily.

"And that squirrel," added Aldric.

"Is that normal?" Bastion asked.

"It's not. In fact, it's most *unnatural*. Even Ellie is agitated." Aldric turned and stroked the head of one of the two hooded hawks perched on a wooden frame attached to the back of his saddle.

"We should head back," suggested one of the rangers. From the brief conversation they'd had during the past hour, Bastian had gathered that he was named Stu, he'd been born into a family of rangers, and he was no more than sixteen years old.

"Does the silence frighten you?" asked the thin ranger, Dennis - the one who had seemed eager to shoot Bastian earlier. "We should be thankful that Arwin has blessed us with a peaceful ride. I'll take quiet any day over the roar of a razortooth or the sting of sand in my eyes."

Bastian looked around. The first hour of walking next to the horses had been treacherous - sun burning his exposed skin, sand stinging at his eyes - but the hour after that had been much more pleasant. Now the wind had stopped completely. The acacia trees were deadly still. No rodents scurried between holes. Even the nearly perpetual motion of the tumbleweeds had ceased. It was as if Bastian and the rangers had been put in a jar and someone had sucked out all the air.

The eerie quiet of the savanna sent a chill down Bastian's spine. It reminded him of something, but he couldn't quite bring the memory to the surface. He shifted uncomfortably and his hand gravitated toward his dagger.

"A storm is coming," said Sir Aldric.

"Can we make it there and back before it hits?" asked Bastian.

Aldric looked at the map Bastian had given him. "Hard to say. If your map is to scale, the oasis should be coming up any minute. I'll send Ellie ahead to scout." Aldric reached back and unhooded one of his hawks. The bird didn't hesitate to take off. It squawked, turned, and headed directly back towards Arwin's Gate.

Bastian could see a look of worry spread across the old knight's face.

"If she's so eager to seek safety," said Aldric, "we would be wise to do the same."

Bastian wanted to agree with him. He knew he was right. And yet, he couldn't. He couldn't go back to Isolda empty-handed. He couldn't give up on his chance to be with Ori. "We must press on."

"Even if your bird isn't brave enough to scout ahead, I am," said Dennis.

"As you wish," said Aldric. "But you should be careful not to confuse bravery and stupidity."

Dennis smiled and whipped his horse far too enthusiastically. It whinnied and charged ahead out of sight.

Aldric, Bastian, and Stu continued on. Within minutes, the clear sky had turned dark and stormy. The clouds were low and thick, nearly black on the underside. Bastian could hear Stu softly chanting prayers to Arwin.

The oasis soon came into full view. It was nothing more than a pond with a spindly tree and a few patches of grass. A man in brown robes sat cross-legged at the base, and beside him was a purple shield emblazoned with a golden scorpion sigil. Scales of justice balanced on the scorpion's tail.

"Rashidi," growled Sir Aldric. He dismounted and drew his sword. "I've seen plenty of filth in the savanna - razortooth tigers, wanderers, even those filthy bandits that have the audacity to march under their own tiger's head banner - but never a Rashidi." He charged toward the man. He looked like he was ready to cut the Rashidi in two, but then he skidded to a halt.

"Stand and fight, Rashidi scum," demanded Aldric.

The Rashidi stayed seated. His eyes were closed. Did he not care at all that he was about to be slaughtered?

"I said stand and fight!" yelled Aldric. His eyes searched the ground. "What kind of trap have you set? A spear buried in the sand?" Aldric spat on the ground. "You sand-eaters took my brother's leg with one of those. You'll pay dearly for that."

The Rashidi opened his eyes and stood shakily. "Forgive me for not standing sooner, traveler," he said in a thick accent. "These old bones don't move as easily as they once did."

Bastian ran towards Aldric and the Rashidi. The Rashidi's face was wrapped tightly in brown fabric. What little skin was left exposed was heavily scarred. And it almost looked like a few strands of blonde hair were sticking out.

Was this the man he was supposed to meet? There was only one way to find out. "You look tired, good man," said Bastian.

"Even gods must rest," replied the Rashidi with a small bow.

Sir Aldric turned and looked at Bastian. "What kind of queer greeting was that?"

"This man is my contact," said Bastian.

"We rode all this way to meet with *this*?" said Sir Aldric, his voice thick with disgust. "What treachery is this?"

Bastian stepped forward to get between Aldric and the Rashidi. "I thank you for your protection, Sir Aldric, but this man poses no threat."

"Of course he poses a threat. He's a Rashidi. He probably has a hundred men buried under the sand, ready to jump out and strike..."

Nut scurried over to the man and sniffed his robes.

"Nut likes him," said Bastian. "That's good enough for me."

"My lords," interrupted the Rashidi. "I have no hidden soldiers. I am here only on business. Do you have the armor?"

"Yes, I have it," said Bastian. "Sir Aldric, would you be so kind as to wait by the horses? This transaction is not meant for your eyes."

"Discretion is important, but in this case, haste is paramount." The Rashidi looked over his shoulder.

Bastian followed his gaze. The horizon had been replaced by an advancing wall of swirling sand that stretched from side to side and top to bottom as far as the eye could see. An errant gust of wind swept through the oasis, ruffling the leaves of the single acacia tree. Behind him, the horses whinnied and stomped their feet.

As he looked back at the Rashidi, the wind blew and Bastian thought he saw a multi-colored tunic underneath the man's brown robes. The Rashidi quickly smoothed his robes and glanced nervously at Aldric.

Bastian poured out the contents of his satchel - fifty golden drachmas and the golden gauntlet.

The Rashidi collected his payment and then produced a small round piece of glass from deep within his robes. He held it to his eye and inspected the gauntlet. "Most intriguing," he noted.

As he inspected it further, a horse galloped out from the storm.

"Was that...?" started Bastian.

"Dennis' horse?" said Sir Aldric. "Yes. And the empty saddle tells me that he wasn't cut out to be a ranger. Stupid rather than brave, that one."

The horse galloped past them without slowing.

"It does fit the description," said the Rashidi.

"Is it genuine?" asked Bastian, keeping one eye on the approaching sandstorm. The calm had now been replaced almost entirely by an ever-intensifying swirling wind.

"One can never be sure, especially without seeing the entire specimen. But yes, I believe it is."

Lightning crashed and illuminated the approaching storm. For a moment, Bastian thought he saw the silhouette of a winged man standing within it. And in that moment, he remembered why the eerie calm was so familiar. He was four, standing in Scarfort with his father, as a man in black robes muttered incantations over a chained, naked messenger. Prince Anton Talenov had sent the messenger to discuss terms of surrender, but Bastian's father wanted none of it. He had the messenger bound and instructed his mage to perform whatever magic necessary - even blood magic - to ensure that the Hornbolt army never crossed the Scar. As the mage cut the messenger and muttered his incantations, the air was sucked from the fort. Everything was still, except for the man writhing in pain as the mage carved symbols into his skin. And then the storm began. The wind...the lightning...Bastian now remembered it vividly. The sky attacked the castle. Wind pulled men from the ramparts while lightning blasted holes in the walls. And then the men in the green cloaks appeared...

Bastian blinked and returned to the present. He was covered in a cold sweat. The storm was nearly upon them. "We must leave," he said reaching for the gauntlet.

The Rashidi pulled the gauntlet out of his reach with surprising quickness. "My apologies, but I will need to take this for further inspection. May the gods watch over you in your travels, if it is their will."

"But..." started Bastian. The dirt swirling in the wind pelted his eyes and filled his lungs. As he wiped the dirt from his eyes, he could have sworn he saw the Rashidi walking through a wooden door in the center of the tree trunk.

A door?

Another wind gust forced him to close his eyes again, and when he opened them, the door was gone. And so was the Rashidi.

"Get ready to mount!" yelled Stu.

In a second, the horses were upon him. Bastian grabbed one of the horse's manes as it flew past. He struggled against the wind, but he finally managed to pull himself up into the saddle. He pulled his bandana over his mouth just as the sandstorm hit them in full force. Wind swirled. Sand stung at his squinted eyes. He was just about to crack the reins when he looked to his left. Sir Aldric was still standing in the savanna.

For a second he considered dashing back to Arwin's Gate, but he couldn't do it. Sir Aldric had saved him from the razor-tooth tiger. Now it was time for Bastian to repay that debt.

Bastian pulled up on the reins and looked back for Aldric, but he could see nothing. It was impossible to see more than five feet in the thick, swirling sand.

"Sir Aldric!" he called into the darkness. His voice was barely audible over the howling wind and crashes of thunder. He dug his heels into the horse and pulled hard on the reins. The horse reluctantly capitulated to his will, wheeling around and heading deeper into the storm.

Each lightning bolt provided just enough light for Bastian to get a glimpse at his surroundings. On the third bolt, he thought he saw Aldric holding onto a tree. "Grab my hand!" he yelled as he rode towards Aldric.

Twenty feet, ten feet, five feet.

"Grab my hand!" yelled Bastian again through his bandana. He reached out and pulled Aldric onto the horse just as a lightning bolt scorched the sand where Aldric had been standing. He rode for what he thought was the edge of the storm, dodging lightning bolts that the storm seemed to be directing specifically at them. He didn't let up on the reins until the storm was well behind them, and even then, he kept the horse at a steady canter.

"Impressive riding," said Sir Aldric, clapping Bastian on the back.

Bastian ignored him. "Nut?" he called, looking around the horse. "Nut?" *Please be here, little buddy.* He held his breath until he heard a little chirp. Nut poked his head out of the satchel and coughed up a glob of sand. "Nut!" Bastian rubbed his squirrel's head. "I can't believe we made it out of that alive. What a story that will be."

"Aye, a grand story indeed," said Sir Aldric. For the first time, he was smiling. "It's a shame I can't let you live to tell it."

"What?" asked Bastian. But it was too late. Aldric's fist crashed into the back of his head.

- CHAPTER 47 -

ISOLDA

Isolda slowly pulled the torn piece of fabric away from her face and coughed up some dust. The winds had finally died down, at least for a moment.

It probably would have been wise of her to stay put. To ride out the end of the storm in...

Isolda looked around to see where she was. When the storm had hit, she'd just gotten up the switchbacks to the top half of Arwin's Gate. She'd ducked into the first building she'd seen, which, judging by the looks of it, was someone's house.

She had to get back to Vulture Keep. She had to warn her family about Sir Aldric before he got to them. *Or is he already there?*

Before she could change her mind, she put the torn piece of her dress back over her mouth, flung open the door, and ran out into the street.

The sky was still black. The winds were still swirling. But it wasn't as bad as it had been. She could make it.

Seeing the city so empty was odd. It reminded her of the time she had been to Deseros after Reavus razed the city. It had been bone chilling to see a once vibrant city reduced to an empty shell. That's what would have become of Arwin's Gate if she had falsely accused her husband of treason. Reavus would have razed the city.

As she rounded the corner into Garus' square, a winged man in black robes swooped down from the temple roof. His wings caught in the wind. For a second it almost looked like he was flying. Really flying.

But of course, he wasn't. He was just a mummer wearing fake wings swinging on a rope.

At least, that's what Isolda thought until he flew by and slashed her side open with his sharp claws. Isolda let out a scream, but the wind and thunder drowned it out.

She clasped her hand against her side. The fabric of her dress was already soaked with blood. *No.* She bit back another cry of agony. Isolda stumbled backward, away from the beast. She could barely stay on her feet.

"Help!" she cried into the winds. But no one could hear her screams. The blood coated her hand and her head started spinning. Was she hallucinating?

The winged man circled through the air and then landed in front of her. He was dressed a lot like the mummers in the parade, but his mask was solid metal rather than clay. And his eyes flickered with cracks of bright blue, almost as if there was a lightning storm raging inside of them.

As he stood in front of her, the wind seemed to curl around them.

Isolda pressed her fingers against her side to try to stop the bleeding. She reached for her ironwood hairpin, but it wasn't there. *Marcus' tourniquet.* She hoped with every fiber of her body that the tourniquet had saved his life. Because it looked like it was going to end hers.

"Where is the body?" said the man in a raspy voice, like wind scraping against metal.

Is he talking about the relic? "I don't have it," said Isolda.

The lightning in the creature's eyes flared as it tilted its head up. It looked like it was sniffing the air.

And then the lightning died. The creature went limp and slumped to the ground. An arrow was sticking out of its back.

But Isolda had no time to be thankful. The arrow had blue and silver fletching. *Aldric's arrow.* She looked around for Aldric, but couldn't see more than a few feet in front of her.

The wind that had been dampened by the creature's presence was back in full force.

She didn't know what that creature was, but Aldric was just as dangerous, if not more. Isolda held her side as she ran for the castle gates. By some miracle, they'd been left open when the storm hit. She charged across the bridge. The wind was getting stronger every second. One gust actually blew her off her feet. If she hadn't crashed into a barrel, she would have been flung off the bridge.

In that moment, she realized she wasn't going to make it to the castle. The wind was too strong, and with each step she felt more and more faint. But she might make it to the dovecote. It was just at the edge of the bridge.

She gripped the ledge and pushed through the wind, one step at a time, until she was at the dovecote.

The second she twisted the doorknob, the wind blew the door open the rest of the way. She had to use all her strength combined with a temporary lull in the wind to get it closed again. She locked it and pushed a table and chair in front of it.

Her side throbbed. She looked down and saw the entire left half of her dress was covered in blood.

I might die here, thought Isolda. And if she did, the secret of Aldric's treachery would die with her.

She couldn't let that happen. Not after all the searching. Not after what he'd done to Marcus.

She stumbled over to the writing table on the far side of the dovecote. She grabbed a thin strip of parchment and dipped a quill into the inkwell, but it came out dry. *Blood it is,* she thought, dabbing the quill against her wound. She scrawled a few bloody words on a sheet of parchment. Hopefully whoever found her body would spread the truth.

A pounding at the door made her jump.

"Isolda," called Aldric. "Let me in! It's too windy out here."

Her heart raced. *Does he not know that I suspect him?* She wasn't sure. Seeing Nesta's dress might have alerted him, but Isolda wasn't sure if Aldric had even been at the tournament. If he did think she was on to him, he probably would have shot Isolda rather than that thunderkin, or mummer, or whatever it was. But maybe he *had* been aiming for her and the wind had blown his arrow off course.

"Isolda!" he called again. He was banging on the door. Cracks were starting to form around the knob.

She was running out of time. And if he burst in and saw the letter she had written...

The letter! Of course. She should have thought of it sooner. She was in the dovecote. She could write letters and send them to anyone in the kingdom. Whether she survived the storm or not, her letters would survive. The entire kingdom would know of Aldric's crimes.

She dipped the quill into her bloody side and wrote a second letter. Then she ran over and grabbed two pigeons - one from a cage labeled Bloodstone, and one from a cage labeled Icehaven. She rolled the letters into tiny scrolls, sealed them with hot golden wax, and tied one to each pigeons' foot. One was for King Ivan and the other was for her sister Katrina.

Now how do they get out? she wondered. She scanned the dovecote. The walls were forty feet high, lined with cages filled with birds from all over Pentavia. Rickety looking ladders on little wheels stretched to the ceiling. And then she saw it: about ten feet up, there was a tiny shuttered window just small enough for a pigeon to fit through.

She rolled a ladder over to it and cradled both pigeons in one arm as she climbed with the other. The pain in her side intensified with every step and her hands were slick with blood. She barely made it to the top without falling.

More banging on the door below. "I'm going to die out here!" yelled Aldric.

Good.

Isolda unlatched the window. The wind blew it open. It nearly knocked her off the ladder, but she was able to regain her balance just in time. She blocked the wind with her hand as she squinted out the window. She could barely see five feet. Sand was swirling everywhere. It was practically pitch black.

The pigeons would never make it through that.

More knocking on the door nearly made Isolda fall off the ladder. How much time did she have left? A minute? A few seconds?

Come on, she thought. *Come on!*

It wasn't quite the lull she had been looking for, but for a second the wind seemed to die down.

She kissed each pigeon for good luck and sent them out into the storm. They twisted and flapped in the wind. Isolda held her breath as lightning streaked through the air a few feet from one of the birds.

"Come on," whispered Isolda. "Come on. You can make it."

Just as they were about to disappear into the storm, a hawk swooped down and grabbed one of the pigeons in its talons.

No.

Isolda climbed down the ladder and ran towards the table. She had to write more letters. She had to send more pigeons.

She was only halfway there when the lock burst and the door swung open. The table she'd put in front of it skid across the floor.

Aldric stepped into the dovecote. Wind was swirling all around him.

"Sir Aldric, thank Arwin you've found me," said Isolda. "I was attacked by...a monster." She held up her bloody hand to show the evidence of her wound and immediately hunched over. Without the pressure of her hand, the pain was unbearable.

Aldric removed his hawk head helmet and approached Isolda. "This morning, in the savanna, I encountered something most unusual."

"I need stitches. There's no time for stories."

"Oh, but I think there is. You see, as fortune would have it, I happened upon a man named Bastian this morning. I thought he was a bandit, so you can imagine my surprise when he showed me a letter bearing your seal. And my surprise only grew when I saw what he was carrying. I hadn't seen that gauntlet for decades. Not since the night I buried it deep in the old gold mines."

So much for feigning ignorance. "You killed my father," spat Isolda. She instinctively reached for her hairpin, but again, she came up empty.

"I did," said Aldric. "But it didn't have to happen that way. I'd intended to save him."

"Save him? From who?"

"From your husband." Aldric smiled wickedly.

"Leave my husband out of this."

"But how can I when he's such an integral part of the story? He was going to kill your father. Did you know that? He and Julian were working together to steal the throne."

"You're lying," said Isolda. She clenched her jaw, trying to resist the need to cry out in pain. Each breath felt harder than the last.

"I think you know that I'm not. You've seen your husband's anger. Imagine how he would have reacted when he found out that his father and Duke Garrion had been killed at Horn Harbor. He was furious, and he blamed the king. He and Julian hatched a plot to assassinate King Bogdan. And your brothers. They were probably going to kill you and Katrina too. Wipe out the entire bloodline. Julian was going to take the throne, and Garrion was going to be elevated to the rank of duke and get Dory's hand in marriage."

Isolda looked around the dovecote. There had to be something she could use to her advantage. She just had to keep him talking.

"I don't believe you," she said. Her eyelids were starting to feel heavy. *There must be something I can use against him in here.*

"Neither did your father. I snuck into his room that night to warn him that he was going to be killed. I expected him to reward me with a county. Maybe even the title of duke. I'd saved his life. I'd killed all three Zaberwald triplets. Without me, the war would have been lost. But do you know what he gave me? His thanks."

"So you killed him?"

"Yes. I slit his throat. And then I stole his most valuable relic: the body of Arwin."

The way he said it so calmly made Isolda feel sick. Or else she was losing too much blood. She clasped her hand tighter against her side.

"I figured I could give it to Julian as proof that I'd killed the king for him. If your father wouldn't make me a duke, maybe Julian would. But it never got that far. Garrion stopped Julian from killing your brothers, and then he and Reavus destroyed Deseros. I still thought I could use the body to show my loyalty to Garrion, so I brought it to Arwin's Gate. But then he married you."

"And you didn't think he'd appreciate you killing his wife's father?"

"Exactly," said Aldric. "I thought he might promote me anyway. We were good friends. I figured he'd make me wealthy, even if he didn't make me a count. But instead he forgot about me. The whole kingdom forgot about me. The bards sing songs of the Rhino's Slaughter. No one cares about how I killed the Zaberwalds. I've been wasting away patrolling the savanna for the past twenty years."

"And now you're going to end up with your head on a spike." Her knees wanted to buckle, but she forced herself to stand up straight. Aldric was going to pay for everything he did to her family.

"No. No, I don't think I will. I'll end up on a battlefield. I'll lead Treland to victory against Sultan Zand. Bards all across Pentavia will sing my name again."

"And how do you plan to make that happen? Your trick with Marcus' armor almost worked, but the sandstorm postponed the end of the tournament. You failed."

"There are other ways to start a war. Can you imagine if you were found dead after this awful storm? Garrion would be outraged. Surely he'd blame Reavus. Or a Rashidi assassin.

Either way, it would cause quite a war." Aldric unsheathed his dagger.

Before Isolda could respond, Aldric sliced the blade across her throat and let the life pour out of her.

- Chapter 48 -
Terric

Terric wiped the dirt from his eyes and slowly opened them. He felt groggy. *What happened?* He looked around. *And why am I in this bush?*

Then it all started to come back to him. How Marcus had been injured in the joust. The alarm horn blaring. Isolda almost getting stampeded. Garrion chasing after her.

All the commotion had provided Terric with the perfect opportunity to escape this city once and for all. He just had to get back to the castle to get his things.

The last memory he had was when the sandstorm hit. It wasn't like when the summer rains usually came. Those were big storms, but nothing like this. This was the strongest wind he'd ever experienced. And it had thrown him into this bush.

Terric crawled out of the foliage as quickly as he could, but everything ached and prickly thorns kept tearing at his clothes. If he hurried, he'd be able to sneak into the castle, grab his things, and make his escape. By the time they sorted through the destruction of the storm and realized he was missing, he'd be long gone.

He was almost across the bridge when movement up ahead made him duck behind a barrel. He peered around it to see someone coming out of the dovecote. No, not *someone*. His father. And his hands were covered in blood.

Terric held his breath as he hid behind the barrel. Why would his father have blood on his hands? Had they taken Marcus to the dovecote? No, that didn't make any sense. He peered back around the barrel, but his father was gone.

Part of him wanted to ignore the dovecote, to just run away and forget about his old life. But he couldn't do it. He already knew Garrion was capable of murder. What if his murderous father had struck again?

His heart raced as he stopped outside the doors. There were a few drops of blood on the rocky ground.

Father Percival was in charge of the dovecote. What if his father had hurt him? Terric didn't want to be a religious man, but that didn't mean he wanted all religious men to be brutally murdered. He slowly opened the door.

"Father Percival?" he whispered and stepped inside. Maybe there was still time to save him.

A gust of wind slammed the door behind him, causing Terric to jump forward. He almost tripped on something. He looked down at a body lying on the stone floor.

"Mum?" Terric's voice quivered. His knees buckled and he fell to the ground.

The pigeons hooting softly was the only response.

"Mum, wake up." He put his hand on her arm.

She didn't move. She didn't blink. Her eyes were frozen open in horror.

"Mum, wake up!" Terric shook her shoulders. "Mum!" A sob escaped his throat as her arm rolled to the side, revealing deep gashes across her stomach. "Mum, no! Wake up!" He shook her again.

"No," he sobbed, embracing her in a hug. "Mum, I need you. Wake up," he mumbled into the fabric of her dress.

This can't be happening. He pushed himself backward. He slid back until he hit a cage of pigeons. They cooed angrily. *No. This isn't real.* He stood up and shook his head. The fear on her face killed him. He should have followed his father instead of trying to escape. He knew that he couldn't be trusted. But this? How could he?

Terric tried to wipe the tears from his cheeks. "Mum?" he whispered one more time, praying to a god he didn't want to serve. He put his hand over his mouth. There were no prayers that could fix this. His father had to pay. He ran back out of the dovecote and ran straight into someone.

Ori's face looked blurry in front of him because of his tears. "Ori!" He threw his arms around her.

"Terric, what's wrong?" She hugged him back. "Talk to me. What happened?"

"It's Mum. She..." He couldn't make himself say the words. "She..." He swallowed the rest of his sentence and pulled back from Ori's embrace.

The rest of his family was standing there. Except for his mother and Marcus. It felt like someone had stabbed his chest. Rixin and Reavus were there with Reavus' guards.

Terric stared at Garrion. Nesta was holding onto his leg as if she was scared he'd get hurt like Marcus. Little did she know that Garrion was the one causing the hurt.

As far as Terric was concerned, Garrion was no longer his father. He was a murderer. A liar. A traitor. And he deserved to be banished over the wall he pretended to protect.

Terric pointed at Garrion. "He killed her."

"What?" Ori gasped. "Terric what are you talking about?" It looked like she might faint. Rixin stepped forward and wrapped his arm around her waist.

"Son, what are you..." Garrion started.

"I saw it with my own eyes!" Terric yelled. "He ran out of the dovecote with blood on his hands! He killed my mum! And he murdered King Bogdan! And he...he tipped Marcus' lances!" All the secrets came pouring out. All of his father's vileness was out in the open. It felt like a weight had been lifted off his shoulders.

"Terric, what are you talking about?" said Garrion. "I didn't kill anyone. I found Isolda like that." He turned toward Reavus. "I was going to get help when I saw you coming toward the dovecote. I was just about to tell you."

"Father," Terric choked. He shook his head. The word sounded bitter on his tongue.

Nesta let go of Garrion's leg and stepped back from him. Her lip started to tremble. "Is Mama okay?"

Reavus swung the door to the dovecote open. He stood there for a moment, completely still. Then he stepped back and turned towards Garrion. "Garrion Hornbolt, you're under arrest for the murder of Lady Isolda. For the assassination of King Bogdan. And for the attempted murder of the participants of the joust." Reavus smiled.

"Terric!" Garrion yelled. "Terric, tell them you didn't see me do it! Tell them the truth! I loved your mother. I would never hurt her. Tell them, Terric!"

"I have told them the truth." Terric felt Ori wrap her arms around him. He melted into her embrace.

"Reavus," Garrion spat. "Reavus is behind this! He's wanted me dead ever since the Wizard's War. Arrest him! Not me!"

The closest guard pulled Garrion's arm behind his back.

Selina stood there in shock. Nesta ran over to Terric and Ori and threw her arms around both of them. "Where's Mama?" She started crying. "I want Mama."

"It's going to be okay," Ori said. But her shaky voice betrayed her.

Reavus turned to look at the siblings huddled together. The smile fell from his face. "Guards, arrest the other members of the Hornbolt family."

"What?" Rixin stepped in front of them.

"Garrion is a traitor. He'll be executed for treason. His whole family will suffer the same fate."

"Not on my watch." Rixin stayed firmly rooted in front of Oriana, Nesta, and Terric. "They haven't committed any crimes."

Selina shrieked as a guard shackled her wrists together.

"By association they have."

"They're your sister's children," Rixin said. "Stand down, Reavus. That's a direct order."

"My sister is dead thanks to him." He pointed at Garrion. "You may outrank me, but the king's laws outrank us all. I'll arrest you too if I have to."

Rixin grabbed the hilt of his sword, but more of Reavus' guards had crowded around them. He cursed under his breath and released the hilt. He turned to Ori and took her hand in his. "I'm outnumbered ten to one. I can't fight them all off alone. But I will fight this." He smiled, but it seemed forced. "And we'll be married. Just like we'd planned. I'll fix this, I promise."

"Rixin!" she screamed as one of the guards pulled her away.

He clenched his hand into a fist.

Nesta continued to cry for her mama as a guard lifted her over his shoulder.

Terric blinked as the shackles were secured around his wrists. This wasn't what he thought would happen. But he should have known. Reavus always annihilated the families of traitors. And his father was a traitor. So now he was too. It just made his hatred for Garrion grow even more. He wanted to kill Garrion with his own two hands.

Marcus was most likely dead. His mother was dead. And the rest of them were going to be executed. Why had Terric come back?

"Wait," Reavus said and walked over to Terric. "Release him."

What? Terric grabbed his wrists when the shackles were removed.

"You've done well, Terric," Reavus said and slapped him on the back. "I could use a squire like you. One that isn't afraid to tell the truth, despite the consequences. One who will serve me loyally." Reavus slapped Terric on the back again. "We'll make a knight out of you yet."

A knight. Terric watched his remaining family members being dragged away. His whole life he had dreamt of being a knight. But not like this. He swallowed down the lump in his throat. It didn't feel like the start of his whole life. It felt like his whole world had just crumbled in front of him.

"Come along," Reavus said. "I'll need you to recount everything you saw. Don't worry, I'll make sure your father pays for this."

Terric felt like he was going to be sick. He had no doubt in his mind that Garrion deserved to die. But he never wanted his whole family to be punished for Garrion's crimes. Losing their mother was torture enough. *What have I done?* With one last glance, Terric turned his back on his family.

END OF BOOK 1

AFTERWORD

What a journey!

No, I'm not saying that about my own novel. That would be weird and conceited...although I do hope you enjoyed reading it. I'm talking about the journey to create and publish it.

It all started half a decade ago when I went to see one of the Hobbit movies with my family. Afterwards, a few of us said to each other, "We should write fantasy novels!" And I did. But the book just wasn't very good. The story was decent, but the characters weren't developed well enough and the world was half-baked at best. So I went back to the drawing board. I spent time reading fantasy novels and analyzing what I liked and what I didn't like about them. And I spent time doing more world building than necessary. Is it really necessary to know how the Barcovan Empire celebrated the summer solstice? No. But I figured it out anyway. I learned about medieval commerce, early astronomy, wind patterns, and a million other things. In hindsight, I may have been procrastinating writing and developing a nasty Wikipedia addiction rather than doing actual research...

But even after all that, something still felt missing when I started writing. The characters were missing emotion. Isolda was a brick wall, Terric was a little pervert (maybe he still is...), and Garrion was a raging idiot. I wondered why the characters didn't feel as real as the characters in my wife's novels. And then I had an epiphany...why not just join forces with her and let her work her magic. She did, and she also added a bunch of characters. Without her, Nesta never would have happened, which would have been a travesty.

Together, we finished the novel and then painstakingly edited and reedited every chapter until we both wanted to throw the manuscript across the room. For such a fiery ginger, she's also surprisingly patient. So thank you, Ivy Smoak, for coauthoring this book with me. You made it what it is...which is hopefully wonderful. If people think it's terrible, I still give you credit.

Also thank you to R.A. Denny who helped with countless hours of world building and beta reading. And thank you to all of our other beta readers.

Thank you to Eric Gross for the amazing cover painting and all of the interior illustrations. You did an awesome job of bringing my horrible sketches to life.

And thank you to anyone who got this far in this afterword (and book). I hope you enjoyed reading this book as much as I enjoyed writing it. In fact, I'd love to hear about what you thought of it. If you could leave a review, that would be amaze-balls. It's like that old adage about kittens dying and angels getting their wings, only in this case, every time Be Careful What You Joust For gets a review, I write another paragraph in Book 2.

Ryan Hauge
February 19, 2018

APPENDIX

HOUSE TALENOV
Truth Rising

His Majesty,
Ivan of House Talenov, First of His Name
King of Treland
Lord of the Trelish, the Shielders, and the Coastmen
Blood of Arwin
Defender of the Realm

Members

King Ivan Talenov

    his wife, *Saxa (Frostborn)* - died while giving birth to Rixin

        Crown Prince Rixin - "The Shadow Prince", former squire to Reavus

    his oldest brother, *Anton* - killed in the Siege of Scarfort

    his older brother, *Costel* - lost at sea when the Sea Fang sunk off the coast of Tujira

    his younger brother, Reavus - "The Hammer"

his younger sister, Isolda - married to Duke Garrion Hornbolt

his youngest sister, Katrina - married to King Magnus Frostborn

Ancestors

Ivan's father, *King Bogdan Talenov* - assassinated at the end of the Wizard's War

Ivan's mother, *Griselda*

Sir Oleg - founder of Bloodstone

Traveling with Reavus

Arwin's Voice - Archpriest of Arwinism

Blacksmiths - Reavus' elite guards

Princess Navya - daughter of Sultan Zand Sakar, hostage of the crown

Axion Oswald Kadavis - tutor to Navya

Knobbly Knees - jester

HOUSE HORNBOLT

Armored in Truth

His Grace,
Garrion of House Hornbolt
Duke of the Shield
Lord of Arwin's Gate
Defender of Arwin's Wall

Members

Duke Garrion Hornbolt - "Arwin's Rhino"

    his wife, Isolda (Talenov)

        Marcus

        Oriana

        Selina

        Terric

        Nesta

    his older brother, *Reggie* - died of disease at age 10

    his younger brother, Jax

Ancestors

Garrion's father, *Count Reginald Hornbolt* - died at the battle of Horn Harbor

Garrion's mother, *Oriella*

Sir Garus - founder of House Hornbolt

Garrion's Council

Sir Aldric Alsight - Master-at-arms

Father Percival - Master of Truth, Master of Spies, High Priest of Arwin's Gate

Axion Tobias Crane - Master Axion

Brother Savaric - Master of Coin, Master of Ships

Quentin Harlow - Steward of Vulture Keep

Household

Peter Harlow - squire to Garrion

Roger - Smith and Armorer

Warin - Stableboy

Sister Morel - tutor to Garrion's daughters

Conrad - Cook, former cook of King Bogdan Talenov

Bella - Oriana's handmaiden

HOUSE HYPOSA
None Shall Pass

(extinct)

His Grace,
Philip of House Hyposa
Duke of the Shield
Lord of Deseros
Defender of Arwin's Wall

Last Living Members
Duke Philip Hyposa - killed in the Battle of Horn Harbor
    his wife, *Anna*
        Julian - killed in the Sack of Deseros, traitor
        Dory - executed after the Sack of Deseros

HOUSE ZABERWALD
The Forest is Watching

(extinct)

His Arcane Majesty,
Bruno of House Zaberwald, First of His Name
Archmage of Pentavia
King of the Huntlands
Lord of the Forest, the Hills, and the Scar

Last Living Members

King Bruno Zaberald - "The Mad Wizard"

    his wife, *Amelia (Kobald)*

        Zara - "The Orange Witch", killed by Sir Aldric during the Wizard's War

           Brutus - killed by Sir Aldric during the Wizard's War

           Otto - killed by Sir Aldric during the Wizard's War

Bannermen during the Wizard's War

Duke Leon Kobald - Lord of Hexton

Count Erasmus Stone - Lord of Scarfort, killed during the Siege of Scarfot when the castle exploded

Duke Felix Gormont - Lord of Horn Harbor, elected King of the Huntlands after the Treaty of Islos

ABOUT RYAN HAUGE

Ryan Hauge is the author of the bestselling Gods of Pentavia series. When he's not writing, you can bet that he's distracting his wife from her work, handling a toy emergency, or whipping up something delicious in the kitchen.

Twitter: @RyanHaugeAuthor
Facebook: RyanSmoakAuthor
Goodreads: RyanHauge

ABOUT IVY SMOAK

Ivy Smoak is a bestselling romance and fantasy author. When she's not writing, you can find her binge watching too many TV shows, taking long walks, playing outside, and generally refusing to act like an adult.

Twitter: @IvySmoakAuthor
Facebook: IvySmoakAuthor
Goodreads: IvySmoak

Made in the USA
Coppell, TX
09 December 2022

88270709R00270